USA TODAY BEST

DALE MAYER

A Psychic Visions Novel

SOUL LEGACY

SOUL LEGACY
Beverly Dale Mayer
Valley Publishing Ltd.

ISBN-13: 978-1-778863-54-7
Print Edition

Books in This Series:

Tuesday's Child

Hide 'n Go Seek

Maddy's Floor

Garden of Sorrow

Knock Knock...

Rare Find

Eyes to the Soul

Now You See Her

Shattered

Into the Abyss

Seeds of Malice

Eye of the Falcon

Itsy-Bitsy Spider

Unmasked

Deep Beneath

From the Ashes

Stroke of Death

Ice Maiden

Snap, Crackle...

What If...

Talking Bones

String of Tears

Inked Forever

Insanity

Soul Legacy

Coveted

Psychic Visions Books 1–3

Psychic Visions Books 4–6

Psychic Visions Books 7–9

About This Book

Coming back home to work in the local hospital suits Dr. Cameron Wingford. Buying land from an old woman who'd needed the money cements his plans. Then the old woman's granddaughter returns home, and all the rumors begin—rumors that connect her to some weird event at the hospital every Halloween, an occurrence he had yet to experience, as he'd just moved there in November of last year.

Living on the fringe of society, Danica's strange family was an oddity that everyone in the community either mocked or avoided. She had never felt welcome, especially after being suspected of killing her own mother. She hated returning home. Hated everything about it—except for her grandmother, her last living relative. And now, her dying grandmother's request cannot be ignored. *Keep the property intact.* That meant approaching Dr. Cameron about the piece he'd bought, an act her grandmother regretted … and an open wound to their legacy.

Open wounds bleed, and, as Danica finds out, this wound can only be healed in one specific way. Even then, a huge sacrifice is required …

Sign up to be notified of all Dale's releases here!

https://geni.us/DaleNews

PROLOGUE

"TONIGHT IS A lovely, quiet evening." Dr. Jonathon Wingford beamed, as he glanced around the emergency room. After thirty years of working here, he always thought of this as his home away from home. Still, this was Halloween, and he'd expected more craziness than this. But it was a small town, so maybe they would dodge that particular bullet tonight, although it was still young. "How odd for a Halloween night. No one's here."

"Sure, there is," the orderly said, nodding toward the big emergency room door.

Jonathon turned to see a blood-covered woman standing on her own, with a shell-shocked look in her eyes.

Two nurses raced to her.

She held out her hands and then slowly, ever-so-slowly, like a cartoon, crumpled to her knees and then to the floor before the nurses could catch her. Jonathon raced to her side, checking for wounds. A moment later, puzzled, he sat back, frowning at his patient, then looked to his nurses and shook his head. "She doesn't appear to have any open wounds. Let's move her to a bed and do a full workup."

They quickly laid her on a gurney and wheeled her into the next open cubicle. After transferring her to a bed, they did a full workup to see just what was going on.

The patient opened her eyes a few minutes later and

stared up at him. She reached up a bloody hand, grabbed his lab coat, and whispered in a pained tone, "Help."

He gave her a reassuring smile. "It's all right. You're in the hospital now. Take it easy. We're trying to figure out what happened. You don't appear to have any injuries, but you're covered in blood."

"Not my blood," she whispered.

He knew that. He could see that. But where had the blood come from?

"My head hurts," she murmured.

"Right. It does appear to have some bruising, but I don't see any open wounds."

"Inside," she whispered. "My head's pounding inside."

"Where's the blood from?" he asked, trying to keep the urgency out of his tone. "Tell me who's injured."

"Accident," she whispered. "There was an accident. She's been hurt."

Jonathon frowned and asked the nurse, "Where did she come from? Do we have any idea what kind of accident? Was she alone? Have the local authorities been called?"

Behind him, the other nurse said, "I'll go find out," and she took off.

Jonathon looked down at the young woman. "What's your name?"

"Daisy," she whispered. "Daisy. Danica. Daisy. Where's Danica?"

She kept repeating both names, so he tried asking again. "Is your name Daisy?"

She stared up at him. Her eyes grew wider and wider, and then a weird cry erupted from deep inside her throat, like a high-pitched whine. The unholy sound rattled his soul.

He tried to calm her down, and then, without warning,

the sound shut off, and she collapsed back onto the bed, unconscious. He ordered a CT scan to see just what was going on with her head, plus an X-ray to confirm any internal injuries they might have missed. The swelling on her head was his main concern. But he needed to know how bad it was and if she had any other injuries he couldn't see.

With her stabilized and barely conscious, he stepped back, as his patient was quickly wheeled out of the room. He looked over at a nurse standing there, a notepad in her hand, frowning.

"What did you find out?" he asked her.

"The sheriff said they received a call of an injured woman covered in blood, walking on the street. They found her. She was alone and barely coherent and was calling out for Danica. They called an ambulance for her, but she disappeared into the trees somehow, and they've been looking for her since. They have no idea how she got here."

He looked toward the hospital bed, rolled down to the end of the hallway, waiting for the elevator. "Do they have a name for her? We didn't find any ID on her."

At that, a security guard came in through the emergency double doors and said, "I followed the blood." He took a moment to shake his head. "There's quite a trail all the way back out the parking lot and across the road, before disappearing into the trees."

Jonathon had that thought running through his mind, as he added, "So she may have walked here on her own." He stood there, staring down the hallway at the woman who'd now disappeared into the elevator. Something about her was familiar and yet distant. He couldn't quite explain it. Her cry had been unnerving, but the fact that she was completely coated in someone else's blood, with only a slight head wound? Well, that was an odd one for him. He glanced back over at the nurse to see her studying him oddly. "What's the matter?" he asked.

"I don't know," she said hesitantly. "When did you change your lab coat?"

"What do you mean?" He grabbed his coat by the front edges and gave it a shake. "I didn't change my lab coat."

She frowned, glanced at his lab coat again, and then dropped her gaze to the floor.

He looked at his lab coat and at the floor where she was staring and said, "I don't get it. What's wrong?"

"She grabbed your lab coat," the nurse said quietly, her gaze darting to his face and then away. "Remember that bloody hand?"

"I know," he bit off. "Of course I remember. What's that got to do with anything?"

"Your lab coat. … It's clean. As if she never touched it."

His eyebrows shot up, and he quickly took off the lab coat and checked it. He looked back at the nurse to see several other nurses and one of the orderlies walking toward him, all with the same look on their faces. "I didn't change my lab coat," he said in disbelief. "You saw me. I've been here the whole time."

She nodded. "I know, and that's the problem. It *was* bloody after she grabbed it. I don't know what happened. I don't know how it happened, but somehow all that blood … disappeared. And honestly … there ain't nothing good about that at all. Something spooky about that damn girl in the first place," she said, shaking her head. "But right now, that lab coat is seriously … *wrong*."

He laid his coat over the back of his chair, wondering just what was going on. Could they have been mistaken?

Maybe the woman had only reached for him? No. He remembered the tug, as she'd grabbed on. He couldn't imagine that none of that blood had transferred. More than a little unnerved, he headed back to write up notes on the case and quickly phoned Radiology to ensure all was well with her scans.

The head of the department, in a testy tone, said, "I don't know what you're talking about. I haven't done any scans in the last hour. … More like two hours."

"I sent a young woman up for a CT scan."

He said, "Well, I haven't seen her yet." And hung up on him.

Jonathon went to Radiology himself to see the CT results firsthand. Yet, when he got up there, he found the place empty. He wandered around and then went in search of the one orderly he'd seen take the stretcher here.

When he finally met up with him, the guy nodded and said, "I took her there, then was called away. Why? Is something wrong?"

"Yes, according to Radiology, they haven't seen her." At that, Jonathon summoned security, and they did a sweep, clearing room by room, searching the small hospital. Thirty minutes later, when everybody reported back to Jonathon, he had to admit one truth that he was still struggling to realize: *the woman was gone.*

There was no trace of her. A bed was found in the hallway, but no blood was on the sheets. So, if this had been her bed, there was no easy way to prove it. But Jonathon couldn't stop staring at the clean sheets, remembering his lab coat …

The same nurse who had commented on his lab coat spoke up in an eerie tone. "I tell you, that girl's nothing but trouble. I don't know who she is, where she came from, but the last thing we need is a ghost around this place."

Startled, he turned and looked at her, and she nodded.

"I've been here since time began, almost as long as you, and it's because of incidents like this that I rarely work Halloween night. Something like this has happened before. Almost exactly like this."

Jonathon shook his head. "I've heard the rumors, but honestly I hate everything to do with Halloween, so generally take my holidays around this time. But yes, I've heard talk."

"It started quite a few years ago," she admitted in a low voice. "I would have to look up just how long ago. We had the same case of a young woman coming in, completely bloodstained, and she disappeared from the hospital. She had no visible wounds, also was covered in blood. She was sent for all the same tests, but she disappeared, and nobody ever saw her again."

At that, several of the other staff members spoke up.

"I heard about that."

"Yeah, I did too."

"Do you really think that's the same person? Or ghost rather?"

At the word *ghost*, silence fell around Jonathon, as the staff all turned toward him, as if they expected him to have answers.

He was still wrapping his head around the fact that they were missing a patient. "I don't know what is going on now," Jonathon said, his hands on his hips, "but I know I was treating a flesh-and-blood woman."

"Sure," the nurse said, looking at him pointedly. "A flesh-and-blood woman who didn't leave any bloodstains on your lab coat."

The other nurse looked at him and whispered, "So what the hell does that mean?"

Jonathon had no answers. Who could? All he knew was that the young injured woman had asked for his help, and, before he could do much, she'd disappeared.

But to where?

CHAPTER 1

Almost One Year Later …

DANICA HARTLING WALKED into the hospital and glanced down at her clipboard to confirm the name of the person she was supposed to contact. Her short-term memory seemed to be getting worse every day. She shrugged, then looked over at the receptionist with a smile and stated, "I'm here to see Dr. Wingford."

The woman at the front counter frowned at her. "He died last year."

Danica rechecked her clipboard. "Dr. Wingford?" she repeated.

"Yes, old doc Wingford died late last year."

"That can't be," Danica said, shaking her head. "I spoke to him yesterday."

The lady sitting next to the receptionist interjected, "I think she's asking for Dr. Cameron Wingford."

The receptionist queried the woman at her counter, "Dr. Cameron? That's Dr. Jonathon Wingford's son."

"Yes," Danica stated, "Dr. Cameron Wingford. I didn't realize there was a father and son pair here."

The receptionist waved her hand around. "There was the father, and now there is the son. He's on duty in the ER, and it's a little busy right now," she noted.

Danica nodded. "Right. He did tell me that he would

likely be busy."

"Yes, he's very busy. Maybe you could come back at another time?" The receptionist looked at the clipboard in Danica's hand, trying to hide her emotions. "Or maybe you could tell me what your visit is about, and I'll have him call you when he gets a moment."

"Which means he'll never call me at all," Danica stated, with a laugh. "That's okay." She glanced around at the fairly empty hospital waiting room. Yet she wasn't at the ER area, and she heard noises coming from the busy nurses' station behind her. She turned to the receptionist again. "I'll go grab a cup of coffee and a bite to eat. I'll come back afterward to see if he's not so busy. Do you know when he's off shift?"

The receptionist winced. "We're so short on staff that I couldn't possibly say."

"Right," Danica agreed, "and that's a problem in itself."

The receptionist appeared nervous and kept glancing at Danica's clipboard.

"It's all right. I'm not here to question how many hours he's working or whether you guys are following the board regulations or not," Danica shared, with a smile.

Again the receptionist asked, "Maybe you could tell me why you are here?"

"I think it best if I wait and talk to him personally," she pointed out gently.

The receptionist dropped her gaze to the paperwork Danica still carried.

"It's fine," Danica stated. "He's not in any trouble, but I do need to see him face-to-face."

"If you say so," the receptionist muttered.

Danica glanced around, looking for signs to direct her to the cafeteria. When she pivoted back to the receptionist, the woman pointed down the hallway. Danica smiled. "Thanks. Let him know I'm here, will you?"

"And who are you again?" asked the receptionist in a dry tone.

"Danica Hartling. Sorry." She brought out the card she often used and handed it to her. "He's expecting me."

The receptionist looked down at the business card. "Medical supplies?"

"Yes and no," Danica replied, with a laugh. "He'll know the name." With that, she turned and headed to the cafeteria. There she sat, with a hot cup of coffee and a sandwich, while she went through her notes.

As she sat here, lost in her own world, she heard a voice calling out to her. She looked up and around but couldn't see anyone looking for her. Frowning, she went back to her paperwork. When she heard the call again, she twisted around, looking, but still found nothing.

Frowning, she sat back and studied the other people in the room. There didn't appear to be anybody she would know, so she went back to her paperwork.

Work, work, and more work. That had been all there was for her lately. She was tired and had been on the road a little more than too much. She was only back in town because of her grandmother.

Then she heard her name being called again. Frowning, she glanced around but still found nobody asking for her. *Daisy*, she thought with a groan and then promptly dismissed the notion. Other people started to look at her curiously. She frowned and looked back down at her paperwork, determined not to look up again.

She had no idea if or why Daisy would even bother. When her phone rang, Danica was glad for the distraction.

She checked her Caller ID and answered, "Hey, Nana. I'm at the hospital."

"Did you talk to him yet?" her grandmother asked testily.

"No, not yet."

"I told you. He's a busy man."

"I know that," Danica agreed. "He also told me to come to the hospital and see him."

"You could have set it up more as a date, you know," her grandmother declared, with a touch of asperity in her tone.

At that, Danica snorted. "No way I'm setting up a call like this as a date."

"It's not as if you have a line of men sniffing at your heels. Too much spooky stuff scares them all away."

"The men are not being kept away by anything spooky."

"Really? So how come you've been looking around the damn room for the last twenty minutes, trying to figure out who's been calling you?"

Danica froze. She pinched the bridge of her nose, then bowed her head and whispered, "Was that you?"

Her grandmother laughed and laughed. "Child, if it had been me, you wouldn't have had any doubt about it," she snapped.

Of that Danica was certain. "Then who was it?" she muttered.

"I don't know that it was Daisy, but, should that call come through, you sure as heck better be answering."

"I'm not answering," Danica retorted. "As you are fully aware, that's not a good thing for me."

"And you and I both know that you don't have any choice in the matter. Ever since you were a little girl, that stuff has been happening around you, and you can't stop it.

Some things are fated."

"I don't want it happening around me," she snapped a little too loudly. She softened her tone, knowing her grandmother meant well. It's just that Nana didn't quite understand all Danica went through with this woo-woo stuff.

"Yes, I do understand," her grandmother countered, once again reading her mind.

"I wish you wouldn't do that."

"It's not my fault you keep transmitting, left, right, and center, child. I really don't have any choice but to hear them," she said, with a chuckle, "and you know yourself that you would do the same thing."

"But I don't *want* to do the same thing," she whined. "I want to be normal."

After a long pause her grandmother whispered, "I'm sorry, sweetheart, but that will never be your life." And, with that, she ended the call, leaving Danica staring at her phone with a stricken expression.

She looked around the hospital cafeteria to see if anybody had been listening in, but it seemed that everybody was much more concerned about their own personal problems than hers, which made a lot of sense, considering where she sat. She was here for a completely different purpose than most, and her heart went out to those who were experiencing tough times right now. No words could ever convey the worry of someone with a loved one in here.

When her name was called in a loud preemptory tone, she turned around with a start to see a man striding toward her. She frowned as she studied him, realizing who he was, yet stunned that he still looked so much like he had before.

He stopped in front of her, a frown flashing across his

face, only to be rescinded almost immediately. He held out a hand. "I'm Dr. Cameron Wingford," he stated smoothly.

She smiled and shook his hand, then introduced herself and motioned at the seat beside her. "Have you got a moment?"

"Yes, but only that," he shared. "This would equate to my break. Things are stable for the moment, but it can turn catastrophic from one moment to the next."

"Of course," Danica noted.

"What's this about anyway?" Then he stopped, eyed her, and leaned closer. "Good God, Danica?" He waved his hand impatiently. "As in, *Danica*, Danica?"

She groaned and then nodded. "Yes, Danica. Danica Hartling."

"Good God," he repeated in shock, sitting back to stare at her.

"Yeah, I seem to get that reaction a lot."

"Honestly I don't think anybody would have ever expected you to return to this town."

"Not sure I wanted to," she replied, trying for a calm tone. "As you know, it wasn't a very easy place for me to be back then."

He winced. "I'm sorry. That was very rude of me."

She shrugged. "Maybe, but it was also honest, and I'll take honesty over anything else that I'm getting."

"You're back for your grandmother's sake, I presume," he asked mildly.

She smiled and nodded. "Yes, and I know my grandmother is another reason a lot of people choose to avoid me."

He sighed. "She is a character. And the fact that she has that uncanny ability to do all kinds of things that some of us would love to do, while others wish she wouldn't," he whispered, with a small smile in her direction, "just adds to the oddness."

"No need to add to the oddness. When your own mother attacks you in a small town like this, with a grandmother who is one step away from being certifiable"—Danica gave a wave of her hand—"it makes for a rough go."

"I'm sorry," he repeated, with a hint of sorrow in his tone, and it sounded genuine. "High school was rough on all of us, and I was what? … Maybe two—no, three—grades ahead of you?"

She nodded. "Something like that, yeah."

"How are you?" he asked intently.

She shook her head. "I'm fine," she replied, adding a note of firmness to her tone that she didn't really feel.

"Yet, you're here."

"I am here, but it has nothing to do with medical equipment. That's just an old business card. I don't work for them anymore, but it does open doorways."

He stiffened and was put on guard. "So, what does this visit pertain to then?" he asked, his gaze searching. "I really don't have time to waste."

"I understand," she responded curtly. "I am quite concerned about my grandmother, but obviously I could book an appointment, if that is the issue."

"I would hope that you *would* book an appointment," he suggested, picking up on her words, "and, yes, it's probably a good idea if you did. I love her dearly, but …" He just let the word hang.

"But she's different. She's odd, perplexing, and a whole lot of things I absolutely love. However, I know a lot of people don't feel that way."

"The last time I saw her in person, she told me that one

of my best friends from high school was about to have twins and would lose one, if I didn't do something to help out," he shared, with a sigh. "I wasn't even in town at the time, and she did have twins, and she did lose one. As you can imagine, they left town shortly thereafter to help forget about that loss."

"Yes, my grandmother has always had the sight," Danica murmured, staring down at the paperwork in front of her. "Unfortunately, having the sight hasn't helped any of us."

"True. She seems to have been plagued with a lot of bad luck," he confirmed, frowning.

"Exactly. And that's one of the reasons I'm here." He waited for her to continue. She shrugged. "I don't really know what to say, except to just say it. It's regarding the property."

"The property?" he asked in astonishment.

She nodded. "Yes. The property. Her property, … which is now your property," she pointed out.

He nodded thoughtfully and stared off into the distance. "And what about it?" he asked, looking at her sideways. Before she could answer, he noted, "I would have thought you got that scar fixed by now."

Her eyes widened. "I've thought of it, and then I get scared and back away from it. So, I haven't done anything about it yet."

He nodded. "It really … isn't that noticeable."

She snorted. "Yes, it really *is* noticeable," she countered, "but I've come to a point in life where, if that's what people want to focus on, then whatever. That's up to them."

"And that's not necessarily fair," he pointed out, "because people may not want to focus, but it's right there on your face. So they may need a chance to get comfortable looking at you without staring."

"Which appears to be a problem," she conceded shortly. "Besides, this isn't even about me."

"No, of course not," he conceded, "but if you ever do decide to get it fixed …"

Her fingers instinctively reached up to her cheek and the long scar that slashed down that side.

"Even if it's just the reminder to you," he offered unsurely, "I'm sure looking at that every morning is not a memory you want."

"I ran from it for a long time," she shared, "but now I've come home to help my grandmother. So, it appears to be something I'll deal with for a while longer."

"I don't understand," he said in a confused tone.

She frowned, not sure exactly what she meant herself, so she just shrugged. "That's not the issue. Can I buy that piece of land from you?"

He looked at her in astonishment. "You mean, my home?"

"No," she clarified. "You bought two sections of land. One has your home, and the other one is empty land, adjoining my grandmother's house."

"Why would you want to buy that?" he asked, frowning. "It's not very usable land."

"I understand," she agreed, "and that's one of the reasons my grandmother sold it to you in the first place. Yet I know that she would very much like to have it back. It's just empty land and the creek," she pointed out.

"The creek, which she already has access to," he rebutted.

Danica nodded. "And again, I know that. … I just … she asked me to come ask you. It's important to her, so here

I am." Again she waved her hand. "I seem to be struggling to accomplish an awful lot of things right now that are important to her."

"I understand," he replied, as he rounded his fingers on the table beside her, obviously thinking about it. "I won't give you an answer right off the bat. Honestly I'm not sure how I feel about it. While I'm not using it, and I don't really need it, I also like not having neighbors too close by."

"Yet you do have my grandmother as a neighbor."

"I know," he grumbled, with an eye roll and a laugh. "Honestly she's a very quiet neighbor, so the best kind to have."

Danica nodded at that. "And she comes from the heart, and that's why I'm really hoping you will open your heart and see a way to let that happen for her."

"Did she tell you why she wants it back?"

Danica shook her head. "No, she didn't, and I have been asking," she stated reluctantly. "However, she's not being very open about it. When it comes to my grandmother, she gets—" She hesitated and then shrugged. "When she gets stubborn like that, there's no budging her."

He chuckled. "My nan was like that too." His buzzer went off just then. He looked down at the pager and nodded. "And that will be the end of the conversation for the moment."

"Think about it, please," Danica added, as he started toward the ER.

"Will do, but I'm really not sure that I want to let it go." And, with that, he disappeared through the double doors and back into the emergency department.

Danica sat here for a long moment, wondering what she was supposed to tell her grandmother. And yet, knowing that her grandmother already knew the answer, a tap came on her shoulder. She turned to see another familiar face, one that she had hoped to never see again.

Jacob, the bully from her high school days, stared at her in shock. "Good God, it really is you, isn't it?"

She stood up, hating the towering advantage he had always had over her, and she nodded. "Yeah, it sure is." She picked up her clipboard.

"What the devil are you doing here?"

She stiffened ever-so-slightly and replied, "My grandmother lives here—in case you've forgotten."

"Oh, who could forget that old bat?" he noted, with a harsh laugh. "What I do know is that this town doesn't need you. It's bad enough having to deal with her. We were hoping she would die soon, and we could all live in peace."

Silence came from the room around them, as everybody suddenly overheard the discussion.

She smiled at him and stated, "She hasn't passed on yet." With that, Danica turned and walked out, without another word.

In the silence behind her, she could have heard a pin drop, as everybody settled in, understanding what had just happened and who had returned to town.

The daughter of the woman who was either murdered or committed suicide. No one seems to know for sure.

It was bad enough that they all knew Danica had almost died—or had died, in fact. It was bad enough that everybody already held her grandmother and her mother against Danica. But now, once again, everybody would know who Danica was and why she was here, which was obviously too much for the townsfolk to deal with. Especially since they weren't happy about her return and were very vocal about it.

And that was something else altogether for Danica to deal with.

CHAPTER 2

CAMERON RETURNED TO the emergency room, smiling at his head nurse. "Thanks for the call."

"Hey, I wasn't exactly sure what you wanted it for, but, when the doctor says to give him a twenty-minute warning call, hey, I'm happy to help out." She looked over at him curiously. "Who was that woman anyway?"

He turned to her and smiled. "How long have you lived here?"

"All my life. Why?"

"Do you remember—" He stopped and shook his head. "Damned if I remember the woman's name. But do you remember the woman who tried to kill her daughter—and slashed up her face pretty good before knocking her out?"

Her eyes widened. "Danica. Jesus, was that Danica?"

Cameron nodded slowly. "Yeah, it was Danica."

"Good God," she mumbled, her jaw dropping. "Why would she ever come back here?"

"I asked her that," Cameron shared, with a headshake. "She's here for her grandmother. Yet I'm not sure what she told me was the truth, at least not the whole truth." He'd come back after his father had died, so who was he to judge? Still, coming home wasn't all that it was cracked up to be.

"Why would she? I'm sure she's all about secrets." He looked at her, surprised. She shrugged. "After what she went through here? I'm surprised she ever showed her face again."

"How bad was it?"

She nodded. "It was bad. The people here were terrified of her."

"She's back. So, if they're *still* terrified of her, they should all face her sooner or later."

"Some people won't face her at all. They'll try to run her out of town."

"Yet her grandmother's here."

She frowned, nodding. "That's right. She is, isn't she? That one's pretty crazy too."

"I don't know about crazy. She's my neighbor, you know." At that, she tilted her head, surprised, and he nodded. "I own the land adjacent to her grandmother's home. I bought it around the beginning of the year."

"Good God," she gasped, staring at him in fascination. "That's pretty gutsy of you."

He laughed. "Why is that?"

"Everybody says it's haunted."

"I don't know about haunted," he replied, with a smile, "but I'm building a house on my parcel. So, it's not as if anything is left to haunt—at least on my piece." Just then, his pager went off, alerting him that an ambulance was on the way. He headed back to work.

Several times throughout the afternoon, he caught his head nurse staring at him. When they got their next break, he asked, "What's the problem? You keep staring at me, as if I've grown horns."

"It's not that you've grown horns," she replied. "I'm just still stunned that Danica's back."

He frowned. "I think she's had a tough-enough life here already. Yet she is here for her grandmother, who is getting up there in age. Regardless, I can't imagine coming back was easy for her."

"No, I can't imagine it was either," she acknowledged. "I'm just surprised."

"Did you know her well?"

"Nope. Nobody knew her well. At least not after the attack. We were all friends up until then. Of course after that, I wasn't allowed to hang out with her anymore."

Cameron turned to face her. "What?"

She nodded. "Everybody thought Danica was bad luck or something. None of us were allowed to have anything to do with her." He stared at her, and she shrugged. "What can I say? Small-town people got pretty unnerved over what happened to her."

"She was victimized," he reminded her. "Twice."

"Sure, but that's how life works," his head nurse replied. "So don't go looking at me as if I did something wrong."

"I didn't mean to. It's just a surprise to hear that."

"You went to school with her too. How did you treat her?"

"I was several years ahead of her, then off to college and med school. So I had no idea she was going through any ostracization."

"She was, and believe me, that was for the best. Something was very worrying about that whole family."

He didn't say anything and just stared off into the distance.

She leaned back and narrowed her gaze. "I don't like that look in your eye. I'm telling you that weird shit happens around those Hartling people. If I see her grandmother in the street, I cross to the other side."

"Seriously?"

"Absolutely," she declared, staring at him. "If you were smart, you would too."

"I don't know about that," he replied, almost taking offense. "I can't say I've ever given in to reactions like that."

"Maybe you need to live here longer, and then you'll probably find yourself doing exactly the same thing." And, with that, his head nurse turned and stalked off, clearly irritated at him.

Throughout the rest of his shift, Cameron asked several other people on staff—those he knew had been around town for a long time—and got basically the same answer. Danica had been treated pretty roughly back then, and it didn't seem that things had gotten any better.

When he made it home, he pulled into his front driveway, parked in the garage, and stepped out of his vehicle. As far as houses went, his was pretty decent. He liked building houses, and he'd gotten the basics of this one contracted and done. He decided he would do the rest as part of his therapy routine for destressing from work. It had seemed like a good idea at the time, but, every once in a while, he wondered if he'd bitten off more than he could chew. It was a job that never ended. He didn't mind doing a lot of it, but working two shifts back-to-back at the hospital all too often, like today, all he wanted to do was crash.

As he stepped into his living room, he was surprised to see his brother Jace was here, sanding down one of the balustrades going up to the second floor into the main bedroom area. "Hey, I didn't expect to see you today. Where is your truck parked? Did you walk here?"

His brother popped his head over the handrail and smiled. "You'll never get this house finished at the rate you keep putting it off."

"It's not that I'm putting it off," he explained, with a smirk, "but I'm tired, and the hospital work I do isn't exactly easy, not to mention all the extra hours."

"They need to get more staff in there," his brother agreed. "The thought of your being the only other doctor is just ludicrous."

"Meaning, if you get hurt or injured again, you're not coming in?"

"Nope, I'm sure not," he declared, with a laugh. "Anybody with a brain in their head would realize that you're overworked, underpaid, and you shouldn't be there by yourself."

"Maybe, but I don't exactly have that option. So *overworked* is what it'll be."

"Ah," Jace responded, then popped back onto the railing job again. "I won't worry then."

"Besides, you're doing a great job with the house and all."

"Yeah, but I'm only doing this to help out a little. You're the one who wanted this as *your* project," his little brother reminded Cameron.

"I really would like the chance to do just that, but you're right. Finishing the house is taking forever, and that's time I don't have. It's also taking energy I wish I had but don't."

He walked into the kitchen, and his brother called out, "Please tell me that you at least have a plan for food."

Cameron closed his eyes briefly and called back, "I can rustle up something."

"Good," his brother hollered, "because, if you can't pay me, the least you can do is feed me."

With that, Cameron headed to the fridge to take a look at what was there. His brother was right. The least Cameron could do was feed him. Since Jace's wife had left him and had promptly filed for divorce, that was also partly why his brother came—to be fed—and right now the last thing Cameron wanted to do was prepare a proper meal. Yet his brother probably wouldn't eat otherwise, and Cameron wasn't sure he would either.

With that, he reached for the pack of ground meat in the fridge and called out, "You okay with a burger?"

His brother called back, "I'm always okay with a burger but make it two. I'm starving."

Soon the barbecue pit was on, and Cameron popped open a beer. As he sliced the fixings to go on top, his brother showed up a few minutes later, slowly stretching his shoulders. "How's that arm?" Cameron asked.

"Sore, still stiff," he admitted, his tone curt, hating questions about the accident that had set him back physically.

Jace seemed to be looking at Cameron's house as his own therapy too, just like Cameron. "We're a hell of a pair," Cameron noted, as he handed his brother a beer.

"Speak for yourself," Jace ordered. "My life is fine."

"If it were fine, you wouldn't be hiding out at my place."

Jace snorted and didn't say anything more.

Cameron flipped the burgers, then looked back over at Jace intently. "Do you remember that woman who tried to murder her daughter?"

"Yeah. Who was that? Crazy Daisy and her daughter, Danica? Yeah, something was weird about them. And something went wrong. And Danica got slammed afterward."

"I didn't realize she had it so hard back then. I guess I didn't see much of her after I moved away."

"You were at college. I wasn't. So I saw her, and this

whole town treated her like shit."

"I don't understand that," Cameron admitted. "I was talking with a couple nurses today at work, and they both told me the same thing. They were more or less saying that, if Danica were to show up at the hospital, they wouldn't even treat her."

"They're all superstitious as hell, the whole lot of them."

"Yet what sense does that even make? Danica didn't even do anything, so why be so superstitious?"

"Her mother tried to murder her, but she survived, and it seemed that it would have almost been kinder if she hadn't lived. That scar?" Jace gave a shudder. "I'm sure she's gotten it fixed by now, but jeez."

"She hasn't fixed it though," Cameron stated, his tone short. "What difference does it make?"

"That scar was visible, like seriously visible. You couldn't even talk to her without your gaze locking on to it."

Cameron winced. He hoped Jace would have been better behaved than that, but it had been such a shock to Cameron to see her, that he wasn't sure he had reacted any differently.

"Why the questions? And what do you mean, she hasn't had it fixed? Did you see her?" Jace asked, staring at him in shock.

Was that fear underlying Jace's tone? Surely not. Cameron explained the strange visit.

"So, you spoke to her?"

"I got a call from her and told her that, if she needed to see me, she was welcome to stop by," Cameron shared, "but I wasn't exactly thinking in terms of real estate."

Jace's gaze went back to the window. "Good God, I can't believe you talked to her."

"Why wouldn't I?" Cameron asked in exasperation,

frowning at his brother. "It's not as if she's got some contagious disease."

"The hell she doesn't," Jace argued, with a bark of laughter. "She has the ability to empty a room faster than anybody I've ever seen."

"Now you're making me feel bad for her."

"Oh no, no, no, don't you go on that kick," his brother countered, raising his hand. "There's no joy possible from having any relationship with them."

"Who said anything about a relationship?" Cameron asked in exasperation. "They are my neighbors, but you're making me realize that she's had a pretty raw deal, and maybe people should be nicer to her."

"Now why would you want to?" Jace asked, with a headshake. He motioned at the burgers. "Come on. Aren't those suckers ready yet? I'm starving."

Ignoring his brother's unusual attitude, Cameron proceeded to check the burgers and flipped them one more time, before plating them. As soon as they dressed their burgers, they sat outside on the back deck—which wasn't finished either, but was getting there.

Cameron looked out at the surrounding property and smiled. "That's the piece she wants to buy back." He pointed off to the side. It was a piece that Jace had already told Cameron that he should sell, if for no other reason than to get some cash, which could be used to hire people to get things done on his house and then some.

"I wouldn't want you to sell it back to her," Jace noted, shaking his head in protest. "That's just bad news."

He rolled his eyes at his brother. "You keep saying that, like she's some pariah."

"She is," he stated flatly. "Don't you make the mistake

of getting involved with her."

"I didn't say anything about getting involved. She asked me about the property. That's it."

"The answer is no," his brother declared, glaring at Cameron. "That's all there is to it."

Cameron stared, as Jace put down his burger. "What the hell does that mean?"

"You know what that means. You would be absolutely crazy to let that freak live beside you."

Cameron had never heard his brother talk like that before, and he let out his breath in a gush. "Oh my God, are you serious?"

"Of course I'm serious," he snapped. "You sure as hell won't see me around this place if you sell to her. The last thing I want to do is look out the window and see that."

"*That*?" Cameron sat here, staring at his brother in shock. "*That*, as in a woman injured through no fault of her own? Do you even hear yourself?"

"Me? Do *you* even hear *yourself*?" Jace stared at him. "Good Christ, Cameron. You can't just take in every orphan off the street."

Cameron bit down hard on his burger. He didn't fight with his brother often, but, man, when they did, it could end up being a doozy. And this one was heading that way. What he didn't know was why. *Something* must be behind Jace's attitude, and Cameron would not likely get it out of Jace easily. His brother was typically private where his personal life was concerned, but something had to be there. Cameron looked over at Jace. "Were you sweet on her or something?"

His brother jerked back hard. "Christ, no." He raised his hands in protest. "No way." He glared at Cameron. "What about you? Were you sweet on her?"

"No, … well, maybe. Yet I was years ahead, then left. I did my schooling and residencies all over the place, but I eventually came back. And, funnily enough, I'd barely heard about her since being back."

"I wonder why?" Jace asked, staring at him. "Don't you even go down that pathway. I'm warning you."

"Don't threaten me, Jace," Cameron stated, striving for a mild tone. "I don't know what your problem is with her, but I don't have one with Danica, or Harriet."

"Good. That's fine. I'm glad you don't have a problem with her and her grandmother, but do not sell her your property." And, with that, Jace threw back the rest of his beer, popped the last bite of his burger in his mouth, and announced, "I'm going home."

Cameron didn't want to say it, but on the tip of his tongue had been a hearty *Good riddance*. This was not the brother he knew, nor the issues Cameron had expected to discuss over a burger tonight. On the other hand, it gave him his house back sooner, as his brother left much earlier than he typically did, and tonight Cameron needed that. He was tired, worn out, and more than a little confounded at the attitudes of everyone around him. It made no sense to him at all. Surely Danica was just another victim.

He didn't mean it in that way. It wasn't that she was *just another victim*, as if she had no value. Of course she had value. A lot of things could cause people a tremendous amount of pain, and he didn't want to be one of them for Danica. He also didn't understand what any of this had to do with his brother and why he was so angry about it. It was the fear underlying the anger that surprised Cameron, and he knew something had to be behind it, but it would take a while before his brother would loosen up enough to talk.

ODDLY ENOUGH, AT work the very next day, after a surprisingly good night's sleep, Cameron got more answers than he expected.

When he walked in, Jenny, the oldest nurse on staff, looked over at him and nodded. "I hear you saw Danica."

He turned to her warily and nodded. "I did."

"Good," she stated in a flat tone. "How is she doing?"

Surprised at the worried tone in her voice, he shrugged. "Adjusting slowly, I think. Seems it's been hard coming back."

"It would be. The town wasn't very good to her."

"I just don't get that," Cameron admitted, a bit of exasperation in his tone. "I went to school with her, but I was a few years ahead. Then I went off to college and into med school, and all of that with Danica seemed to have happened while I was away."

"It was pretty rough, and especially hard on her," Jenny shared, giving him an odd look. "As you know, … people here have long memories."

"They might have long memories, but I don't understand why they would hold anything against her. Surely she was the victim in this case."

"She absolutely was a victim, and the problem with being a victim, particularly in circumstances like this, is that it scares people."

"I talked to my brother briefly last night, and he flat-out told me to stay the hell away from her."

"He would, wouldn't he?" Jenny said, with a laugh.

Cameron stared at her, puzzled.

A look of realization dawned on her face. "You don't know, do you?"

"What don't I know?"

"They were sweet on each other at the time right before the accident."

Cameron stared at her, as if unsure. Deep down, he noted a grain of truth to it though, and it would partially explain how Jace had acted. Yet contradicted what his brother had told Cameron last night.

She nodded. "But he ditched her. I don't know how quickly afterward, but they certainly weren't an item beyond that. Now, it was a pretty new relationship," she added cautiously. "So, I'm not trying to paint him in a terrible light."

"Anything you're saying comes across as putting him in a terrible light," he pointed out.

"I know. So why don't we just stop the conversation and leave it there?"

"No. How about we don't? How about you just tell me what you know, and then I can talk to him about it because he was really upset. Over-the-top, you know?"

She shrugged. "All I know is that they were dating. I don't know for how long or even how serious it was. I have no idea how close they were. After the attack—and nothing else to call it," she declared, "and after her mom died, Danica was in the hospital—trying to recover. She arrived DOA. You know that, right?" She sent him a sideways glance.

He frowned. "Sorry?"

"Danica was dead when she arrived. Her mom succeeded in killing her. Then somehow"—she glanced back to the first cubicle—"somehow she came back again."

"*Somehow*?" he repeated, raising an eyebrow.

She nodded, with a small smile. "Yeah. At the time, several people questioned why anyone would revive her because her face was pretty badly mangled." He stared at her, and she nodded. "I know. I know what you're thinking. She at least deserves a life. She at least deserves to have a chance. And I'm all for it," Jenny declared, raising her hands, "but I'm just telling you that, back then, people thought they should let sleeping dogs lie. And then suddenly she was alive and breathing again."

"As in she was so badly damaged that she couldn't be treated?"

Jenny shrugged. "People aren't always the nicest," she murmured.

"Yeah, I'm finding that out," Cameron muttered. "Honest to God, I thought I knew the people in this town, but—"

She laughed. "Not when you bring up something like that. Then you start to know the people of this town a little better."

"But you've lived here all your life," he protested. "Surely you love it here."

"I *have* lived here all my life, and, yes, there is a lot that I love here," she agreed, "but also an awful lot that I don't love. Some of the people here, their attitudes, their ingrained superstitions, all of that makes a big difference as to who these people are on the inside."

"So, you think some superstition affected my brother?"

"I don't know. Would you have said he was superstitious?"

"No, I wouldn't have said that at all," Cameron replied, thinking about it. "And I also didn't think he would break up with her either, not after something like that had happened."

"But what a man does and what a man's family thinks he does are two separate things," she declared pointedly. "You might have expected him to stand by her side and all that jazz, but they were young and pretty innocent."

"But she was a victim. She was also innocent. Or am I missing something else here?"

"No, you're not missing anything, … except you may not be aware of the rumors. Supposedly she wasn't attacked, but she tried to murder her mother herself, and her own wounds were a result of her mother fighting back."

Cameron stared at Jenny in shock, unable to swallow that alternate theory.

She nodded. "That's really what's behind it. The townsfolk are all afraid that we saved a murderer and that she got off scot-free."

CHAPTER 3

DANICA SAT IN her grandmother's car, praying it would last another six months, while waiting for Nana. Danica had ordered groceries online for pickup but had forgotten a few things. So Nana *had* to go inside, as per usual. As Danica waited, she got a sinking feeling in her stomach, that foreshadowing nudge. She looked around quickly, but nothing noticeable or obviously disruptive loomed ahead.

However, she hadn't gotten where she was without recognizing that something was approaching. She wasn't sure whether she should turn on the car engine and drive away or hunker down and try to appear as if nobody were in the vehicle.

As she waited, her phone rang. It was her grandmother.

"I need you in the store," Nana stated in that preemptive tone that brooked no argument.

Danica groaned. "No, I don't want to come into the store."

"You can't hide forever," Nana declared in an irritated tone.

"I could try."

"It won't work, Danica."

"Why won't it work?" she snapped.

"I told you that before. Now you should just suck it up."

"And if I don't suck it up?" she asked, with a groan.

"It still won't make a difference. Come inside the store. I need you."

"Fine," Danica muttered, "but sometimes your idea of *need* and mine are two different things."

Her grandmother cackled. "Maybe so, but I still need you in here."

Danica exited the car and headed toward the supermarket, going straight to the back. There, she walked over to find her grandmother, standing in front of the cottage cheese. "What on earth did you need me for?" she asked, looking around and seeing no sign of trouble.

Her grandmother pointed at the cottage cheese. "I can't read the label anymore."

She stared at Nana, realizing she'd been had, then groaned and quickly plucked up the first container, reading it off to her.

"What about the other one?" her grandmother asked, pointing to the one beside it.

Danica picked up the second cottage cheese container and read that label too. Her grandmother frowned, trying to make a decision. "It's cottage cheese," Danica declared. "Just pick one, and let's go."

Her grandmother stared at her. "Nothing is wrong, you know."

"Yet I'm sensing something," she murmured.

Her grandmother visibly sniffed the air, a habit that drove Danica wild. "Not a problem for me," Nana said, with a chuckle, "although it might be for you."

Danica pinched the bridge of her nose, a habit she was becoming all too accustomed to, as she tried to deal with her grandmother. "If it's something that I don't want to deal with," she stated, "then I really don't want to be here and don't want to be forced to deal with it. So, I'm going back out to the car."

Her grandmother shrugged. "You can run, but you can't hide."

She stiffened at that. "Maybe not, but I can at least stay hidden for a little bit longer."

"It won't help." Her grandmother shrugged and motioned behind Danica.

Slowly, with her heart sinking into her stomach, she turned to look at the crowd standing around her.

Several people just stood there, with widened gazes. Then they rapidly looked away, snatching furtive glances again and again.

Danica stared at them calmly, waiting for somebody to say something, knowing it was unlikely that any of them would, and, if they did, it wouldn't be nice.

Her grandmother knew that, but, unlike Danica, Nana always felt hiding was no good. Her grandmother believed it was better to face the world head-on and to ignore everything they had to say, especially if it was stuff you didn't like.

Immediately Nana called out to one of the women in the crowd, "Hey, Angel. Isn't this great? My granddaughter's back."

Angel stared, her shocked gaze going from one to the other. She then slowly backed up, turned, and raced from the store.

Nana howled with laughter. "I knew that would set her on the run," she declared, still chuckling. She smiled at several other people, who had also backed up.

By the time Danica turned around to see who was still here, she realized they were all gone. "Did you scare them away, just like that?" she murmured.

"Sure, I did. Just think. We won't have a line to deal with at the checkout now," her grandmother replied.

Danica stared at Nana in horror. "Please tell me that you didn't just do it for that reason."

"I don't want to stand in line, do you? Besides, it's already all over town that you're here. They might as well get a good look-see at your face, and then they'll leave us alone."

"Wouldn't that be nice?" Danica muttered bitterly. "Yet you also know that they won't leave us alone."

"They will, but it'll take a bit," Nana admitted. "I just figured it was faster to do it this way."

Danica couldn't reply to her grandmother in the way she truly wanted to. By the time she got home, she was furious.

Her grandmother shrugged and softly said, "Deal with it, dear. People will be people. The sooner you let them be people, the sooner they'll get over it."

"And if they don't get over it?" she asked in frustration.

"You knew it was a problem, but you came back anyway. I appreciate that. Yet I won't sit here and let everybody stare at you."

"They'll do it anyway," Danica stated. "I find it much easier to get through the day by ignoring them."

"But you're not ignoring them. You're just hiding," her grandmother corrected, with a bite to her tone.

Danica groaned. "It's not that I'm hiding. It's more a case of trying to find a peaceful answer without upsetting the apple cart."

"Yet you *should* upset the apple cart. *You* didn't do anything wrong," her grandmother snapped. "They have treated you like a leper for too long, and it's time it stopped."

"But it won't," Danica grumbled, turning to face Nana.

"You know that as well as I do."

"We can debate that until we're both blue in the face, and we will still not change each other's mind."

"I guess we can agree to disagree."

"Fine. But, for now, can you help me get these groceries inside? Then you can go off into that little camper of yours. God only knows why you won't live in this house."

Danica didn't say anything, and Nana knew perfectly well why Danica wouldn't live in her grandmother's house.

"Did you give him a deadline?" Nana asked.

"No, I didn't give Cameron a deadline," Danica declared. "No point in saying, *Hey, sell it to me or else, and you only have five days.*"

"He should sell it to you just on principle," her grandmother insisted.

"Just on *what* principle? He didn't have anything to do with this."

"No, but I had to sell it to pay off the medical bills," she noted. "I just want to get it back again."

Danica winced. "Thanks for the reminder," she muttered to herself. As it was, it wasn't her grandmother's fault. The medical expenses down here were something else, and that would cripple anybody. After her mother's death and Danica's subsequent hospitalization, and the rest of the pain and the hellish problems that her grandmother had been through, the medical bills had crippled her financially.

Nana had been forced to sell some of the land, and now all she wanted was to have it back again. The trouble was, getting part of it back was one thing, but she wouldn't get it all back. Maybe she would come to terms with that in a way. Yet, in other ways, Danica didn't think her grandmother would ever make peace with it.

From her grandmother's perspective, the property was still her home in her heart, and, even though Nana understood intellectually that it wasn't, she still found it hard to accept. Given her age, that may be understandable, but it didn't change the fact that nothing she could do would give all that property back to them. Besides, Nana could barely keep up the property she currently had, so going after more of it wouldn't be easy or practical.

Honestly Cameron hadn't done anything wrong by buying it. And certainly he had no reason to give up the land between Nana's home and his, just because her grandmother wanted it back. She'd sold it fair and square, and he'd bought it that way. As far as Danica was concerned, that was it. But, if Cameron was willing to sell a part of it back, Danica would gladly take that piece and build a home for herself. It was definitely something she could do. She would live there by the creek and be very happy. But only the creek area and only that part of the woods. The rest of it was haunted, as far as she was concerned, and the main haunting party was her own damn mother.

The last thing Danica wanted to do was to see Daisy's evil face every night before going to bed or waking up to that same damn smirk every morning. So, maybe something could be said for Cameron's *not* selling it to them after all. The trouble was, they were neighbors regardless. All Danica was trying to do was corral them into a livable space.

WHEN DANICA WOKE the next morning, she felt a little more in control again. There were good days, and there were bad days. She hopped up, took care of her morning ritual, and then, with Benji at her side, she stepped out and went for a walk. The dog had been a stray that had found her years ago, when she'd desperately been looking for a friend.

Technically Danica wasn't allowed to go on the property she'd asked to purchase, but it was still a place that Benji wanted to go to all the time. So, hoping that the good Cameron wouldn't mind, Danica stepped out and took Benji for a walk. They got in a twenty-minute ramble over the property, finally returning through the backyard of Nana's place. They waited outside the house until Nana opened the door.

"There you are," she said, with a smile. "Come in. Come in."

When she hesitated, Nana glared at her. "Get your butt in here," her grandmother snapped. "Let's not be stupid about it."

Danica frowned and stepped closer, but, as soon as she neared the doorway, she couldn't enter.

Her grandmother glared at her and then, as if seeing what was happening, her shoulders slumped. "I am so sorry, child. … It's not letting you in. At least not right now."

"I know," Danica said softly. "Why do you think I haven't come in yet? Do you think it's because of me?"

"Child, it's because of her. Daisy's a very agitated soul. She's adrift."

"If she would at least be at rest for a few moments, it would be a whole different story. But she never is," Danica muttered, with a broken smile.

"I've tried so much to help her, but she just won't leave. If she won't leave, it's because she has something that she needs to do, which should deal with you. It's one of the reasons I wanted you to come home—so your mother's soul can rest."

"*You* might have wanted me to come home," Danica pointed out, "but I'm not sure it was the best idea for me."

Her grandmother slowly nodded. "And that might be true too," she conceded, "but to have both of you so unhappy just breaks my heart."

Danica nodded. "I'll sit out here. The weather's good enough anyway." She stepped over to the patio table with its twin chairs.

"The weather is always enough to grumble about."

"I could do with a good old storm to clear the air, but then all we get is mugginess," Danica said, with a laugh.

"A lot of it is due to your mother too."

"I know, but I keep hoping that one day she'll leave us in peace, but it's not likely to be anytime soon. Especially not now that I'm back."

"I know. I know. I was really hoping that having you home would change things."

Danica just let her ramble.

Danica's mother was an odd spirit and not a happy spirit at that. But Daisy's mood was well past anybody's ability to fix it, ever since she had passed. Danica hadn't seen her mother's spirit since returning, and, for that, Danica was grateful. The last thing she wanted was that visual to go along with everything else. She had already heard Daisy calling Danica's name on a regular basis. The sound drove through her spine and up to her head, until she wanted to scream.

Sometimes it even seemed that Daisy was begging. If Daisy wanted forgiveness, Danica knew she was supposed to forgive, but, damn, it was hard. The fact that her mother had been mentally ill should have made it easier, but somehow it didn't. There didn't seem to be any justice.

Danica caught sight of her face in the nearby window and deliberately turned away. No good could come of looking at that. It was bad enough dealing with the pain and the pressure already, but to see the scar on a regular basis just added insult to injury.

"It's not that bad, you know," her grandmother noted, bringing a tea tray with her.

She smiled over at her. "You're just trying to be nice."

"You could always get it fixed," Nana suggested.

"I could, but you also know that, anytime I've gone to a doctor, something stops me."

"That could just be fear," her grandmother pointed out quickly, then took a seat beside her granddaughter. "It doesn't mean that it's definitely your mother trying to stop you or that she wants her damage to be there forever."

"Maybe, but since we haven't figured out another answer, that's where it stays."

Nana nodded and handed her a cup of tea. "Let's sit and relax. It seems that life is just harder these days."

Danica didn't say anything, but privately she agreed.

Nana asked, "How's work going for you?"

"It's going."

"You say that, and it's always the same. I don't know how you can do any work in that *machine* of yours."

"It's an RV," Danica clarified, with a chuckle. "And it's big. Huge, as a matter of fact, especially for just me and Benji. I have power and water, since I'm hooked up now, so it's perfectly fine. I also have internet, so I can do my work."

"And you're still doing graphics stuff, *huh*?"

The way her grandmother said *graphics stuff* always made Danica chuckle. The poor dear had no idea what *graphics* even meant and had not one iota of interest in finding out about it either. "Yep, I do *graphics stuff*." Her grandmother just glared at her. "And seeing how it's paying the bills right now, it's going just fine."

"Maybe it's fine," Nana replied, "but I don't think it's good. You're isolated, and that's not right. You're alone, and you shouldn't be alone."

With that, Danica faced her grandmother, declaring, "We're not going down that path again. You know perfectly well why I'm alone, and you can see it in town every time I go there. I don't even know why I wanted to come back here."

"You wanted to come back because you want closure, the same as I do."

"Sure, but I don't think closure is to be had."

"I'm not so sure about that. I just can't get past the feeling that, in order for your mother's spirit to be happy, we should solve what happened."

"You mean, outside of what everybody thinks happened?"

Her grandmother looked at her and snapped, "*You* know what happened."

"No, I don't. I lost a lot of my memories, remember? Due to shock, pain, horror, *death*," she stated in a sarcastic tone.

"You brought a little bit back with you too," her grandmother pointed out.

She stilled, looked over at her grandmother, who nodded.

Nana added, "You think I don't know that? I can see it, and that bit of energy is not healthy. It's not good at all."

"Exactly," Danica agreed. "I don't know how to get rid of it, and honestly I'm not sure I give a damn enough to even bother trying."

"It could kill you, Danica. And it could ruin whatever chance you have at happiness. At a future."

"Since we don't even know what I've attracted," Danica pointed out, with a smile, "maybe it won't make a damn bit of difference. Maybe it's just energy."

"We know it's energy," Nana stated, eyeing her calmly. "But it's a matter of what that energy wants, and why it's attached to you."

"It's attached to me for the same reason we talked about last time," Danica replied, with a frown. "It's attached to me because it doesn't know how to reverse it."

Her grandmother wore a solemn expression as she spoke. "Child, I know you don't like hearing this, but I'm pretty sure that's also the reason your mother is hanging around."

At that, Danica frowned at her. "You mean, besides guilt, besides wanting forgiveness, besides trying to kill me or you? Which of those things—"

"*All* of those things," her grandmother stated bluntly. "I know it's hard for you to hear this, but I'm not really sure that your mother killed herself. I'm also not sure that your mother attacked you."

Danica lowered the coffee cup and stared at her. "What are you talking about? Who else could it have been?"

"It's something I've been meaning to bring up for a long time. I spoke to your mother a couple times. You know that."

"I do know that," Danica acknowledged, "but I won't listen to the ramblings of a crazy woman, be it on this side or the other."

CHAPTER 4

SEVERAL DAYS LATER, Cameron was at the hospital, completing yet another back-to-back shift, when he caught one of the orderlies looking at him hesitantly. Frowning, Cameron motioned the employee over. "Hey, Diego. How are you doing?" Cameron inquired. The orderly just shrugged. "Something bothering you?"

Diego just shrugged again.

It was a common phenomenon with employees. They didn't always speak up, and sometimes it took time for them to get comfortable, especially with a new doctor. "Is the job going okay for you?" Cameron asked. Diego nodded. "You seem to have something to say to me. If you do, please just speak up."

Diego shook his head but still grinned.

"Meaning that you *do* have something to say, but you don't want to speak up?" Cameron tried to clarify.

Diego choked out a smile and shrugged.

"Look, Diego. I won't be offended, if you need to say something, even if it's something I won't like, I would rather you share it," Cameron explained. "Particularly when we deal with emergencies in a small town, where you probably know a lot of people. I was born and raised here, but I didn't stick around for all those years afterward because I had to go off and do my schooling."

The orderly frowned and then slowly nodded. "That makes sense. I thought I recognized you from before."

"You did?" Cameron asked cheerfully. "My family lived on the outskirts of town," he added, "but I was bound and determined to be a doctor. So sticking around was never part of my plan. And honestly, coming back home again wasn't really part of my plan either," he said, with a laugh. "Yet, at the end of the day, family is family."

Diego smiled, and this time it was a real smile. "Ain't that the truth."

"Of course, since coming back, I realized that I haven't really reconnected fully because I haven't had time," Cameron shared. "It's been a surprise to see how things have changed."

The orderly nodded, intently studying Cameron, as if weighing his words and wondering if Diego should speak up or not.

"So, what is this about?" Cameron asked, looking at Diego carefully. "Does it have anything to do with Danica, who was here recently?"

At that, the orderly frowned.

Cameron continued. "Apparently everybody already knows she was here. No, she's not sick or anything, in case you were worried." But Cameron knew that no way was Diego worried about Danica. This was about something else. When the orderly still hesitated, Cameron just decided to blurt it out. "Are you trying to warn me about her?"

Diego's eyes lit up with relief, and he nodded.

"It's okay," Cameron replied. "I've known her for a long time."

"But it ain't her," Diego said suddenly.

At that, Cameron stopped. "What do you mean, *it isn't*

her? It isn't her I should be careful of? Or it isn't her—as in she's not who I thought she was?"

Although old and seemingly on his last legs, Diego's mind was still sharp. He slowly nodded. "That's a good way to put it, and I guess both would be true."

"If it's not her I'm supposed to be worried about, who is it then?" Cameron asked, looking around to ensure nobody could hear them. He leaned in. "I would really appreciate your telling me."

The elderly orderly hesitated and then whispered, "You should be worried about her mother."

Cameron straightened. "You mean her dead mother?"

He nodded, obviously relieved that his message had been delivered and understood by the doctor.

"Is she haunting this place?" Cameron asked. He didn't believe in ghosts, but he knew this town had taken on an eerie superstitious overtone that he would do well not to knock or to ignore.

Again Diego nodded. "She's *still* haunting this place." His tone was low, as he glanced around. "Everybody knows it."

"Do you know why?"

"Daisy was murdered," he whispered. "Also something everybody knows."

Cameron straightened and eyed him carefully. "I thought Daisy committed suicide, after trying to kill her daughter."

The old man shrugged. "That's what they say, but what if it's not true?"

"So, if it's not true, who killed her then?"

The old man looked at him steadily. "The rumors say the daughter did it."

Cameron froze. "I heard that mentioned. Can't say I believe it though."

He nodded. "They say that she was the one who killed her mom, then made it look like her mom had attacked her."

"Good God," Cameron said in shock. "I've never heard anything like that."

Diego shrugged. "That's what they say."

"And what do you say?" Cameron asked Diego, looking for any signs of lying or subterfuge, but the old man stared back at him steadily.

"I think she's innocent," Diego stated. "I don't know what happened back then, but, because Danica doesn't know either, Daisy still haunts the place, has for years, since she died."

"And how often does she haunt it?"

Diego glanced around, as somebody walked behind them, yet appeared to be completely uninterested in their conversation. "Every once in a while, and we don't know why, she comes through our ER or the one in the next county, as if she's dying. She's covered in blood, but it's not her blood. She grabs a doctor's lab coat, leaves her bloody handprint, and then she's taken up for X-rays or whatever else you send her for, only she disappears along the way. And then the lab coat where she grabbed is clean, as if she had never touched it. What's even worse is something happens to the person she grabs onto."

The hairs on the back of Cameron's neck rose. "Are you serious?"

Diego nodded, his gaze steady. "In case nobody warned you," he began, "if a young woman who looks like Danica comes through here, step away or else."

"All those years of these hauntings and nobody's investigated?"

Diego gave him a half-cracked smile. "Who'll investigate it? Nobody wants to get close to those hands, just in case they're next."

Cameron let out his breath with a *whoosh*. "So people believe that Danica killed her own mother and made this look like, what, an accident?"

Diego shrugged. "I don't know about an accident. I just know that most of the people here believe that her mother, who was disturbed, didn't kill herself, and that the most likely candidate who did it would be Danica."

"You say *Danica* as if you know her."

Diego hesitated.

Cameron just waited. It was often the best technique with people to remain silent until they fessed up to whatever they were trying to hold back.

Finally the old man replied, "I know the grandmother."

"Ah." Cameron smiled. "Harriet's my neighbor, you know."

He looked at him and then slowly nodded. "That makes sense."

"Why does it make sense?" he asked in confusion.

"Because you're connected." He glanced around. "So, watch yourself, Doc. The last doctor who saw Daisy's ghost died."

JACE WANDERED THROUGH his brother's house, hating the chill that had set in since finding out that the witchy Danica was back. He had a little history with her, not anywhere near enough, yet still way the hell too much. As soon as she'd had her accident, he knew something was different about her, something was wrong. And not just the facial scar but everything else. She'd haunted Jace's dreams ever since, and he was sure something was off about her.

He didn't know how to make his brother understand that Cameron needed to stay away from her. The fact that he'd been away when so much of it had happened here blew Jace away because, although it was old knowledge, it was still something that everybody knew and that nobody liked to talk about.

When his phone rang, he glanced down to see his buddy calling him. He answered it, happy to have a distraction, only to hear the first question out of his friend's mouth.

"Hey, did you hear that Danica's back?"

"I heard," he snapped, "and I can't say I'm happy about it."

Colby laughed. "Yeah, I didn't think you would be. You tend to go off on a rant every time you find out the conversation's heading in her direction."

"She's a witch," he declared.

"Whoa, whoa, whoa. That's pretty strong language. I know you don't like the chick, but I surely will not give her that power."

"You might not, but it's the power she has."

His friend chuckled. "That's because you don't understand why you were attracted to her in the first place."

"It's not about *that*. She was young and pretty … and available. Like, what the hell? I was hormone-driven, so that's not hard to believe."

"Yeah, but then what happened afterward?"

"I'm pretty-damn sure she killed her mother. That's what happened, and you know it."

"I know that's what you keep saying, but do you really

believe that? Because, if so, then she's back again, and maybe this is a good time to make her pay for it."

"Make her pay how?" Jace asked hesitantly.

"Go to the sheriff and his deputies. Come on. That's what they're here for. If Danica murdered her mother, then she should go down for murder. It's pretty damn simple. Stop your caterwauling or do something about it."

At that, Jace started to get angry at his friend.

Finally, after a few minutes of Jace's ranting, Colby stated, "I'll just leave it there. You go talk to whoever you want to talk to, but right now you need to chill. Either have a couple beers and relax, or do some exercise or something, but I don't need to listen to this shit." And, with that, he rang off.

Jace stared down at his phone in consternation. He hadn't meant to go off so hard, but just something about knowing Danica was back hit him in an ugly way.

It wasn't desire. That's for sure. To be honest, it was fear.

CHAPTER 5

DANICA WOKE TO the sound of a vehicle pulling up beside her RV. Benji started barking at the door, which would bring attention to the fact that she was inside the RV. Not what she wanted a visitor because absolutely nothing was good about *that* vehicle, and she didn't need to look out the window to know that it was a cruiser.

As she pulled the curtain to the side, she groaned because, of course, the local deputies were here. Two of them. Obviously everybody knew that she was in town, and, although she'd been aware that this could and would likely happen at some point, she hadn't really been prepared for the idea of it happening right away. But then again, this town was nothing if not full of superstitious old bats.

She quickly dressed, expecting to hear them knock on her door, but instead they went straight to her grandmother's house. She watched them from behind the curtain, as she brushed her teeth. As her grandmother opened the door, she had a big smile on her face. But then that was her grandmother. She loved everybody, or at least gave them that appearance. She said it was important to keep up appearances, so people didn't see her the wrong way.

The trouble was, everybody saw Nana as she was, or as they thought she was—a crazy old lady who thought she was psychic, yet had just enough uncanny accuracy to make everybody uneasy around her, which is why Nana had no friends. It broke Danica's heart to see her grandmother always attempt to be friendly, yet get rebuffed again and again. Nothing was wrong with Nana. She was blessed with the sight—or perhaps cursed, depending on your point of view. Danica didn't know; she'd had plenty of problems of her own.

The fact that she was back was a testament to the relationship she had with her grandmother, because Danica would make this attempt for nobody else in the world. Yet Nana was failing physically. Danica could see it, even if her grandmother refused to acknowledge it. Watching as the smile fell off her grandmother's face, Danica winced, quickly put on sandals, opened the door to let out her dog, then stepped outside and called out, "Good morning."

Immediately the new arrivals turned to look at her. One of the men winced, as he caught sight of her face. She stiffened and stared at him directly. "Were you looking for somebody?"

Her grandmother called out, "It's all right, honey. They're just checking up."

"Checking up on what?" Danica asked coolly, as she studied the two men, who shuffled uncomfortably under her piercing gaze. She'd often found that the only way to deal with people who were out to cause trouble was to face them directly and to make them face themselves, if nothing else.

She looked over at the one man, and a memory twigged. "Hey, Aaron. Is that you?"

He nodded, formed a half smile. "Hey, Danica. Yeah. I'm a deputy in the sheriff's office now."

"That is good news," she said. "I know that's something you always wanted."

"It is, thanks. How are you doing?"

She smiled at him. "I'm doing okay. How about you?"

He shrugged. "I'm okay. Sandy and I managed a few years, but it didn't last," he muttered, kicking a stone in front of him.

"I'm sorry to hear that," Danica said, from the heart. "No surprise though. She had been after bigger and better places. This town was never really where she wanted to live."

"Right, and she's long gone," he muttered, with a shrug. "I got my boy though."

"You have a son?" she asked in delight.

He nodded bashfully. "Yeah, and she didn't want custody because she was heading to Hollywood," he grumbled, almost spitting onto the ground.

"Maybe she'll find whatever it is she's looking for," Danica suggested, "and you've got your boy. How old is he?"

"He's four and a half," he stated, beaming.

"That's lovely," she murmured. "Again something you always wanted."

"I did," he admitted, "except I was thinking about having a whole baseball team to myself."

She chuckled. "Pick the right woman next time. I can see that it was definitely part of your ultimate vision of family life."

"I come from eight," he added, cracking a smile. "It seemed so natural to want the same number." Such bewilderment filled his tone as he continued. "I just don't understand why she wasn't up for it."

Danica shook her head. "Because Sandy never planned on being a housewife and a mom," Danica pointed out. "Lots of women would be happy doing that, but Sandy just wasn't one of them."

He nodded and then caught sight of the sharp look from the man at his side, who glared at the two of them.

Danica smiled at the other deputy. "Hi, I don't think we've met. I'm Danica." She reached out a hand, but he almost tripped over himself, trying to get far enough away. She kept the smile plastered on her face, even as Aaron looked uncomfortable at his partner's actions.

"This is Deputy Trent Smith," Aaron rushed in to say.

"That's okay," she replied, still with a smile and a nod. "I don't bite. Of course my dog might." The deputy glared at her, and she chuckled. "I am used to that reaction. So, what's up? Any particular reason you're here?"

Deputy Smith glared at her. "Yeah, we heard a stranger was in town."

"Really?" she asked in confusion, wondering at the weird sense of familiarity to his face. He was older than Aaron and appeared more seasoned, senior even, but he didn't want much to do with her. "No strangers are here. We were all born and raised here. Unless it's you. Are you new to town?" she asked him. "Yeah, you must be. I've never seen you before."

He continued to glare at her.

She realized she probably shouldn't be pissing him off, but it was too much fun. Besides, that reaction from people was getting very old. She had a scar on her face, but it was hardly anything that made her look like a gargoyle. For the first time, she had to laugh at herself because it really wasn't that terrible. It was disturbing, sure, distressing and probably scary to little kids, but to adults? It shouldn't have any effect at all.

"So, now that you know I'm here, is there anything else I can do for you?" She walked toward her grandmother, then put an arm around her small shoulders, and added, "I'm here to help look after my grandmother. I'm sure you can agree that's a good thing to do."

Aaron smiled, looking over at Nana. "It's been a while since I've seen you, Harriet."

She beamed at him. "I'm always here. Anytime you want to pop in and have a cup of tea, come on by."

He nodded, then looked back at Danica, this time a little more nervously. "It was good to see you, Danica." He nudged his partner. "We just wanted to stop in and to confirm who was here."

"Now you know," Danica stated, giving them both a bright, mocking smile. "Stop in anytime."

And the two of them hastily returned to the cruiser and pulled away.

Danica and Nana remained outside, standing on the grass, watching the sheriff's cruiser go on down the road.

Her grandmother looked at her. "You know, if you were nicer, they might have come in."

"If I was any nicer, they might have taken me down to the station and charged me," she snapped.

Her grandmother sucked in her breath. "I hope you don't believe that'll happen."

"I *hope* it won't happen," she shared, "but I am perfectly aware that plenty of people around here would like to see me arrested. It's not even that they think I did anything wrong, but simply because I'm different, and that makes them all very uncomfortable."

"That just displays *their* faults," Nana declared. "Not yours."

"I know that, Nana. Yet it was funny because, while Aaron was here talking to me, I saw the new deputy's reaction.

Meanwhile, I had just admitted to myself that my face isn't that bad. It's a bit of a shock, yes, at first glance. And it might be something that people have to look at a couple times before they're more comfortable with it," she added, with a chuckle. "However, it's not something to recoil from, the way the new deputy just did. So, definitely something else is going on."

"It's the same as the rumors I told you about."

"Right, those rumors," Danica noted, with a shake of her head. "Do people really think I killed my own mother?"

"I think they don't quite understand, so they're looking at everything. Plus scared people always lash out," Nana explained, patting Danica's hand. "Remember that."

"I know. Scared people hurt people."

"Hurt people?" Nana repeated.

"Exactly, and they don't know they're doing it, so we can't blame them for it." She looked at Nana. "Have you been doing anything around town to make them leery of you?"

She snorted. "No, I sure haven't, but occasionally something pops up, and I do feel compelled to tell people about it."

"Of course you do." Danica let out a sigh. "You also know that's guaranteed to make them afraid of you."

"Maybe, but I still think that, if somebody is in danger of getting hurt in the next few days, I need to tell them about it. And that will never change."

"No, and, because it won't ever change," Danica replied, with a smile, "none of this will ever change. You will always be on the outside."

"Just like you," her grandmother pointed out shrewdly.

She smiled and nodded. "Yes, just like me."

"But you think you're on the outside because of your looks."

"No, I'm on the outside because my own mother tried to murder me," she stated, shaking her head. "Even worse, old ideas and fears stick around. However, I've never really expected anyone to think I might have had something to do with my mother's death, so I'm surprised to find they've jumped on that bandwagon to begin with."

"I don't know why they would have jumped on it either," Nana said. "It was never fair to you, but I suppose there really is no such thing as fairness."

"No, that's very true. They're not thinking. They're reacting. And, when people *just* react," she added, with a shrug, "all kinds of shit happens."

Her grandmother smiled. "Come on inside. Let's get you some coffee. I wish you would sleep in the house though."

"That won't happen, as you very well know," Danica argued, "not when we know who runs the house."

"If you ask me, is there a choice?"

"No, there's not. If I try to stay in this house after dark, you know perfectly well what will happen."

"We could work on that," Nana suggested somewhat hopefully.

"My RV is parked in the driveway, Nana. I think that will be close enough in this situation."

"I would still prefer that you were in the house."

"Maybe, at some point, but, for now, it seems that this is as far as I can go." Danica swung her arm around, noting the grassy side yard they stood on.

"You could ask Daisy nicely," her grandmother offered in a charming tone.

Rolling her eyes at that, Danica walked up to the steps,

looked at the house, and asked, "May I come in for coffee?"

The door opened but just a tad.

"See? I can come in for coffee if I ask politely," she noted in a mocking tone, "but only because it's daytime. As soon as it gets dark out, you know that the house won't want me in here."

Her grandmother winced. "I'm sorry, dear." Nana opened the door wider, and they both stepped inside.

"Me too, but let's not forget that she's also your daughter," she murmured. "Plenty of pain for all of us."

"Indeed," Nana said. "I still struggle to understand why she would have done that to you."

"Yet you also know that, in the last few years before it happened, she couldn't stand the sight of me." She looked around the room, bright and colorful. "In a way, it would be nice to know. Why does anybody choose to kill someone they should by all rights love?" She sat down at the kitchen table, filled with an odd sense of discomfort. The house had never been home to her, certainly not since she'd left. After coming back, it had a definite *You're not welcome* energy to it.

"Did she ever tell you that she loved you?" her grandmother asked from the far side of the room.

Danica thought about it, then shook her head. "Honestly, no. I don't think she ever did. She wasn't into that lovey-dovey stuff, and she sure as hell wasn't into hugs and cuddles and looking after people," she added, "but you already knew that."

"Of course. I couldn't get a hug out of my own daughter," Nana sadly admitted. "I don't know what I did wrong."

"Why do you assume that *you* did something wrong?" Danica asked. "My mother was a force unto herself. She did as she pleased, and the rest of us were just on the edges of her life, if she let us, and, if not, we weren't. In the end, I'm not sure Daisy was really all there."

"I think that's an easier way for you to look at it too," Nana replied, bringing a tall silver pot of coffee over to the table. "It's hard for me to think about what she did, but it's got to be even harder for you."

"I try not to think about it at all," Danica shared in a quiet tone. She waved her hand. "Now, let's talk about something much nicer."

"We could, but that would mean telling you that the hot water heater seems to have quit completely last night."

She stared at her grandmother and groaned. "Seriously?"

Nana grimaced. "I don't think I did anything to break it, but it's not acting right today."

"Of course not," Danica said, with a sigh. "I'll take a look at it."

"You don't have to. I can call somebody in. I'm sure somebody will come and look after it."

Danica looked over at her grandmother and shook her head. "Are you sure? Because I'm not. I'm not sure at all. Too often, as you and I both know, the people who come aren't ones we can trust. The people who come end up causing us all kinds of trouble and likely have a negative purpose."

"That talk is practically guaranteed to make people not come at all," Nana noted, with a laugh. "Sure. I sense all kinds of ghosties in this place, and some of them are pretty-damn cranky about your being here at all, but I also know that some of them aren't bad. They're just people attached to the home." Her grandmother sighed. "I'm in an odd mood these days. We're not to that point yet, but you do know that the spirits are calling me daily."

"Tell them to *F-off*," Danica demanded, glaring at her grandmother. "I didn't come all this way to have you up and die on me."

"No, and I do appreciate the fact that you did come all this way, even if I don't quite understand it." Danica glared at her grandmother, and her grandmother smiled. "I know you don't like it when I talk like that, but it's confusing for me, sometimes a little more confusing than intended."

"Of course," Danica replied. "Don't you worry about a thing. I'll get the hot water heater fixed."

Nana shook her head. "Do you have any money to get it fixed?"

"I have some money. The rest, we'll find a way."

Her grandmother nodded slowly. "I don't know what I would have done if you hadn't come home."

"I'm here now, so let's just deal with that and forget about the rest."

"In that case, maybe *you* should take a look at the hot water heater," Nana suggested hopefully. "I don't know if you can do anything to fix it, but I would really like a shower."

With a crack of laughter, Danica nodded, smiled, and got up, heading down to the ancient basement, where all the utilities were. As she walked up to the hot water heater, she sighed. "Come on. Do you really want to knock off now? Can't you wait just a little bit longer?"

And it almost seemed as if she got a message across, as she heard something.

It wasn't a voice in her head. It may have been a noise, yet it wasn't. She'd always found that equipment talked to her, though she knew that would sound foolish to anybody else.

She glanced around the room. "How about holding on a little bit longer? Just a little bit. I don't suspect Nana's got more than six months, but what are the chances that you can give her hot water for that time?" She placed her hands on the actual hot water heater itself, checking out what she could feel, and it wasn't long before she realized that it just needed to be relit.

She bent down, checked the pilot light, and looked for the lighter she'd left down here years and years ago. Sure enough, there the lighter was, and she quickly relit the pilot, listening as it fired up again.

She made her way upstairs to her grandmother, who stood at the top of the stairs with a hopeful expression on her face. "The pilot light had gone out again," Danica shared.

Her grandmother cackled with joy. "I'd already checked that damn pilot light," she stated, "and it wasn't out before."

"It's working now," Danica confirmed, with a smile, "so you can have your shower in a few hours."

"That's good to hear," her grandmother replied. "If nothing else, having you home always keeps the equipment running smoothly." As she walked back to the kitchen table and her cup of coffee, her grandmother asked her, "Did you ever think to make … *repairs* work for getting money?"

She frowned at Nana. "You mean, as in creating money?"

"I don't know, just anything to make it so you're not always quite so desperate and on the edge of financial problems," her grandmother pointed out.

"Did I say I was on the edge of having money problems?" she asked.

Her grandmother frowned. "You never tell me anything

when it comes to money."

"Nothing to discuss," Danica stated, with a chuckle. "I'm okay, and that's all I care about. Food on the table, dog food for Benji. All kinds of things in life I don't need but might be nice to have. Yet I don't choose to worry about it." She sipped her coffee and then asked, "Do you know the other deputy?"

Her grandmother shook her head. "It may have been Simon's boy, but I don't know that for sure."

"Ah. Simon's boy." Danica frowned. "I guess that makes sense."

"Why?" her grandmother asked. "What about any of that makes sense?"

"Simon has always been scared of us, scared of the gift, believing the superstitions," she replied, chuckling. "So his boy has probably picked that up from him."

"Yeah, but that boy is hardly a boy. He's a man, but he's a man full of prejudice. Yet where did it come from? They almost always have a source, and, in this case, it would have come from Simon. What's his son's name?"

"Aaron introduced him as Trent. Yet, back in the day, I thought everyone called him Casper," she shared, staring off in the distance. "Maybe it's a nickname."

"Casper, like the ghost?" Nana chuckled at that. "Maybe it's a good name after all, making fun of his superstitions." Nana studied Danica, watching her facial expressions, awaiting her response.

Danica shrugged. "You just never really know with things like that," she replied, with a smile. "Don't worry. I have no intention of talking to him or causing him any pain, unless he continues to show up here."

"You do know your very existence upsets him."

"Oh, I know that much," Danica agreed, with a smile. "I won't do anything on purpose."

"Good, glad to hear it. On the other hand, if you would do something nice for people, maybe they would learn to forgive."

"I've done nothing for them to forgive me about," she declared, looking at her grandmother.

Her grandmother winced and went silent. "I know that, … and I didn't mean it the way it sounded. Nothing that happened was your fault. Still, I always find myself looking for ways to make amends."

"We can all make amends," Danica suggested, "yet you should just give up trying to make amends when the people choose not to see past their own prejudices. So don't you worry. I won't cause you trouble. I won't get anybody else irate over my being here. They seem to do that all on their own. Yet I'm just trying to look after you."

"Partly why I wanted you to come home was to make peace with your past before I'm gone," she explained in frustration. "I don't really want you to go through this nightmare every day of your life. The only way we'll solve it is if we find out who killed your mother. At least then people will stop thinking it was you."

"Sure, and what will they find out? Except that Daisy killed herself. You and I both know that, and absolutely no way is anybody else ready to hear that. So, what am I supposed to do?" she asked.

Her grandmother's shoulders slumped. "You're right, and I'm sorry. I hadn't really considered how the rest of the world always looks at you."

"I'm not looking at them in any other way either. I'm just ignoring them. And, with any luck, people will slowly get used to my being around again."

"You'll stay? You won't let them chase you away?" her grandmother asked, fear and hope intermingled in her facial expression.

Danica reached across the table and picked up the frail, pale, papery-thin hand of her grandmother, then smiled. "I won't let them chase me away."

Nana smiled and relaxed. "In that case, we need to go grocery shopping."

Danica shook her head. "Oh, no—hell no. We just went grocery shopping. I'm not going out for you to parade me around and to tell everybody that I'm home again."

"It would be good if we did though," Nana replied cheerfully. "At least let's go get ice cream this afternoon."

"Don't you have ice cream in the freezer?" she asked suspiciously.

"Maybe, but it doesn't really matter because ice cream from the parlor has a very different taste than ice cream from a store."

"Maybe it does," Danica conceded, shaking her head. "However, it looks to me as if you're just trying to get me back out in public."

"Would that be so bad?"

"*So bad*? No. But so good? Absolutely not." And speaking of which, she placed her empty coffee cup on the table. "I didn't take Benji for his walk."

"You go do that." Nana smiled at her granddaughter. "As soon as you return, we'll eat breakfast and then plan our day."

"Plan our day?" Danica repeated. "I work, remember?"

Her grandmother's face fell. "Right, I forgot that."

But seeing the disappointment on Nana's face, Danica

offered, "I could take maybe the rest of this morning off and work this afternoon."

Her grandmother's smile blossomed again. "Now that," she declared, "would be lovely. Thank you."

"No promises on how long that'll last though," she warned. "I must work in order to keep the money flowing."

"Got it," Nana said cheerfully, yet completely ignored her warning. "I still think it'll all turn out okay."

"Me too. Otherwise I wouldn't have come back," Danica stated. "I didn't sign up for this without realizing what I was up against."

"No, maybe not, but you did it for me—" And Nana stopped, as if finding the right words.

"Don't feel guilty, Nana."

"What?"

"You heard me. Don't feel guilty about my coming back and all that went on before. Please do not feel guilty."

"I don't want to feel guilty, but, if things don't go well now and if I've ruined your life by bringing you home again," she shared, "that will be very hard."

"You haven't ruined my life at all. This is a choice I made. I'm here, so relax. I'll take Benji for a walk now."

"You do that." Then she suddenly asked, "Pancakes?"

Danica glanced back at her grandmother. While not hungry in any way, but knowing perfectly well that her grandmother needed something to do, Danica nodded. "Sure. Pancakes would be lovely." And, with that, she escaped out the back door, hearing her grandmother get up and happily bustle around the kitchen behind her. Benji, absolutely delighted, darted around outside, racing toward the creek ahead of her.

She stopped at the edge of the water and smiled. Something was so soothing about the ripple of the water, the beauty of the overall scene, the clear blue stream allowing everything below to be seen. The creek made her heart feel calm and peaceful when she was here. Something to be said for having acreage with a creek on it.

With that thought, she turned and glanced in the direction of Cameron's property. She had no idea how he felt about her request. She could only hope that he would consider it in good faith because that's how she had presented it to him, in good faith.

She did want to stay with her grandmother. She didn't think her grandmother had all that much time left and certainly didn't need the property in terms of that time frame. Yet it would be something that would put her grandmother at ease, just knowing the land was back together again.

And, if her grandmother did pass away sometime soon, Danica wasn't sure what she herself would do. How did one plan for that eventuality, when absolutely no one else was in her world? It was just the two of them, and to lose that one connection to another living person who cared about her would hurt, and in a big way.

She could only hope that would be a long time away. However, Danica knew in her heart of hearts a date. A date that was emblazoned in her mind, and it was only a few weeks away.

A few weeks to store up memories of a lifetime, and then her grandmother would be gone, and Danica would be all alone.

She wandered for the next twenty or thirty minutes, trying to find that sense of peace again, that sense of connection to the land. It really was the only reason she would consider staying after Nana was gone. This connection to the land was all she had. Yet, with so much conflict in town, couldn't she find a better place?

Still, she really didn't have a choice.

She needed to stay—at least for now.

The more she walked, the more peace soaked into her soul. She found a good spot to stop. She sat down by the creek, picked up a few rocks, and tossed them aimlessly into the water beside her. She worked on finding that inner core, that place of concentration and peacefulness again.

Every time before she worked on a project, she took a few moments to pull back out of the real world and to become something of a creator again, opening up the wells of creativity to allow her to do the work that she did. She was working on all kinds of things at the moment, some personal, some private, some for clients. All of which meant that, when she was on, she needed to be on, and she was on. She needed to focus. Right now, what she needed to do was shut it all down.

The official visit this morning by two deputies had rattled her in a way that she hadn't expected. She thought for sure that most people would have forgotten about her by now. Yet she always knew that some of the old memories would remain. However, she hadn't really seen just how bad it could be, not until she saw the reaction of the one deputy. While Aaron's reaction should have calmed her, his partner's had just highlighted what she was up against.

Now she realized that her notoriety had grown instead of shrunk, and that wasn't good. She hadn't done anything to make people treat her the way they did.

Yet habits died hard, and people, especially those with small-town mentalities, were especially brutal about taking it out on others. So, whether Danica liked it or not, she would deal with this, at least until some of the disgruntlement died down.

She didn't know what that would take, but she was prepared to let it go because her grandmother was here, and that was all that mattered.

Hearing a *crunch* beside her, she stiffened and turned to see Cameron walking toward her. Benji raced over to greet him, his small body vibrated with joy at the sight of him. She checked to ensure that she was still on her grandmother's property and noted she was probably right on the border. "I'm still on Grandma's property," she said smoothly.

He looked at her in surprise, glanced back, and nodded even as he crouched down to greet Benji. "It never occurred to me to doubt or to question that," he replied. "It's not exactly something I worry about."

She nodded and smiled. "That's good to know. I wouldn't trespass on purpose."

"It's a minor point," he noted, "particularly since this is clearly a space that you really love."

"It is," she murmured, "but, if it's a space you love too, then that makes life a little more difficult."

He chuckled. "How's your grandmother doing today?"

"In a way, she's better, I think," she shared. "The day in the grocery store was a little distressing, but—" She quickly told him about the incident, and he nodded.

"Small towns. It's one of the reasons I couldn't wait to get away from here, once I grew up," Cameron admitted, with a hint of longing in his tone. "I was heading for the big city, you know, the big-time."

"Why did you come back here?" she asked, looking at him before glancing to make sure that Benji hadn't wandered too far away but instead he'd stretched out on the ground a few feet away. "When you think about it, I'm sure an awful lot of other places need doctors."

"There are, no doubt about that," he agreed, with a smile, "but my father had passed away, and eventually family becomes the bottom line."

She nodded. "I'm sorry to hear that. That's why I'm back too. I never really thought I would return," she conceded, cracking a smile. "And it was all I could do to get away fast enough."

"Of course, particularly after what you went through."

She glanced back and nodded. "I presume somebody filled you in on that."

"I've heard a bunch of variations at this point," he shared, with a smile. "It seems you have grown bigger than a mere local legend."

"That's the last thing I ever wanted," she muttered, with a sigh. "I would much prefer for everything to be calm, peaceful, quiet, and for me to be completely ignored. How's that sound?"

"I don't think that'll happen anytime soon," he stated, smiling at her. "I suspect that the more you ignore it, the better off it'll get."

"That's my hope," she said. "I don't want Nana upset. The deputies were here first thing this morning too, which doesn't exactly make things calm or quiet." When he looked at her in surprise, she shrugged. "I knew one of them. I went to school with Aaron. The other one, maybe a new deputy, was Trent, or *Casper* was his nickname, if Nana's memory serves," she shared, with a shrug. "He took one look at me, fell backward several steps, then basically stuttered his way through interrogating me as to why I was home again."

"Did he really interrogate you?"

She sighed and shook her head. "That's not fair, I guess. He didn't *directly* accuse me of anything, but he did say they were checking around to determine what *strangers* were in town."

"That doesn't sound very normal."

"No, nothing normal about it," she declared, "but it's very typical of what I deal with here."

"I'm sorry. I didn't realize it was that bad."

She shrugged. "Doesn't matter. Did you think about what I asked you?"

"I haven't really had much of a chance," he replied, taken aback. "Sorry, this walk today was just me trying to find a few minutes to destress from work. Part of the problem with moving back home was the fact that I knew it was a small town. I knew that there weren't very many doctors. It's another of the reasons I came back, but, with so few providers, I'm working way more than I should, and I just haven't had five minutes to myself."

"Aah. That makes sense too. I hear a massive shortage of skilled doctors are everywhere."

"There are, so any thought about leaving just makes me feel guilty because what will I do? Desert the people who I grew up with, leaving them without a doctor and poor odds of getting another?"

"Yet you can't be held responsible for everybody," she pointed out. "If you need to leave for your sake, then you need to leave."

"I know. I've thought about it a couple times—believe me."

She nodded, liking his quiet admission because it was the truth. She couldn't imagine trying to deal with everybody here. “Is it the people here or is it just the workload?”

“It’s the workload,” he stated, giving her a smile. “Just no end to it, and I can’t catch a break. I’ve been working seventeen, eighteen, close to twenty days in a row again now,” he replied, “and that’s with overtime too, and still no end is in sight.”

She winced. “Twenty days of overtime without a break? I’m not even sure that’s legal.”

“It probably isn’t, but what else are we to do, when nobody else handles car accidents and the like? Plus, people come to the ER at night, so they can get treated. That says a lot about the town.”

“Several other towns are close by,” she noted. “Surely they could go to one of those.”

“They could, but not if it’s an emergency. Or maybe it’s more convenient because I’m closer.” He smiled and sat down on a tree stump beside her, releasing a big sigh. “It’s really peaceful here, isn’t it?”

“It is,” she agreed. “It’s one of the reasons why I would love to buy that piece of land.” She looked at him intently. “It’s just the place for me.”

“Would you stay though, or would you leave? I would hate to see land like this sold back to the family and then have you turn around and sell the whole thing off again.”

“I’m not even sure what I can do about that,” she admitted. “My grandmother’s land is tied up in all kinds of trusts and things.” She gave a wave of her hand. “I don’t think my mother could ever leave because of that.”

“Couldn’t or wouldn’t?”

“Both. Daisy wanted to. She really wanted to. She was pretty desperate to get away from here. This was not any place for a person like my mother. She was after the nightlife.

She wanted to go places, to be places. Yet she was never really stable enough for it. Every time she had a partner or a boyfriend, something would go wrong, or he would be the small-town type and didn't want to leave. It drove her batty."

"What about your father?"

She shook her head. "I'm not even sure who he is," she shared. "I don't particularly care. He was just another stranger I didn't know, one more face in a world of faces who didn't care, … so whatever." She hoped that she sounded at least a little convincing in that regard. She had thought about her father quite a lot in the last few years, especially as her grandmother had aged. Danica realized where things were heading and how alone she would be at the end of it.

"Are you alone in this world?" Cameron asked.

It was almost as if he had read her thoughts. "After my grandmother? … Yes." She nodded. "I'm not now, but I will be."

"Will you search for your father?"

"Who knows who he even is?" she stated, with a shrug. "For all I know, he was a traveling salesman. My mother was unhappy, desperate to get away, desperate to not be associated with my grandmother. Daisy did drugs for a time. She did anything she could, … just to forget, to live, to be somebody. She was always very unstable, so that had an effect, and, over time, the impact was very negative, very damaging," she murmured.

He nodded but didn't say anything for a minute or two. "But you, you never went that route?"

"No. Not me. … I love my grandmother, but I didn't feel as if her second sight affected me. I didn't feel that it should. What affected me most was being the daughter of my mother," she clarified, with a sigh. "It's hard when people saw her almost as the local whore—and honestly I don't mean that in a bad way, just that she changed boyfriends frequently, to the point that nobody felt safe, and that included married men as well. The local women hated Daisy because of that and wondered if I were the offspring of their husbands, which just made life even more complex."

"Wow," Cameron muttered. "That couldn't have made for an easy childhood. I don't remember any of that from our school days."

"No, and, to a certain extent, I thought I had dealt with it. You grow up thinking you've got it all locked down, but then things blow up, and you wonder if you understand anything at all in the world. I do get that the world is not kind to people who are different," she pointed out, then took a moment, as if collecting her thoughts. "The world isn't kind to anybody with a mental illness or to anybody who is different or has a disability, even if it isn't readily apparent."

"Meaning your scar?"

"Meaning my scar," she agreed.

"And yet you could have it fixed."

"I could have fixed it, and I still might at some point."

"Sometimes you find it useful, do you not?" he murmured. When she glanced at him, he smiled and nodded. "I see all kinds of things in my world, remember?"

"How would you think that my scar would be useful?" she asked curiously.

"Because it keeps people away," he noted. "I'm sure you can count on one hand the number of people who have gotten past that barrier."

Her lips crooked, as she looked at him. "You're pretty

smart, aren't you?"

"I am," he confirmed, with a chuckle. "Also, apart from your scar, some of what I would call the *woo-woo* stuff going on with Harriet has everybody petrified."

"I know that, but I'm not sure how much of it is for real and how much is not," she pointed out. "I guess the jury is still out, in a way."

"Even with your grandmother?"

"Yeah, even with my grandmother. It's not the easiest thing having her as my relative either," she shared, with a smile. "Everybody looked at us like some party joke for a while. *Hey, bring Danica to the party, and she can read people and tell us if we will all get our tall, dark, and handsome boyfriends.* You know, that sort of thing," she murmured.

"Did they really do that?" he asked.

"Yeah, they *really* did," she confirmed, with a laugh. "Again, desperate to be welcomed and included, I would go and do all kinds of stuff," she admitted, with a headshake. "I would have been much better off staying home."

"So, were you ever right?"

"I was right more often than I wasn't," she said sadly, "but people don't want the truth. They want what they want, and sugarcoated at that. Just so they can believe in a happily ever after and not worry about it."

"Oh, ouch," Cameron replied. "And I suppose you told them they weren't getting their happily ever after then?"

"It wasn't a choice. I didn't really even think about it," she admitted. "I just told them the truth, and sometimes that meant telling one of them that her boyfriend was sleeping with her best friend. As you can imagine, that caused all kinds of drama and cemented my reputation and popularity back then."

"Sounds like a raw deal, if you ask me," he replied.

"It wasn't easy at the best of times. As my mother degenerated, and my grandmother got a little bit wilder and looser with her tongue about things happening around her—even stopping people in the streets and telling them they should go home and lock up because they were in danger—only to have an ex-husband come and attack them the following day. It got pretty wild there for a while." Danica shrugged. "I left as soon as I could, and stayed away as long as possible. Yet I can't leave Nana on her own at this stage of her life, so it is what it is."

They sat in companionable silence for a long moment with Benji back to wandering around them, sniffing everything in his sight.

Then Cameron announced, "Since I'm selling the property to you and not to Harriet, I'll do that."

She looked at him in delight. "Seriously?"

He nodded. "If nothing else, I can see you need a home." When she stiffened, he smiled at her. "No, I'm not doing this out of charity. I don't do charity and certainly not when it comes to my own property and my own home. I'll figure out just how much of the land I want to sell."

"It's one title, and, though you could split it, my preference would be to have as much of it as possible."

"Since I bought that from your grandmother, I also picked up the land on the other side of me," he murmured. "That's why my house is more to that other side than this side," he explained. "So, in theory, it would be okay if you had this whole piece. I'm just not sure I'm ready to say that yet."

"No rush," she murmured, but there was, because she felt joy starting to sing inside her. "I would really, really,

really, really love it if you would, though."

He nodded. "Let me talk to my lawyer about how to make this happen."

"Of course, and we should still come up with a price we can both agree to," she pointed out.

"We should, but I'm sure we can reach an agreement on something. You know where property prices are at, I presume?"

"They're not bad around here right now," she replied, "though, for a while there, they were pretty scary."

He laughed. "Depends on what you mean by *scary*."

She smiled. "I just know that I'll never sell my grandmother's place, unless somebody wants a haunted property as part of his group of properties," she murmured, "yet it's still worth something."

"It is. I'll get an idea of what a fair assessment is on the land parcel, and then I'll get back to you. How's that?"

"Thank you." Danica smiled with delight. She gave him the first real and honest smile from her and beamed at him. He froze, staring at her for a long moment, as if transfixed, then she slowly let her smile drop away. "Is something wrong?" she asked, as she got up stiffly, wondering what she'd done.

"No. Nothing's wrong at all. It's just … I saw you really smile and it, … it was really beautiful."

She stared at him in surprise, then shook her head. "Nobody else would agree with you."

"I don't give a shit what anybody else thinks," he said, with a chuckle. "I just know that was one of the most beautiful, natural smiles I've ever seen in my life." He grinned. "And it was really nice to see." At that, he got up. "Now that I've made you uncomfortable, I'll head home and grab some breakfast."

She laughed. "Sounds good."

"Maybe you'll come over and have breakfast with me one day."

She looked at him in surprise, and it was obvious, no matter how she tried to disguise it, that she was shocked by the invitation.

He stopped, frowning at her. "You really don't have any friends, do you?"

She slowly shook her head. "No, I sure don't. People are too scared of me to be close to me."

He nodded. "Maybe so. I prefer to make my own decisions. So, as far as I'm concerned, it's all good. If you want to come for breakfast one morning, that would be nice. If you would rather not, that's okay too. Whatever. I'm happy either way." And, with that, he turned and strode off.

She was left, staring at him in consternation. She wasn't even sure what she was supposed to say, but somewhat belatedly she yelled back, "One time, that would be nice."

He raised a hand in acknowledgment, without breaking his stride, and continued back toward his house.

Smiling, she glanced back again, and the doctor had gone from sight. The location of his house made more sense now, something she'd never understood before, when he had all this land over here. She'd been grateful for it because it left her grandmother's place mostly quiet. Now that Danica had heard how he had the property on the other side as well, that additional purchase probably made selling Nana's property to Danica a bit easier to let go of. As she thought about it, she recalled a big meadow over there, which was quite pretty, peaceful even. It all made far more sense to her now. It made sense that he would choose that space.

But she preferred the wild spaces.

She preferred the *alone* spaces.

She preferred her own home ancestry, and that was really what this was all about.

Now, with a buoyant bounce in her step, she headed back to tell her grandmother the good news. As she walked into the kitchen, she saw no sign of Nana.

She called out to her. Seeing that the stove was still on, with pancakes burning, she quickly shut off the burner, removed the pan, and raced around the rooms, calling out for Nana, heading to the bathroom first and finding nothing. Stepping out to the front yard, she heard Benji barking like crazy. As soon as Danica rounded the corner of the front porch, she saw her grandmother, lying in a garden bed, unconscious.

CHAPTER 6

HARRIET WANDERED THROUGH the maze, and she knew where she was, a familiar place, whether she liked it or not. She'd spent her life here. But she was on a mission—her mission to help her granddaughter before it was too late. Danica needed help, whether she liked it or not. "Damn it, Stefan, where are you?" A muted grumble came, and she grinned. "Nice to know you're still around."

"As if I have a choice," Stefan muttered, slowly showing up in front of her. "What's going on?"

"I told you that trouble is coming."

"I know. You have a time frame or any other information?"

"No, I don't. I just know it's coming, faster and faster."

"And you still think it has to do with your daughter?"

"I know so," Harriet murmured. It was hard to see him in this frozen state.

"What happened to you?" he asked.

She hesitated. "It doesn't matter. I don't know who did it, but I don't think it's related."

"How can you think it's not related?" Stefan asked, no humor in his tone. "You were attacked, and now here you are, walking in our frozen world, trying to warn me about your granddaughter. Yet I need you to look after her."

Immediately Harriet gave him a headshake.

"You know you should," Stefan stated.

"No, I don't know," argued Harriet. "I also understand it's a task I cannot complete, as you well know. Looking after Danica requires more than I can do." Harriet nodded slowly. "She needs help."

"Help she will get," Stefan agreed gently, "but I can't protect her from here."

"Cameron owns the property, the old part of the property," Harriet said. "I asked Danica to see if he would sell it back to us, so we could be whole again."

"Yet it's not about the property," Stefan pointed out.

"No, no, it's not," Harriet whispered. "As you well know, it's about keeping things safe."

"You think it's connected to the property? Have there been any incidents since Cameron showed up, since he bought the place?"

"Yes and no," Harriet replied. "I'm not sure what the problem is, really. If I knew, I would tell you. But I figured that, if Danica can buy it from Cameron, maybe that would close the loop."

"It might not have anything to do with the ownership of the property," he reminded her.

"People are often attached to a place," Harriet noted.

"Do you think your daughter is being threatened?" Stefan asked.

"I don't know," Harriet replied, almost frantic, "but something is very wrong."

"*That* I agree with," Stefan said, his tone soothing. "You know that your time's coming,"

She shook her head violently. "It can't. I can't go yet," she cried out. "Don't you understand? Danica's not ready."

"I hear you, but some things happen in their own way."

"But not this. She's already paid enough. She doesn't need this too."

Stefan sighed, a gentle whisper of a sound that crossed time and distance effortlessly.

With that, Harriet finally smiled. "I know you think I'm just a crazy old lady," she murmured, "but this crazy old lady has one goal in life, and that is to keep her granddaughter safe."

"For that reason alone," Stefan replied, "I am here talking to you now. You know she's gifted. You've watched her. You've kept an eye on her." He chuckled. "It's instinctive. Whenever somebody moves through the ethers who has power yet isn't trained—you and I both know how dangerous it is."

"Sure, but I couldn't train her. I didn't have the time or energy, and then she left. She wouldn't have anything to do with us. Even now, I'm sure she would fight tooth and nail to not acknowledge even the basics of her gift."

"She might surprise you," Stefan stated.

Harriet felt the intensity of his gaze, the strangeness of it, even though he wasn't anywhere close to her. "You're checking me over," she murmured.

"Of course. You are a constant in my world these days," Stefan shared. "I'm trying to see where and what is going on."

"If you figure it out, let me know," she murmured. "Some days are good, and some days I feel as if I've lost it."

"Some days *are* good, and some days you *have* lost it," he agreed, a smile in his tone. "That doesn't mean it's bad though."

"Doesn't mean it's good either," she whispered in despair. "Danica's suffered enough."

"Yet she's grown stronger," Stefan declared, keeping his tone calm and contained. "She has grown stronger, but, without training, that in itself just isn't enough."

Silence came, as if he were peering into the distance. He very well could be, as he was incredibly powerful. Harriet didn't know anything about him, except that she managed to communicate with him, and that, in itself, had been a gift.

Over all this time, she'd never met him in real life, had never seen him in person in her conscious world, had no clue what he really looked like—only that he was here on the ethers. He was a lifeline for those like her, who couldn't easily work within the world anymore, who struggled to find normalcy in a life that just wasn't normal, who struggled to find any commonality with the world around her. For that reason Harriet spent a lot of time in the ethers.

"You have taken grave chances coming here at this time," he murmured.

"I had to," she whispered. "I had to. It's all about keeping Danica safe. It's all about keeping her gifts safe."

"But does she even know about *her gifts*?"

"She knows, just not the extent, not the depth. In truth, not really any of the details." Harriet released a hard sigh. "She never wanted to, not with her mother acting out, setting bad examples of what not to do."

"Of course," he acknowledged gently, "but hiding isn't an answer."

"Might not be an answer, but it sure seems to be a solution for Danica. You need to help her."

Within the silence he contemplated her words.

Harriet knew Stefan wouldn't walk away. No way he could. It just wasn't in him. Neither did it affect just him.

He groaned and added, "She needs to know."

"I know she needs to know, but she won't accept it. So, anything I tell her, she will refute, before even giving it a chance for her to listen, to agree, much less to understand just how intricately woven she is in this world of energy."

"Yet that in itself isn't easy either," he whispered. "It won't be easy for her."

"It will never be easy for her," Harriet noted sadly. "What her mother did to Danica caused such heartache that I don't know if Danica can ever open herself up to this again."

"Did Danica ever open up her gifts in the first place?"

"I don't know. Maybe she did and kept it all hidden. Maybe it was already beyond her at that time."

"What about your daughter? How were Daisy's gifts?"

"Crazy, wild, uncontrolled."

"How much of that was her own personality?"

"A lot of it," Harriet whispered. "Daisy didn't want anything to do with her gifts if they wouldn't bring her fame and fortune. She didn't understand helping others for the sake of helping others. She wanted us to be free, to have things." Harriet's tears clogged her throat. "She was my daughter, and I loved her, but I never understood her, and I couldn't get her to understand me. The harder I tried, the more she balked. I would like to think, had she lived, that we would have found a way to communicate, but we never had that chance."

"Daisy was tormented," Stefan said.

"Too tormented," Harriet murmured. "And nothing I could do seemed to help her. It was the one and only time that I despaired of these gifts. What's the point of gifts if you can't do any good for the people you love? I lost her, but I will not lose Danica."

And, with that, she waved her hands, sending off and out of the way both Stefan and the world she was in. She slowly opened her eyes and woke up, staring around at a sterile white room, knowing with a sinking heart exactly where she was.

CHAPTER 7

DANICA SAT OUTSIDE her grandmother's cubicle in the ER. She knew Cameron wasn't working today, but she wanted to call him in to ensure that her grandmother would be okay. Yet, in her heart of hearts, she knew that her grandmother wouldn't ever be okay. Not really. Danica could hope for a little bit more time with Nana. Still, Danica suspected that her grandmother had a perfectly good idea of when her passing would come. Nana wasn't psychic for nothing, though even that term made Danica wince.

Her mother had made a mockery of everything her grandmother stood for. And Danica, growing up with the two of them, had made a mockery of anything resembling a family life. Only after her mother had died did her grandmother ease back and open up to Danica about that strained relationship, revealing how much torment had existed between Nana and Daisy. It was sad because her mother had been torn up about the whole second-sight concept and had not been happy to have any association with it. Yet, at the same time, Daisy had been the one who had used and abused her gifts to get favors from people.

Her mother had been mentally ill. Yet nobody ever gave her credit for it or recognized it. Mental illnesses here in this town weren't treated properly, and, in her mother's case, it wasn't treated at all.

People just saw Daisy as loose and strange. Something for the boys to play with on a night out, but nothing to bring home to mama. Yet Daisy had desperately wanted to be brought home to mama. However, after she'd had Danica out of wedlock, without any father hanging around, Daisy's reputation had been cemented, and not in a good way. Small towns were very unforgiving. They were even less forgiving when it came to the local witch, which is what Daisy liked to call herself. Not a term that her grandmother appreciated in any way because that's not how Nana had presented herself.

But, when life happened, you found the pieces you could live with, then tried to ignore the rest. At least that's what her mother had done. Danica didn't hold any animosity toward her mother. If anything, Danica was just sad, sad for Daisy's life that could have been so much easier and so much better, but it was hard to put broken china back together again. And, if her mother had been one thing, it was broken china. Daisy used to come home from a date, burst into tears, then throw herself down on her bed, feeling worthless, believing herself to be worthless because the men would treat her that way, and Daisy would allow it.

She was so desperate to get out of what she saw as her nightmare of a life that she would do anything with anyone if they promised that they would take her away from it all. Of course the men promised her everything in order to be with the witch at least once. It almost became a rite of passage in town, something Danica struggled with as well. When she found a lot of the younger men at school, even those just a few years ahead of her, like Cameron's age, had gone out with her mother just for the experience, Danica was heartbroken.

They did it for the experience, for the laughs, for the

giggles, for the *chalk one up on a bedpost*, as everybody else did. It had been truly soul crushing. Then the girls had laughed at Danica more times than not because her mother was being bounced around the place, like she was nothing but a toy to be played with and then discarded. Because of that, Daisy had believed she *was* a toy to be played with and discarded, and thus Danica's life had been hellish right from the beginning. It still broke her up when she thought about it, even now. However, she could do nothing about it back then. She'd been a child herself.

Danica had tried hard to speak to her mother about this, but Daisy wasn't into listening to the up-and-coming version of herself—Danica—who was trying desperately hard to keep herself clean and out of the same lack of morals her mother had fallen into. That had just made Danica seem like a preachy do-gooder, and her mother had hated Danica for it. She wasn't that way at all, but there had been no coming back—not when her mother saw Danica as competition, saw her as having a chance to get away from it all, having an opportunity for a better life than Daisy had had.

That had been one of the final straws in her mother's psyche that had taken her to the last stage. It had been painful for all of them. While Danica had never wished that her mother would die—and certainly not for the attack that she'd put Danica through—it had still been a relief in a way to realize that Daisy would never wake up again.

That made Danica feel like a horrible person too, and her life became messier, as Danica had tried to deal with it while growing up herself. She had talked to a therapist, but nobody really understood the whole psychic part, so Danica had always downplayed that in order to make it seem as if she wasn't quite so crazy as she came across. Yet, if she couldn't ever tell the whole truth, how would Danica ever get the full value of therapy? How did you tell people that your mother was psychic and that it drove her crazy because she desperately didn't want to hear the voices in her head, while she desperately wanted a better and bigger life?

But feeling sorry for her mother wouldn't be something Danica could do now either. She paced, just waiting to be allowed into her grandmother's ER cubicle. When the ER doctor stepped back out and looked at her, he frowned.

She frowned right back.

"You know that your grandmother is quite ill, right?"

"I do know that. That's why I came back home again."

He shook his head. "It looks like she just blacked out, and she's likely to have more of those blackouts as time goes on."

Danica asked, "Are you sure she wasn't hit in some way?"

He shook his head. "No bruising. No sign of any injury to her head or otherwise. I know that would be an easy answer for you, but it's not the answer in this case."

She sighed. "It's better than thinking somebody may have come up and hit a defenseless woman," she murmured, "but I understand what you're saying."

"Good," he replied, with a nod. "I want to keep her here a little bit longer to ensure that she's fully cognizant and ready to handle life back home again. Do you live with her?"

"I live on the property," she replied, evading the question.

He nodded. "That's good. I don't want to see her living alone anymore."

"Maybe not. Yet it's not easy to convince her to go anywhere."

"I can make it happen," he declared, shooting her a look.

Immediately Danica's back went up, and she declared, "My grandmother is fine. I'll be there, and I'll look after her."

He stared at her intently. "I would like to see that you do, but I don't want to see her back in here for the same injury."

"You might not want it," she replied, "but that doesn't mean you won't see her back for that or for a different injury, if she's fallen again."

"No, of course not," he noted, giving her a look. "You can't keep an eye on her all the time."

She didn't really like anything in his tone, and it was hard when people were so judgmental because Danica wasn't sure what she was even supposed to say. She would do the best that she could do, but her grandmother still went out shopping and still walked out in the fields on her own, and Danica wouldn't try to stop that. It's what made her grandmother happy.

As soon as the doctor filled out some notes, he added, "I'll keep her through this afternoon. I'll check on her then, and, if she's doing fine, then you can take her home."

She thanked him, watching as he walked away.

She didn't know anything about him, but his threat of being able to move Nana and to not let her go home was something Danica hadn't really considered and certainly didn't want to consider at this point. To take away her grandmother's freedom would be brutal. Nana didn't want to go into a home, and there was no need for her to do so.

Not now that Danica had arrived.

She just needed everyone to understand that her grandmother was no longer alone and was possibly a victim of the circumstances around her. Danica didn't know what the hell was going on, but the sooner people realized that she was here and that Nana would be fine at home, the better.

She strode into the small cubicle to see her grandmother sitting up and smiling. "See, I'm fine," she declared, with a smile.

"You might be fine, but the doctor did threaten that he could keep you from going home. And he threatened it in such a way that it made me wonder if he meant *forever*."

Her grandmother narrowed her gaze at Danica. "You do know that power goes to some of these people's heads, but, short of a court order or something of that nature, I doubt he could do much."

"If you're deemed incapable or mentally incapacitated …"

"Sure, but barring that, they can't do it without my permission." Then she froze, looked over at her granddaughter, and asked, "You wouldn't do that to me, would you?"

"Of course not," Danica said. "I'm the one who just warned you, so that whenever *that* doctor is in your vicinity, ensure you are acting as normal, as whole, and as complete as you possibly can."

"Duly noted," her grandmother stated soberly. "It's a sad world when you fall down, hit your head, and they think you're not capable of looking after yourself."

"It is, indeed, but it's the world we live in. As you well know, we are always under suspicion."

Her grandmother stared at her for a long moment, then nodded slowly. "Yes, you are right there," she agreed sadly. "Even if I didn't want it to be that way, it is a consideration we must keep in mind." She pleated the sheet covering her waist, as she leaned her head back against the pillow. "When can I go home?"

"Soon enough. He wants to ensure that you're doing okay into the afternoon. So he wants to keep you here for a few more hours."

She winced. "He just wants the bills to go higher."

Danica frowned at her grandmother. "Is that your feeling, or is that more than a feeling?"

"It's common sense. If he can charge us more, then he will."

Danica considered that, then headed out to the main desk, and asked for her grandmother's bill.

"Is she being released?" the receptionist asked.

"Yes, the doctor said, now that she's doing much better, he'll check on her one more time, but I wanted to pay the bill, so we were ready to go as soon as he comes back by."

"Okay." The receptionist quickly spat out the numbers, handing Danica a copy of the bill, and they were high enough to make Danica's eyes water. The woman asked her, "Don't you have insurance?"

"No, we don't." Danica stared at the bill and shook her head. "Therefore, I'm pretty sure these numbers can come way down." The receptionist pursed her lips. Danica stared back calmly. She and Nana had not had medical insurance for a very long time, and thus Danica knew the ins and outs. She was well aware that the bills were inflated massively for those with insurance versus those without.

As she waited for the receptionist to respond, Danica pulled out her phone to check the last time she had had a medical bill to see what the percentage had been for her ultimate reduction in bill. She thought she may have paid something like 40 percent of the original amount.

The receptionist clicked a lot of keys on her keyboard

and then announced a number approximately 40 percent of the original bill for Nana today.

Danica nodded. "That sounds more like it."

"You might want to consider getting insurance," she suggested.

"My grandmother has a pre-existing condition, does she not? So, as you know, the insurance costs would be exorbitant. I can't afford it, and neither can she."

The receptionist frowned but stayed quiet.

After all, what could she say? It was the truth. The medical system was broken, and a lot of people didn't care one way or another because they had insurance. So, it was good as long as they were covered. But the minute something changed within their own coverage, their tune changed as well.

Danica had learned from the best on how to negotiate medical bills. Even as she pulled out her credit card, she withheld it, stating, "It should be at least 15 percent lower if I pay cash."

Both the receptionist and the other woman seated beside her stared at Danica oddly, then glanced down at the bill and frowned. Danica put her credit card back into her wallet and pulled out the cash that she kept in the back section of her purse. It was a decent amount of money, but she thought she could cover Nana's current bill, as long as the hospital bill continued to drop.

Finally the other woman grumbled, "We don't usually do that."

"Actually you do," Danica corrected, staring at her. "Maybe you don't like it, but cash is instant, and you don't pay the credit card fees associated with those other payments."

The woman quickly checked on her computer and then nodded. “I don’t think I’ve ever had anybody do this.”

“There’ll probably be more and more of this happening,” Danica suggested, “when you consider the costs of medical bills these days, and the cost of medical insurance.”

The other woman finally smiled. “That’s fine. We don’t sell insurance here, and almost everybody is covered one way or another,” she said apologetically, looking at her.

“This is how we cover ourselves now,” Danica stated, as she counted out the bills carefully and handed them over.

The receptionist counted the bills too, making sure it was all there, and then she nodded, but she didn’t give Danica a receipt. Danica asked for one. The receptionist repeated, “You need a receipt too?”

“Yes, I surely do.”

The receptionist shook her head and started printing it off. Danica wasn’t sure why the lack of a receipt bothered her, but it did.

When she finally had it, she checked it over carefully, wincing at the numbers that were still incredibly high for an old woman who had just come in to get checked over. “I probably should have taken her to the vet. It might have been cheaper,” she mused.

The receptionist eyed her to see if she was joking, then shrugged. “It probably would have been, but it wouldn’t have been as good.”

Danica thanked them and walked off. She wondered about that. She knew some vets who were pretty damn knowledgeable, and they would certainly have been able to treat her grandmother right—and for a fraction of the cost.

When her grandmother realized that the bill had been paid, she laughed. “That’s a good idea. Let’s go. I won’t stick around for them to close the door on me and to not let me out."

"They would need the deputies involved for something like that."

Her grandmother, amid throwing back the blankets and sliding to the floor, stopped and shot her a look.

"What?" Danica asked Nana. "Do you really think any of the deputies around here will let you go, based on your word or mine?" she asked. "If you *do* think that, you need to remember where you are and what you've been through before." Danica held up her hand, silencing anything Nana would say at this point. "No, … I do remember, and it sucks," she retorted.

"It sucks, but it's also reality," Nana stated. "So, it doesn't matter how we feel about it. We need to ensure *you* understand exactly what's going on and how it'll be affecting you," Nana declared. "I love you dearly, but you didn't used to be foolish, nor I."

"I am neither of those. Today was a temporary lapse," she added, with a smirk in her grandmother's direction. "Come on. Let's go."

And, with that, they both slipped out of the room and toward the front exit. Just as they reached the front door, Danica heard a man calling out from behind her and urged her grandmother to continue. "Go on." Turning back, she saw Cameron walking into the hospital from one of the other doors.

"Hey, are you all right?" he asked, frowning at her.

"My grandmother fell and hit her head. I'm just taking her home after being checked."

He glanced back at the emergency room. "I'm sorry to hear that. You sure she's okay?"

"Yeah, she's fine," she said, with a bright smile. "However, I don't want to leave her alone, so I'll see you around." And, with that, she quickly followed her grandmother. Knowing that even though she didn't want it to be so, she turned to see him standing there, staring at her, his hands on his hips, as if trying to figure out what they were up to—and why it all felt wrong.

She could only hope that he didn't realize until afterward. Yet he was smart, and absolutely nothing was slow about him. If he got any inkling that something funky was going on, he would be all over it.

The good news was he didn't know her, at least not yet. The fact that he would likely get to know her a whole lot better was something she refused to look at. After all, what do you say to a guy when he has no clue that you're about to become lovers?

Her visions, when they came, were hard, fast, and never wrong. What she could see in that moment was the two of them, hot and heavy in the sheets. But what she also realized was that she wasn't angry about it, and that would be a huge step up for her.

CAMERON TOOK A few more steps toward the ER department, only to see Bridget, one of the older nurses who had been here since forever, staring at him. "Was it my imagination, or did those two act like they were escaping?" he asked.

She nodded. "I would take it the same way," she murmured.

"Problems?" he asked, looking at her.

She shrugged. "She paid the bill in cash, after making sure to knock it down quite a bit, so obviously some level of experience there."

"They don't have insurance?" he asked, freezing in his tracks and frowning at Bridget.

She shook her head. "We've known the old lady has never had insurance, so I'm not surprised that the granddaughter doesn't either. Yet it's much more common these days to have it."

"But it's all too common," he added, "that people cannot afford it, particularly if it's not included with their job."

"The granddaughter wasn't very forthcoming with any information, and, because she paid cash, I couldn't really get too much out of her. I didn't ask what she did for a living, but honestly she didn't seem to be very open to answering any questions."

He nodded. "Can't say I blame her. Her reception here hasn't been that warm." The nurse frowned at him, as he nodded. "Ah, you haven't been here that long then?"

"Sure, I have," she stated. "Since forever."

"Like ten or twelve years?" he asked.

She pursed her lips. "Twenty-five plus."

"Do you know anything about the attempted murder that happened way back when?" he inquired.

She nodded. "I heard the rumors about it. Some mother tried to kill her daughter, and then the cops weren't so sure that the mother did it. Something like that. Maybe it was the other way around."

"*That* was the daughter of the mother in question, plus the mother's mother," he shared, motioning toward the glass doors.

Her eyes widened, and she stared back outside. "Seriously?"

He nodded. "As far as I understood, the local verdict was

very much that the mother did attack the daughter. The daughter spent quite a bit of time in the hospital herself."

"I heard that, but then someone told me that it was all a cock-and-bull story and how the daughter got away with murder," she shared, looking around, and then freezing, as she looked back at him. "In fact, I think your brother told me that," she stated.

Cameron stared at her in surprise. "Jace said that?"

She nodded. "I think so. Though I don't know why he would have said that. He's had a bone to pick with Danica for a long time. They used to go out in high school before all this happened, and then he turned against her."

Cameron stared at her, not sure what to believe and what not to.

"Believing that she killed her own mother? That's enough reason to turn anyone against you," she noted, as she walked back to her desk. "Doesn't change the fact that we still should treat her."

"We treated the daughter today?" he asked.

"No," she stated. "The older lady, the grandmother, I guess."

"Okay," he muttered, with a nod. "In a way, that makes sense."

"Why?"

Just then one of the doctors, Dr. Patrick, walked up to the reception desk and asked about Harriet Hartling. "I was coming to check on her, but apparently they've absconded," he noted in a heated tone. "We can't keep them here legally, but I do wonder at times."

"What do you mean, you wonder?" Cameron asked, eyeing him carefully.

"I'm not sure Hariett should have left," Dr. Patrick stated, pausing, then shrugging. "I'm probably the reason for it though, because I told the granddaughter that I could keep the grandmother here if I thought she wasn't fit to be left alone."

Cameron exhaled sharply. "Wow. How badly injured was Harriet?"

"She wasn't injured at all that I could see," Dr. Patrick replied. "I don't know. Just something about it seemed off. The granddaughter had asked me if there were any injuries that suggested her grandmother might have been struck on the head."

"So, whoa, whoa, whoa, hang on a minute," Cameron interjected. "What are you talking about?"

"The grandmother was brought in by ambulance, unconscious, and we did the usual. She woke up. She came to on her own," Dr. Patrick clarified. "She doesn't have any visible injuries. She wasn't disoriented, and, by rights, I didn't have any reason to keep her here. But I did make a comment to the effect that, if we weren't sure her grandmother was stable, in good shape, and well-looked-after, we were in the position to refuse to release her."

"Which, as you well know, isn't true." Cameron frowned, as he looked at Dr. Patrick pointedly. "That was just a fear tactic on your part. What I don't understand is why you would do that."

Dr. Patrick bristled. "What I don't understand is why you care."

"Because that's not how we operate," Cameron stated, staring at him. "Why would you even do that?" Cameron asked, incredulous.

"Because she's a murderer," Dr. Patrick snapped. "Some of these people might have forgotten, but I haven't. The last thing I want is to see that old lady killed by her granddaughter, just like her mother was."

"You don't know that," Cameron retorted sharply, "and that talk is not welcome here."

"It's not your hospital," he sneered. "So, I wouldn't be pushing your weight around too much. We all know everything to know about that young woman, and none of it's good." With that, he turned and walked away.

Cameron was shocked that this was even a consideration, as it went against all ethical norms. He turned and looked over at Bridget, who stared at the departing doctor. "Is that really a sample of the ethics going on around here?" Cameron asked.

She shook her head. "No, it shouldn't be. Obviously, if we have a concern, we call Family Services. But nothing I saw warranted concern. Then again … I didn't speak with the patient."

"If you have a concern, then I am all for somebody doing a follow-up," Cameron stated. "I am not against due diligence. … What I am against are threats being thrown around, particularly for someone who's already struggling to come back to her hometown."

"Maybe she shouldn't have come back," Bridget suggested. "It doesn't look as if anything is here for her."

"How can you say that? Who are we to decide? It's her family home," he responded, his tone adamant. "She has every right to be here."

"Maybe, but these people have long memories," she cautioned. "So having the right to be here is not the same thing as making a good decision to return. You might want to keep that in mind." As she turned to walk away, she added, "You might also want to remember that Dr. Patrick's on the board, and no guarantee now that he'll vote to keep you here."

"You mean, because I'm against his breaking the law?" Cameron asked, disbelief coloring his tone.

She nodded. "Exactly."

"In that case, I would be happy to leave," he replied, flint in his tone, "and believe me that there would be a hell of an investigation into this hospital's ethics."

With that, he turned and stormed off to his office.

CHAPTER 8

DANICA SAT AT the kitchen table, across from her grandmother, her gaze intense as she studied Nana. "So, you want to tell me exactly what happened?"

"I did tell you," her grandmother replied, somewhat testily.

"No, you didn't."

"I fell," she repeated flatly. "That's all there is to it."

"No, that's not all. I'm not sure what's going on here, but the more you keep me in the dark, the more suspicious I get, and the harder it is for me to look after you."

"You don't need to look after me," Nana declared.

"That's not true. Somebody needs to look after you, particularly after that doctor made those threats."

"He had no business doing that."

"Maybe not, but he obviously feels like he needs to," Danica noted, staring off into the distance, still trying to process the amount of hate she had encountered since her return. "Whether it was directed at you or me, I don't know. I honestly didn't realize how long the memories would be for the townsfolk. I was more concerned about my own memories and handling being back. I hadn't really considered how much active hate I would come up against here."

"You shouldn't be coming up against any of it," her grandmother snapped. "It's ridiculous that they would think that you killed Daisy." Nana brushed her wispy white hair from her face. "I can't believe they would even accuse you of that."

"They did plenty of accusing as soon as I got out of the hospital," she murmured. "Everybody was torn as to whether I could have done it myself. Nobody even contemplated that I had no reason to kill my mother," she added, shaking her head.

"*You* have never considered that you had any reason—yet you've had lots of reasons," Nana clarified. "Still, that would have been a long time ago, not at the stage when you were ready to leave."

"I *was* ready to leave, and not just that. I made sure I did leave. Just no place for me here after that," she shared, pausing as she reflected on her words.

"I missed you so," her grandmother began. "With your mother gone and then you leaving, this place was awfully lonely and quiet for a long time."

Danica winced and sighed. "I'm sorry for that too. It really never occurred to me, to be honest. I was in so much pain that I just wanted to run and hide, and that's what I did. I took off and didn't even consider what you might need or would be going through." She stared at her grandmother in remorse. "I'm really very sorry for that. I want to say I was young, but I was certainly old enough to know better."

"Oh, heavens, child, stop blaming yourself. You weren't responsible for me, and you sure as heck weren't responsible for what your mother did. It was just tough to find my world so completely upended like that. I went from having my family, who I love so dearly, all around me, to suddenly having no family around me at all. And harder still, the friends I thought I had back then just turned out not to be my friends at all. I think that was the hardest thing."

Danica nodded. "Exactly. Even for myself, I had friends—or people who I thought were friends. I had a boyfriend—I thought," she added, shaking her head. "Who knew that Jace would take all of it as being something evil—in his words. I didn't even realize he was religious."

"I don't think religion had anything to do with it."

"You need to be more careful," Danica declared, searching her grandmother's gaze. "Are you sure nobody came up and bopped you on the head or anything?"

Her grandmother looked at her in surprise, then gave a rueful shake of her head. "No, no, no, don't even go down that pathway. It was nothing like that."

The trouble was, Danica couldn't quite shake that possibility from her mind, and she kept thinking about her grandmother's response the whole time. Something was just off about it, and Danica didn't know what she was supposed to do about it. If her grandmother wouldn't fess up and tell her, Danica would be operating in the dark, and that was not the way she wanted to do things in a situation like this.

When her grandmother announced that she would be taking a nap now, Danica nodded and then sighed, watching Nana walk slowly to her bedroom.

SITTING IN HER RV, ostensibly trying to work, all the doors wide open and the big living room window popped out, Danica thought about everything that had brought her to this moment in time. She would do anything she could to make her grandmother's last days, weeks, or months as comfortable as she could. She doubted it would be more than that, certainly not years, but if that's the way it was to be, then it would be fine. Yet Danica still wasn't where she wanted to be and wasn't doing what she thought she should be doing.

That thinking brought to mind the question of the property request. Why was she even trying to buy it back? It was important to her grandmother, but, when Nana was gone, then what? Would Danica keep it for herself? Why would she even want to do that? She didn't know. She really didn't. She sighed as she contemplated life, a cold beer in her hand.

Her grandmother had gone to bed early, after the bump on her head, and now Danica was out of sorts. There had to be something she could do to make herself feel better, but instead it felt very much as if—and she didn't want to say it—a case was being built against her; and it all just felt wrong.

When she heard footsteps crunching outside, Benji jumped up and started to bark. Looking up, Danica wasn't surprised to see Cameron standing outside her open door, his hands on his hips, as he surveyed the RV.

"Is this where you're staying?" he asked, when she popped her head out.

She glared at him and nodded. "You got a problem with that?"

"No, not at all," he said, giving her a crooked grin. "I often wondered about getting one of these and just traveling all over America by myself."

She nodded. "I did quite a lot of that myself. It seemed that I could never quite settle anywhere, and every place felt wrong somehow. Eventually I ended up here, hoping that I would find—I don't know—home again," she said, for want of a better word.

"Do you think you could really settle here? I know you want to buy the property and all, but—"

"I don't know," she admitted. "I kept thinking that maybe things would clear up here, and I would be okay, but I sure didn't expect the reception that I'm getting."

He stared at her for a long moment, then slowly nodded. "I'm surprised you came back. I understand the reason—your grandmother and all—but it can't be easy."

"It's not easy, not at all. It makes no sense that people are still thinking that I killed my mother," she shared, shaking her head. "I don't even know where they got that answer to begin with. The local authorities made it very clear that they knew exactly what had happened, and I know my mother attacked me," she murmured. "Yet it seems as if everybody else wanted me to be the bad guy. I just—I guess I thought that would have gone by the wayside by now, but people still haven't wised up to it." She cringed. "I don't understand why it's still a thing." She brushed her hair off her face, took another sip of her beer, and stared at him. "But that's not why you're here."

"I'm checking to ensure your grandmother's okay,"

She stiffened, her gaze narrowing.

He held up a hand. "I also wanted to apologize for what Dr. Patrick said. If there are obvious cases of abuse or neglect, we are obligated to contact social services. However, we are certainly not allowed to keep someone at the hospital if they don't need to be there."

She didn't say anything but stared at him. He shifted slightly in place, making her realize just how uncomfortable she was making him. She relaxed ever-so-slightly, noticing his energy shift back too.

"So, I'm sorry for what my colleague said to you," he

added.

She nodded. “He’s quite the dick,” she muttered, letting go of the need to censor herself.

He stared at her, shocked for a moment, then laughed out loud. “I’m not sure that’s a comment I would have made,” he noted, with a smile, “but I can see that it might be a choice phrase for you. He had no business even saying what he did and no need to keep Harriet either.”

“If it were just to ensure she was doing okay and he was erring on the side of caution, that’s fine,” she clarified, not wanting to say what she was thinking.

“Why do you think he was keeping her then?”

She took a moment to answer. “I don’t know. As far as my grandmother is concerned, it was to jack up the bill.”

He winced. “That would not go over well,” he replied. “You don’t have insurance either, do you?”

She shook her head. “Nope, never had. My grandmother has never had insurance, nor my mother before me. Anytime anybody has had to go to the hospital, it would damn-near break the bank. And it doesn’t just break the bank once. It does so every month thereafter, while we work to pay it off.”

Even if she wasn’t explaining that very well, he nodded. “I get it. I hear the same thing from a lot of other people.”

“Insurance is supposed to help if major calamities happen, and yet, with a pre-existing condition, the insurance companies do absolutely everything they can to get out of paying for it.”

“I know.” Cameron nodded in agreement. “One of the sad parts of being in the medical profession is seeing all the people who won’t get proper medical help because they don’t have coverage.”

“My grandmother doesn’t need help,” she stated. “I was

concerned that she may have been hit over the head. I was here at the time, but I was walking out back from talking to you with Benji, so I didn't see anything."

"*Huh.*" Cameron frowned. "Did the doctor say anything about that?"

"He told me that there were no wounds, but he's lying," she said, with a shrug.

His eyebrows shot up. "What do you mean, he's lying?" he asked.

"She's got a swollen noggin and an egg-shaped bump on her head," she explained.

He stared at her. "Was it there at the hospital?"

"I don't know," she admitted, "but it's plenty evident now. That's for sure. But, if he didn't see it, what kind of doctor is he? Why would I take her back to someone there if they can't even see an injury like that?"

"Where is she now?" Cameron asked, looking back toward the house.

"She's gone to bed," she responded.

His frown deepened. "And you don't like that either?"

"No, because, if she's got a head injury, I don't want to see her to go to sleep and have further problems," she clarified. "Look. I'm no expert on medicine, but she looked much better when I put her to bed."

"Sure," he replied, "but head wounds are tricky. Would you mind if we walked in and checked on her?"

She hesitated and then hopped to her feet. "Benji, come on. Let's go check on Nana." With that, she headed to the house, mentally begging the house to open the door for her or to at least unlock the door. She sighed in relief when she could turn the knob and actually enter the house, Cameron on her heels. "I wish you wouldn't put things that way," she muttered. "Now I'm worried."

"Maybe we need to be worried," he replied, as they moved through to Nana's bedroom.

She knocked on the door, mentally again asking for entrance, then pushed it open slightly. "Nana, are you awake?" A mumble came from the bed. Danica looked back at him and said, "Wait here."

Stepping into the room, she asked again, "Nana, are you awake?"

More mumbling came, but it was indecipherable. Fearing that her grandmother had gone into one of her psychic episodes, Danica walked over and gently placed a hand on Nana's shoulder. "We just need to check up on that head wound."

More mumbling came, and Danica noted that her grandmother wasn't cognizant of what was going on around her. "Easy, Nana, just take it easy," Danica murmured, gently stroking her shoulder.

She glanced over to see Cameron had stepped into the room and was frowning at her. "Are you sure she's really talking? To me it seems like she's more incoherent than anything, and that's a concern."

She hesitated, then looked at him and shook her head. "No, in this case, it isn't."

He stopped midstep and frowned at her.

She sighed. "I get it that you don't understand, and that's fine. I don't really care if you understand or not, but it would be nice if people would believe me when I say, *She's fine.*"

"How can you say that she's fine if she's incoherent?" he asked gently. He stepped up beside her grandmother and studied her features. "Mumbling incoherently like that is not a good sign."

"It's not a good sign for the *average* person," Danica stated, "but it's a normal sign for my grandmother."

Confused, he just looked at her.

Danica sighed and added, "When she's having her psychic visions, she's often like this."

His expression cleared, as he looked down at Harriet. "Interesting. I don't know if you heard, but my grandmother used to have visions too, but she would sit in a chair on the porch and *shift*—stare up at the sky, and her eyes would close off."

Danica nodded. "Nana does that too. But, when she's asleep, she'll do this," she explained, motioning at her grandmother. "It's not that she's incoherent by any means. She's just not here right now."

"When you say 'not here,'" he asked cautiously, "where would you say she is?" He looked at Danica curiously.

She wasn't sure if this was a test or something else, but she shrugged and gave him half an answer. "Presumably she's off talking to someone."

He didn't appear to be satisfied with that either.

She went a different route. "I never heard anything about your grandmother having the sight."

"It's not something that was ever advertised," he replied calmly. "Honestly, most people gave her a pass because she was always doing so much charity work. Yet she did the charity work to make up for not being able to help a lot of the people who she felt needed help."

"I get that too," Danica noted. "Yet it's also hard to *not* help because you know it's not welcome. However, you also know that the outcome in the end is something that nobody will be happy about, but you can't stop it. It's already underway, and that's just the way it is."

He smiled. "That sounds like personal experience talking."

"It is. I saw my mother slowly go nuts. But did I ever have any indication that she would turn around and attack me, try to kill me? Or do this to my face? No, not really. Would you ever think that someone you love would become so jealous of you—a younger version of themselves—becoming so frustrated with their lives and everything they've done, that they would do this? Of course not. Even if I had known, it's not as if I would have had any ability to step in and to change it," she admitted.

With a shake of her head, she continued. "When you're young, the world doesn't give you any power, and, when they finally do, they don't trust you with it, so others step in to hinder you. So you're left still trying to make your life happen, even though you no longer have the ability to do so." She shrugged and turned to him. "As you can see, my grandmother is totally fine." She motioned for him to back off, to exit the bedroom.

"Let me just have a look at her head," he suggested, "and I would like to ensure she doesn't have a fever."

Danica watched as Cameron carefully assessed her grandmother, his touch gentle, accepting, not intrusive, and in no way judgmental, as he carefully looked over Nana. Finally he nodded and stepped back. "Keep an eye on her overnight. I know that, for you, all that mumbling and whatnot is common but, from my perspective, not so much."

"Yet you've seen your own grandmother when she was having visions."

"I have," he agreed, with a nod. "That's why this isn't as disturbing to me as it might be for a lot of people."

"Ain't that the truth."

"Still, we don't want it to be something other than what we're expecting to see," he stated. "It's one thing if you see a vision happening from start to finish, and you know what it is, but, when you step into something like this midway, you're already predestined to assume it's a vision. But what if it isn't? What if this one time it's a case of her injury affecting her?"

"Not a whole lot I can do at this point except keep an eye on her," Danica replied.

"That's all I ask." Cameron gave her a smile, as he followed her back out to the living room, and she headed straight out the door.

"Is there a reason you don't stay in here?"

"Yes," she said, but she didn't elaborate. Nobody would understand that. As soon as she got back outside, she stopped and took several deep, long breaths.

"It's almost as if going in there hurt you," he noted.

She stiffened and then shrugged. "There aren't any good memories for me in there."

"Ah, I hadn't considered that."

"It's fine. Nana and I get along peaceably," she said, nodding. "We don't have any issues, and, depending on how long she has, we'll find a way to make it work," she murmured. "But I won't be leaving her, especially now that I know that nobody here at that hospital will give her the care she needs."

"That's not fair," he noted in a mild tone. "I'm certain they won't hurt her."

"No? That other doctor of yours?" she pointed out. "I'm pretty damn sure he doesn't like anything about my grandmother or me. He's dangerous—to you, to Nana, to me."

"Yet he's not the one who hired me, and the hospital needs doctors, so I'm not worried about losing my job," he responded.

An insight suddenly slammed into Danica, and she murmured, "You should be because he's already mounting a campaign against you."

He stared at her, then slowly nodded. "I had a nagging feeling about that earlier, and I just put it off, thinking they wouldn't be so foolish as to get rid of their one and only new doctor, still with not enough staff on board," he shared, with a smile.

"You're wrong," Danica told him.

"I know, … and I'm not foolish enough to discount what you tell me, so thank you."

She frowned at him.

He shrugged. "I know you don't trust me. You maybe don't believe me, and I get that. All I'm trying to say is that I won't discount what you say. I'll keep an open mind."

"If it did happen, and he managed to get you fired, would you leave?"

He shook his head. "Maybe the hospital," he replied cheerfully, "but I could just open up a general practice. They need one of those here too."

She smiled at him. "That would be a good idea, but you should take your payment in chickens and deer meat," she offered, with a laugh.

He grinned, and his face suddenly lit up, exuding a boyish charm that she found incredibly attractive.

That just reminded her of her earlier vision of them in bed. She stomped on her smile that even now threatened to blossom under his attention. "Now that you know Nana's okay, you can go on home."

His smile slowly faded, and he nodded. "In a way, I guess that would be sensible, wouldn't it?"

"It probably would be." She nodded.

"Yet I don't want to," he challenged, looking over at her with a small smile. "I like your company."

She shook her head. "Now that will definitely get you fired."

He smiled, giving her a lazy look. "Maybe, but maybe I don't care."

She stared at him. "What?"

"I understand. You don't get it, do you?"

"No, not only do I not get it," she began, "I don't think anybody around you will get what you're saying either. In fact, I suspect that your brother would be absolutely horrified."

He nodded. "You knew my brother, didn't you?"

"As it turns out, no," she stated. "I thought I knew your brother, but he had hidden depths I didn't have any idea about."

He winced. "I gather he was pretty rough on you back then."

"Is that what you call it? I was still trying to survive my injuries when he lit into me like you wouldn't believe," she explained. "I had no idea what the hell was even going on, and he was screaming at me for trying to kill my mother. And yet I'd never even thought something like that could happen, much less be so misunderstood that he would accuse me of doing it. I'm not sure his head was on straight. He said many harsh and cruel things. I'm not sure it is over even now."

"No?"

"Yeah. When you do drugs like that, … that's often a

side effect," she added. Then she noted a stillness overtaking Cameron's expression. "You didn't know about Jace taking drugs?" she asked tentatively.

"No," he muttered in an odd tone. "I didn't. Did you do drugs with him?"

"No, I didn't do drugs. It was one of the sore points between us. He thought I should, but it wasn't my thing. I had seen enough of my mother's boyfriends to realize that drug use wouldn't be a part of my life, no matter how much Jace asked," she explained. "I refused to be my mother."

"How close were you?" he asked curiously.

"Not very, apparently, though I had once thought we were heading down the pathway of true love." She gave a bitter laugh. "He immediately botched that thought, and I'm pretty sure he thought I was just like my mother. Another mark on a bedpost, and he would be the first to take it," she admitted, casting a hard look in Cameron's direction. "Which is also why I'm not exactly sure why you're here and just what your game is. So, if you have any inkling or idea of that happening," she declared, "just forget it. I am not my mother. I wasn't then, and I'm not now. I won't ever be like her."

CHAPTER 9

CAMERON KNOCKED ON his brother's door, and, when no answer came, he frowned and headed around the back of the small dilapidated rental property. Cameron had questions—questions that needed answers. Questions that he knew his brother wouldn't appreciate, particularly given his current mental state.

Heading around to the pastures at the back, he walked to the fence line and stared out across the fields. No sign of him. Yet his truck was here. Cameron shook his head, then walked back to the house, just in time to see his brother blurrily open the door and stare at him in confusion.

"What's up?" Jace asked, rubbing the sleep from his eye.

Cameron stared at him. "Why are you asleep at this time of day?" His brother got defensive, reminding Cameron that he had to watch what he said and the way he said it. Otherwise his brother tended to blow up.

"None of your fucking business," he snapped. "What do you care anyway?"

Cameron looked at him. "Of course I care. I thought you would do something today."

His brother glared at him. "So this is just a visit to ensure I'm on track, doing work for you?"

"No, obviously not," Cameron said patiently. "I'm just checking up on you."

"No need to check up on me," he snapped once more. He went to shove the door closed and then groaned and looked at Cameron with frustration. He sighed loudly. "Obviously I woke up on the wrong side of the bed, and that comes from people waking me up when I'm not ready, so go away."

"Great. Sure. No problem," Cameron replied. "By the way, I talked to Danica today."

"And? What's that got to do with me? She's one crazy bitch. Keep her away from me," his brother said.

"Interesting," Cameron replied. "She mentioned a few things that I wanted to argue with her about, but she seemed pretty adamant." At that, Cameron watched his brother process the information through slitted eyes, as Jace glared at him.

"You shouldn't be listening to anything she says about me. You should know that by now."

"I don't know that," Cameron argued, "because one of the things she told me, by accident, was that you were heavily into drugs back then and tried to get her to join you."

Jace snorted. "Of course she would say that, wouldn't she? Miss Goody Two-shoes. She would never do drugs," he said in a mocking tone. "She wouldn't be like her mom. She was more like her mom than you would think," he stated, with a sneer.

Cameron stared at him, one eyebrow slowly raising. "So, is it because of her or because of something else that you're so hell-bent on dissing her?"

"Doesn't matter what I'm hell-bent on. She's nothing but trouble. I keep telling you that, and, if you aren't smart enough to stay away from that bitch, it won't matter what I say. You'll do whatever the hell you want to anyway."

Cameron was stunned at the vehemence in his brother's words. "I don't think we've ever had a conversation where you got so riled up so quickly over nothing."

"It's the *over nothing* part you better get a handle on," Jace declared, "because that bitch will ruin everything you try to do."

"So, maybe you should tell me exactly what your relationship with her was like," Cameron began, staring at his brother in shock. "Because I'm not recognizing who and what you're talking about right now."

"Of course not. You were probably hot on her tail back then too," Jace stated, slapping the doorframe. "Every-damn-body was."

"But having only met her a couple times in high school—and she was obviously somebody in a bad spot—that's hardly the definition of a relationship, is it?"

"I don't know," Jace spat. "It would be typical of you to go find yourself a partner right now, while the rest of the world went to hell in a handbasket."

"What the hell are you talking about?" Cameron asked, staring at his brother.

Jace glared at him, and then his shoulders slumped. "It doesn't matter," he muttered. "I have my own demons to deal with. You've got yours, so whatever."

When the door slammed in his face, Cameron slowly turned and walked down the sidewalk and back to his car. He stood at the driver's side door, staring around the neighborhood, wondering what the hell he was supposed to do with this. His brother had been much more antagonistic lately, due to the circumstances in his life, which now Cameron had to question. What did he really know about the truth of his brother's life?

Was his wife correct in that Jace had been abusive, or was his brother correct? Was his wife just wound up, looking for child support and custody of their one-year-old son? Cameron didn't dare contact her for fear of alienating his brother even more than they had already become. Plus, Cameron really hadn't been around Jace's wife that much, not even after moving back home most of a year ago—not with burying both his parents, building his house, working godawful long shifts at the hospital. So how would he know whether Jace's ex-wife was lying or not? What if she told Jace about any such discussions? Nope. That would be too much pressure on their already strained brotherly relationship.

So Cameron had no idea what to even think about Jace and his personality change, but something was definitely off here, and he could see how even the mention of Danica sent Jace into a shitstorm.

Frowning, Cameron got into his vehicle and drove back to his place. Needing to destress, he got out, walked into the kitchen, and made himself a coffee. Putting it in a travel mug, he headed outside to the property he had agreed to sell to Danica. Questions ran through his mind at a million thoughts per second, and his mind was spiraling.

Should he sell it?

Should he not sell it?

He didn't need it.

What was Danica's reason for wanting to keep it anyway?

He wasn't sure whether it was Harriet who wanted to keep the property together, or just Danica. Frowning, he wondered how Harriet was doing and again worried about her head wound, which he had seen for himself. Had it been caused by a fall, or was someone else involved? He hadn't even thought to ask Danica about where she had found Harriet or to check out the area for himself.

His feet almost instinctively led him to Harriet's place, but he froze at the edge of the property line, realizing that he would need to deal with Danica. That shouldn't be an issue, and, in a way, he was looking forward to it. Yet it had become an issue, just because of his brother's words. While he stood here, staring, the door of the RV opened, and he watched Danica lean against the open doorjamb, a question on her face.

"What are you looking for? Me?"

He shrugged. "Maybe. I'm not sure yet," he replied in a half-joking manner.

She smiled. "When you figure it out, you know where I am."

On impulse, he asked, "Did you check the area where your grandmother was found?"

She turned back to look at him. "You mean, … check the ground?" she asked, trying to sort through what he was really asking.

"You found her on the ground—but where?" he asked, moving an arm in the direction of the house from left to right. "Exactly where did you find her? That head wound came from something other than what we thought, maybe. You don't know what happened, do you?" he asked in confusion.

"No, I don't. I just found her collapsed." She hopped down, with Benji following eagerly, racing over to say hi to Cameron. He bent down to pet the small Heinz 57 mix that seemed to be a cross between a Chihuahua and something along the lines of a wiener dog. A very strange-looking dog, yet as friendly as he could be, and that's what mattered. Benji was a darling, and Cameron spent a few minutes petting him.

When he looked up, Danica walked toward him. She had slipped on a pair of sandals. "Follow me," she said, and, with that, she headed to the side of the house and pointed to an indent on the ground.

He looked around at the area and asked, "No sign of anybody else here?"

"No," she murmured, staring down at the ground where she found her grandmother.

"What was her pose?" he asked.

Startled, Danice frowned at him and then dropped to her belly with Benji running over, thinking this was a new game, trying to lick her face, making her laugh. But then she rolled over with her hand at a bent angle, one arm over her head, the other arm bent at the side, and one knee bent upward.

Seeing what he would have stated was a typical crime-scene pose, he nodded. "You didn't see anybody? You didn't see a weapon or anything along that line?"

She shook her head. "No, I didn't see anything." He just nodded. "Why?" she asked, and then sat up and turned to look at him.

"I don't know, but she definitely has a head wound, and, if she had fallen, she would have fallen right where she landed. That bump on her head is fairly substantial, but she didn't hit herself when falling," he noted, as he waved his hand around. "Nothing is here but soft grass and dry dirt, so nothing she could have hit her head on. I expected to see big rocks. Plus, she fell off to the side ever-so-slightly, as if she were turning to look at someone or was twisted around, and they came up behind her," he explained. "I'm definitely not law enforcement, so I don't know how all that works, but I do understand how wounds work. This is something I would say we should be wary of."

She stared at him for a long moment, as he shifted uncomfortably under her direct gaze. Finally, rolling it on her tongue, she asked, "We?"

He flashed a smile. "I'm not against you," he stated intently. "I am in no way afraid of you, upset at you being here, angry at you, or whatever other adjectives you might want to use. I am happy that you're here, happy that you're looking after your grandmother, and very sorry for all the problems you've had."

Surprise lit the dark depths of her eyes, and he could understand why, now learning more about her life and how others had treated her.

She dropped her gaze to the ground and muttered, "I didn't see anybody. I had walked around the property, thinking of the same issues, because, if she didn't hit her head, somebody else hit her head for her." She lifted her gaze to look at him intently. "But that would imply somebody had deliberately targeted her, or they came upon her suddenly and surprised her."

"True, but this is her property, and it happened close to her house."

"So, what were they doing here?"

"That is an issue," he noted, with a small smile. "Have you had any break-ins or anybody bothering you?"

"No," she replied, looking around. "Not since I've been here, though I haven't really had a chance to ask her. Maybe she would have something different to say."

"Would she keep something like that from you?"

Startled, she looked over at him. "I want to say no, but the answer is probably, yes, she would. My grandmother is very protective of me, and, if she thinks something would upset me, she might very well try to avoid that discussion."

"Even though it might impact your own safety?" he asked curiously, his gaze darting to the RV that he could just see the back end of. "I don't think your watchdog will be much of a hindrance to an intruder," he stated, with a note of amusement, as he dropped down to pet Benji again.

"Maybe not," she agreed, with a small smile, "but he's a great early warning system."

"Now to that I will agree," he admitted, "although I'm not sure I heard him barking when I approached."

"He let me know that somebody was out here," she murmured. "Plus, he also knows who you are at this point."

"Not really," he countered, frowning at her. "I've been here what? Once or twice?"

"Sure, but nobody else has been here in all that time either. I take my grandmother out for the shopping that she needs, and she no longer has any friends who come by to visit."

He winced at that. "I think everybody should have friends, particularly at this late stage of life," he muttered, as he turned his attention toward the front door of the big house. "Nobody should be alone when they're old."

"Yet that's what happens, isn't it?" she asked.

"It's exactly what happens. Hopefully you'll stay with her right through until the end."

"That's not likely to be all that long," she muttered, "so that is the plan."

"Not all that long?" Had Danica really said that? He studied her features for a long moment. "Is there something I should know about her health?"

Danica snorted. "No, absolutely not. You're not her doctor, and we can't afford doctors. So, it really doesn't make any difference."

He winced. "I guess I know that. I want to lecture you on having no insurance, but I won't."

"Good thing," she declared, with spirit, "because it won't do any good."

He burst out laughing and grinned at her. "Glad to see you have some fighting spirit."

"That's what I do have," she agreed, with a nod, "maybe too much of it."

YOU NEED TO tell her … repeated the voice in the darkness of Harriet's mind.

"I know. … I know," Harriet murmured. She felt the chill come over her soul. Her time was coming to an end. It was too soon. And in many ways too late.

Of course we know that. Such mockery and amusement filled that voice. *We've been waiting for you. You will come and join the rest of us, but she must be told.*

Harriet pulled the blanket tighter around her shoulders, as she shifted in the bed. She looked around the room and the house that she had both loved and hated—her prison and yet her mansion.

Mansion reiterated the same voice again. *It was never a prison.*

She kept her thoughts to herself on that one, even though it seemed like that voice always knew what she was thinking. She shifted again, feeling the weight of her body on her sore bones and joints.

Your time is coming, the voice said gently. *Don't fear it.*

"I don't fear it," she murmured. "I just dread telling my granddaughter."

Maybe you should have told her a long time ago.

"The way I told my daughter?" she whispered.

Silence was the first response to that. *Of course that didn't go well, did it?* Came the now-soft voice in the darkness of her mind.

"No, And now I must find a way to tell my granddaughter so that she doesn't have the same reaction."

But you were happy with these choices.

She smiled in the darkness, staring around at the faded beauty of the gorgeous old house. "I was very happy with the choice. And yet I sit here now in my waning days, wondering if I made the right one." She could almost sense the start of surprise from the voice in the darkness. "I know," she admitted, with a wave of her hand. "Not only does it not matter anymore, it's way too late to do anything about it."

Laughter rippled through her mind. *Way too late* was the agreement. *Now you need to sleep. You haven't many more sleeps left.*

"And why Halloween?" she whispered to the darkness around her.

Maybe you should ask yourself that. Why did you choose Halloween to tell your daughter?

Harriet shuddered, slipping down under the blankets, keeping the one wrapped around her shoulders, even as it bunched up underneath her neck and head. "I didn't think."

No, you just reacted, and reactions have consequences.

"I know they do, but I didn't think the reaction would have such strong consequences."

This is the consequence of not thinking.

She hated the smartness of all the answers. Yet she felt a certain comfort in knowing that there would always be answers, along with a certain amount of pain, knowing that the answers would often not be to her liking. She turned off the lamp beside her.

The voice in the darkness whispered *Good night* in her ear.

She smiled. There really was a comfort in knowing that she was never alone. The trouble was, she would become one with that voice very quickly. And her granddaughter had no idea. Resolutely Harriet turned, curled up underneath the blanket, and closed her eyes. One thing she desperately needed was time. Time to make good on her promises. Time to do good for the sake of her granddaughter. Even her daughter. Some things needed to be dealt with, and Harriet needed that amount of time in order to do it.

Feeling the *tick-tock* of her heartbeat match the *tick-tock* of time, she closed her eyes and sank into a deep sleep.

CHAPTER 10

DANICA HESITATED, AS she stared at Cameron's face. "I was thinking that somebody might have attacked her," she admitted cautiously. "Yet I saw no sign of anybody when I arrived and have seen no sign of anybody since."

He nodded. "Of course you didn't call the sheriff, did you?"

She shook her head. "It would take a lot for me to call the sheriff," she declared, her tone formal.

He winced. "Vestiges of your time here before?" he asked.

"Absolutely. Plus, based on the most recent visit I just had here."

"So tell me then. I don't quite understand the motive behind the request to buy the land from me."

"Because of my grandmother," she replied, with a shrug. "I know it bothers her, and, if I can find peace for her at this stage of her life, I'm happy to do so."

"Not for yourself?"

"Sure. I would prefer to live on it," she replied.

He looked around at the house and again asked, "Why are you in the RV and not in the house?"

"Because I prefer it," she repeated. No way she would try and explain how houses had memories, houses had energy, and, in her case, no *good* energy was attached to this one. She could go in during the daytime, but she certainly couldn't go in once it got dark. She wasn't sure whether that was her mother's doing or not. Maybe it was still left over from her grandmother. So much pain was tied up in this location that Danica was okay to not have anything to do with it.

"I'm surprised you would settle here. There doesn't appear to be much here for you."

She gave him a nod. "You could be right," she admitted. "Definitely a lot of energy is here, memories that I don't feel great about," she murmured, wrapping her arms around her chest, as she looked at the acreage around her. "My grandmother has always called this home, and, now that I'm back again, I realize how much this place, *the land*, feels like home to me. It's just that the house itself is not necessarily comfortable."

"I'm sure you would be happier in other locations, other states even."

"Maybe," she said, with a glance in his direction, "but something can be said about coming home. However, I might feel differently after she's gone."

"Coming home is one thing. Coming home to a place where you're obviously ..." He hesitated.

"Not welcome?" she added, her voice rising.

"I didn't mean it that way."

"No, maybe you didn't, but it doesn't change the reality of it. That's exactly what it is," she retorted.

"They think you got away with murder," he shared bluntly.

She laughed. "At least you call a spade a spade. I prefer that to people tiptoeing around, with veiled glances and sideways looks," she murmured. "I did not kill anybody. I did not attempt to kill anybody, and, if you had been the visiting physician or one of the doctors at the hospital at the time, you would have realized it just wasn't possible. But nobody would vouch for my injuries or clarify in any way what had gone on. So, everybody's rumor mill superstitions just went into overdrive."

"I never thought of that," he noted. "I haven't looked at your case."

"Can you?" she asked, looking over at him.

"I don't have access to the sheriff's records, and I don't really know that I would or should have access to your medical records," he replied.

"Then it's just the slight dubiousness about accessing somebody's record for voyeurism versus an actual desire to help," she pointed out.

He looked at her sharply. "The only reason I would be accessing those records is if I could find a way to reassure people, particularly those around us, that you could not have self-inflicted those wounds."

"It wouldn't help. Don't you realize that, even though my wounds couldn't be self-inflicted, as far as the locals are concerned, they were supposedly inflicted by my mother as I tried to kill her?" she asked, with a hard glance. "People will take whatever information they want, and they will twist it so it appears to answer the questions in the way they want at any given time. The truth isn't what this is about. It's about vilifying me, no matter what."

"Right, but why?" he asked, staring at her, feeling troubled.

"I don't understand why," she murmured. "Because they're afraid of me, I think. More than afraid, to be honest."

"Because you died?" he murmured. "We have a lot of people who die on the table and come back."

"Sure, but do they wake up in the morgue?" she asked.

He stared at her in shock and then slowly shook his head. "I've heard of that happening in various places," he replied, "but not in North America."

"Right. So that's just one more of those little oddities that people don't like about me," she stated.

An awkward silence passed for a moment.

She looked to see him studying her carefully. She shrugged. "What?" she asked. "What is it you're now suspecting?"

"I'm not suspecting anything," he said defensively. "The questions running through my head are not really appropriate either, but I can't stop thinking about them," he admitted.

"Such as?" she queried.

"What did it feel like?" he asked. "To wake up in a body bag?"

"Suffocating," she said bluntly. "It wasn't a body bag though, if that's what you're thinking. I was in a cold-storage drawer at the morgue. I woke up, and I couldn't get out, and I felt like I had been buried alive," she murmured, staring at him, feeling the same remnants of fear running through her system. She shuddered and wrapped her arms tighter around her chest. "People don't understand just how it changes you."

"I'm so sorry. I can't even imagine," he murmured. "When we were in med school, we used to fool around like that every once in a while. You know, get the experience of what it was like to be in a drawer. I hated it. It was pretty damn freaky," he confessed.

"It is freaky," she murmured, "but it's more than freaky. It's … life-changing, but that doesn't even do justice to the feeling. When you wake up, and you are the one in that drawer, pounding for somebody to let you out—only to have the drawer come open and everyone run away because they realize you are alive? Instead of thinking that something bad had happened to you—like an accident, and you were pronounced dead in error—they take off, thinking that you're a ghost, a demon, or some other godforsaken thing," she muttered.

She glared at him, remembering the horrific looks she'd gotten, as she had been moved to the ER department, where the doctors could check her over. "Then to find out that *nothing*," she said, with air quotes, "nothing was wrong."

"What do you mean by *nothing wrong*? You were stabbed multiple times, weren't you?"

"Oh, I was," she confirmed. "Absolutely I was. But … You might as well just go read my chart. Then, if you have any questions, feel free to come back and ask them." He hesitated and she shrugged. "You'll do it to satisfy your medical curiosity. At least this way, I can give you permission, and you won't feel like you're breaking the law, violating my privacy or whatever."

He winced and nodded. "You don't pull punches, do you?"

"No." She cast a lopsided look in his direction. "That's never done me any good. I know that people do the shit they always do, bend the rules all the time. In your case, you do have a reason to check it out, and you have access," she noted, with a grin. "So, you might as well look at it. Then you can tell me what you find. It's not as if anybody ever tells me anything."

"Right. You don't have a copy of your medical file or the sheriff's investigation, do you?"

"Nope, not exactly. It's not something that's easy to get."

He nodded.

"Go," she urged him. "I know you're dying to run away."

He hesitated. "You've certainly got my curiosity up," he conceded. "So I would very much like to take a look and see what I can find. I'm not even sure how much of your file is there."

"Hell, I wouldn't be surprised to find out that it's been burned or something," she noted, with a mock smile. "Believe me that the superstitions in this town are something else."

"And yet you want to stay."

"I want to stay for my grandmother's sake. I'm not sure how I feel about staying overall."

"Yet you are buying my land, and you will own the rest after your grandmother's gone. She would leave it in your possession, I assume."

She nodded slowly. "Yes, and, in a way, it would be a good thing for me to have a home base, but I guess it also depends on whether that home base will be something I can live with or if it'll be a place where I am never accepted."

"I can't imagine, given what I've seen for a reaction from the locals so far."

"What if they found out the truth?" she asked, looking at him slowly. "If they realized that most of the rumor-mongering was coming from one specific corner, would that change things?"

He stared at her and then slowly nodded. "Over time, it would. Although I would have thought that a lot of these people would have forgotten what had happened already."

"So would I," she agreed, with an odd expression. "So, somebody, somewhere along the line, has kept a lot of this alive, and I just don't understand why."

"Did your mother have any other family here?" he asked.

She stared at him and then shook her head. "Why do you ask?"

"I just wondered if we're missing another connection here, if your mother knew something or was related to somebody or something else. Was she here all the time?"

"She was here most of the time. A couple times she ran away, and we thought maybe she was gone for good. I do believe I heard something about her having disappeared for long periods of time before I was born as well," she shared, with a shrug. "I know that sounds absolutely horrific, and I don't mean it that way, but it was par for the course with Daisy. I do remember one particular time when I was still in school, but I don't remember what grade." She frowned, trying to dredge the memory from the back of her mind. "I really don't know anything about it, but she was gone for quite a while."

"Then she came back?"

She looked over at him and nodded. "Yes, she came back. As my memory serves, she was different in a way. But again, I was just a young teenager, so I'm not sure I have an idea of what *different* really means," she said, with a laugh.

"Maybe it's something we can ask your grandmother about, when she's feeling better," he suggested.

"Why?" she asked, looking at him intently. "What do you care?"

"I don't like to see injustices like this," he said, looking off to the side. "For one thing, your grandmother doesn't have an easy road ahead of her as she ages, and you won't have an easy road ahead of you as you try to make the rest of your grandmother's life comfortable, all the while dealing with this level of prejudice from the townsfolk."

She smiled. "If you really want to help, why don't you start with your brother?"

HARRIET LISTENED TO the conversation from the sanctuary of her bed, wondering how long she could hold off before everything blew up in her granddaughter's face, through no fault of her own. Harriet wanted to trust the doctor, but they'd tried trusting doctors in the past, and it hadn't worked out so well. She knew her granddaughter needed somebody to be there in her life, when Harriet was gone. It was interesting that Danica had talked about waking up in the morgue and that he felt compelled to look at her charts.

Harriet was sure that would be a HIPAA violation or two, something along those lines, but, Danica having given Cameron permission, that was a whole different story. An interesting twist too.

Her granddaughter typically avoided men like the plague. Harriet wasn't even sure Danica had ever had a long-term relationship. It's not something they'd ever discussed, and it wasn't all that surprising. It's not as if men had been very kind to Danica, particularly not since she'd woken up in that damn drawer.

If a single experience could take away her granddaughter, it would be that one. It would be bad enough to find out that you'd been declared deceased, but then to find out that you'd been locked up in cold storage, all ready for a grave, only to wake up trapped in that horrific metal prison? It was a nightmare that had kept Danica from sleeping for a very long time. Harriet couldn't even begin to count the number of days, months, possibly even years that she'd sat at her granddaughter's side, trying to convince her to go to sleep, reassuring her that she wouldn't wake up dead again.

Sadly, waking up dead would have been a piece of cake, compared to what Danica has had to endure ever since. Her granddaughter had made that very clear. So much easier. She got teased, harassed, and pestered about it from the start. Nobody seemed to have anything but fascination for the young woman who had woken up, after being pronounced dead. Nobody looked at the incompetence of the doctors. Nobody ever looked at the doctor at the time, who had been more of an old fuddy-duddy than competent. That was the problem when everybody protected their own.

Even though Harriet and Danica had spent many, many years here—Harriet's entire life, for that matter, and Danica's childhood as well—they were still outsiders … because of Daisy's behavior.

Then the family had been ostracized for a very long time. Harriet's own mother had probably started the process, and, with Harriet's own abilities, that hadn't helped. Yet Daisy's psychotic breaks, as Harriet liked to put them, had finalized the deal. From then on, they'd been *that family*; the family everyone hated to be close to, hated to be around.

Of course Danica finding out that her mother was hell-bent on killing her because Danica was young, pretty, sexy—the epitome of everything Daisy wanted to retain, but she couldn't rewind time—which must have been awful for Danica. Daisy had been ruled by sheer jealousy and greed. Or maybe it was just a weariness of the whole aging thing. Maybe Daisy had been planning on taking her own life the whole time. Just something else they wouldn't know the answer to.

For all her abilities, Harriet had yet to speak to her daughter in the afterlife. To have that conversation would have helped her a lot, but her daughter wouldn't give her that satisfaction. Daisy hadn't been a hard child to raise, not until she hit puberty, and then she'd become impossible.

Slowly, with a sigh, Harriet pulled back the blankets and sat up, wishing the room wouldn't spin quite so badly around her head. The last thing she needed right now was to show weakness. Not only would that make her granddaughter worry, but it would also show weakness on the ethers—something Harriet couldn't afford to do.

She groaned as she sat up a little farther and made her way to the bathroom. "You can't get old now," she muttered to herself, ignoring the fact that, for many people, she already was old. *Very* old. Her daughter had been born to Harriet late in life, and maybe that had contributed to Daisy's instability. Harriet couldn't provide the world she wanted for her daughter. She couldn't provide anything, apparently.

She'd been spending all her evenings working on healing her daughter while Daisy slept, and yet nothing ever seemed to work. Harriet had read that sometimes you couldn't heal some afflictions, but she had refused to believe it. It was her only daughter, her only child, and this hadn't been something Harriet was prepared to live with. Seeing the end result, even now, all these years later, still tore her apart. Yet no need for it. No reason for Daisy to have gone the way she had, unless it was a result of the energy work. And then, of course, she got into drugs.

When Daisy got into drugs, everything had gone wild. Harriet had tried to get help from the local sheriff's office.

She had also tried to get help from the parents of the other kids. But either nobody would help her or nobody knew how to help her. She blamed the lot of them for a long time, but, of course, it wasn't their fault. Daisy had made decisions on her own, and Harriet couldn't help Daisy with those any more than the other parents could help their children. Once Daisy had gone down that addiction pathway, it was just too hard to try and regain control of her.

After using the bathroom and slowly washing her face, Harriet studied her reflection in the mirror. Looking closely at her head, recognizing the wound that she had tried so hard to keep hidden, she realized no way Danica hadn't seen it. She shed her nightgown, removed her pants and shirt from the hook on the back of the bathroom door, and got dressed. As soon as she stepped back into her bedroom, her granddaughter rushed through to see her.

Danica stared at Nana, surprised. "You shouldn't be up," she scolded her.

Harriet smiled. "Of course I should be," she argued, brushing it off. "I fell. It's really not that big of a deal."

"So, if you just fell, how did you get that bump on your noggin?" Danica asked, staring at Nana.

Danica was always way too perceptive, that one. Too smart, too intuitive for her own good, and too strong energy-wise. Yet Danica didn't really understand what she was doing on the energy level.

Because Harriet tried so hard to protect Danica, to not have her go off the rails like her mother, Harriet had withheld all the training and all the energy work knowledge from Danica, and now Harriet feared it was way too late.

Harriet's eyes widened, when she watched Cameron walk in. "I don't need a doctor," she stated briskly, wiping her still damp hands on her pants. "What I do need is a cup of tea." She brushed past both of them and headed for the kitchen.

In these moments, where she had to appear strong and decisive, were her downfall. She knew that, and it would make her more exhausted than anything. Yet the appearance of strength was everything, particularly in the eye of the enemy. She had yet to sort out whether Cameron was a friend or foe. His brother was definitely a foe, but that didn't mean that Cameron was too, or that he even understood the war his family was involved in.

Harriet sighed as she put on the teakettle and then made her way to sit at the kitchen table. As she glanced at her granddaughter, standing there, arms crossed, glaring at her, Harriet smiled. "I'm just fine, you know," she declared, catching sight of the tears in her granddaughter's eyes. She sighed and opened her arms. "I know it'll be a shock for you, but one day I will go." She waved her hand at her granddaughter, trying to bring her in. "And there won't be anything you can do about it."

Danica nodded, as she gave her a hug. "I know that. I understand that completely, yet we don't want to bring that time to us any faster than we should."

"Says you," she muttered, with a smile. "There are plenty of days when I'm more than ready to go."

"If that's an issue, then we need to talk about it," Danica stated firmly. "I have no intention of dragging your life out longer, especially if you have no wish to do so. But neither do I want you becoming so morose that it becomes all you talk about and worry on."

"I'm not worried about dying," Harriet said, her gaze going from her granddaughter to Cameron. "I'm only concerned about leaving you behind."

"Of course you are," Danica agreed, and she sat down beside her. "I will be fine, Nana. You know that."

"I do know that." She patted her granddaughter's hand. "You were always the one who would be fine. No matter what, you will always be fine. The trouble is, you never really let anybody in to help you."

Danica laughed. "Other than you, nobody has been around to help me, as you well know."

Wincing at her bluntness, Harriet stiffened and glared back over at Cameron.

He just shrugged and walked over to the now-bubbling teakettle. "How do we make the tea here?" he asked.

Harriet laughed. "What? Is this somebody who's willing to help?"

He looked at her, surprised. "I've helped lots of people, and I've lived alone for a long time," he shared, cracking a lopsided grin. "I can manage a cup of tea. I just didn't want to open up every cupboard door and make you think I was being intrusive just because I don't know where the tea is." At that, he opened the closest cabinet. "But it's right here. Where else would it be?"

"Exactly." Harriet smiled. "Where else would it be?"

He made up a pot of tea and brought everything over to the table, then sat down beside Harriet. "Now I'm not sure how that bump didn't show up in the hospital, or, if it did, how my esteemed colleague missed it." A patent disbelief filled his tone. "But I would like to know how you got that smack on the head."

She looked over at him and said casually, "Somebody hit me, of course. What else could it be?"

CHAPTER 11

DANICA STARED AT her grandmother in shock. "You were attacked?"

She shrugged. "Yes, if that's the word you want to use. I'm not sure I want to use that word, but let's just say I thought I heard somebody behind me. I turned around, and, the next thing I knew, I woke up in the hospital."

"Who in the fucking hell was it?" Danica snapped.

"If I could tell you that, I would solve the problem and do so. But I can't tell you because presumably that's why he hit me when he did, just as I was turning around to see who it was. Yes, I know that'll get you all in an uproar, but I'm fine."

"You're fine," she repeated, staring at her, "but you weren't fine. And if somebody hits you on your own property, that is something to be concerned about."

She smiled and shrugged. "Maybe, … but it's also not something to be overly concerned about because he's obviously gone."

"What if he comes back?" she asked, clearly worried.

Harriet gently gripped Danica's hands. "It'll be fine." She looked back over at Cameron. "What are you doing here?"

"I came to check up on you," he replied, his gaze completely ignoring the hard look Danica shot in his direction.

"As you can see, I'm totally fine."

"Good," he replied, lifting the teapot and pouring three cups, obviously with no intention of leaving.

Harriet sighed. "You really don't need to worry about me."

"Just because you say so doesn't make it true," he pointed out bluntly, "and having seen the size of the lump on your head, I won't just let it slide. If you don't want to contact the sheriff, that's fine, but I will."

"No, you won't," Harriet declared, the sharpness of her tone cutting through the small room like a knife.

Danica stared at her and shot back, "Why not, Nana? What on earth could that possibly hurt?"

"What it could do is bring up an awful lot of old memories and old hurts that really have nothing to do with it. The last thing I want is to have any of that old stuff brought back up again."

"And you think it would?" she asked. "Is that what's going on here?"

"I don't know," she replied, as she smiled gently at her granddaughter. "And I don't care. I just want it all to go away." She looked over at Cameron. "I'll need milk in my tea, please."

Surprised, he hopped to his feet, walked over to the fridge, pulled out a jug, and brought it to the table.

"What difference does it make if it does bring all that back up?" he asked, not to be deterred.

DANICA WASN'T SURE how much of this conversation was happening because her grandmother didn't want him involved, yet he was being fairly insistent. And, if he went to the sheriff—which Danica wasn't against, although she would hate the process—her grandmother would likely get quite irate yet again. The last thing she wanted was to upset Nana. "I think it's probably a good idea if we do bring in the police," Danica shared, not wanting to let it go, especially when she had a vote in her corner. Never ever had that happened before.

Her grandmother frowned at her and shook her head. "The local authorities haven't changed," she murmured. "It's still the same people, the same fear, the same overt hatred."

Danica winced. "True."

To which Cameron muttered, "You were attacked at your home, so nothing else should matter."

She laughed bitterly. "Nothing else *should* matter, but it will," she stated, a hard edge to her tone. "You don't have any idea how that was for us."

"You keep saying that, but it's been a long time, and it should have been well and truly over long ago."

"Agreed, but it isn't," Harriet said.

Then Danica caught sight of her grandmother's pale face again and frowned. She didn't want the same old drama either, but doing nothing wasn't an option. "Neither," she told her grandmother, "can I have you getting attacked, particularly on your own property."

Her grandmother shrugged. "Wouldn't it be nice if we lived in a perfect world, and assholes weren't out there," she said, her language surprising both of them. She chuckled. "Forget about it. I'll be fine. It wasn't major, and we won't dwell on it."

"How can you not dwell on it?" Cameron asked, studying her. "What if it isn't you next time? What if it's your granddaughter?"

CAMERON GOT UP and left soon afterward. As he walked out to his car, he heard a shout. Turning around, he saw Danica jogging toward him. "I *will* contact the sheriff," he repeated firmly.

She smiled. "That's what I was hoping you would do. Just be aware that my grandmother will likely hold that against you."

He shrugged. "She can hold it against me, but my question to her is still very valid. What happens if it's you next time? Harriet may not care about her life, but I'm hoping you don't have such a cavalier attitude to something so precious."

"No, I don't have a cavalier attitude to something so precious," she said. "Yet I can understand her not wanting to bring up everything we've already been through. You weren't here last time, and you don't know everything that happened."

"No, I don't, but I will be checking in with my brother though to see what's going on."

"Nana and I really would like for Jace to stop spreading his vitriol. If you want to do something concrete, then, yes, start there."

"You want to tell me more? Surely there is more to the story."

"No, I won't tell you about it all. More than enough rumors and chaos are all around for that to come out without involving us," she explained. "I also don't know how dangerous any of this is, so, please, if you're doing this, watch out for yourself."

He stopped, studying her expression, as his lips quirked. "What's the matter?" he teased. "Would you miss me if something happened?" She shuddered, and he watched the color strip from her face.

"Please don't even joke about that," she whispered.

He felt hit with a level of remorse that was completely unexpected. "I'm sorry," he muttered. "I know you've been through an awful lot already."

"I have," she agreed forcibly, "and, until you have experienced such a thing, it's hard to imagine. And don't joke about something like that. You're a good doctor, and this town needs you. It would be a shame if something happened to you, God forbid. I also know that people would say any accident that befalls you was because of your association with us."

He felt himself stiffening at that concept, wondering if that's the only reason she would have any regret. But deciding it wasn't time to push it, he just nodded. "I'll be careful. By the same token, you also need to be careful. If someone would attack your grandmother, they would certainly attack you as well."

"I know. I know," she muttered, turning to glance back at the house.

"You should probably sleep in the house."

She looked over at him and, in a bold statement that he didn't understand, said, "As much as I would like to, that's impossible." Turning, she headed back to her grandmother and disappeared from sight.

He was left standing here, pondering her statement.

BACK AT HIS house, Cameron wandered through his property, wondering what to do, and then finally decided it would be better to go talk to somebody in person. Hopping into his vehicle, he headed to the sheriff's office. Even with this extra stop, he knew he would still end up arriving early for his night shift at the hospital, but that would be par for the course anyway.

As he walked in, several people looked up, smiled, and called out to him.

"Hey, Doc. What's going on?"

"Nice to see you, Doc."

"How you doing, Doc?"

He smiled, waved, and asked, "Is Deputy Peter Benson here?" He'd patched up the man a few months ago, and it was helpful to have a familiar face to talk to, especially under these circumstances.

"Yo," came a call from a side office.

Cameron looked over to see somebody he at least knew personally and had worked with at the hospital on several cases. It usually involved domestic violence, though a couple accidental injury cases were involved too. He walked over and asked, "Hey, you got a minute?"

Benson looked up, smiled, and nodded. "Always for you, Doc. Come on in. Grab a seat. What can I do for you?"

Cameron sat down and looked over at him, waiting to gauge the expression on his face, and asked, "What do you know about Danica Hartling?"

Immediately his expression changed, and he looked down and shuffled the paperwork in front of him. "Ah, it's going that way," he muttered.

"I sure get odd reactions, depending on who I talk to."

"I'm sure you do. I wasn't here at the time and just know what everybody has said afterward, since I've been here a long time now," he murmured, "but that name still causes all kinds of chaos when you mention it."

"I've seen that myself," Cameron noted. "I wasn't here at the time of the big event, but my brother was." He got a look from the deputy, who just nodded. "Apparently my brother has more than a lot to say about it to everybody, but he's not being very forthcoming with me."

"What is it you want from me?" the deputy asked, folding his hands and resting them atop the desk.

"Did you … Are you aware that old lady Harriet—Danica's grandmother—was attacked and hit over the head today?"

At that, Benson's eyebrows shot up. "No," he said, sitting upright. "I did not know that." He frowned, shaking his head. "It's odd that I don't, since that report should have crossed my desk as soon as it came in," he added, looking across his desk in multiple places, as if searching for the missing report.

"Nobody reported it because they don't believe anybody'll care."

He winced at that. "I can see where they might have gotten that attitude from a long time ago," the deputy admitted, "but it's not as if that still prevails today."

"They had a visit several days ago by two deputies." Cameron shared what he'd been told, trying to keep his tone causal. "They seemed to be questioning Danica's presence, while at her grandmother's house."

"Of course." The deputy sighed, slouching back in his chair and looking over at Cameron. "We can't always stop the superstition and rumor-mongering that goes on around here," he began, "but I would like to think that, if there were attacks causing injuries, somebody would let us know, so we could put a stop to it."

"Which is why I'm here," Cameron stated. "I just wasn't

sure how this all was supposed to work its way through the system, particularly if the system isn't exactly there for those two women."

"Oh, it's there for them," he declared, waving his hand. "Again, absolutely nothing to do with me. But I do know there are very long memories around here."

"What are those long memories all about?" Cameron asked curiously, looking at him.

"Some of the staff here have been around for a long time, and, although I'm sure a lot of those memories have twisted over the years, that impression still remains, and none of it's good."

"Of course, but Danica was also a victim," he pointed out.

Deputy Benson nodded. "I know. Trust me when I say that I've had this argument with several of them over the years, whenever the subject has popped up, inevitably around Halloween."

Cameron leaned forward. "You're kidding. Why Halloween?"

The deputy stared at him. "Surely you know about the hauntings at the hospital."

"Yes, in a secondhand way from other staff here, but I haven't done a Halloween here yet to see for myself."

"I have had some firsthand experience," the deputy said, with a laugh. "I don't know that it happens every year, but apparently it happens enough times that people get freaked out and won't work the hospital shifts on Halloween. Then again, maybe people won't go to the hospital either, especially if they're freaked out about what might show up while they are there," he suggested, with a shrug.

Cameron nodded. "Every time I bring it up, I get weird

answers, and people clam up." He looked over at the deputy. "Don't you get those reports?"

"Nothing has been filed officially," he stated, "and definitely not on the Halloween stuff."

"Okay, so that's bizarre."

"Oh, it's all bizarre," he declared, with a nod. "Yet, if anybody is attacking anyone in my town, I want to know about it."

"I wasn't sure if it was something that would even come across your desk."

"It would because we're a small outfit, and anything like that is definitely a no-go. Now I need to go talk to her."

"You might not get a warm welcome."

"Of course not," he muttered. "That would be way too simple. Regardless, someone has been hurt. Why would anybody not want us involved?"

"Someone's been hurt, but the person in question is the one who's definitely grumpy about it."

He chuckled. "I've met Harriet several times, but she's always been nice and easy to talk to."

"I would agree with you. But, in this instance, I don't know that that'll hold true, considering she's the one who was attacked."

"I should check at the hospital for a report."

"You could," Cameron agreed, "and I'll tell you something else that I found to be strange. They let her go with a head injury, yet no mention of the head injury is in her case file. I saw it for myself when she was at home."

"Are you sure?" Benson hesitated, watching Cameron nod. "I know this will come across as completely crazy, but is there any chance that the granddaughter may have inflicted that injury after the fact to throw you off?"

Cameron just stared at him in shock. "What?" he asked, unable to get anything else out for few moments, trying to wrap his head around the insinuations. "Honestly, I'm stunned that you even asked that."

"If the doctor at the hospital didn't see a head injury, yet you go to the house and see a head injury, why wouldn't you at least contemplate the possibility that the granddaughter, Danica—about whom we have all kinds of crazy reports—didn't attack the old woman?"

"Good God," Cameron muttered, sitting back.

"I'm guessing you didn't even think of that."

"No, I didn't think of that," he stated, calmly trying to gather his wits about him, "because that's just ludicrous. She has absolutely no reason to do something like that."

"Was she happy to show you the wound, or was she trying to fight it?"

"She was protecting her grandmother's privacy and trying to get her permission to a certain extent," he replied, frowning. "I don't think it was to stop me from seeing *her own handiwork*, as you propose. Besides, I did talk to Harriet about it myself."

"She couldn't tell you who hit her?"

"No," he said, frowning.

"Exactly. Now, I'm not saying that's what happened, but is it possible that the head wound developed after the fact and just didn't show up at the time of the hospital visit?"

Cameron slowly shook his head. "Yes, it's possible, I suppose, but not common. She has a large head wound," he noted, carefully choosing his words. "I don't know how she got the head wound, who gave it to her, or anything else about it, only that she has one, and her head has a definite swelling."

"Is it severe?" the deputy asked.

"No, but, according to Harriet, she heard something behind her, turned, and was knocked out."

"It also could have been Danica then as well."

Cameron stared at Deputy Benson, feeling the sinking in his stomach. Was the Deputy prejudiced against Danica and her family? Was he causing harm by being here? He wasn't sure, but there was something … off in the guy's speech.

Benson nodded. "See? That's what people will say."

"You don't even sound surprised."

"Nope, I'm not because that's the stuff that goes along with anything to do with her."

"That Danica attacked her own grandmother, trying to make it look like it was somebody else? Come on. Harriet was taken to the hospital unconscious."

"Sure. But you don't know who made her unconscious," he pointed out. "All I'm saying is that I'll take a look. But you have, in your own words, just basically asked what happened. Harriet turned, got hit from behind, can't identify who hit her, yet no injury showed up until after she got home again. That doesn't make sense then, unless Danica hit her twice."

"Good God," Cameron snapped. "You're telling me that Danica supposedly hit her grandmother over the head enough to knock her out, races her to the emergency room, and then, with everybody thinking it's just a fall, gets her home, hits her again, then puts her to bed with a head wound?"

Benson just sat there and looked at him. "What? You got another explanation?"

"No, I don't," he snarled, "but that's not a logical explanation either."

Benson shrugged. "I get it. You don't like it. I don't like it either," he muttered, with a shrug. "So, if the granddaughter did hit her grandmother, we need to know about it because that *is* something I can do something about."

"What can you do about it?"

"I can arrest her and charge her for attacking her grandmother," he replied.

Cameron sat back with a *whoosh*, a sinking feeling in his gut. "That's not what happened."

"Then you explain it," he said, looking at him. "I'm just going by what you've told me."

"No, you're not," Cameron declared. "*That* isn't what I told you at all."

"It is. You're just not listening. Maybe you're under her spell, just like everybody else was at the time."

At that, he stiffened. "What do you mean, *like everybody else was at the time*?"

He looked at him. "Oh, you really don't know very much about what went on back then, do you?"

"No, I don't. I wasn't here. I told you that."

"Yes, but do you also understand that back then," he added, using air quotes for emphasis, "she was *suspicious* at the very least?"

"Why? Because of her mother?"

"Oh, her mother was a whole different ball game," he noted, "but you've got to remember that the apple doesn't fall far from the tree."

"What, so she's guilty, without having done anything, just by association of her blood?"

"Hey, hey, hey, I'm not saying that," Benson replied, waving his hands. "Don't go putting words in my mouth."

"It sure feels like you're putting them in my mouth,"

Cameron said, staring at the man he thought would be an answer to this quandary. Now he realized he'd probably just made things even murkier and more confusing for Harriet and Danica.

"You go do what you need to do," the deputy replied, waving him out. "I'll make an official report and go see her. Don't worry about it," he added.

"Don't bother. Instead I will check on her."

"What? So now you're telling me that you don't want me to go talk to her?"

"No. I don't think I do," Cameron said, with an odd smile.

"Doc, you've got to understand that you came this far because you realized that this old lady was in trouble," the deputy pointed out. "So, the least you can do is let me ensure she is safe where she is."

"I know she's safe," Cameron declared, scrubbing his face. "I just can't believe that this is the outcome of what I thought would be a helpful investigation. Instead I think I've made it worse."

"Maybe you need to take a closer look at the people involved," the deputy suggested. "I'm not saying that this group of people are crazy or would do something like that, but I'm just listening to your words."

"No, no, you're not," Cameron corrected, staring at him. "You're listening to rumors, superstitions, something completely different."

The deputy eyed Cameron suspiciously. "Are you doing okay?"

"I'm starting to realize that maybe this town is not doing okay at all anymore," he murmured, standing and turning to leave.

"I'll still stop by and talk to them," Benson called out.

"You do you," Cameron responded, with a wave of his hand. "I'm no longer concerned about your input."

"Maybe that's more of an issue," Deputy Benson said, as he got to his feet and headed out after Cameron. "Maybe you should be concerned, and the fact that you aren't just makes me even more worried."

"I'm fine," he said, turning to face him. "I just hadn't realized how deep the poison in this town has spread."

And, with that, he walked out of the station.

CHAPTER 12

DANICA STAYED CLOSE to her grandmother for the rest of the day. It was evening now, and she was surprised the house had allowed her to stay inside after dark.

When her grandmother glared at her and announced, "I'm not an invalid."

"No, you're not," Danica agreed calmly, "but you're also not feeling great."

"Now, how do you know that?" she snapped.

She looked at her and smiled. "I can see it."

Her grandmother grumbled for several minutes and then slunk into her chair. "I could use another cup of tea."

"Okay, I'm happy to get you a cup of tea. I'll also heat up some soup, and, if you have a bowl of that, you'll really make me happy."

"I'm happy to have soup," she grumbled, with a dismissive wave of her hand.

"Maybe. But you're obviously distraught about something, and you're not talking to me. What I'm afraid of is that you know who hit you."

She looked over at her granddaughter and shook her head. "No, I do not. I wish I did, but I'm afraid that this doctor will be more trouble than we want."

"In what way?" she asked.

"If he goes to the sheriff, you know that they'll come

over and start poking and prying."

"Somebody attacked you," Danica replied in exasperation. "Maybe they should."

"No, they shouldn't." Nana glared at her. "You need to stop doing anything that will bring people into our world like that."

"I understand that part," Danica noted, "but I won't let anybody attack you and get away with it."

Nana sighed. "But you also know, or you would if you thought about it, how it'll look when they get here."

"No, I don't have a clue what you're talking about. What do you mean?"

"I didn't have a lump in my head when I was in the hospital, but I had one when I got home. So, who do you guess they'll think gave it to me?"

Danica stared at her grandmother and slowly sank into the chair beside her. "They wouldn't think that, would they?" she muttered, her thoughts running rampant, disbelief draining the color from her face. "Why? It's not as if I have any reason to harm you."

"Considering that people will kill each other over a cup of coffee, I'm not sure that's a fair assessment of the situation," Nana argued, with half a smile. "That's why I didn't want Cameron to go to the sheriff. I wasn't thinking about me at all," she declared, looking at her granddaughter.

"I really don't give a crap if they do think that. What will they do? Charge me?"

"They might," Nana snapped, looking at Danica intently. "You know that an awful lot of people here would be happy to see you go away. Permanently."

"Sure, but *permanently* is hardly going to jail for attacking you," she said, giving a hysterical laugh. "That's ridiculous." Yet, as she thought about her words, she realized that a certain amount of truth was in her grandmother's concern. "Good God," Danica muttered. "I can't even imagine having to deal with that crap again."

"No, and that's part of the problem. You might not want to think about it, but that doesn't mean it won't happen."

"I won't think about it right now either," she snapped. "Somebody attacked you, and that is my concern."

"Your concern, but not mine," her grandmother clarified.

"Why is that?" she asked, eyeing her grandmother.

"Because I'm not worried," her grandmother responded.

"Going back to all that cryptic stuff again, are we?" Danica studied Nana, long enough to make her grandmother uneasy. "I have a couple questions to ask." She watched the almost visible wince on her grandmother's face, then nodded. "Don't you think it's about time you told me what was going on between you and my mother?"

"Going on?" her grandmother asked in astonishment, staring at her. "What do you mean?"

"I don't know. I really don't, but obviously something occurred between the two of you that Daisy could never find peace over."

"No, she couldn't ever find peace, and that was because of those abilities of hers."

"Abilities? They were for real?"

"They were for real, but she kept using them for less than good. What I know is that, when she started pulling that crap, all kinds of things went wrong."

Danica stared off into the distance. "I wonder if she ever would have found peace," she murmured.

"I don't know that she could have. She wanted out. She wanted away from here. She didn't want this lifestyle, and I didn't have anything to give her other than this," her grandmother shared, turning to Danica. "I thought that maybe when you were born, it would be enough for her."

Danica smiled. "And yet you and I both know that she wanted nothing to do with me. Why did she even go ahead with the pregnancy?"

"The truth? Is that what you want?" her grandmother asked.

"Yes, I really do."

"Because it was too late to do anything about it," she stated. "You were already too far developed for her to get an abortion."

Even though Danica had figured the answer would be similar to that, to hear it was still a sucker punch to the gut, and one that brought a physical, almost visceral reaction. It was all she could do to not bend over and cry out in pain, but she covered it somewhat, though her grandmother saw it anyway.

"That's why I didn't tell you. There are just some things you shouldn't know."

"Maybe I shouldn't know them," Danica admitted, breathing when she finally could, "but the fact that I already basically knew it doesn't change the fact that it's not the same as the truth. I'm all about the truth right now."

"Even if it hurts?" Nana asked.

"Especially if it hurts because, when you're gone, I would like to know exactly what happened. I was kept out of so much back then. I didn't even understand—until the kids started to accuse me of killing my mother—that was how they all viewed me," she shared, her tone pained.

"It was a big enough shock as it was, and it was just so wrong that they even did that," her grandmother stated stoutly. "Of course you didn't hurt her."

"No, but Daisy's still dead. She killed herself instead of being my mother," Danica snapped, glaring at her grandmother.

"That's something I live with too." Harriet nodded. "I know. It's a messed-up world for all of us."

"I'm sorry you had to deal with that as well." Danica tried hard to push back the tears, trying to imagine what it was like for her grandmother.

"Of course I did. She was my daughter, my only child. I was so absolutely delighted to have her. And yet, from the moment she was born, Daisy's health was a roller coaster of concern for me. When she hit puberty, her mental decline accelerated and just never quit," her grandmother murmured, staring off into the distance. "She was a very unhappy soul."

"Was there anything we could have done to make it easier on her?" Danica asked, looking over at her grandmother. "I couldn't figure out how to even talk to her back then."

"That's because she didn't want to talk to you. She saw you as the epitome of everything she could no longer be."

"What I can't understand is why?" she said. "I stayed out of her way. I didn't have anything to do with what went on in her world. I stayed away from her boyfriends. I just … I didn't do anything."

"You didn't *do* anything," her grandmother explained gently, "except *exist*. For Daisy, who wanted to get away and to live a life of freedom and luxury, having you around was, in her mind, a millstone on her neck. I don't mean it that way, but—"

"No, but it's true," Danica accepted. "That's exactly what I was, whether I like it or not. But I had hoped that she would at least find her way out of here and find a way to be at peace."

"You and me both," Harriet muttered. "Daisy could never find anybody to take her away, and I had no money to send her away. So, we were both trapped in this situation, where I saw Daisy's deterioration, but I just didn't know how to help. I didn't know how to fix it," she admitted, tears coming to her eyes. "She was my daughter. I absolutely loved her, adored her. Yet it didn't seem as if anything I did helped her."

WHAT A BITCH.

It was early morning. He watched the woman putter around in the front garden. He was safely hidden. Hidden from sight and, hopefully, out of mind, but a part of him wished Danica would disappear from this earth, never to return. He normally wasn't one to have those kinds of thoughts, but the trouble she had brought into his life was unbearable now.

And then, of course, there was her mother.

That was too much to even begin to think about. Those things kept him up at night, wondering whether he should have done something or could have done something. He wasn't sure he should be blamed for anything. Yet he couldn't stop the guilt—the guilt that he could have done more, even if he wasn't the best messenger for it.

Now, as he watched her in the garden, it drove him nuts to think she was happy and carefree, while his world had been torn apart.

Did she even know?

Did she have any idea just how much torment she had brought into his life?

Was she so unbelievably oblivious to it all, numb to it all, and maybe even blind to it all?

He didn't know how much her mother had told her, how much her grandmother had told her.

That was another issue he would love to get answers for, but what answers would he ever get?

It's not as if they wanted to talk to him, and honestly he didn't want anything to do with her. He was much better at skulking in the shadows, rather than trying to go out there and say hello. What would he say? The words choked back in his own mind. It's as if he could not convey the feelings of disgust and antipathy he felt toward her.

It was just—it was wrong. He needed to leave their place. No reason for him to be here.

He continued to watch her for a long moment, fear warring with anger and frustration from so long ago. Finally he forced himself back off the road and over to where he'd parked his truck. He'd been here multiple times already and almost got caught once by that old biddy.

She should have had her lifetime shortened a long time ago too. That would have made him happy. Nobody else would give a shit. That was the problem. In fact, everyone else was just not even worth his time.

Feeling the same lethargic apathy that seemed to pervade his world these days, he got into his truck and headed back home. He didn't know why he tormented himself so much. It would be so much better if he could just ignore that she was back. He had no problem ignoring old Harriet being around, since she was almost as crazy as her daughter had been. But for the granddaughter to come back? That was just adding insult to injury. Even though he could tolerate Harriet somewhat, he certainly didn't want the granddaughter pushing her nose into his business either.

He pondered that as he parked, got out, and walked toward his front door. He wondered if he could do something to make Danica disappear again. He wanted her to realize that she wasn't wanted here, never had been, and never would be. The best thing she could do was go away and leave them all alone.

Only as he got to the front step did an idea hit him. He stood here for a long moment, contemplating it, and a smile broke out across his face. For the first time in a very long time, he felt a joy in his step, as he walked inside and promptly crashed on the couch.

Finally something he could do. He wasn't sure exactly how it would pan out, but he had an option now, and options were always good. If nothing else, they made him feel that he was getting somewhere, and that was priceless.

CHAPTER 13

DANICA SAT IN her RV, working on her laptop, with the windows and the doors open, enjoying the early morning breeze. She heard a vehicle drive up, the crunch of the tires on the gravel giving easy warning of the arrival of the visitor. She wasn't sure who it was, but, as she mentally reached out, it didn't appear to be anything she wanted to deal with. She groaned and looked down at Benji, who sat at the open door.

The hairs on the back of his neck stood up, although he was not yet growling, but had definitely bared his teeth at the oncoming visitor. She didn't know whether the person was coming to visit Nana or her. When a *Howdy* was called out in her direction, she sighed, got up, and walked to her open front door, and looked out to see a deputy's cruiser. She nodded calmly at the man standing there. "Hello," she murmured. "What can I do for you?"

He studied her and smiled. "I'm Deputy Benson. I spoke with our good Dr. Cameron late yesterday."

She nodded but didn't say anything and just studied his face. Something was off about that genial look. "What can I do for you?"

"I understand that you believe your grandmother was attacked."

Again she just nodded and didn't say anything.

"Do you want to give me some details?" he asked.

"I'm sure you got the details from Dr. Cameron," she murmured. "So, not a whole lot more I can tell you."

He looked at her. "How about you tell me what you do know?"

She shrugged and gave him a quick reply. "From what I heard, the doctor at the hospital said that Nana didn't have any swelling or bruising at the hospital, correct?"

"At the time, it wasn't evident. You checked?"

"No, I did not check then, so I have no idea."

"Right," he replied.

Such patent disbelief filled his tone that she stiffened and glared at him. "Is there a reason that you're here?" she asked, bristling.

"I should ensure that your grandmother is okay, shouldn't I?"

"No, I'm not certain that you should," she replied, staring at him. "As a matter of fact, you're on private property. So, unless you have a real reason to be here, I suggest you leave."

He looked at her and frowned. "Now, hang on a minute. I'm here to help."

"No, you're not," she argued, trying to calm down, chastising herself internally. "You've more or less just accused me of hurting my grandmother, something I would never do. And I don't care whether you believe me or not."

He flushed bright red. "Look. I didn't mean it that way."

"Yes, you did," she declared, cutting him off with a wave of her hand. "I get it. You don't want to believe that the doctor may or may not have seen an injury. Therefore, if it wasn't there at the hospital, it must have happened at home. But you're wrong, and the facts don't matter because you won't listen to anything anyway. So just take a hike. Nothing to see here." She motioned for him to get back in his vehicle and leave. He looked at her, opened his mouth, and then closed it again. She nodded. "Exactly."

"I'm not trying to cause trouble here," he said. "Obviously I've come across a little too harsh."

"Ya think?" she asked, openly mocking him now. "I'm not sure that you came across too sharp. You already had your mind made up before you got here. The least you could have done was check out the facts first and not just assume you had them."

"But you haven't given me any facts," he said in exasperation.

"No, but Dr. Cameron did. So, if you're planning on arresting me, do it now."

At that moment, Nana called out from inside her house, "You better not arrest my granddaughter. She hasn't done anything." Slowly her grandmother made her way out to the front step.

Danica hopped down from her RV and raced over. "You shouldn't be moving."

"I'm fine," Nana said, brushing Danica off with a wave of her hand. "Besides, if this BS will go on, you can bet I won't sit on my butt and let another travesty happen."

Danica glared at Deputy Benson and tried to tell her grandmother who he was, even as her grandmother raised her voice. "I don't give a shit who he is or what he's doing here. He can leave now."

Looking at the openly hostile old woman, Deputy Benson shrugged. "I was just coming to ensure you hadn't been attacked."

"No, you weren't," she snapped. "You were coming because you had a sense of duty to come and to check on a report. But now you can go back and say you checked on it. Everybody's alive. Duty done. That's all you care about, right? It's got nothing to do with the facts. It's got nothing to do with right or wrong."

"If you were taken to the hospital and you had no apparent injury, and yet you come home and find an injury, what am I supposed to think?"

"I wouldn't try thinking at your age. It's obviously a strain on your brain," Nana retorted.

At that, Danica giggled. Her grandmother was nothing if not sharp.

Nana continued her scathing remarks. "For you to even think about accusing the one and only person in my world who absolutely loves me, who would do nothing to hurt me, is complete and utter bullshit. You're obviously not here because you truly care about us." She pointed to his official cruiser. "So just get in that vehicle of yours and get lost."

Deputy Benson shifted uncomfortably. "Ma'am, I'm a sheriff's deputy. And if somebody attacked you—"

"Oh, just go away. You're one of the superstitious cult in town," she declared, cutting him off. With that, she walked back inside and slammed the door hard.

Danica burst out laughing. "You see, Deputy? That is my grandmother. No way anybody'll pull the wool over her eyes."

"Yet you were worried enough to take her to the hospital," he pointed out.

Her smile fell away, and she nodded. "That's because she was unconscious, but apparently that isn't of interest to you either."

He slammed the hat back on his head, walked toward his

vehicle, then looked back at her and called out, "There better not be another incident."

"On that, we can agree," she snapped, now glaring at him. "Yet it won't be my doing if there is."

He shrugged. "Says you."

"I can't say I have anything to prove my innocence, but you're not looking for proof of that anyway, are you?" she snapped right back. "All you want is to see something that's not here," she murmured. "So go back to your office. You're perfectly safe. Nobody here will hurt you."

He flushed at that and asked, "Are you threatening me?"

"Of course not," she said, with an eye roll. "You came already terrified, without my having to threaten you in the least," she explained, with a bright smile. "Now, go on, go on. You'll be fine. You survived a visit to the Crazy Ladies' House. Not to worry," she assured him. "No need to come back ever again."

And, on that note, he got into the cruiser a little too quickly and raced down the driveway.

Her grandmother stepped back out of the house and said, "You really shouldn't antagonize him."

"Me?" Danica asked, looking at her. "What about you?" she cried out.

Her grandmother shrugged. "What? I'm too old to care, but, in your case, they might hold it against you."

"I really don't give a damn," Danica replied. "I'm surely not staying here once you're gone anyway."

Her grandmother looked at her, sorrow in her eyes, and whispered, "No, Danica. That makes me very sad too."

"It shouldn't. You know as well as I do that no way anybody here in this town will ever accept me." And a certain sad knowing settled into Danica's soul.

"You don't know that," her grandmother retorted. "Some people appear to be on your side, like that nice doctor."

"You mean, like the nice doctor who somehow gave the deputy the impression that I attacked you?" she asked, one eyebrow raised.

Her grandmother winced. "It's really not his fault. From a medical perspective—and those people have very limited thinking, you know—it really does make sense that you would be the one who attacked me."

She stared at her grandmother in shock. "What?" she cried out. "You really think I would have attacked you?"

"No, of course not," she stated. "Don't be silly. I know you didn't attack me, but, for these people, who only see what's in front of them and don't know the difference, it makes sense to them. Because an injury appeared, after there being no injury, they don't know what to think about it."

"Yeah, you want to tell me what you did?" Danica asked, finally seeing the sense in that.

Her grandmother gave her an innocent smile and then chuckled. "While I was healing, I held it off while I was unconscious for a while," her grandmother explained. "But then I really struggled. I'm not as strong as I used to be. So, while I fell asleep again, all of it just popped up, even though I was trying so hard to keep it down so you wouldn't worry."

She stared at her grandmother. "So, all that time you were unconscious, and I was worried about you, you were in there trying to heal yourself?"

"I was trying to rest," she stated, with a sniff in the air. "And with rest comes healing. So, it's not as if I did anything wrong."

"No, but you could have told me that you needed to

take some time out to heal," Danica complained, looking at her intently. "Instead you let me worry. Why?"

"It's not as if I let you worry," she said, suddenly looking frailer than Danica had seen her in a long time. "I'm just not as strong as I was, so I can't do what I used to do as easily."

Immediately Danica walked over with a forlorn look on her face and muttered, "I'm so sorry."

"Getting old is not for the faint of heart." Her grandmother chuckled.

"No, it sure isn't," she agreed, giving her a pat on the cheek.

"You need to stop worrying. My time will come, and I will go in peace, the same way I've always lived my life."

"Oh, right. Will you try to tell me that you've always lived in peace? Now I know you're lying," Danica declared, stiffening at the thought. "There was no peace when my mother was around and not likely all that much peace since she's been gone." Danica hesitated. "You've never once told me if you ever talked to Daisy on the other side." Her grandmother looked at her, tears in her eyes, which made Danica feel awful. "I'm sorry. I shouldn't have asked."

"Of course you should have asked," her grandmother responded. "I'm surprised you didn't ask before, but the answer is, I've tried, and I haven't been able to make contact."

"Do you think she doesn't want to make contact or isn't capable of it?"

"I would suggest she isn't capable. She was a pretty sick woman here, and we like to think that the minute you cross over, all the disease in the world that plagued you while you were alive is gone, … but that's not the case. I am genuinely surprised that you didn't ask before."

"I wanted to ask," Danica admitted, "but I didn't want to bring up any more harsh memories."

"Right. We're both bound by those memories, aren't we?" her grandmother muttered. "And it permeates everything in our world, whether we like it or not."

Such sadness filled her grandmother's words that Danica once again wrapped her arms around her and held her close. "I'm so sorry. I shouldn't have brought it up."

"You might as well have. I'll cross over and meet her sometime soon anyway."

"Maybe that's what she's waiting for. Maybe she has her own things to apologize for."

Her grandmother looked at her and laughed. "Don't ever expect apologies when you're on the other side," she stated, with an eye roll. "Sometimes people over there are just plain angry."

"Maybe it's not that they're angry. Maybe it's more that their own perspective prevails," she suggested, rearing back and looking at her grandmother.

"If you wanted to reach out, you could," Nana mused.

Danica snorted and stepped back and asked, "Even if I could, why would I?"

Her grandmother looked at her shrewdly and replied, "So you could get answers."

"She won't answer me," Danica retorted. "I asked her at the time, and she was in such a blinding rage. She couldn't do anything but slash and cut," she described, glaring at her grandmother. "I doubt her answer will be any different now." With that, she looked back at Benji, who was whining beside her. "I need to get back to work."

"Fine," her grandmother muttered, "but you can't run and hide forever."

"Yes, I can," Danica replied, as she stepped into the RV. "I can certainly run and hide long enough to avoid Daisy. There will be no good day for me to come face-to-face with my long-dead mother."

"One of these days, you should deal with it."

"Maybe, but not today. You guys might have fun with all that reunion stuff. I had more than enough fun when I woke up in the morgue," Danica declared.

With that, she stepped into her small RV and got back to work, struggling hard to refocus on what she was doing before the deputy had arrived, yet knowing that she had to work. She had to produce. It didn't matter what distractions were going on around her, there just wasn't anybody else who would help pay her way.

Other than her grandmother in her childhood years, there never had been anyone for Danica. Once she had turned eighteen and left, she had only herself to rely on. Danica doubted that would ever change. Besides, she was happy being independent. It gave her a lot more than she had been expecting, and it was good for her. At least as long as she was independent, she didn't worry about people betraying her. She was done with that. She'd been betrayed by the very person who should have looked after her, and instead all she'd done was try to kill her.

YOU CANNOT WASTE any more time.

The urgency in his tone was unmistakable. Harriet shuddered. "I know. I know, but—" she muttered.

No buts. You're out of time.

She nodded and stared out at the distance. "I know," she whispered.

You've tried to talk to her many times, but you keep stopping and not telling her what she needs to know. Now you've left it too late.

"No, I haven't," she snapped. "I still have time."

Soon it is Halloween, as you well know.

"So I still have time," she repeated softly.

But not much. Not much. The whispers rolled around her. *You know what it'll be like, if we're the ones who tell her.*

She winced at that and nodded. She got up slowly, feeling old, sore, and tired. It would end soon; she knew that. She was grateful to know that the end was very soon, but she had so much to do first, so much that had to be dealt with.

It's true. You do have a lot to do, and yet you keep wasting time.

"No. She's had a terrible time. We don't even know who attacked Danica all those years ago," she muttered.

Do you want us to find out? the voice asked.

She shook her head. "There's always a payment, a cost due."

Sure, it takes energy to sort through people's minds, to figure out what somebody may have done and what they may not have done. If you don't want us to do it, that's fine, but you still need to do your part.

"I am," she muttered. But she was losing hope of anything changing, anything interfering that would make this something she didn't have to do. It was her responsibility to do it; she knew that. But that didn't make it any easier.

None of this will be easy, but it doesn't change the fact that you should do it.

And, with that, the voice faded once again into the distance in Harriet's mind.

CHAPTER 14

"WE NEED TO go into town and get some groceries," her grandmother announced abruptly over their afternoon tea.

Danica looked at Nana and nodded. "Where do you need to go?"

She frowned and thought about it. "To the butcher and down to the small veggie stand. We'll need a few other basics, but, if we can at least get that, it's a good start."

"Sounds good," Danica murmured, but, inside, her heart sank because, every time they went out, it got a little bit worse than the last time. She had no reason to expect an issue, but these escalating problems just kept happening.

As her grandmother looked her over a bit, she shrewdly noted, "Unless you sense any reason why we shouldn't."

"Remember how I'm not doing that woo-woo stuff," Danica stated, as she glared at her grandmother.

"Doesn't matter if you're doing it or not," Nana declared. "You know perfectly well that it's all around you."

"Maybe, but that was your thing, and this is my thing."

"Meaning, it won't ever be your thing?" she asked sadly.

"You can't blame me for not wanting anything to do with it," she replied, looking at her grandmother. "It drove Daisy to insanity."

"I don't know if anything would have kept her sane.

Honestly, she was so desperate to get out that leaving was all she cared about."

"Was it to get away from me?" Danica asked, hating the faint pain that still remained, a remnant of long ago.

Her grandmother looked at her in surprise, and then her shoulders slumped. "Probably from you and me," she agreed, with a sad smile. "It's not as if she left us any answers."

"From all her screaming and shouting, she was definitely trying to get away from us and this town. So, we can hardly think of it as anything other than that."

"That could be true," Nana admitted. "I keep thinking that my daughter didn't hate me as much as she appeared to. Yet I lose that argument on a regular basis."

"Of course you do," Danica agreed, looking away from the intense gaze of her grandmother. "As do I."

"Do you still think about her a lot?"

Danica nodded. "However, I try not to because the thoughts are never happy and because there are no real answers. No good answers are there," she said, struggling to keep the conversation on track. "Why don't we go out for dinner?"

Her grandmother looked up with interest and then slowly shrugged. "There really isn't any place where we can be alone."

"We could pick up something and bring it home at least," Danica suggested, looking at her hopefully. "We used to do that all the time."

"Now that we did do," she replied, with a chuckle.

"I don't know what we would pick up though."

"There's that little fish-and-chips place."

"Is it any good?"

"Oh, I think that's Jerry's place now," she replied, "and

it's really good."

"Jerry," she repeated, looking at her grandmother. "Homer?"

"Yeah, that's him. You remember him, don't you? Oh, that's right. You were friends in school, weren't you?"

She nodded slowly, thinking about it. "We were. He was a terrible student in school," she noted, with a smile. "I used to help him with his homework all the time."

"Or he was just sweet on you, and that was his excuse," her grandmother offered, with a twinkle in her eye.

"Maybe, but he wasn't sweet on me afterward."

At that, her grandmother's smile fell away. "That really did stop everything in your life, didn't it?"

Danica nodded. "Yes, that whole event—the combination of events, I guess, is a better way to put it. But whatever. Let's go get fish and chips."

"Are you sure?" her grandmother asked, looking at her anxiously.

"Are you worried that I'll be upset at anything Jerry says? No, I won't. I've been up against tougher people than him," she shared, with a laugh.

"Okay, as long as you're sure."

"I'm sure. Don't worry about it. Let's go shopping."

They managed to get to the butcher shop and the little veggie stop, so they had fresh fruit and vegetables for at least a few more days. Danica's appetite wasn't very good, but she was making a point of eating to ensure her grandmother ate. Yet Nana had cut down quite a bit.

As they left the veggie store, Danica pointed out, "We didn't buy very much."

"I'm not sure we need very much," her grandmother said. "It's not as if we're eating a whole lot."

"I worry about you though."

"And I worry about you," Nana said, with a smile.

"You're not eating much."

"Neither are you," her grandmother stated right back.

Danica groaned. "Do you always have to be this snappy?"

"Do *you* always have to be this snappy?"

At that, she sighed. "All right, fine. Let me stop by the house and put up the meat and the produce really fast. Then fish and chips it is, but you'll eat them."

"Fish and chips it is," Nana agreed, "and you'll eat them too."

Now chuckling, the two women were still smiling as they pulled into the fish-and-chips shop.

"We could just pick it up and take it home," her grandmother mentioned, staring at the restaurant with an odd loathing on her face.

Sensing something that finally might be important, Danica waited for Nana to say more, and then asked, "You want to tell me why?"

"No, I really don't want to."

Danica groaned. "Okay, but I don't want to go in there if something is wrong and if you aren't telling me what it is."

"Nothing's wrong." Nana shook her head. "It's just, you know, those memories."

"But those memories count," Danica said. "What on earth about Jerry could possibly make you upset?"

"It's not Jerry. … It's just, you know, Jerry's family."

"Do they work here too?" Danica asked, looking around.

"No, I don't think so."

"Well then, let's just go in and have fish and chips, and then we can return home." As they got out of the car, Danica stopped, looked at Nana, and asked, "Are you thinking that they won't serve us?"

"I have no idea," Nana replied, looking at her. "I've never been here."

Danica hesitated, then the door opened. A couple came out laughing and joking and walked around them, heading to their vehicles. She looked over at her grandmother. "Seems they enjoyed their meal."

Nana just nodded and stared at the restaurant.

"If you've got something to tell me …"

"I can't really have anything to tell you," Nana muttered, "considering you won't believe in this stuff."

"But I believe in you," Danica said gently.

Just then the door opened again, and a man bellowed, "Danica. Is that you?"

She stopped to look at Jerry, who had come out on the front step.

"Somebody inside told me that you were out here," he said, with a big beaming smile. "I couldn't believe it." He snagged her up into a big bear hug. "Good God, I haven't seen you in forever."

Danica laughed. His exuberance was hard to argue with, and it helped lighten the atmosphere around her. She hugged him back and added, "I haven't been back for very long. I was just trying to coax my grandmother to come in and to have some fish and chips."

He looked over at her grandmother and smiled. "Come on in, Harriet. I haven't seen you in forever either."

She nodded and gave him a tentative smile. "It's been a little bit tough these last few years," she murmured.

"Oh, it has been," he concurred affably, completely unaware of what she was saying. "Come on. Come on," he urged, dragging them inside and seating them at the far side of the restaurant. "You'll be comfortable here," he said calmly. Soon he came back with water and menus, then left them alone for a few minutes.

Danica looked over at her grandmother, who was staring down at the menu but was obviously uncomfortable. "You need to tell me what's wrong, Nana."

Her grandmother looked at her. "If you would open your senses, you would feel it."

"What on earth does that mean?"

Her grandmother sighed. "I can't say anything here."

"Okay, fine. But, when we get home, we'll have a talk."

Her grandmother stared at her and slowly nodded. "You're right," she agreed in an odd tone, as the color in her face came and went. "It's definitely time to have a talk, but you should stay for all of it."

"Don't worry," Danica replied. "I've been waiting a lifetime for this talk."

Her grandmother winced and then slowly nodded. "You could be right," she muttered, then gave her head a shake. "It's probably time we cleared the air, but that doesn't mean you'll like anything you hear."

"No, it doesn't. But I don't like very much about what's been going on in my life for the last few years either."

Just then Jerry came bouncing back in their direction. "What can I get for you?" he asked. "I'll put your orders in, and then I'll grab something to drink and come and sit and visit a bit," he said pointedly, looking at Harriet. "Then you can tell me what the hell's been going on with you."

Danica quickly ordered fish and chips for both of them, and Jerry bounded off. True to his word, he returned with a big Coke in his hand and sat down across from her.

"Now what on earth," he asked Danica, "brought you back?"

She pointed to her grandmother. "It's simple really. I just wanted to spend some time with her before there wasn't time to spend."

His face immediately scrunched up, and he looked over at Harriet.

Harriet just shook her head. "I'm fine," she murmured. "That's just my granddaughter."

"Ah. But you know that, if she says something, you should listen to her," Jerry stated, with that same affable smile.

Danica looked at him and asked, "What does that mean?"

"Oh, you know very well what I mean," he said, with a chuckle. "Every time I asked you a question back in school, you always had the answer, and it was always correct. I never went against what you said. If you told me that it would be a rainy day, I prepped for rain, and, sure enough, it would rain. If you told me that it would storm that day, then believe me that I prepped for a storm. If you told me that we would have a test that day, then we would have a test. Absolutely nothing you could tell me that I wouldn't have believed," he declared.

"Yeah? How did that work out for you though?" her grandmother asked with interest, leaning forward to register his facial expressions.

He laughed. "She was always right," he stated with admiration, as he looked over at Danica, his grin kicking up a notch. "She was *always* right. It was so uncanny. We used to talk about it all the time. Man, she was good."

Danica groaned. "I had forgotten all about that."

"How could you forget?" he asked. "You're the one who kept me alive back then."

"Kept you alive?" her grandmother asked instantly.

"He's joking," Danica said.

"Not really," Jerry argued. "She got me through school. She's the one who told me who was sweet on me and whether the girl I was sweet on was sweet on me too," he shared, with a laugh. "We're married and have three kids now," he announced, with a big grin in her direction. "You were a godsend when I needed it."

Danica smiled. "All you needed was a little confidence."

"That confidence and your insight," he noted, with a burst of laughter. "It's the insight you helped with. Glad to see you now," he murmured. "How have you been?"

She shrugged and smiled. "I'm fine. It wasn't the easiest time when I first left, but we all grow and change out of necessity, if nothing else."

He nodded. "Man, those were some wild rumors they passed around here for a while. I'm really sorry. Anytime I heard anybody speak bad of you, I just—damn, I got myself put in jail for beating up so many people."

She stared at him in shock, and he gave her a huge, affable grin. "Hey, I meant it. You were the answer to everything for me back then, so I wouldn't listen to nobody spouting off about all that shit. I don't know what happened. I don't care," he continued. "You're good people. That's all that matters."

Her heart warmed, listening to him. "Thank you. It means a lot to hear that. Some people haven't been so welcoming since I've been back."

He stared at her, anger crossing his features. "They better not let me hear them," he warned, "because *that* I will not tolerate. You're always welcome here, and, if you ever need a hand, you just let me know."

Hearing a bell in the distance, he hopped up and grabbed their meal, then brought it over for them. "Here you go," he said, waving his hand. "I'll leave you to eat in peace, but you come back and visit, you hear me? I want to catch up on everything you're up to, and besides," he added, with a big grin and a wink, "I might have a few more questions that need answers." And, with that, he disappeared.

Her grandmother eyed Danica in surprise.

Danica shrugged. "Can't say I remember much of that."

"Can't remember much of what?" Nana asked, staring at Danica suspiciously. "The fact that you used to help him out?"

"I knew I helped him out with schoolwork a lot," she clarified in a confused tone. "He wasn't exactly brilliant in the book department."

"No, but it sounds like he's done okay since."

"I think so," she murmured. "At least, I would hope so. He made it sound like he was doing just fine."

"In which case, you've got nothing to worry about."

She nodded. "He did sound happy. So, in that case, I'm happy that whatever I told him worked." She shook her head. "I don't remember any of the particular questions, just that he always used to bug me about stuff." She laughed. "And he's right. He would phone me and ask, *Will it rain today?* I would instinctively know yes or no, and he would just go for it." She was still chuckling over the memories. "But who would have thought that anybody would listen to my word on that?"

"People often do, particularly when you're right all the time," her grandmother pointed out. "You've always been a very good seer."

At Nana's words, Danica felt her smile fall away.

"I know. I know. It's a word you don't like." Nana raised her hands. "Yet it's not exactly a word I can stop using. It's a part of my world."

"It might be a part of your world," Danica noted, "but that doesn't mean it's part of mine."

And, with that, they quickly ate in silence.

Danica went to the cashier to pay, but Jerry would have nothing to do with it. "Nope. Nope. Nope," he stated vehemently. "The least I can do is cover this meal for you," he murmured. "I'm just so damn happy to see you doing so well," he added, with a smile.

She thanked him and quickly led her grandmother out to the vehicle, and then drove them home.

When they got back, her grandmother suddenly announced, "I need to go lie down."

Watching her grandmother, now with that old woman walk going on, Danica had never remembered seeing her grandmother so slouched over, so slow, so hesitant, even with the head injury.

Nana slowly made her way to her bedroom, where she closed the door.

Danica sat in the kitchen for a long moment, until she felt that nudge that it was time to go. She walked back outside with Benji, as the door to the house quickly slammed shut and locked.

"I know, Benji. It's stupid. I won't acknowledge the supernatural energies all around me, when the damn house has its own personality, its own likes and dislikes, and I'm on the dislike list," she murmured. "How can there not be seers and witches and healers and a million other crazy things, when

I'm living on the outside of a house that gets to decide who goes in and who doesn't?"

Benji had no answers for her, but nobody ever did. Danica slowly walked back to her RV and settled in for the night.

"DANICA," SOMEONE CALLED out.

She bolted upright from a deep sleep and stared around her. She hopped out of bed, put on a few clothes, and quickly opened the door. "Who called?" she whispered softly.

But nobody was there. Nobody that she could see or note and nobody that Benji was particularly bothered about.

Danica looked around but saw nothing. Hesitating, she was about ready to go back to bed when the front door of Nana's house opened. It just swung wide open.

She glared at it. It's only ever let her in the house when it wanted to, but that also meant that there was likely a reason she needed to go in. With Benji at her heels, she slowly approached the front door, and, when it let her pass, she knew that there must be a problem with her grandmother.

She raced into her grandmother's bedroom to see her sitting up, tears running down her face. Danica sat down on the side of the bed. "Are you okay?"

Her grandmother just looked at her, and the tears kept running faster and faster.

Danica held Nana's frail body, knowing her heart would break when her grandmother's time came and went. When she saw her like this, something that she had never, *ever* thought to experience—seeing this strong woman brought to tears by something in her world—it just broke her heart. "I can't help you if you don't tell me what's going on," she murmured.

"But you don't want to help anyway," Nana muttered.

Yet no heat was in her tone, just the sadness that made Danica pull back and look at her. "What help do you want?"

"You know," she wailed. "You already know, but it's not a world you want anything to do with."

Danica hesitated and then noted in exasperation, "Yet I'm asking the damn house for permission to come in. So, what on earth am I supposed to believe if not that *some* of this woo-woo stuff is true?"

"Some of it?" Nana asked, her voice gaining in strength.

"Okay. I don't even know what I believe anymore," Danica admitted. "I just know that some of it I can't discount."

"That's something at least," Nana replied, "but I really need you to step up and to not hide."

"Stepping up and not hiding is a whole different story than being active in any of this," Danica murmured. "It's one thing for me to find a belief. It's another thing for me to just blindly go with it."

"Of course," Nana agreed in a sage manner. "You probably want proof."

"I don't want proof. I watched you and Mother all my life," she replied in a frustrated tone. "I already know how real a lot of this is. I'm the one who woke up in a damn morgue drawer, remember?"

Her grandmother cracked a smile at that. "You know, in a way, I wish that had been me."

"Yeah, well, in a way, I wish I had been you too," Danica declared in a burst of frustration, "because there wasn't anything nice about it."

"Yet, for many, it would have been a hell of an experience."

"It *was* a hell of an experience, but not necessarily an experience I wanted," Danica pointed out, shaking her head. "A lot of things in life we want, and a lot of things we could do without."

"You could have done without your mother, I know."

"No," Danica countered sadly. "I could have done *with* my mother. Not living *without* a mother would have been nice, but, because I couldn't control that, it's just what life was for me." She hugged Nana closely, trying to understand what was going on.

"We can't hang on to the past and be sad and upset because of what didn't happen. We're already well past that now."

"What I want to know is what's bringing on all this pain and tragedy into your world?" Danica asked.

"It's fine," Nana muttered. "I just got really sad."

"But why? What's making you sad?" she asked. "You scare me when you do things like this."

"Sometimes I just feel the pain. Everybody's pain. Right now I'm feeling somebody's pain, but I don't know whose it is," she explained.

Danica frowned, as she held her grandmother. "Is it important to know who it is? Or can you just send some healing energy without knowing?"

Her grandmother stared at her and then nodded. "Maybe that is the best answer, especially in this case."

"Regardless of what case it is," Danica added, "I would think it's always a good answer. Just because people have pain doesn't mean they want anybody else to know about it. So you might want to keep that in mind."

"I feel very disconnected from what people want in this

world," Nana shared, looking at her granddaughter. "I've had so much in my life, so much of my space taken up with the work that I do, that I feel very out of it now."

Her words brought a question to Danica's mind. "Do you want to tell me exactly what work you've been doing all these years? I've always wondered how you made money and what you did."

Her grandmother chuckled. "I healed people. That's what I do."

"But—" The words just failed her. Danica sat back, studied her grandmother, and asked, "From here?"

"Yes, from here," Nana confirmed, "and, a lot of times, people do pay me. They pay me in real money. Sometimes they can't pay me, and sometimes that's okay too. If somebody needs healing, I've never held back."

"How?"

"I belong to multiple groups. Remember when you got me hooked up on the internet years ago?" Nana nodded wistfully. "I managed to join a group of healers, and, since then, I work with people all over the world."

"Remote healing?" Danica asked, almost doubting it.

"Ever since your mother passed on, I felt the need to help others. I couldn't help Daisy, but I could help others."

"Ah, yes, God love the guilt," Danica murmured.

Her grandmother nodded. "I recognize the guilt, and I understand it. It doesn't matter whether there's any believability in it, or if I can do anything, or if I don't feel guilty about it," Nana explained, "because healing was just something I needed to do."

"That's fine," Danica replied. "I doubt anybody would begrudge you the opportunity to heal somebody."

"You would be surprised," she replied, "but thankfully a

lot of people out there know the good that we can do. So I can do it from a distance. There are groups of us," she added. "I don't manage them. I did at one time, but now I just show up at a certain time. Other than that"—Nana faced Danica—"I don't need any money."

"We all need money to a certain extent," Danica clarified, looking at her grandmother. "Whether it's to pay rent or to put food on the table."

"I'm fine. I don't care about money, and money is in the bank if I wanted it. But I don't spend it if I don't have to."

"That I can see."

"Long ago I didn't know how much longer I would have in this world or what worries I would face, but I figured it would be best if money wouldn't be among my worries, so I began to live much more economically."

"Money won't be a problem for you now," Danica shared, "because I'll ensure that you're fine."

Her grandmother smiled at her and asked, "What about you? How will you survive?"

"My freelancing has paid the bills for years. I'm a big girl. I can make decisions for myself."

"I do want you to stay here when I've gone."

"You may want that, and I may even want that, but this house has a mind of its own on the matter."

Nana groaned. "That could be true, but, if you would accept it and believe in it, it wouldn't have so many problems with you."

"Right. You always go right back to the woo-woo stuff that takes us so far off the topic."

"It doesn't matter whether it does or not," Nana noted, with a smile. "The house is here to protect me. It was gifted to me by my grandmother—and I would love to gift it to you, but …"

"Yeah, but it doesn't like me. You and I both know that."

"Yet, despite what you say, it called you tonight."

"It certainly opened its doors and let me in. Whether that was you or the house, I don't know." Danica gave her grandmother a look. "You also know there's no way I can explain to anybody that the reason I can't live in this house is because it won't let me in."

Her grandmother's lips twitched, and she nodded. "I know." Then she frowned at her intently. "Do you remember when it first began to happen?"

"Yeah, when I came back from the undead," Danica replied, "just to make me feel even less like I belong in the world," she murmured.

"I was trying to figure out what caused it."

"Why would you even care at this point?" she murmured.

"Because I still would like to pass this house on to you. It's still got a lot of good years left."

"Maybe, but it's also got some very defined notions of who should live here," she pointed out, "and you and I both know I'm not on that list."

Her grandmother didn't say anything for a long moment. "I never could figure out why," she murmured. "It makes no sense to me."

"It doesn't matter," Danica noted, "but I figured that, somewhere along the line, only people with gifts were allowed inside."

Her grandmother slid her a sideways glance. "Yet you are more gifted than any of us," she murmured.

Danica winced. "I'm not going down that pathway."

Her grandmother groaned. "Of course not, and normally I'm okay to leave it at that, but today? I just got a little melancholy. What will you do with the house, if nobody else can live in it?" she asked.

"That's not my problem because it won't ever become mine."

"And yet it will be yours, in monetary value if nothing else."

Groaning, Danica replied, "I don't know what I'll do then. You and I both know it doesn't like me and has never liked me since I came back from the hospital that day."

"Yet, on a psychic energy level, that makes no sense. I've been trying to puzzle it out, but I have never asked anybody who might have any answers." Bolting upright, she added, "That's what I should do. I should ask Stefan."

"I was going to ask if you could ask questions of somebody about all this stuff, and there you go."

"He doesn't really like it when I ask him questions because I don't make an appointment. I just spirit walk and hit him up with questions out of the blue," she said, with a laugh. "But I don't think he really minds it. In fact, I think he likes that I come to visit. And usually I know when he's a little low in spirits and could use a little boost."

"And who is this?" Danica asked in fascination.

"His name is Stefan," Nana replied. "I really don't know very much about him. I tripped into his world a while back, surprising both of us. Now we have this regular highway that we can travel. I stop in and talk to him on an irregular basis." She shrugged. "He's a busy man. It's not as if I can just have a cup of tea with him every day, although sometimes it would be nice."

Danica looked at her grandmother in wonder. "So, you

have somebody you can talk to psychically? And you just happened into his world, and he just happened to talk to you?"

Her grandmother looked at her, paused for a long moment, and then nodded. "Yep, that's how it went."

"Good God," she murmured. "And what? He doesn't think you're nuts?"

Her grandmother laughed. "If I'm nuts, so is he. Therefore, I'm pretty sure neither one of us thinks we're nuts."

"Maybe not," Danica muttered, "but it's hardly normal behavior."

"No, but I'm not sure anything is normal about us anyway." She looked over at her granddaughter and added, "I can go back to sleep now. You better get back to bed too."

"Oh, you think so? Has the house decreed that I should leave now?" she teased, giving her grandmother a mocking grin.

"In a way, yes, and it's time for me to go back to sleep," her grandmother replied. She gave Danica a quick kiss on the cheek, signaling that it was time to leave.

Danica got up, moved out toward the living room, then glanced back at her grandmother's bedroom. To the house, Danica declared, "You better look after her. I'll be pissed if you don't." And, with that, the front door opened, and she stepped outside, only to have it slam shut behind her with the force that she was used to.

She'd been at odds with this house for a long time and still didn't know what to blame it on. As far as she was concerned, she hadn't done anything, but the house seemed to hold a very serious grudge. She glanced back at the house and muttered, "I didn't do anything."

And, with that, she strode back to her RV for the night.

CAMERON WORKED THROUGH the night shift. He didn't get much of a break, but it also wasn't at a pace that was enough to exhaust him. So, halfway through, he still felt pretty good. He glanced over at Denise, one of the night nurses.

"How long have you worked here?" he asked her.

She shrugged. "Not all that long. I came in on one of the incentive programs for new grads. So, I'm staying as long as I can, and then I'm out." He looked at her, surprised. "It's way too small-town for me," she murmured.

He nodded thoughtfully. "I guess if you weren't born and raised here, not a whole lot for someone is here, right?"

"Even if you *were* born and raised here," Denise replied, with a wry look in his direction, "still not a whole lot for you here."

He grinned. "That may be true, but I have family here."

"But family still isn't necessarily a reason to bury your life here," Denise argued, looking at him curiously. "You could get a job anywhere. The whole country is screaming for doctors. Why limit yourself to this?"

"They need doctors here."

"Sure, they do, but they could also go to the hospital in the next county over."

"I go over there and do hours too," he shared.

She nodded. "I've heard something about that. So, again we know that you could work anywhere. I don't understand why you would come back here."

"Don't try to convince him to leave," interjected Bridget, as she came over. "We're already so short-staffed. For a while there, it looked like we might even shut down."

"We should if we can't get anything better than the old-timer back there," Denise stated, with a nod to the doctor who had been on staff for fifty-plus years.

"He's still better than nothing," Bridget countered, "so be respectful."

"I'm not being disrespectful," Denise declared, "but there comes a time when somebody should call it quits. And this is definitely that time for him." With that, she picked up one of the files on the nurses' station and walked away.

Bridget looked at him and said, "Please pay her no mind."

"Not at all," he replied, shrugging. "I was wondering what the staffing was like here anyway."

"It's rough," Bridget replied, "and it won't get any easier with the dwindling numbers around town. I'm surprised they have enough money to even keep the hospital open. We're down to pretty basic supplies now, pretty basic services. If it's bad, we send them off to a bigger hospital."

"But at least we're here if the locals need us."

"I've been here all my life, and it gets pretty hairy at times. Enough that I would hate to see it shut down."

"Speaking of pretty hairy, I've heard a couple rumors about Halloween."

She looked at him and then slowly turned. "What about Halloween?"

"Not every Halloween here," he clarified, looking at her sideways, as Bridget's skin had paled ever-so-slightly, "but enough Halloweens that apparently it's a bit of an ongoing problem."

She stared at him, giving him a shrug. "People like to talk. They like to make up sensational rumors to make themselves feel important. Don't you be paying it no mind either."

"So, no ghosts come into the ER or the OR on Halloween?" he asked, with a smile.

She shook her head. "Nope, they don't, and I wouldn't worry about it if there was a ghost."

"Why is that?"

"Because we're good people, and the Lord protects his own," Bridget declared. "I am not afraid of any ghosts around this place."

"So, you work on Halloween?"

She stiffened and glared at him. "No, I don't work on Halloween. Haven't worked Halloween since I came here," she shared, with a stiff nod. "That is an event I always share with my grandkids and the other neighborhood children."

"Right," he replied calmly, watching her. "Maybe you could tell me what it is that happens on Halloween that most people are talking about?"

"I would just as soon not," Bridget stated, sounding a bit bitter. "I don't like to gossip, and that gossip won't do anybody any good."

"Yet, if I don't know what is going on—or what people are saying is going on—I won't have a clue what I'm supposed to do come Halloween."

"Do what you always do, heal people," she suggested in a matter-of-fact tone, and, with that, she turned smartly on her heel and walked away.

It never ceased to amaze Cameron how people could either talk so much or not at all about such issues. One group of people couldn't stop talking, and then another group wouldn't open their mouths about it. That he had spoken to one side just made him want to seek out one of the others, so he could get more information on this hot topic. How was he supposed to understand exactly what was happening here if nobody would tell him?

As he walked toward the front desk again, Dr. Cumberback called out to him.

Cameron walked over to see him. "Hey," he greeted him, with a smile. "How are you doing tonight?"

"Tired," he snapped. "I am more than ready to go home. I guess I should have gone home a hell of a long time ago."

There wasn't a whole lot Cameron could say to that, but Dr. Cumberback was right. They were so short-staffed, and, as a doctor, he cared. Granted, Dr. Cumberback had been a doctor for just over fifty years, and maybe he needed to retire. He'd stuck around longer than he should have perhaps, but he was here, and that had to count for something.

"I appreciate your helping out," Cameron said. "It's not been easy around here."

"No, it hasn't," Dr. Cumberback muttered. "We should have shut down this place years ago. It's getting worse and worse every year. That damn bitch," he snapped, venom spewing from his tone.

Surprised, Cameron said, "I'm sorry?"

"You're too young to know, and you haven't been here long enough to find out, but, ever since the haunting started," he began, shaking his head, applying pressure to his temples, "this hospital's damn-near reached the breaking point."

Cameron frowned at him. "Would you care to explain that?"

"No," he snapped, "I won't explain it, and I'm too damn tired and too crotchety to give a shit. Ask one of the old people around here. They'll tell you. Most of them will belly up fast with old wives' tales that will last all day."

"Sure, but then I'm listening to gossip instead of someone who potentially has dealt with the reality," Cameron retorted. "I've been here most of a year now and haven't seen anything."

"Nope. That's because it's not Halloween yet," he responded. "Believe me that, come Halloween, you'll see it, all right. And it's not every Halloween, which just makes it worse when it does happen because you think maybe it won't, and then *boom*. Then the next Halloween it doesn't happen. Yet, in the meantime, everybody is so edgy, you don't know what you're supposed to be doing. I have one hard and fast rule—I don't work Halloween. Just in case …"

"Just in case of what? What happens?" Cameron asked.

"We get a patient in. She's bleeding terribly. Not a wound on her, but we don't know that because she's completely covered in blood. We send her up for X-rays, but she disappears from the hospital."

"A flesh-and-blood woman?"

"Yes," he snapped, "a flesh-and-blood woman, every damn year, or other years if I'm not on shift. And then we send her off, obviously thinking that she's hurt and needing X-rays, CT scans, or something. She disappears from the hallway. Nobody ever knows what happens. The orderlies who are moving the gurney turn around to open the door or something, and, when they turn back again, she's not there. It's incredibly unnerving and very disorienting, especially if she grabs your lab coat. Don't let her touch your lab coat."

"What about the lab coat?" Cameron asked curiously.

"Yeah, she grabs somebody's lab coat and leaves behind a bloody handprint," he shared bitterly. "Then she turns around and disappears. Meanwhile, they are still wearing their lab coat, and now there is no longer any blood on it," he stated, glaring at him. "Oh, I get it. Everybody thinks it's just some big joke. Unless you're the one who's wearing the lab coat she keeps reaching for."

He didn't know what to say to that. "So, never any blood left?"

"No, never any blood left. The lab coat's clean. I swear to God, she's a flesh-and-blood woman we've been treating. And of course the doctor who treats her dies … like your father did … But now, every Halloween, I am absent," Dr. Cumberback shared, with a chuckle. "I just don't want to be here, just in case."

"Do you recognize her?"

He shook his head, but it was almost too fast of a headshake to be believable.

"Surely somebody must recognize her if she's coming all that often."

"What? With all the blood, we are distracted. Plus, you think we have a registry for ghosts around here?" he asked, staring at him. "None of us have a freaking clue who she is, and I don't want to know either. I want her to fucking leave me alone." And, with that, he harrumphed and took off.

Cameron stared at him. One of the other nurses came up and noted, "He's pretty touchy on the subject."

"I would say so," Cameron agreed mildly, looking over at her. "Wouldn't you be a little huffy if you were the one she might grab?"

The nurse looked at him thoughtfully and nodded. "When you put it like that, it's something I have wondered."

"Wondered what?" Cameron asked.

"He's got a pretty strong opinion on the haunting. Maybe it's because he's afraid?"

"Maybe no other doctors wanted to work that night,"

Cameron suggested, looking at her curiously. "Or do you know?"

"Not as far as I can remember. There have been other residents and certainly other people around. He may be the only living doctor to have experienced her visitations. The orderlies get pissed off too, but, because she looks so real, nobody ever says anything,"

"I see." Cameron frowned. "Have you seen her?"

"No, I would like to though."

"Why is that?"

"Because I have a suspicion that I know who she is," she shared, "but it would open a can of worms like you wouldn't believe."

"Halloween is coming up in, what? Just a few days I think."

She nodded. "I'll volunteer to work this year," she added.

If Cameron didn't know any better, she said it with a bit of excitement.

She continued. "Most people here avoid it. Just don't let her touch your lab coat."

"That's been mentioned before. And how long has it been going on?"

"I want to say ten years, but maybe a lot longer than that," she replied. "I don't really know. The gossip, when you bring it up, just makes it sound like it's been going on forever, but I'm pretty sure it hasn't been that long."

"Interesting," he murmured.

"Yeah. I'm looking forward to it," she declared, her eyes lighting up. "It's one thing to hear these stories. It's another thing to see it for yourself." With that, she headed back to her own work.

Cameron thought about it over his shift, throughout the rest of the evening and into the morning, wondering why something like that would occur. He didn't know anybody who dealt in this stuff, except Harriet of course. He wasn't sure that she was the one to ask though. However, he did have a good excuse to go check on her. Not that he would necessarily get a decent reception, depending on what he asked.

No matter what, all of it did pique Cameron's interest in Halloween night. He just needed to know the truth, and maybe he would get his wish soon.

CHAPTER 15

DANICA WOKE UP in the wee hours of the morning, startled and unsettled. She bolted out of bed and peered around the curtains to see what was upsetting her. The house appeared normal, and she need not worry about Nana, safely inside the house, because Danica knew damn well that the house would protect her. It wouldn't even allow Danica entry, unless there was a problem with Nana. Otherwise Danica would have a hell of a time convincing the house to let her in. Yet, for the moment, Nana would be fine, as long as she was inside. It's when she left that she could get into trouble, which was what happened in the garden recently.

Sending a message mentally to the house and feeling like an idiot, Danica warned, *Something is afoot. Take care.* There wasn't any response, but, then again, what response did she really expect?

It was a damn house, and every time she did something like this, it made her feel like a fool. But she couldn't deny that the house had a soul, a spirit, so to speak. The question was how? And why?

Of course there were never any damn answers.

That was one of the things that really bothered her, not to mention the fact that, if anybody found out, they would just label her as crazy. She'd spent enough of her childhood listening to people call members of her family crazy. She would do a lot to avoid that, particularly if it was pointed in her direction.

Uncertain, Danica quickly dressed. With Benji leading the way, she headed outside into the predawn coolness and walked around the property. There didn't appear to be anything amiss, but her nerves had noted that definitely something was going on—someone, somehow—yet no danger was visible. However, the unseen was here, the unseen that she often refused to even acknowledge, just because of shit like this.

When she heard a man call out to her, she turned to see a stranger walking toward her. She frowned, as she called Benji closer. The man stopped a good distance away, and it was hard to see him. An eerie glow was around him. "Who are you? What are you doing here?" she snapped. "This is private property."

He shimmered before her, making her even more unnerved. She bent down and picked up Benji, knowing that he would provide absolutely no defense, yet he gave her comfort.

When the glowing presence replied, "I mean you no harm," his tone was soft, gentle, caring—almost.

She frowned as she asked, "Do I know you?"

"In a way, maybe," he replied, with a chuckle, "but then again, maybe not."

She shook her head. "Can't say I like cryptic conversations," she muttered. "Again, why are you here, and what do you want?" She started backing up. Then she froze, with this sense of being restrained. "What's going on?" she gasped.

"I would like to talk to you, but don't be afraid."

"That's nice," she snapped. "I've spent a lot of my life afraid. What is it you want from me?"

He replied, "How about an open mind?"

She sneered. "At five o'clock in the morning? Is it even five?"

"I don't know." He chuckled. "You tell me."

The note of amusement in his tone confused her. She glanced around at the predawn light, just starting to soften the world around her. "Close to sunrise, yes," she confirmed, "but that's got nothing to do with anything. What are you doing here?"

"There is an easy way to do this from my point of view, but it might be harder from your point of view." She glared and he nodded. "Fine, but don't say I didn't warn you."

And then came an instant *clap* in her head. She dropped Benji and slapped her hands over her ears. "What the hell was that?" she cried out. When the man spoke this time, his voice was inside her head.

My name is Stefan. I keep an eye on your grandmother, he explained in a soothing tone. *She's not long for this world. In order to get her through her days and nights, I sometimes come and help.*

Danica's jaw dropped. "Did you just speak inside my head?" she asked in an ominous tone.

He sighed. *You know, if there was an easier way to get people to accept this, I would definitely use it.* He sounded amused. *Yet there isn't. In your case, you need to be aware and to get rid of some of this defiance that you're so quick to send out.*

"Defiance?" she repeated, her tone turning bleak. "Is that what it is to you?"

No. It's fear. I recognize it. I'm sure if you were to look, you would recognize it as well. You've had good reason, and maybe you still have good reason, he added. *I don't know. I do know that your grandmother needs you, but you need to realize that she needs you on another level that you haven't been able to help her with.*

"No, of course not," she retorted. "She wants me on that woo-woo level."

Which you already are a part of. You just haven't told her.

She frowned and asked, "How do you know?"

Because I can see your energy. His laughter ran through his tone. *I am talking into your mind right now. Your grandmother likes to talk to me while she's asleep.*

"Yes," she murmured. "That was how she used to call me in the nights when I was younger, when I had horrific nightmares."

Don't forget the times when you were older and still had horrific nightmares, he murmured, his tone full of compassion.

"What do you know about me?" she asked, trembling. "Did she tell you?"

She didn't have to tell me. I can see it. Unfortunately for me, sometimes I see too much pain from too many people, and the secrets that they want to hide aren't something that can really be hidden. Not with somebody gifted like me, he shared. *So, can I see your past? Yes. Do I look? No. Can I see your future? Some of it. I really don't look at that though. What I can tell you is that your grandmother is quickly fading. She's not done today and maybe not done tomorrow. However, she doesn't have long, and there are things that she needs to tell you. What I need from you is for you to shut up and listen.* His tone brooked absolutely no nonsense at that point. *I know you don't want to hear it, but she needs to explain some things to you. And you need to hear them. Do you hear me?*

"I hear you," she replied, aiming for calm in a world that

was anything but. "I don't understand what this has to do with you. Or why it matters so much that I listen?"

Because it's your heritage—a heritage that you are utilizing to some extent, but she doesn't know that, and it would make her rest so much easier if she did, he explained. *There's also some secret she's hiding. You need to know what that is. You can't make a decision if you aren't fully informed.*

"You mean, she would have peace if she knew that I was using some psychic ability?" she questioned. "I don't even know what I'm doing," she muttered, with a wave of her hand. "And if it means having people in my head like this, I really don't want to know either."

He chuckled. *On the other hand, you're never alone,* he noted. *In case of emergency, there is always somebody to call. You've been alone so much of your life, and, with your grandmother's imminent passing, you will be alone in a way you've never felt before,* he noted. *Yet there are things that need to be dealt with first, and this house is one of them. I've never seen anything quite like it.*

"Yeah, well, it's also one of the reasons why I can't *not* deal with some of this stuff," she snapped. "Do you know what it's like to have a house that has control over whether you get to go inside it or not? I threatened once to burn it down. I think that's why it holds a personal grudge against me."

Stefan's laughter rippled through her mind, making her smile.

"I don't know who you are or why you care. Yet I know the house looks after my grandmother. So, for that reason, I tolerate everything."

Of course, he agreed. *For you, your grandmother is your heart and soul. She has been there for you all this time, and she's doing everything she can to stay longer. Yet you also know that her time is coming very quickly.*

"With all this information," Danica asked, "why is there no way to stop that from happening?"

Because it's the Circle of Life, child, Stefan stated, a bit of exasperation in his tone. *No matter. Nothing you or I want matters. This is a circle that will continue until time ends.*

"Will time ever end?" Danica asked, the tears choking her. "Because that is not a time period I want to have happen. She's very special to me."

She is, and you are very special to her. But she will not die in peace, and she will not leave you in peace, if you do not give her a chance to tell you everything that you need to be told. Then you have a big decision to make.

"What difference does it make?" she asked, a weariness that she hadn't expected filling her soul. "It seems like life, so far, has just been incredibly hard. If she's about to dump more on me, I'm not sure I can take it."

You can take it, Stefan declared in a soothing tone. *You're young, and you have perseverance, and you have the will. Not only can you take it, you need to take it. She cannot be asked to carry more of the load when you are perfectly capable of taking some of it from her,* he asserted. *So, remember that your grandmother has done more than her fair share, and now she needs time to rest. When it's time for her to go, she needs to go with a clear conscience and to know that you are capable of handling what she leaves behind.*

On that weird cryptic note, he disappeared from her mind, leaving her almost bereft, and yet, at the same time, overwhelmed with joy.

She was so exhausted that she walked back to her RV and crashed. She managed a few hours of sleep. By the time she woke up, rushed inside the family home, and made breakfast for her grandma, it was later than her usual routine.

While they sat at the table, Nana studied Danica intently, as if thinking what was on her mind. "What are you so heavy in thought about?" her grandmother asked.

Deciding there was no time like the present, she shared, "I had a visitor last night."

Her grandmother's eyebrows shot up, and she looked out at the yard. "Like a male visitor overnight?" she asked, with interest.

Danica rolled her eyes at that. "No," she replied.

"Too damn bad," her grandmother muttered. "You can't stay a hermit forever."

"Yes, I can," Danica declared, "and I'm quite happy to at this point."

"No, you're hiding," her grandmother insisted.

Not wanting to go down the same pathway again, she waited for her grandmother to stop the old refrain about how Danica shouldn't be single and how she should move on and have a family, as if that were even an option. "His name was Stefan," she divulged.

Her grandmother stiffened and glared at her. "You talked to Stefan?"

"I'm not sure that I talked to Stefan as much as Stefan talked to me," she clarified, with a note of humor.

Nana's shoulders slumped, and she nodded. "That sounds like him."

"He seems to think that you need to talk to me about something."

"I've been trying to talk to you since forever," her grandmother replied, "but you don't want to hear what I have to say."

"He says it's important," Danica concluded.

Her grandmother nodded and stared down at the plate in front of her. "It might be important, but it's still not something you want to hear."

"Doesn't matter if I want to hear it or not. I don't want you to take something painful to the grave."

"Something painful?" her grandmother asked, with a broken laugh. "There has been nothing but pain."

Danica suddenly realized that she really didn't know a whole lot about her grandmother. "Then tell me," she urged. "What is it that I need to know?"

"For one, it has to do with your mother's abilities," Nana began but didn't continue.

Danica winced and, noting Nana's hesitation, Danica spoke up, for it had been too long to let it go now. "I'm sitting here, prepared to listen."

"That's something at least," Nana muttered. "Anyway, you know that your mother had abilities?"

"Yes, I know that," she said calmly.

"I suppose that's part of the reason why you spent so much time avoiding her."

"That's not why I spent so much time avoiding her," she countered, shaking her head. "Yet it was one of the issues I had to deal with as a child. Everybody had their own version of what they thought was my mother's problem," she explained, with a broken laugh. "Her psychic abilities were much vaunted and talked about."

"Yet you had that friend of yours at the fish-and-chips place," Nana added. "Jerry what's-his-name?" Danica shrugged, and her grandmother nodded. "He obviously thought you had abilities too."

"I just answered questions," she muttered, with a wave of

her hand. "Most of the time, they were questions that anybody could have answered. He really liked a girl. It was obvious that she really liked him too. But his insecurity was stopping him. So, when he asked me if she liked him and was somebody who cared for him, I told him yes because that was the truth. She did really care for him, so, yes, it could work. But, of course, like everything, it takes work. It takes time. It takes commitment. If he was prepared to do that, then it would be fun."

Her grandmother nodded. "So that's what you did. You just answered basic commonsense questions, with basic commonsense answers."

"Yes," she agreed.

"But you also told me that, when Jerry would ask you questions, you had no problem seeing the answer?"

"That's the truth. I did," she confirmed, "but I don't need it to be chalked up to psychic energy or any such gobbledygook," she added, with a snort. "And if you're wondering whether I'm using that energy now, yes, I am," she declared, with a hint of bitterness in her tone.

Her grandmother stared back, a mix of astonishment and joy evident on her face.

"Yes, Nana, but don't get excited, I don't use it very much. I don't use it often, only when it's necessary. For example, with Stefan last night. He was quite the handful, and, when I gave him a hard time, he ended up communicating directly into my mind," she grumbled, with a touch of annoyance. "I can't say I needed that or particularly enjoyed that experience."

Almost immediately his voice rumbled through her head again. *No, but some people are stubborn, and it's the only way to get through to them.*

She glared at her grandmother. "See? He just called me stubborn—in my head too."

Her grandmother snorted. "You can't argue with that because you are stubborn."

Her shoulders slumped, and she nodded. "Maybe, but my circumstances weren't always the easiest."

"No, child, they weren't the easiest, and they may not get easier coming up either."

"Why is that?" Danica asked.

"Halloween is coming," her grandmother stated gravely.

It was almost as if she knew the answer to that, but still asked, "And?"

"Your mother died on Halloween."

Danica paused, then replied, knowing the full weight of that date. "I know she died on Halloween. I almost died on Halloween. No," she corrected herself, "technically I *did* die on Halloween. Why do you think I avoid everything to do with that so-called holiday like the plague?"

"Right. Because she died on Halloween, it's also when you died."

"Exactly." She looked over at her grandmother. "Do you ever think it was a mistake that I was brought back?"

"God, no," her grandmother exclaimed in shock. "I always felt it was a sign. A sign that you needed to do more."

"Oh, *great*," she responded sarcastically. "So, just because somebody made a medical mistake, I'm now supposed to be some … energy worker or whatever you call it?"

"Not just an energy worker," she retorted. "And being brought back has its own pain."

"I know," Danica snapped. "I'm the one who went through it, remember? Waking up in that drawer isn't something I care to experience again."

Her grandmother winced. “I know,” she whispered.

Just then came a pounding on the front door, a pounding so forceful it seemed the entire house rattled. Danica looked at her grandmother in shock, then jumped to her feet and approached the door, whispering, “What the hell?” An unsettling rumble came around her.

“You’d better be on the lookout,” Nana warned.

As soon as she opened the door, Jace raced in, glaring at her in a fury, “You fucking bitch. What the hell are you doing here? Go away. Crawl back into whatever hole you came crawling back from,” he roared. “How dare you come back and mess things up between my brother and me.”

“Jace, I’ve haven’t seen you in God-knows how long. How are you?” she retorted, with as much sarcasm as she could muster considering her shock that the house let him in. “Obviously you’re not doing all that well. Apparently you have issues with your brother again. Now I don’t know what that has to do with me, but, as far as I’m concerned, it doesn’t.”

He glared at her. “If you weren’t here, I wouldn’t be having this problem.”

“You certainly don’t belong here in my house,” she reminded him.

“It’s not your house, remember?” he sneered. “It’s your grandmother’s house, or that dotty mother of yours.”

“My mother is long gone, and she may or may not have inherited it, but that isn’t an issue now.”

“So, what then? Are you planning on offing your grandmother now to get the house?”

She stared him down as she shot back, “The door’s behind you. Use it.”

He shook his head defiantly. “I’m not going fucking

nowhere until you promise to get the hell out of this town. I want you gone tonight."

"That's nice," she snapped, her eyes narrowing. "I'm not going anywhere. So, get that through your thick skull and get the hell out."

"You don't belong here."

"If I believed the sheriff and his deputies would do anything, I would call them. But I think I'll skip that step and go straight to your brother."

Jace continued to glare at her. "Yeah, you would, wouldn't you? Anything to mess me up."

"I don't even know who you are," she declared, with anger in her tone. "I haven't seen you in years, and here you are, busting into my grandmother's house and causing trouble. So, I've got no problem telling your brother what you did today. Now get your ass out of here, before I call him right now."

He shoved his face close to hers. "Do it," he dared, bellowing in her face. "Just fucking do it."

Nana called from the kitchen doorway, "Don't you threaten my granddaughter like that," she snapped. "I don't know who you think you are, but nobody comes into my house and does that."

He turned and scowled at her, then pivoted back to Danica, as if afraid to take his gaze off her. "You're nothing but a burnt-up old witch," he said, sneering. "Your days are done. Get the hell out of town, both of you. And you," he added, turning to her grandmother, "you can just fucking die, … like you should have many years ago." And, with that, he turned and stormed off.

The house slammed the door shut behind him, but Danica was so irate that Jace had even been allowed entry inside that she turned and started yelling at the house. "What the hell are you doing letting that happen in here? You're supposed to look after Nana. You're supposed to protect her," she roared, "not let some psycho like Jace get in here. If he ever comes around here again or tries to get in, you know what you're supposed to do. So, ensure you do it. I don't give a shit about me," she snapped. "Obviously we both know you don't either. But letting Jace inside this house was something inconceivable; he is somebody who should never have come through my grandmother's front door."

As if in response to her roaring, the house started to slam windows and doors all around, until her grandmother yelled out at both of them.

"Stop it. Stop it, both of you," she said, glaring at her granddaughter. "The house did his job. I wasn't hurt. You know perfectly well that, if this had gotten worse, the house would have stepped up and done something about it."

Danica buried her face in her hands, aiming for control, but it was hard. "How the hell do you argue with a house?" She dropped her hands and looked over at her grandmother. "We can't let this stand."

"Absolutely we can," she replied, "and we will. Jace's irate and upset, and that's his fault. However, we won't add to his pain."

"Why is he so upset? Why is he upset at us?" she asked, staring at her grandmother. "It makes no sense. Come on. Let's go back to the kitchen. Let's sit down again and talk." She extended her hand.

Her grandmother shook her head. "Honestly, I need to go lie down. I'm feeling pretty tired again."

With concern, Danica watched as her grandmother unsteadily made her way to her bedroom. "You sure? Is there anything I can do to make you feel better?"

Her grandmother just lifted a hand. "I'm fine," she murmured. "I just need to rest."

That worried Danica, but something else was so unnerving about the house's blind acceptance of Jace, who had just blasted into Nana's house, and Danica felt the need to confront someone about it.

She grabbed her phone to see if she could find Cameron's number. When she couldn't, she put on her shoes, and, with Benji in tow, headed over to his place. He might not be home, but, if he was, he would get an earful.

As she approached, she looked up to see him standing outside with a cup of coffee, talking on the phone.

He caught sight of her and waved and ended his call, a big smile on his face. But the smile fell off quickly as he took in her expression. "Obviously not a social visit," he remarked, with a shrug.

"Well," she replied, "let's just say it would have been a much more social visit if your brother hadn't just shown up at Nana's house. Jace had absolutely nothing nice to say, including threatening me and telling me to get the hell out of town, not to mention shouting at Nana and telling her to just die," she added, feeling the tears threaten to spill as they choked at the back of her throat.

Cameron's facial expression turned thunderous as he listened, while she detailed what had happened. "I … I don't know what's gotten into him."

"Something has," she interjected. "He ditched me way back when pretty-damn fast, but I got over it. Believe me that I got over it really, really well. Yet he burst into the house like we were old enemies. I don't know what's going on, but I don't have any animosity toward him. I don't know what he thinks I've done or haven't done, but I need him to leave Nana alone."

"Yes, of course," Cameron replied, shaking his head.

Honestly, she couldn't hear anything but sincerity in his words.

Cameron muttered, "Right. … He has become someone I don't recognize myself."

She nodded. "Ditto for me too," she muttered. "I went through hell before. I really don't need him giving me hell again. However, his threats were pretty-damn clear."

"Will you tell the sheriff?"

She snorted. "No," she replied too quickly, scrunching her nose. "They already seem to think that I beat up my grandmother, an idea you gave them apparently." She shot him a hard look.

"No, I did not," he declared. "Benson jumped on that as a possible idea for how your grandmother got injured and why she didn't have a wound show up at the hospital."

She nodded. "My grandmother was afraid that would happen, which is why she had been so worried about you going to the sheriff's office. But I, of course, didn't listen. So now I am the number one suspect in attacking my own grandmother," she declared in a fury. Suddenly it was almost too much for her. "Sometimes I wonder why I even came back."

"I'm sorry about Jace, just adding to everything else for you and Harriet. I too question why I'm here sometimes," he admitted, with half a smile. "This hospital is pretty small in many ways, and it does need people, but it could be amalgamated into the next county. It would be an inconvenience for some people here, but I'm not sure it would be that much of an inconvenience."

She nodded. "I guess that's always a possibility, isn't it? Anyway I don't know what the answer is regarding Jace, but I wanted to tell you." She turned to head back, calling out, "Benji, come on. Let's go home."

"You sure you don't want to stay for a cup of coffee?" Cameron asked.

She shook her head. "No, Nana was feeling poorly when I left, saying she needed to lie down. Honestly, she looks like she could go any day now. That head bang has had quite an effect on her."

"Let me come back with you," Cameron suggested. "I'll take a look."

"She probably won't even let you," Danica muttered in frustration. "She's very against anybody looking after her or finding out about her." She looked over at him. "You know that everybody thinks she's a witch, which is why they run away when she comes around."

"Do they?" he asked, frowning.

"Yes, they do," she confirmed, her tone odd and sorrowful. "I'm pretty-damn tired of it myself. Forget about selling me the property," she murmured. "I'll leave as soon as my grandmother's gone. Nothing is here for me." She thought about the house and winced. "Chances are I can't sell the place."

"No, you probably can't," he agreed, thinking on it. "At least not for a while, until old memories die down."

"I thought maybe they had died down," she shared, "but then your brother showed up and proved that nothing has died down at all. He's still got a chip on his shoulder like I can't believe, though I never did anything to him in the first place. I don't know why he's got such a big hate on for me."

"I don't know either," he admitted, "but I'll talk to

him."

She nodded. "I don't know that he'll listen, but maybe. If so, then I thank you ahead of time."

And, with that, she turned and walked back the way she'd come.

CAMERON COULDN'T BELIEVE what Jace had done, but watching Danica stride back toward her grandmother's house, Cameron didn't doubt it. Absolutely nothing in his mind suggested in any way that Danica had made this up. As far as his brother went, that was taking things a bit too far, even for him. Cameron got on the phone, but his brother didn't answer. So Cameron waited a few minutes and called again. When his brother finally answered, a weariness to his tone made Cameron wonder about what was going on here. "You want to explain what you just did?"

"What did I do?" he asked, his tone belligerent, but the knowing tone was evident, almost like a don't-ask-me-brother tone.

"You threatened two women alone in their own home. Are you nuts?" Cameron cried out. "That behavior will get your ass thrown in jail."

"I don't give a shit," he replied, "and it's not me who'll get put in jail. It should be that bitch for what she did to her mother."

There was such an off tone to that remark, and Cameron didn't understand. "I guess I don't understand what relationship you had with her mother that makes you feel this way."

There was dead silence at first, and then he stammered, "I didn't say I had a relationship with her. Don't put words in my mouth."

"I'm not. But every time anything related comes up, you're always talking about Danica's mother. It's as if you think you know that Danica did something to her mother. You blame her, as if she is responsible for taking her mother away from you … or something like that," Cameron explained. "And yet you were dating the daughter, so please don't tell me you were screwing the mother at the same time."

"You don't know anything. You don't know anything, Cameron. You don't know fucking anything." With that, his brother ended the call.

Cameron struggled to identify the emotions, but it seemed to be hurt and maybe grief in his brother's tone. Fear even?

Cameron glanced around his house, wondering at the wisdom of even coming back to this town. At times like this he wondered why he stayed. He'd been given other offers, and now he had to question if maybe he wouldn't have been better off taking one of them instead of living here, with all the secrets and mysteries and rumors and gossip.

It seemed that the town had changed in his absence, as if Daisy's death and Danica's resurrection had been so horrific that so many people had changed all around him too. His brother had changed, and Cameron didn't even know how or why. This wasn't the brother he knew.

Although Cameron had been back, coming up on a year soon, he had thought that they were getting closer. But now? It's like they were further apart than ever. Yet why? How could Jace possibly have been so involved over ten years ago to care so much about Danica's mother being murdered or dying by suicide? Either way it went beyond Daisy being dead. It was a fear that Danica had murdered her own mother, and that made no sense at all.

Just as he went to make coffee and to put on some breakfast, his phone rang again. This time, it was Danica. "Can you come?" she asked, fear in her tone. "I'm afraid she won't wake up."

He turned off the coffeepot and bolted out the door, running the last few yards to her house. When he got there, the door was already open, and she stood just inside the kitchen, trembling. "Are you okay?"

She nodded. "Please, go see her."

He bolted through to where the woman was lying in her bed, as if she hadn't gotten up this morning. She opened her eyes, looked at him, and whispered, "You know it's time for me to go."

"I don't think your granddaughter is ready for that," he replied gently.

"No, but she never will be," she murmured. "It's just that she doesn't know so much."

"Then stay," he whispered, knowing it was futile. "Stay, at least long enough to tell her."

"I tried. I tried so many times to tell her this morning. That's what I was going to do. And then—that's when your brother came," she murmured. "Just so much anger, so much hatred, and all of it becomes too much."

He reached out, checked her pulse, and nodded. "You could last a little bit longer, maybe for your granddaughter's sake. To tell her what you need to tell her, so you can go in peace."

"I don't know," she whispered. "It's a lot of effort, and I'm so tired."

He looked down at her and frowned. "How old are you?"

She gave him a ghost of a smile. "Old, so very old."

He turned back to the doorway to see Danica, her fist shoved into her mouth to hold back the tears. He went to join her there. "She might last another day or two," he whispered. "Mostly, I think, because she has something she needs to say to you."

At that, Danica nodded. "We were trying to have that discussion when your brother arrived," she said, bitterness in her tone.

"He won't be back again," Cameron stated, "so I suggest you have that talk now. I'll leave you to do it in peace."

And, with that, he turned and walked back out the door.

YOU HAVEN'T TOLD her. The harsh accusation broke through her exhaustion, once Danica had excused herself too.

"I know," Nana whispered. "I've been trying to get there."

Well, get there faster. You and I both know your time is up.

"You could allow me *not* to contemplate that every minute of the day," she snapped.

Too damn bad. She needs to be told, and she won't like it if we have to do it.

Nana shuddered at that thought. "Don't," she ordered. "It's important that I tell her."

Then tell her. You are not doing your job, and you need to. You know it, and I know it.

"I know. I know." She hated the last-minute pressure. To do this—something so awkward and so difficult—would change Nana's relationship with her granddaughter for the rest of her life.

Your life won't be very long, so it's not much of a hardship, came the voice in the darkness of her mind.

"You don't know that," she declared. "A lot of things could go wrong right now."

So fix it. Only then will she be safe.

Nana sighed. "But will she be safe? I don't know. There's more animosity and more hate than I have ever seen in my life in this town. I don't understand why."

The voice gentled as it responded, *Because things are coming to a crux. Every time a big change like this comes, the villagers get restless.*

She snorted at that. "You make it sound as if this has been centuries in the making."

It has been. The voice laughed. *You're the only one who doesn't seem to believe that. We keep telling you, and you keep thinking that we're making a mockery of it, but we aren't. It is true. This is a legacy, and it's not a bad one.*

She wasn't so sure whether it was a bad one or not at this stage. However, it was well past the time of being able to do anything about it.

You've got that right. The voice chuckled. *Everybody has difficulty at this time. You're not alone.*

She smiled at that. "I don't think death is easy on anyone," she muttered.

And yet it's only a transition, the voice stated smoothly. *The same transition everybody makes when they're born. It's just in reverse. Maybe it's uncomfortable for a few months into the pregnancy, as you learn to grow into the body that you will become. And maybe it's uncomfortable through the birth channel as you're born. In the first few years, you are literally this helpless amoeba, waited on hand and foot. Yet that stage ends, and you become that adult, and you are free to make all the decisions you want. With each one you make, there is a related consequence. You don't make them blind. You make them knowing full well what you're getting into.*

She stared around the room and nodded. "I can't hide that. I know that. There is no escaping this."

No, there isn't, but your end isn't the same as everyone else's, though it's still just as final.

CHAPTER 16

DANICA REJOINED HER grandmother, trying not to cry again, while sitting on the bed with the woman who had been a stable home base for Danica over all these years. "Do you really have to leave now?" she whispered.

Her grandmother gave her the briefest of smiles. "If not today, tonight," she shared weakly. "If not tonight, tomorrow. My time here is over. Honestly it's been over for a very long time. I've been waiting for you, hoping you would come."

Danica's eyes filled with tears. "You know if you had called …"

"Yes, but that wouldn't have been the same thing," Nana murmured. "I could have called you at any time, and many times I wanted to," she whispered. "Many times I felt like I needed to, but I just couldn't pull you away from everything that you knew."

"Everything?" Danica asked. "I've only been half living. I've been away for ten years, and it hasn't been any better than the eighteen years when I was here."

Her grandmother smiled. "I know that, and I'm sorry. I'm so sorry for all of it."

"It doesn't matter," Danica replied. "I just know that it's been a tough, very tough lifetime. Now, do you want to explain what it is that you need to tell me?" she whispered.

Nana sighed. "It's not that easy."

"Of course not. What does it have to do with my mother?"

Nana hesitated and then sighed. "Your mother used energy all the time. She used it in any way she wanted. To show off, to flirt, to capture men. She put them under a spell and would seduce them, so that they would take her away. But energy, when used like that, it turns … bad." Nana shuddered. "It always turned out wrong for Daisy, not immediately, but soon afterward, … and she could never quite get away with anybody. She was desperate to have a man, as a grounding rod, somebody who would stay with her, somebody who would love her. But every time she did this, it just caused her more pain and, in many cases, hurt her partners too," she murmured. "She was incredibly beautiful, but she was also so very wanton with her beauty and her gifts. She didn't care about anything except herself. Only herself, in order to get away from here."

"Why did she hate it here so much?" Danica asked.

"Why do you hate it so much?"

"For me, it's the bad memories," she replied instantly. "My mother killed me. I have the scars to prove it. It's memories of a town that hated me. It's memories of a time when I was shunned, and still am," she added, with a broken laugh. "That hasn't changed. I'm not sure it ever will," she murmured.

"You need to know that you are in danger."

She stared at her grandmother. "What do you mean that I'm in danger? You're the one who was hit."

"Yes, I was hit, and, if I had stayed inside the house, the house would have taken care of it."

"Maybe, yet Jace came inside. Now I don't know," Danica snapped, looking around at the house. "This house should have learned to at least look after the yard too, or something."

That brought a smile to her grandmother's face. "And yet you've never asked about the house."

"I certainly have asked about the house, but you've never given me an answer. I asked my mother about the house too, and she wouldn't give me an answer either."

"The answer is a little on the strange side," Nana shared, "and, in some ways, not on the good side."

"What's new there? What's so dense and dark about it? Did you imprison somebody's soul or something?" she asked half jokingly. When her grandmother frowned, Danica wondered if she should have even brought it up. "I meant that as a joke."

"I know you did. The trouble is, you're not all that far off."

"What? Please don't say that."

Her grandmother smiled. "There are things you don't know. Things that you have avoided having anything to do with, but, no, there isn't a soul imprisoned in this house. Yet the house was brought to life through love—for all the right reasons. Now the house stands guard for all the same reasons," she said, with a smile, looking around. "It's not that he has a separate entity or a separate existence, but he is alive in many ways. This house was built by my ancestors and my father and my husband, both of whom adored me," she whispered.

An eerie sense of encroaching darkness surrounded them in this room. And yet it was still morning outside.

"House, turn up the lights, please." Her grandmother chuckled, as a dim light brightened the space around them.

"It's almost as if he can read my mood," she whispered, "and nothing you can say will change it."

"I know," Danica agreed, looking around, worry gnawing at her. "What am I supposed to do with the house when you're gone? He's like an entity all on his own."

"He has protected me time and time again," she whispered. "I know that there isn't any way for you to understand that, but he was built of love … every ounce. Generations of our family have built, renovated, and added on to this house. My father put everything into this house. I was the apple of his eye. He loved me more than anything," she whispered. "As did my husband. So much of the house was already built by the time he came around. But, once he understood what my father was doing, he was right there to help. Every step of the way, every piece of wood was magically treated. Every ounce, every pound, every board, nail, screw—all of it went through a process of their bestowing it with the honor of looking after me."

Nana shook her head in wonder. "I really had no idea that such a thing was even possible. At the time, I didn't really understand what it meant in terms of living with the house, until my father passed away. That's when it really came into being. So, in a way, this house is my father. Maybe his energy is connected here. I don't know," she said, "but it has been a joy to have, particularly on days when I'm alone because I'm never really alone because of him."

Danica looked around at the house and shook her head. "No wonder people think we're nuts."

"The only people who think we're nuts are the people who don't know about the unique things that go on in our world," Nana explained, smiling. "Stefan knows. He's still trying to wrap his head around it. People buy and sell houses with complete disregard to the energy they put into it or give back to it."

"People are takers," Danica muttered, lost in thought.

"You are right about that. They don't give back. They don't take care of these beautiful homes. They just live in them, strip them, sell them, and move on to something else, move on to something that makes them more money or maybe is a better place to live. Nobody cares about the actual essence of a building. Everything is energy. It doesn't matter whether it's a toilet that you flush every day or the house that you live in or the food that you eat. It's all energy, and, if you treat it with respect, joy, love, and gratitude," she rambled on, "that energy just builds and builds and builds. Somehow, when you take care of it, … when they cared about it, … the legacy of this house was born. Did my great-great-grandfather—or whatever relative however far back—realize what he was creating? I don't know. But my father and my husband were all for it," she said, with a smile.

It was odd for Danica to listen to her grandmother talk about her husband because Danica had never met him. He was gone well before she had arrived on the scene. "You never talk about him."

"Maybe not, but he's never far from my thoughts. We were truly blessed to have the great life that we did," she murmured. "When he was here, he knew he wasn't long for this planet either. He told me so himself. He also worked with energy. He knew, and he understood me."

Nana smiled. "I was gifted to have the time that I did have with him. It's also why your mother had so much in the way of gifts, getting that from both sides of her genealogy. Maybe that's what made her so unstable too. I never could figure that out. The gifts, if used correctly, do a lot to protect the person wielding them. But, in Daisy's case, just so much was there, and she wanted nothing to do with reining it in or controlling it. She was wild, irresponsible. Of course, what she really wanted was a man, that sense of something that I couldn't seem to give her," Nana murmured.

Her head fell back, and with tears in her eyes, Nana added, "Daisy was truly the one greatest creation of my life, and yet she truly was also my greatest failure," she murmured. "We were constantly at loggerheads, constantly fighting. It was impossible to live with her. Yet, because she was my daughter, I also knew it was impossible to live without her."

"You have lived without her all these years," Danica pointed out calmly.

"I know. I know. Thankfully I had you," she murmured. "I often wonder what happened to Daisy that night."

"You don't know?"

"No." Nana opened her eyes to look over at Danica. "I don't know. I had various thoughts about what could have happened. I don't have any proof of what did happen, and it hurts. It hurts a lot to know that my daughter may have suffered."

"As long as you know that I didn't do it."

She looked at her granddaughter in surprise. "Oh, my dear, I never once thought you did." Nana took Danica's hand. "Only the crazies in the world wanted you to have done it. You were too special, too sweet to have hurt your mother. I mean, in self-defense, certainly, and honestly you had every right to try and save yourself. But know this, I know that you didn't hurt your mother."

"No, I didn't. But believe me that there are times when I wonder if I should have."

"Of course, child. That inability to fight back against

those who love you is one of the handicaps women often are challenged with. It's why so much abuse is out there. We take it, and we don't realize it's abuse until it's too late."

"Were you ever abused?" Danica asked.

"No," Nana whispered, a smile in her lips. "He truly loved me, and I truly loved him. Even for the few years that we had, we were blessed."

"Did he know my mother?"

"No, no," she said, with sorrow. "He died while I was pregnant. One of the saddest, hardest things I've ever done was carry on. I just wanted to go to the grave with him," she whispered. "If I could have found a way to do that, I would have. But when I found out I was pregnant, I knew I couldn't. No way I could take that step anymore. It's as if he had left her on purpose to ensure I stayed behind. While I don't think even he understood, it was pain and torment for me and Daisy. I never understood what made her that way. I never understood any of it. Maybe it was literally just too much out-of-control energy. The more I tried to teach her to wield it, the less she would listen to me. It just became a constant power struggle. It was all fun and games while she was a child, but then somehow she grew into this angry woman."

"You don't know what made her angry?"

"No." She sniffed as she added, "Halloween is the day after tomorrow."

"You keep harping on Halloween."

"That's because you've been gone, so you don't understand. Daisy comes back every Halloween."

Danica froze, staring at her grandmother. "What?" she asked in shock.

"You heard me," Nana said. "Just like you died and

came back, your mother comes back every Halloween."

"How is that—how is that even possible?" she whispered.

"I do not know. But I can tell you that she comes back and makes life hell. She comes back to the hospital. She always grabs for one of the doctors. Most people—staff and patients alike—try to stay away from the hospital in case Daisy does show up. Sometimes it's this hospital. Sometimes it's the other one a county over. There's never really any rhyme or reason why one or the other. Yet I know several of the staff here will not go to work on that day, just in case Daisy does appear."

"That's awful. No wonder this town can never forget."

"True. She terrorizes them. I don't know what she wants. I don't know why she's still haunting them, but the fact that my daughter lives as a deeply troubled spirit on the other side—as she was a deeply troubled soul on this side—pains me terribly. If I could do something to help give her peace, I would do it. I have sought assistance from so many people," she whispered. "Honestly, if I can last through another Halloween, it will be the one thing that I'll try to do again this year. The one goal I've been trying to achieve before I go is to give Daisy peace, so that she can finally leave and never come back. I just want her to be at peace."

Danica sat back, having a hard time even listening and processing what she had just heard. "That is unbelievable."

"I know," her grandmother agreed, with a soft sigh. "For that, you need to talk to Stefan, because he is likely the only other person who can help Daisy."

"Does he know her?"

"No, he doesn't know her, but he knows me. He's heard the stories. He knows how much it hurts me to know that

Daisy's out there, wandering."

"At the hospital, what does she do?"

"She goes through the emergency entrance covered in blood, and the trouble is, one of the people she deals with at the time ends up dying."

Danica sat back in horror. "What?"

"Yes," Nana murmured. "Again, it's not just at this hospital, although this seems to be the primary place for her to haunt. But she was also taken to the other hospital multiple times in her life. So that became a secondary haunting ground for her. I don't know how she chooses one versus the other. I don't know how she chooses her victims, one or the other," she shared, tears running down her face again. "All I can tell you is that your mother walks on Halloween every year and has done so for the last ten years."

"I don't get it at all. You're saying medical personnel have died every year in the last ten years on Halloween?"

Nana gave her the saddest of smiles. "Yes," she whispered. "That's just one more reason to try to get Daisy to stop. Cameron's father died after the last Halloween, from a heart attack, when he had no health issues. He passed the very next day, after Daisy had left her bloody handprint on his white lab coat."

"*Try* to get her to stop?" Danica jumped to her feet and paced the room. "Oh, good God," she exclaimed. "We should stop her. That she tried to kill me while she was alive is one thing, but to kill innocent people who are there trying to help her is absolutely an abomination. How the hell are they dying?"

"That's the thing. Most of the time it's a heart attack. At least that's what the evidence suggests, and forensics ends up deciding that," Nana shared. "Every time it's some sort of medical emergency that nobody can really explain because these people generally don't have any prior history. But I can tell you that Daisy does pinpoint specific people, and so some of the staff just don't work anymore out of fear that they might be next."

"Good Lord," Danica muttered, sinking back onto the bed and staring at her grandmother. "Of all the things I thought you might want to tell me, this is absolutely not what I expected."

Her grandmother gave her the briefest of smiles. "I understand, and you already know that I'm not here for long. But, if I could change one thing, it would be to give Daisy some peace. … I know you don't want to hear this again, but I really need to rest."

"I still think we have a lot to talk about," Danica noted in alarm, looking at her grandmother, not sure how to voice her concerns.

"There is. There absolutely is, and I promise I will wake up. I will wake up until we can stop my daughter and can put her to rest."

"Why do you want to buy that property back?" she asked suddenly.

Her grandmother never even opened her eyes. "Because it's all connected to the house," she whispered, "and he's been even more erratic and more upset since I sold off that piece. I needed it to put food on the table. Not a lot of people want to pay for psychics," she murmured. "The healings I accomplished have helped a lot, but back then I needed money, and I ended up selling that piece. Now, I need it back so I can make things right."

"Have you thought about, when you're gone, what will happen to the house?"

"Nothing will happen to the house. It's really all just energy. Like all energy, it can't be destroyed." And, with that, Nana fell asleep.

Danica, on the other hand, would not be sleeping anytime soon.

JACE STORMED AROUND his small rented house. While the residence wasn't much, he thought the attached land might calm him somehow.

He poured himself a generous amount of Jack Daniel's before slumping onto the couch, pissed off and shaky from the booze. His doctor had warned him to stop with his binge drinking, but it was damn hard when it was the only thing that allowed him to function. That fact also scared the crap out of him, but he wasn't permitted to tell anybody, especially not that brother of his. Cameron was an unbearable know-it-all at the worst of times. As for the best of times? Let's just say there weren't any best of times anymore. Jace wasn't even sure when things had soured.

But one thing was for sure, things had gone south since Danica had arrived back in town. Jace wasn't even sure what his big hate for her was now. And yet something was there. There must have been, and he was willing to go with it.

He was pretty sure it was something somebody had told him. Yet, in his amused, drunken state, it was way past his ability to figure out why and how. Yet he was supposed to love his brother, and that was getting harder too. What do you do when you have a sibling who's always such a goddamn success that you look like a complete failure alongside them no matter what?

Jace had been doing pretty well until the divorce, and

the divorce wasn't even his fault. His wife just took offense because he'd gone out with one of her girlfriends, and things had gotten a little out of hand.

He'd apologized, for crying out loud. What did his wife expect?

Her girlfriend had been the one who came on to him, so he shouldn't have to pay the price for that. But his wife didn't see it that way. Of course she didn't. She wanted to see it whatever way she wanted, which wasn't working out so well for Jace.

Then, to make it worse, he had a son, but he hadn't seen his son in a very long time. When he did see his son, all he did was squawk anyway. He'd become a mama's boy, without Jace there to guide him.

Now just he and his brother were left. Their father had died after that bitch had shown up at the hospital last Halloween. … His father had had a heart attack the very next day, and their mother had followed him within a few months. Cameron only came home for the first funeral and then the next, staying to help sort out the estate. Seeing the state of the medical staffing issues at the hospital, Cameron had agreed to stay on a trial period.

So now just Cameron and Jace were left in the family. Yet they were on the outs again. They'd been that way a lot as brothers growing up. Then his brother had gone for a higher education degree in medicine, coming home to fill his father's shoes. Unfortunately for Jace, that had only emphasized the success gap between the brothers.

It wasn't Jace's fault. He had tried hard to make a fresh start, and, if that fresh start wasn't working out, why the hell was that his problem? Of course he didn't have an answer when his friends, laughing and joking and taunting him, asked, "Then whose problem is it?"

Jace didn't need to listen to their BS. Which is why he hadn't seen any of them in quite a while now. Maybe that was a problem; he didn't know. This wasn't the time to get his head wrapped around any of this shit either. Friends were supposed to be there for each other. They weren't supposed to gang up and to do an intervention.

He had dumped them out of his life pretty damn fast. And, besides, they'd accepted his getting rid of them pretty quickly too, so surely that meant they weren't really friends, right? His tired brain struggled with it.

He stared out the window, knowing that he should probably go do some work at his brother's house, but he was probably too damn drunk to even do anything effective. His brother did pay him or, at the very least, gave him food and a place to sleep when things got bad, which was happening again. He hadn't paid his damn rent for a while, and he knew where that would lead.

He groaned, buried his head in his hands, and tried to sit up, only to collapse back. When a knock came on the door, he raised his blurry gaze to it and called out, "Come in." When a stranger stepped in, Jace glared at him. "Who the hell are you? What do you want?"

The stranger looked at him and shrugged. "I heard you need money."

"Yeah, I need money. So what does that got to do with anything?"

"I have a job for you," he said, with a smile, "and you should like this one."

"Yeah? Why?" he asked.

"Because you can get rid of somebody you hate."

"I hate lots of people in this world, but chances are that

I'll get caught."

"Not this time." The stranger chuckled. "Besides, nobody will give a crap if this person disappears."

"Yeah, who's that?" he asked.

"Danica. … I know how well you love her."

He stared at the stranger, his brain trying to make sense of it. "Hang on. What do you want me to do?" he asked. "I'm up for anything that gets that bitch out of my life, but I don't know exactly what it is you're asking me to do."

"You don't seem that dense," the stranger stated sharply, "but maybe you're not quite desperate enough."

"I'm not desperate at all," Jace retorted, with a sneer. "I don't know why the hell you would even think I am."

The stranger laughed. "Maybe because you're collapsed here in a stupor, trying to justify your existence, when really there's no justification for it at all. In fact, you're as bad as Danica is."

At that comparison, a red haze filled Jace's mind. He roared to his feet and lunged at the stranger, who sidestepped him nicely, and down he went. He shook his head. "Did you fucking trip me?"

The other man laughed. "Hell no, I didn't, but when you're ready for some money—"

"I don't need money that bad," he interrupted.

"No? You're about to lose your son because you haven't been paying child support, and you'll soon have your truck impounded. You haven't been paying much of anything, including rent. The only job you've got is the little bit of work you do for your brother." The stranger sneered. "Then again, … you're not even doing that."

"How the hell do you know so much about me?"

"Easy. I just hang around the bars and see what lowlife is

in trouble, needing a lift."

"So, are you trying to help me or to hurt me?" Jace asked with a snap. "I'm really tired of people ready to kick me when I'm already down."

The stranger nodded. "That's a really good point," he noted, with a cold and calculated smile. "So, to answer your question, I'm trying to help you. I'm ready to give you a hand up in life. All you need to do is take it."

"Yeah, but you still didn't say exactly what I should do."

"It involves getting Danica to move away or to disappear—whatever method you choose," he replied. "Surely that could be some fun for you."

"I hate that bitch," he snapped. "Now she's got her hooks into my fucking brother too."

"Ah. So, you're about to lose the only job you have and the only support you've got," he noted, with a nod. "I'll leave a number here on the table. When you're sober enough to talk to me, give me a shout, and we'll see what we can do."

"Yeah, but you can't let them take my truck," he added, surging up.

"That depends on you," the stranger replied, looking at him intently. "I'm happy to go pay it off right now and to ensure that your wife gets the money. But—according to the judges—you need to find a way to deal with your ex." He stopped and stared at Jace. "Of course that's another option."

Jace frowned, struggling once again to sort out what the suggestion was. "You're not … you're not suggesting I go kill her, right?" he asked in shock.

"Oh my, I didn't say that. You did."

Jace shook his head. "No, no, I didn't. I would not—"

"I am glad to hear that because, once you get rid of one

problem," he added, "it's so easy to turn around and get rid of other problems too. Just think what your life would be like if you didn't have an ex-wife taking you to court every five minutes. Your son would be here for you, and only you, and nobody else could say a word about it. You would have your truck. You would have your monthly disability money, instead of it going for child support. You could live on it—free and clear. No hoops, no problems, no troubles."

Jace shook his head. "But I don't hate her, for Christ's sake," he muttered in a haze. "I might even be halfway in love with her still."

"Still? How about when she took you for every penny you had? She filed for custody and then fought to have your truck because you weren't paying the child support. You don't realize that boy isn't even your own son. She's been having an affair."

"How did you know that?" At that, Jace glared at him. "That was a fucking raw deal," he roared, his rage coming back to him. "She should never have done that."

"Oh, I agree. Absolutely I agree," the stranger replied. "It's up to you how you want to go through life—like a loser, surfing couches, who's about to lose your truck and the few other things that might have mattered to you? Or will you stand up and take notice? You know where women belong, don't you? A whole world is out there where men are in charge. You're just not part of it."

"I should be." Jace glared at him. "I am the man of the household."

"You were," the stranger said, with a smile. "You were, but you're not now, of course. Though you cared at one point. The question is whether you care enough about yourself to do something to make your life better."

"Yeah, but I won't go off on the mother of my kid," he snapped.

"No, that's fine. How do you feel about Danica though?"

"That bitch?" Jace said instantly.

"That's what I thought. So, you know your choice. Talk to me when you're sober, or stay on the same path you're on." And, with that, he was gone.

He was gone so fast, and Jace had to wonder if he was really even hearing what the guy had said. It was freaky to even think about. That's not who he was. He wasn't the guy to turn around and to shoot his ex-wife. But that voice in the back of his head nudged him. *Who mentioned anything about shooting?*

He collapsed onto the couch in a drunken stupor, wondering at what his life had become. Then he didn't care one damn bit, as the Jack took care of the rest of his ability to think.

IT'S TIME, THE voice in the darkness stated.

Harriet shook her head in denial. "Not yet," she snapped. "Another forty-eight hours."

Dark laughter whispered through her. *What will forty-eight hours do for you? You have no way out of it. This is the commitment.*

"I know," she cried out, raising her hands in frustration, "but you can't blame me for wanting something different for her."

She will have no choice either. It is your family legacy.

"I understand," she protested, "but that's not helping."

It matters not what helps. You need to tell her. And, with that, the voice disappeared.

She sagged back into her bed, tears in the corner of her eyes. Yes, it was time. She would soon die. She knew that. She didn't even care about that. That was just another transit in her mind. And it should be one not filled with as much pain and angst as she was going through. People died, often at peace, yet many feared what awaited them.

That wasn't the case for Harriet.

She knew exactly what waited for her, and she was okay with it. Matter of fact, for years she had felt that she would be completely blessed to have such luck. She wasn't so sure that luck was a part of it right now, but that was beside the point.

What she was trying to do right now was preserve her granddaughter's life after this.

And, of course, because she wanted to save her granddaughter *and* Daisy, everybody else was making sure that wouldn't be an easy thing to do.

Harriet rose from the bed, dressed, only to collapse onto the big chair in the living room, knowing that her granddaughter was outside in her RV, working away, trying to pay the bills. Money was not an issue around here, at least not now. Harriet had tried so hard to utilize the help that had been offered, and then finally she just gave in. As they explained, it made no difference. Money was just energy. It was just another form of currency, and, as she had already bartered away her soul, this little bit extra made no difference.

The tears rolled down her cheeks. Sad, quiet, tired, Harriet grew resigned, as there was no changing what had been put in motion centuries ago. She kept trying to find another way to do it, but only after there had been some terrible failures.

She hadn't even considered this to be wrong until recently, when she realized how much her daughter and granddaughter had suffered.

She hadn't coaxed Danica home. She had come home on her own will. But the man in charge would easily say that she had come home because she knew it's where she belonged.

Danica was following the instincts of generations, whether she liked it or not.

And that was hard for Harriet to take in because, even if her granddaughter didn't want any part of this, it didn't matter what she wanted. It was well out of her hands.

It had always been out of her hands. It was in the hands of people who were more powerful than her.

Harriet had always thought that she had done very well. But she knew that she had utilized a lot of their collective energy to do the good things in life that she had done. Good things were important; it was important to help others. It was important to feel she had some legacy to leave behind. She just hadn't considered what that legacy would look like when it wasn't the one she had dreamed it would be.

Nobody could blame her for wanting more, but everybody would. Everybody would view her in a completely different light, and she wasn't ready for that. Now though, it was well past the time for her to make any of those kinds of changes, and that made her sadder than anything.

She felt the old age in her bones. She had confronted the papery-thin crepey skin with more and more moisturizers, which just seemed to suck it all away, as if the sand in the ocean ran dry with every wave. No holding back this aging tide, she knew that, but she couldn't stop herself from trying.

A preservation instinct remained here, an instinct for herself, and an instinct—even though she wasn't afraid—an instinct as old as time, to stop the inevitable rush of what was coming toward her.

Harriet wanted to believe it was just because she wanted to preserve her daughter and to help her before it was too late, and yet another part of her realized perfectly well that there was no helping Daisy, and she was just—

You should tell her.

"I know. I know," she snapped, getting angry and feeling cornered.

Now, the voice insisted.

CHAPTER 17

BANNED FROM THE house again, Danica worked away in her RV, trying to figure out what she was supposed to do and what the hell was supposed to happen with the house. Was the house dangerous, or was this just some strange possession? When a knock came on her door, she got up and opened up the RV, but nobody was there. Frowning, she turned around. When she heard a knock again, she reached a hand up to her head.

The voice said, *That's where I'm knocking, if you would let me in.*

Frowning, she mentally opened up a door, realizing that Stefan was trying to come in. "What the hell's going on?" she asked, glaring around her small RV. "And how completely freaky is it that you can do this?"

He chuckled. *It might be freaky. Yet it's also a good thing in case of an emergency.*

"Yeah, you say that, but I don't know that I could do it—to call you in the first place, I mean. Besides, will I be dealing with emergencies where I need you?"

Maybe. Did you talk to your grandmother?

"A little bit, but only a little bit. She was nearly ready to collapse again from fatigue. And still I think there's something else she doesn't want to tell me."

Absolutely. I agree. There are things she doesn't want to tell you, but these are things that you do need to know.

"*Great,*" she murmured. "Something about my mother haunting a hospital?"

Yes, I've heard things about that too, Stefan confirmed, a sharpness in his tone. *That hospital is on my watch list.*

"What do you mean, your watch list?" she asked, surprised. "Do you really track this stuff?"

Sometimes. Sometimes I should. It depends on how much damage these entities cause while they're here. If they're just visual, and they scare people, well, I've got other things to do with my time. So I don't worry about that so much, he said, with a laugh. *However, if they're there to cause trouble, that's a different story.*

"According to my grandmother, every Halloween my mother appears badly hurt but has no visible injuries. They end up sending her for X-rays, or whatever, and, on the way, she disappears. But, whoever she grabs at the time, ends up dead. As a result, apparently nobody wants to work Halloween at this hospital."

No wonder, Stefan noted absentmindedly.

"I don't know that I believe it. Yet Nana made it sound like they all supposedly died of natural causes, you know, heart-attack-type things. Which could be just from the visual, and yet it's always the person she touched."

Very interesting, he murmured. *I'll look into that more.*

"Yeah, particularly since Halloween is the day after tomorrow," she muttered. She got up to pour herself another cup of coffee. "I would offer you coffee, but, in your present state, would it run right through you?"

I don't drink coffee, but I do drink tea though. Stefan chuckled. *I don't think I can drink it vicariously through you,* he added.

She shook her head. "You do know that people think we're nuts."

Yep, I've heard that a time or two. Thankfully I'm at a point in my life where I really don't give a damn. He paused and asked, *How about you?*

"Of course I give a damn," she admitted, with a sigh. "Nothing is easy about this, about what I've gone through. I've done everything I could to just shut it down. But some of it, you just can't ignore. It's part of who you are."

It's definitely a part of who you are, and you'll be required to step out—

"I won't," she replied instantly.

After a moment where he pondered her words, he then added, *I don't know whether it'll be on Halloween because of your mother, or something else, but something really ugly is brewing in your neighborhood, and I'm really concerned about your grandmother.*

"Yeah? My grandmother isn't likely to make it to Halloween, in case you didn't know that," she snapped. "She's fading quickly, and I'm just hoping she'll last long enough to tell me everything she needs to say."

She needs to, he declared. *Whatever she is holding back is causing her great stress. That's not the kind of thing that should go to the grave with her.*

"You want to tell me about that stuff—seeing as you obviously know everything about it?"

No, I don't know everything about it. Your grandmother has me blocked from reading her thoughts. However, I wouldn't tell you if I did because it's not my job, he noted in a terse tone, and then started to withdraw. *I'm off to talk to your grandmother.*

"She's sleeping."

No, she's not, he replied, his tone deepening. *That's the one thing she's not doing, even when she should*. And, with that, he was gone.

Danica quickly packed up her work, saved everything she had opened on the computer, and, with Benji at her heels, raced over to the house. The door opened as she approached. As she walked in, she called out, "Nana, are you here?"

When no answer came, she headed into Nana's bedroom and stopped at the doorway. Her grandmother was in bed, and, no, she wasn't sleeping. But Danica wasn't exactly sure what Nana was doing. Her arms were in the air, as if she were open to embracing someone from above.

Danica frowned, as she looked around. "Nana?" she asked, but no answer came.

A weird hum filled the air. She didn't know if that was Stefan talking to Nana or something else, but it was definitely odd. Then again, Danica's whole life had been odd lately. She sat for a few minutes and then realized that her grandmother seemed to be coming out of whatever trance she had been in.

Heading into the kitchen, she put on coffee, hoping to have a cup with Nana, as she finally shared her big secret with Danica. She glanced around at the house and asked, "What will you do when she goes?" She wasn't sure what lengths this house would go to in order to protect Nana.

When it came to possessed houses, that was a little bit beyond anything anybody had ever mentioned to Danica. Maybe that was part of what her grandmother needed to talk to her about. But when? Or would that be just one more of those things her grandmother didn't share?

Danica had been locked out of so many discussions

growing up. All she could have done mentally was to disappear herself, and that had been hard. She hadn't gone the same route as her mother and would have taken offense to anybody who would have implied such a thing.

She stared out the kitchen window, wondering about the wasted life her mother had lived and, to a certain extent, the wasted life Danica herself was living. She'd been living off the grid, trying to stay quiet, trying to stay hidden, trying to not cause waves or to attract attention.

Because that was the worst, … bringing attention to yourself, knowing that people just wouldn't get it. They wouldn't understand, and, because they wouldn't understand, there was absolutely no reason for them to find out anything. Once they found out, Danica's life would change.

She glanced out the window toward Cameron's house and frowned. She thought she saw somebody outside, traipsing around the property close to her place. Not her place, she corrected herself, shaking her head. It was Nana's place. It would never be hers. Even if it was her place on paper, it still wouldn't be hers.

She knew, deep inside, that her grandmother wanted the property back, to be joined again. She just didn't understand why. She'd asked Danica to buy it. She had told Cameron she didn't want it after all, and she hadn't told her grandmother that either. Yet, if her grandmother was that close to death, should Danica even tell her about all that at this point? Or was that one of those deathbed things you had to follow through on, or otherwise what? You would get haunted? She groaned at that thought because that was no joke in her world. Hauntings were all too real.

She shook that thought from her head.

She had certainly known more than her grandmother

had realized, but that had been found out by listening in, as much as she could as a teen, to conversations between her mother and others. Around the time Danica realized her mother was playing some weird games out there, people were laughing, joking, and calling her a witch. Danica just needed to know more. What she'd found out seemed to mock her and her family. Danica had basically tossed it all off as not being possible. Yet inside she knew.

But the rumor mill, once it started, wasn't exactly something you could just ignore. Around here, no ignoring something so prevalent. The townsfolk had done enough to have as much fun with her mother as they possibly could. Then, after the fun was over, they had nothing nice to say. How could the men have nothing nice to say at the same time they were getting her into bed? How the hell did that work?

What if her mother really had done exactly what Nana had said? What if Daisy had enticed every one of them through some witchy energy work to fall in love with her? Her mother had broken up a dozen marriages in this town alone and who knew how many from other places during Daisy's periods of absence. As much as Danica hated to say it, her mother should be pitied for her frantic panic to get away. Yet nobody else cared. As long as Daisy put out, they were happy to take, until she died, and then everything changed.

How did that work?

Danica had no freaking clue. Of course she had always held back with people, like Jace, who had been her friend and maybe a boyfriend of sorts—though they'd never consummated the relationship, not for lack of trying on his part. She'd always been afraid of the risk that she could become a mother in the process.

The coffeepot gurgled along, as Benji trotted to the bedroom to say hi to Nana. As Danica followed him, she poked her head around the doorway to her grandmother's bedroom. She saw Nana was fully awake now, cuddling the small dog. "How are you feeling?" she asked.

Nana looked over at her, her gaze so sharp it was hard to believe she was close to dying. "I feel good," she replied in a surprisingly strong voice.

"Good. I put coffee on. You ready for a cup?"

Her grandmother nodded. "Coffee would be perfect," she said, with a smile.

"Are you getting up, or am I bringing it in here?"

She looked at her in horror. "What? I'm not an invalid. I'll be up in a few minutes." And, with that, she waved Danica off.

Danica headed back to the kitchen, pouring two cups of coffee while wondering how a woman could seem to bounce back so easily. Yes, Nana was a healer, but she was now an old healer. Yet she still seemed to wield her gift. Did it have anything to do with the weird stuff she was doing in there earlier? As soon as Nana joined her at the kitchen table and got settled with her coffee, Danica asked her.

"I was meditating," she replied, with a smile, "connecting to the ethers, trying to stay here a little bit longer so I can tell you everything that needs to be told."

Danica nodded. "I'm surprised you saw that. I came in to ensure you were okay."

"You mean to ensure I was alive?" And then she burst out laughing.

Danica shrugged. "I'm not sure what else I should do when you don't respond. I need to know that you're alive."

"No, you don't. You'll find out soon enough that I'm not. I'm not mad at you for that. We both know my time is coming, and I certainly don't begrudge you the need to check up on me."

Danica frowned and stayed quiet, because something was off about her grandmother's voice.

"What's the matter?" Nana asked.

"Something's different," Danica studied her. "You don't sound the same."

Her gaze narrowed. "In what way do I not sound the same?"

"I don't know. It's hard for me to describe it, but definitely something is different."

"Different isn't bad. It's just different."

"I know that. I'm just saying your voice sounds different."

"No, it's the way you are so hyper-focused on me," her grandmother argued.

Danica took a deep breath. "That is an example right there," she began, trying not to word it too callously. "Normally you wouldn't argue with me. Normally you would just let it roll off your back. Yet, right now, you seem to be riled up about something."

Her grandmother opened her mouth, as if to dispute something, and then closed her mouth again. "Maybe there is some truth to it after all," she mumbled, but she didn't elaborate.

"Do you want to explain that to me?" Danica asked.

"No. … I don't feel like explaining a lot of things to you."

Danica stared at her. "*Okay*. I'm not sure what this is all about, but maybe I should just leave you alone for a little while."

"Maybe you should," Nana declared in a snappy tone, glaring at her.

Danica let out her breath in a rush. "Okay, fine." She slowly got up and moved toward the back door, calling Benji with her.

"You'll just walk away like that?" Nana asked in the same combative tone.

"Not necessarily," Danica replied, "but obviously you don't want company right now."

Her grandmother blinked several times and then slowly nodded, sagging in place. "Maybe you should just leave me alone for a little bit. I will collect myself, and I promise I'll be more normal when you come back," she replied.

The *more normal when you come back* comment really worried Danica. She wasn't sure how to respond to that, so she just nodded. "Do you want me to stay? Or do you want me to go?"

"Go. Just go," she muttered. "It'll be fine."

Danica had no other recourse except to leave, yet it bothered her to see her grandmother in whatever this state was. Danica stepped out of the house and stood on the porch, sipping her coffee. Benji was at her side, whining, obviously not happy with what he had seen either. "I don't know what's going on," she said, petting the dog. "She's definitely different at the moment."

She looked around and then called out, "Stefan, you there?" A grumble came in response in her head. "Did you see my grandmother? She's different, as if it's not really her." Stefan snapped into her head, to the point that she reached up with both hands and groaned.

Sorry, sentences like that are guaranteed to grab my atten-

tion.

Danica groaned. "*Great.* Maybe we could have a quieter discussion, like a phone call or something."

Almost instantly her cell phone rang. She stared down at it and muttered, "I didn't even give you my number."

You want a phone call or not? he snapped.

When she answered the phone, the pressure in her head eased.

"Now, what do you mean that she was different?" Stefan asked.

"She was combative. Her voice didn't sound the same. She didn't talk the same." She relayed part of the conversation and tried to describe what had caught her attention. "She even told me that I should probably leave now, and she would be 'better' or 'different' or 'normal' or something when I came back."

"*Hmm.*" Stefan gave an audible sigh. "Sounds like you've got a hell of a mystery going on at your place."

"I'm just not sure how any of this is supposed to work."

"There is no *supposed to,*" Stefan replied, "particularly when spirits are involved."

"*Are* spirits involved?" she questioned.

"This didn't sound like a spirit. It sounded more like a possession. Somebody may have been speaking through her."

"Oh, good God," Danica whispered. "I really don't like hearing that."

"No, I'm sure you don't. However, you also don't know a lot of the stuff that's been going on in that house, which is starting to affect your grandmother."

"She's lived here all her life. I can't imagine that anything going on in this house is just affecting her at this point," she murmured. "Maybe before, when my mother was alive. Maybe that affected her. I don't know."

"Do you know what happened to your mother?" he asked.

"She committed suicide, after she tried to kill me. No, let me rephrase that." She spoke bitterly. "After she *did* kill me."

Silence came on the other end. "I'm sorry?"

"You heard me," Danica stated, "I was declared dead and woke up in the morgue drawer."

"That was you?" he asked.

She stared down at the phone in shock. "What?" she asked. "You know about that?"

"I know a little bit about that."

"*That's nice*," she quipped. "I don't even know who you are. Yet you apparently know about the strange incident that completely changed my life."

"First of all, waking up in a morgue drawer would change anybody's life," he replied. "That couldn't have been an easy experience. Second, add to that how your mother put you there has to be one of the hardest things to sort through."

"Absolutely," she muttered, "and none of it makes any sense."

"So, your mother did commit suicide?"

"Yes, as far as anybody could say, she committed suicide. Although the townsfolk may believe I killed her."

"Oh, that's fascinating," Stefan murmured in a completely conversational tone.

She stared down at the phone. "I don't even know why I'm talking to you," she admitted, with a hint of a chuckle. "That makes no sense to me."

"You're talking to me because I understand this stuff,

and you have limited people to talk to."

"You are correct on both points. I really don't know anybody who can help me with this woo-woo stuff but you and Nana," she replied.

"If you ask me, that's because you refuse to get involved. … Oh, but you haven't refused to get involved at all, have you?"

Danica sighed. "When it dominates your life, as it's always dominated mine, I'm involved in a certain amount of woo-woo stuff," she admitted, "but I'm not crazy involved, like my grandmother."

"No, but you are doing *some* energy work. So that's good. It should at least allow us to move you faster forward with that as a base."

"Faster toward what?" she asked in confusion.

He snorted. "I really wish she would tell you her secret."

"Yeah, I really wish she would too. But right now, the woman in there, she ain't telling me anything, and I'm not sure she's even the woman I thought she was."

"That's a very disconcerting comment," Stefan noted, as he took a moment. "I'll get back to you." With that, he was gone.

She stepped through the grass, groaning. "It would be nice if things would just fall into place every once in a while," she muttered out loud, "instead of being this massive struggle."

Then someone across the way replied, "Too bad. Now it won't be a struggle at all. You should never have lived. You know that too."

She turned to face the man, just as a shot rang out—strong, steady, and deadly. It pierced through her upper thigh and dropped her in place. Even as she lay here, she heard him calling out, "Excellent," and he was gone.

She mentally reached out to Stefan, but he was there already.

I'm here. I saw what happened. I heard what happened, he stated. *Help is on the way. You stay alive now. Do you hear me? You can't die now.*

"Are you sure?" she asked, almost welcoming the darkness below. "It would be a good end for me."

No, Stefan snapped. *It would not.*

"Yes, it would," she whispered. "Not a whole lot of good has been in my life."

Yet even more good is coming, Stefan shared, *but you must survive this first.*

She would have laughed, but the icy coldness moving up her body wasn't doing anything to keep her in control or cognizant. She closed her eyes and, with a very long, slow breath, whispered, "Say goodbye to Nana for me."

CAMERON GOT UP, dressed, and headed for the kitchen. He was two steps away from reaching for the coffeepot when a thought slammed into his head.

Go to Danica, NOW.

He didn't even give himself a chance to think or to question it. He bolted out the door, barefoot, and raced across the property to Harriet's house.

As he arrived, he couldn't see anything amiss, not until he got closer to the porch and saw a body on the lawn. He raced up to find Danica, staring at the skies, her eyes open. A midthigh wound gushed arterial blood, and it appeared to be a bullet wound. He went into full doctor mode.

In between trying to deal with her and calling for assistance, he didn't even question the instincts that had him running to Danica. Chaos ensued for the next forty minutes, until he got her into the emergency room and up to surgery, where he closed up the leg wound and fixed the arterial bleed.

By the time he was done, he stepped out of the OR to see a deputy standing there, staring at him. Cameron looked at him blankly.

"She was shot, was she?" Benson asked.

Benson's tone did not sit right with Cameron. "Yes," he confirmed. "You should go back to the property to find the bullet though. It wasn't in her leg."

He nodded. "Has she been conscious? Did she say anything?"

"I haven't spoken to her. I found her on her back in the grass, and I just went into emergency mode." He stared at his hands. "I haven't had coffee or even the chance to think."

"You have no idea what happened?" The deputy pressed him for more information.

Yet Cameron had no more to give. "No. I have no idea what happened, and she won't be awake for a few hours."

The deputy pursed his lips. "Damn. I really need to speak with her."

"You can try all you want, but she's still under general anesthesia and will be out for hours," he stated. "So, that will be a waste of time."

The deputy looked way more than stumped.

"Better for you to go back and find the bullet, which I didn't even think about trying to look for because I was trying to keep her alive," Cameron explained, as he walked with the deputy toward the front of the hospital.

"So, you're on call right now?"

"No, I'm not, but Dr. Cumberback was already busy, and Danica needed treatment immediately." He scrubbed his hands over his face. "I'm not even sure what the hell happened. It's been such a blur," he murmured.

"I am sure it has been."

Cameron studied the deputy, trying to decipher his meaning, but then let it go. "Let me know if you find anything, will you?" Benson just nodded as he walked out of the hospital, but Cameron noted his stiff gait. "She didn't do this to herself," he called out.

The deputy turned and asked him, "Are you sure? It would be a hell of a way to throw suspicion off her." And, with that, he quickly left the hospital.

Cameron stared after him in shock. He looked around at the other nurses, but nobody would meet his eye. "Seriously? You guys think Danica shot herself, hitting an artery?"

"The artery would have been a mistake of course," replied one of the nurses, trying not to catch his gaze. "If the deputy thinks it's not impossible, maybe she did."

"It's just a leg wound," one of the other nurses pitched in.

All this grated on his nerves too damn much. He thought about the mess her leg had been in, that he had just tried to fix, and to hear them say, *It's just a leg wound*, made his blood boil.

"I don't think we can consider what I fixed as *just* anything," he snapped, glaring at them. "I don't know what the hell is happening around here or why everybody is all of a sudden on the *I hate Danica* train," he snapped, trying hard to control his anger. "Yet she's a patient here, and she will be treated with the respect and the highest level of care that we offer to anyone in this facility."

When no one spoke up, he growled, "Is that understood?" He turned and glared at the nurses.

One by one, everyone just shrugged and nodded. He knew that Danica would get whatever care they gave, and it might not be the best, which made him sick to his stomach.

If she wouldn't get the proper care here, he would ensure that she was moved somewhere else or that he stayed here with her. And, for the umpteenth time, he wondered if this hospital should even stay open.

If this was how they treated patients they didn't like, maybe it shouldn't remain open.

As long as Danica was here and remained in danger, from her shooter and even this hospital staff, he would stay and keep her safe.

THE BITCH IS in the hospital. Damn. If she hadn't jerked at the last minute, surely the bullet would have done a better job. He racked his brain over the whole incident. He couldn't believe he had just caught her in the leg, when he had aimed for her heart. Afterward he'd been so panicked that he ran off.

Should have stayed to finish the bitch.

He stared down at his hands, then looked back to where she was being slowly moved to a hospital room and realized that he really had no choice. He adjusted the color of his white coat he'd snagged from the doctor's office and considered his options.

Maybe I still can.

Resolutely he turned and followed the gurney, as it carried her upstairs.

CHAPTER 18

DANICA WOKE SLOWLY, the pain muffling her brain, along with some disorienting images. When she finally managed to open her eyelids, Cameron smiled down at her. She blinked several times, trying to clear the wooliness from her brain. "What happened?"

He looked around to check if they were alone, then leaned closer and whispered, "You were shot." Her eyes widened in horror. He nodded, placed a restraining hand on her arm, and added, "Don't move. You're in the hospital, and you'll be fine."

"I don't feel fine," she whispered. "It hurts."

"And it will for a bit," he replied in a soothing tone. "You took a bullet through your leg, and it hit an artery. I had to rush you to surgery, but you will recover. It was a fairly straightforward surgery."

She blinked. "Who shot me?" she asked.

He shook his head. "I didn't see anyone, so I don't know. But definitely a bullet went through that leg. I sent the deputy to the house to look for it. It had to be somewhere in the vicinity."

Her eyelids closed again, as she contemplated what he said. "Why would somebody hate me enough to shoot me?"

"That I don't know," he muttered, "but the deputy is chomping at the bit to talk to you."

She shook her head and shifted in the bed, trying to get up to leave.

"Whoa, whoa," Cameron said, pushing her back down. "You're not going anywhere."

She stared up at him. "I'm not talking to the deputy," she declared flatly. "You just fix me up and let me go home."

He stared at her in surprise and frowned. "I get that you have a problem with being in the hospital, and I realize it's probably the last place you want to be, but I can't let you just walk out of here, not when I know how badly you're hurt."

"But you fixed me up, right?" she asked persuasively.

He still frowned but nodded. "Yes, I did, to a certain extent. But that doesn't mean you'll be 100 percent and certainly not right now."

"I will be 100 percent," she declared. "Honestly there's nothing more you can do for me here that I can't do for myself."

He sat back and stared at her. "I get it. You're completely paranoid about hospitals, after waking up downstairs in the morgue."

"No," she countered, "you don't understand. It's way more than paranoid. Until you've had your life flipped like I did, you don't realize the power of one incident and how it can affect you," she muttered, as she stared up at him. "Surely you can understand that I cannot stay here."

"Not wanting to be here is not the same thing as trying to leave before you're in any condition to do it."

"I don't have insurance, remember?" she snapped. "Believe me when I say that I don't have the cash to cover what you just did."

"So, what was I supposed to do?" he asked, rocking back

on his heels. "Leave you to bleed out on the lawn?"

She shrugged. "That would have been an easier answer all the way around."

He let out a slow whistle. "Whoa, I don't like hearing that."

She glared at him now. "Doesn't matter whether you do or not. You have no authority to keep me here against my will, and I want out."

"You can't even walk," he noted.

"I'll be fine," she stated forcefully. "Just release me and let me go."

He shook his head. "The only way you're getting out and going home is if somebody can look after you, and that person needs to understand how to stop a bleed—in case you open the wound," he explained. "And you don't have anybody,"

She winced. "Thank you very much for that reminder."

"I'm not trying to be mean. I'm just trying to ensure you stay safe."

She looked up at him. "Do you really think I'll be safe in here?" she asked, her anger strengthening her voice. "I doubt even one nurse here would look after me."

That was too close to what he had already wondered and worried about himself. Instantly he felt the heat washing over his cheeks, as he stared at her.

She nodded. "You already considered that, which is why you're sitting here."

"I don't *know* that," he corrected. "I would really hope not."

"This place should have been closed a long time ago," she muttered. "I don't know why you're trying to keep this hospital open, but it needs to be shut down."

"You blame the doctor for what happened to you ten years ago?" he inquired.

She looked up at him. "I don't know that I blame anybody. All I can tell you is what happened, what I experienced. So you tell me. … As a doctor, how could that have possibly happened?"

"I've thought about it a lot," he admitted, "and I don't have an answer for you."

"Right. Exactly. And, if you think I'm safe here, I'm telling you that you're wrong."

"You're possibly correct." He nodded. "And, yes, that's why I've been sitting here, making sure that, when you wake up, I'm here to talk to you," he shared, looking at her intently. "Obviously I want you to know that you'll be okay."

"Sure," she replied, "but you also can't guarantee that, especially if I stay here."

"But you can't look after yourself and your grandmother, and she surely can't look after you," he argued.

"I know that," she muttered, slumping back onto the hospital bed.

"Stay overnight. Let me double-check that you're not bleeding anymore. Then maybe I can get you patched up and out of here," he suggested.

"If you would just go away and leave me alone for a bit, I might be able to heal this." At her words, he stopped and slowly pivoted back to her. "Don't even ask. Just go."

"If *that* works," he declared, "we'll definitely talk."

"No, we won't," she snapped at him. "I've spent a lifetime dealing with this town's conspiracy shit, and I'm not adding to it now."

"Even if you can heal yourself?" he questioned.

"We'll see," she muttered. "That's more my grandmother's trick, not mine."

"What?" he asked in shock. "Are you telling me that she works as a healer?" he asked, dumbfounded.

She groaned, letting out a big sigh. "If you've got questions for Nana, ask her. Now I'm tired." In truth, she was damn exhausted, and it was all she could do to keep her eyes open.

"Then sleep," he said. "It's the best thing for you. And I'll be right here when you wake up," he reassured her.

She snorted. "You don't have to."

"Yes, for some reason, I do."

She quickly closed her eyelids, muttering, "You do you," and drifted off to sleep. When she woke the second time, he was still here. She opened her eyes and glared at him.

He smiled. "Yes, I'm still here," he announced cheerily. "And, yes, you're still in the hospital. No, I haven't released you."

At that, she groaned and whispered, "You should. You'll just cause trouble."

"How do you know that?" he asked.

"Because that's what my world does," she stated. "It causes trouble. Apparently I'm the catalyst for all kinds of shit," she muttered.

"You can't go through life believing that." She opened her eyes, frowning at him. "That's what I've been told by this town and its people all my life—those first eighteen years when I was living here. I'm an adult now, and, no, I don't have to believe it. The problem is, other people do," she pointed out, "and that changes everything." With that, she closed her eyelids and fell asleep again. He stayed.

When she woke the third time, she stared at him

through half-lowered lids. He dozed gently in the chair beside her.

When she moved ever-so-slightly, he bolted to his feet and stared down at her. When he saw her, relief lit up his face.

"I wasn't trying to run away, you know?"

He studied her for a long moment and raised both eyebrows. "But you would have if you could have."

She frowned. "I gather you will condemn me for that?"

He shrugged. "Let's just say, as a medical professional, you, as a patient, are a nightmare."

She smirked. "Maybe," she quipped, as she gently moved her bandaged leg, "but maybe I'm the opposite of a nightmare."

He frowned at her and asked, "What do you mean?"

"The leg feels pretty good. I won't go run any marathons," she murmured, "but I'm not sure it's as bad as you made it out to be."

He walked closer, flipped back the sheet covering her leg, and looked down at it. "I need to change the dressing and check for bleeding anyway." He eyed her closely, his gaze searching. "So, I'll go grab the stuff I need."

"You do that," she said all too cheerily. "I'll just stay here and rest."

"If only I could believe that," he muttered, glancing at her expression.

"I promise," she murmured, wondering at a man who would stay in the room with his patient to ensure she was okay.

He studied her for a long moment and then nodded. "See that you do." Then he quickly walked out of the room.

As soon as he left, she sat up, then rested on the edge of

the bed. Her feet were now on the floor, yet she hadn't put any weight on them. With a deep breath, she stood up, pleasantly surprised that she could stand on her injured leg.

Danica nodded, as a childhood memory hit her. She had never talked about this trick of hers but had known how to do it since she was little. She was never the kind to go to a hospital, or even to the doctor. Now, here she was, once again proving that the power of the mind, the power of energy, was an immeasurable force.

She stood up, evenly balancing all her weight on both legs, then took a tentative step and another and another. She walked to the bathroom, quickly used the facilities, then washed her face and hands. Nothing like the grungy feeling after such an unpleasant experience, both of getting shot and having surgery.

She opened the bathroom door and slowly moved back into her hospital room, keeping an eye on the floor to ensure she didn't trip on anything. Any sudden jarring would hurt the most. She was much better, but she certainly wasn't fully healed yet. When she got an alert in her senses, she looked up to find Cameron staring at her in shock.

"What are you doing?" he asked in a hoarse whisper.

She groaned. "Exactly what it looks like I'm doing," she murmured. "I'm walking to the bed, so you can change the dressing." And, with that, she took the last few steps, clambered up onto the bed, and stretched out her leg.

"You shouldn't be able to walk," he muttered, glaring at her.

She shook her head. "That's because you come from your very narrow-minded physician personality and perspective," she explained, "instead of being open to all the other things in the world that can happen."

He took several deep breaths and then bent over her leg and gently removed the dressing from her wound.

She leaned forward to take a close look at it too. "Okay, it's not doing too badly," she murmured.

He stared at the wound, over at her, and asked, "*Not too bad*? This looks like it's two weeks down the road of healing."

"Yes, but I've always healed quickly," she noted, with a one-arm shrug. "Just accept it and move on."

He repeated, "We will have a talk about this."

She groaned. "Do we have to?"

"Yes," he declared, as he quickly redressed the leg. "Obviously you can go home."

"Thank you," she said cheerfully. "So, something good came out of this after all."

"I'm taking you home."

"Fine," she replied agreeably. "That'll cause no end of rumors though, so you better be prepared for that."

"I really don't give a crap about rumors," he snapped, shaking his head, "but I do give a crap about how the hell you healed your leg."

"I can't really explain. It just … I can't."

"There's always been stories," he muttered, "but I never put any stock in them."

"Maybe you should now," she suggested. "Healers have been around since forever."

"I just never had exposure to any," he acknowledged. "Why the hell, if you can do this for yourself, why aren't you doing this to help your fellow man?"

She stared at him. "Yeah, you mean the fellow man who treats me so well out there?"

He flushed and nodded. "I get it. Probably a few people

in this world are not deserving of your help. However, plenty of people out there are."

She shrugged. "Maybe, but also an awful lot of people out there would call me a witch and would lynch me and would hang me from the closest tree, and this town is full of them," she murmured.

CAMERON WAS STILL in shock over what he'd seen, but Danica was right. The people here would take her healing gifts the wrong way. Hell, even getting her out of the hospital would be a challenge. He walked out to the front desk and went through the process to check her out himself.

The receptionist came over and asked, "What's going on?"

"Danica's leaving."

"Leaving?" she asked in shock. She frowned, nervously sat down, and muttered, "Of course she is. I hope she dies from it too."

He didn't even know what to say, the hate was so blatant. "That's a pretty rough thing to say."

"No, it's not," she argued bitterly. "Every time she's around, something weird and freaky goes on in this place."

Having just seen the evidence of it with his own eyes, he didn't really have a comeback. By the time she finished racking up the bill, he understood one of the reasons why Danica wanted out in a hurry.

It was an enormous amount of money, even with those major discounts Cameron got as a doctor on staff. He quickly used his credit card to pay for it, while the receptionist stared at him in shock. He shrugged. "I need to get her out of here fast."

"Oh, I'm all about that," she agreed. "If it was your family member, we could have taken a bigger discount."

"Then take a bigger discount because we won't have her sticking around, now will we?"

With that, she quickly adjusted the bill yet again, down to a fraction of the original cost. He shook his head. "Now, if only everybody else's medical bills were quite so reasonable."

"Then we wouldn't have the money to run the damn hospital," she muttered. "You've got to keep that in mind too, Doc."

Not anything he could say to that because she was right. Yet some of these bills were just so extreme that it made no sense to him. He had to wonder if they were increased for certain people, and he damn-near asked her about it. He decided it wasn't the time and got the added reduction credited back to his card. With her watching him still, Cameron walked off to Danica's room, where she waited for him.

"The bill is paid. Let's go," he said.

Her eyes lit up, only to be quickly masked with fear. He wasn't sure what the hell was going on with her now, but obviously she wasn't happy that he'd paid her bill.

"Payment is always required," she muttered, looking at him, as he pushed the wheelchair toward her. "I'm not going out in that."

"Yes, you are, and it's not up for discussion," he stated in an authoritative tone that brooked no argument. "Already there is enough cause for people to be scared of you. Let's not add to it."

As she was still in a hospital, she had limited options. She shrugged, and, as if realizing what he suggested made sense, she sat down in the chair. He wrapped his coat around her. dropped the bag of her personal belongings on her lap. He quickly pushed her out toward the front door.

Thankfully the hospital was fairly calm, if not empty right now, so Cameron got her out to his car in no time. With nobody seeing him outside, at least he hoped, he helped her into his vehicle, reminding her to act like she was still badly injured for the sake of anyone watching.

She did as he asked, and, when he got around to the driver's side and drove out of the parking lot, she muttered, "Do you really think anybody will care how I act?"

"I don't know," he admitted, shaking his head. "I don't understand what's going on. This little hospital that I used to love is turning into something I don't recognize."

"That's because the town's prejudice and fear is showing up," she declared. "Remember that we're getting closer to Halloween. They'll probably be a lot nicer afterward."

He glanced over at her, frowning. "What do you know about all that Halloween crap?"

"I don't, really. Remember how I've been gone for the last ten years? So I only know a little bit about what my grandmother told me, and she's still withholding information from me, which kinda pisses me off. Therefore, I can confirm that you won't like hearing even the little bit that I know of either."

"The shit I am hearing is already stuff I don't like, so maybe you could fill me in."

"When we get home, I'll make you a cup of coffee," she offered, "and, if you'll tell me how much the bill is, I'll pay you back."

"You don't need to," he countered in a huff, raising his hands. "Apparently I didn't even need to help you. You could have done it yourself."

"I'm not so sure about that," she murmured. "Some things are easier if I take over, but to have a foreign object go through my leg like that would be really tough."

"Really tough?" He snorted.

"Yes, really tough," she murmured.

He didn't say anything for a long time. Now, back at Harriet's place, he helped Danica out of his vehicle, and she walked slowly to her RV, feeling more tired than she was happy about.

"Not quite so good, *huh*?" he asked.

"All I need is a little more time," she shot back, then looked at him sideways.

He nodded, then waited until she had the RV open and helped her step up and inside. "Where's Benji?" he asked.

She looked around and shrugged. "I'll say with Nana. At least I hope so," she murmured.

"Shall I go check?"

She nodded. "That would be good." Danica watched him leave. He turned to see her slowly close the RV door.

He headed to the main house and knocked. When a shout came from inside, he pushed it open and stepped inside the living room, where Benji greeted him, jumping around his ankles. He smiled, bent down to pet him, then looked over at Harriet. "She's doing fine."

She nodded, albeit stiffly. "Good. So, it's started then." She sat down on the comfy couch, with a *thump*.

"What has started?" he asked, looking at her.

She hesitated, narrowing her gaze at him. "You won't understand."

"No, I might not understand," he countered, feeling the same anger as everybody kept cutting him out of discussions because he supposedly wouldn't understand. "That doesn't mean I shouldn't know whatever the hell is going on. It affects Danica."

Harriet smiled. "Of course. It absolutely does affect her, more than you could possibly know."

"I just brought home a woman who had been shot and should be in the hospital for several more days and thereafter need therapy for her leg, but she's looking damn fine already, walking around, completely mobile right now. So, if somebody could explain how that happened, that would be wonderful."

Harriet studied Cameron for a long moment, then nodded. "Let's just say she's special."

"I already understand that," he declared, "but *special* apparently depends on your perspective."

Harriet cracked a smile at that and nodded. "Put on the teakettle, and I'll give you some of it," she conceded.

"Why only some of it?" he asked in exasperation, as he walked over, found the teakettle, filled it with water, and plugged it in. He pivoted and leaned against the counter, with the teakettle starting to bubble happily behind him. He had an unencumbered view right into the living room, so he could speak directly to Harriet. "I don't understand how Danica did what she did."

"I'm sure you've heard of healers."

"Sure, I have," he admitted. "I've just never seen it happen before my eyes."

"So, this is only new to you because you haven't been exposed to it before," she stated, giving him a smile. "That really isn't anything for you to worry about."

He groaned. "Maybe not, but it's still shocking," he muttered.

"Only if you're not open to it," she argued, eyeing him intently. "And, if you're not open to it, you really don't belong here."

He stared at her for a long moment. "Is it *here* in this house that I don't belong, or is it here in this town that I don't belong?" he asked. Then, without allowing Harriet time to respond, Cameron raved on, "Because there seems to be an awful lot of judgment and predisposition to, shall I call it, *hatred* for you and yours."

"There is. It's gotten worse in the last few years as I've gotten older too," she murmured, "and that's sad."

"Yes, it is sad," he agreed, "but it's not as if anybody ever gives us any explanation to help us understand."

"Why should we?" she asked, looking at him.

"So you don't appear to be a witch," he replied in exasperation.

"So what if I am?" she asked, looking at him, a small smile playing around the corner of her lips.

"If you are," he stated, "I would have wanted you in the hospital, helping some of my patients who weren't doing so well."

"And years ago that's exactly where you would have found me," she shared, with a cackle. "Not that anybody will let me anywhere close to the hospital now." He stared at her, and she nodded. "You should check into that a little more deeply," she suggested, "before you start flinging arrows. I used to go help a lot at the hospital, even before the death of my husband—who was a doctor, by the way," she said pointedly.

He stared at her. "What?"

"Yes," she confirmed, "he was a doctor, and he worked at this hospital. Since his death many years ago, things have started to fall apart."

"I don't even know what to say to that," he muttered. "I had no idea."

"Of course not, and nobody will tell you either," she shared, with a groan. "Nobody will tell you the truth. They'll just give you bits and pieces of their version of the lie."

"But you're not exactly helping to counter that either," he pointed out.

She smiled. "No, I'm not. Can't say I'm too bothered about answering your curiosity as well," she declared, "but, as far as my granddaughter goes, she needs to be protected."

"She told me about waking up dead."

"Did she tell you where?"

He nodded. "In a drawer in the morgue."

"Yes, but even she is unwilling to take a look at why."

"I don't understand."

"Correct. I know you don't," she replied, with a wave of her hand. "That's part of the problem. There's just so much you are capable of understanding, and you're starting from too far away, so I don't have time to get you up to speed," she grumbled.

He felt that same anger whispering through him. "It would be nice if somebody would," he snapped, "because I don't understand what's happening or why Danica's hated so much, all because she woke up from being dead."

Looking at him, Harriet sighed. "And, if they knew how much she could heal herself, the townsfolk would be here in a snap, ready to torch this house."

"You sound as if you have firsthand knowledge of that."

"Sure, I do. They tried once before."

"When was that?"

"A long time ago," she began, "when my husband was

alive. They decided that I was some witch because of my healing gift. So I could never go back and help heal anybody else publicly again." Harriet took a moment to collect herself. "That was a great sadness for me because so many people could use help healing, but what could I do? I have been chased out of the hospital, and, during the night, they tried to burn down my house," she murmured.

"What?"

"Yeah. My husband passed away soon afterward, and my life has never been the same again."

"I'm sorry," Cameron whispered. "It's obviously not easy if you become the brunt of that fear."

"And that's exactly what it is," she stated, looking at him sharply. "It's fear. People were afraid of me, my daughter, and my granddaughter, and that's not fair."

"It might not be fair, but fear is caused partly by ignorance. So, if you don't speak up and explain what's going on, what do you expect?"

She shrugged. "Me? I don't expect anything, especially not in this day and age." She looked into the kitchen, as the teapot whistled lightly. "People are just so busy being full of themselves and not wanting to help anybody else that they aren't willing to get to the real truth."

"Yet I am here, and I am willing to get the truth," he pointed out in frustration, "yet I'm not hearing you speak it."

She snorted. "You wouldn't recognize the truth if you heard it."

He stared at her, a little dumbfounded to hear how strong her voice was and how adamant she was about his position on this. "You really don't know anything about me," he murmured.

"Possibly I don't," she admitted. "So I'm as guilty as you are of falling into that same judgmental trap."

"And it would be nice if you wouldn't do the same," he countered, "because I would very much like to know what's going on. I'm not happy at what I'm seeing in terms of the town's attitude toward your granddaughter."

"Did anybody see you leave and take her out of there?"

"No, the receptionist helped me with her bill, but she wasn't very friendly about it. She became very helpful though, when I explained that the sooner we got it done, the sooner Danica would be gone."

Harriet laughed, but it was a bitter laugh. "Yeah, and she's probably from one of the families I helped for years. Only now I'm some pariah, and so is my granddaughter. People forget and don't want to be reminded that, for many decades, I am the reason a lot of them survived," she murmured. "Now all they do is get things their way and forget about the help they were given."

"And yet you gave the help freely, I presume?"

"Of course," she said. "Help that's not freely given is not help at all."

He smiled at that. "I don't know how true that is—given my profession, where I get paid for helping—but I can imagine that a lot of people would prefer to forget when they got help from a nontraditional healer. Especially if they considered it done in pity or as charity."

She nodded. "They sure do," she agreed vehemently. "That's very unfortunate because people need to remember when they are given help because that person might need help themselves."

"Is that what happened? Did you need help, and nobody was here for you?" He looked at her for a long moment.

"You really don't understand what it's like to be raised in an area where everybody is afraid of you. My poor daughter went through hell here."

"Why didn't you leave?" he asked. "If it was that bad, you could have left."

"I could never sell this place," she muttered, looking around. "I'm tied to it in many ways. My concern now is what will happen to it when I'm gone."

"It's a house. What difference does it make?"

A perceptible shudder shook the house.

He frowned, took in his surroundings, and noted, "I didn't think it would be that windy today." When he looked back at Harriet, a knowing smile played on her lips. He glared at her. "See? You're just holding back secrets, and I'm asking you for the truth."

"Yeah, maybe," she agreed, "and maybe I need to hold back on those secrets, since it will all change, and it will change soon enough."

"And yet you do realize that somebody shot your granddaughter today, right? Am I the only one who's concerned about that?"

"No, I am too," Harriet replied. "I'm trying to figure out who would still hate her so much. My best guess would be your brother."

Cameron felt like he'd been tossed into some crazy storm with her words. "Why would you think that?" he asked hoarsely.

"Because he's threatened to shoot Danica, of course—though people who threaten don't necessarily carry out their threats," she murmured, then looked over at the teakettle. "You can make the tea now."

Feeling like he was in some bad comedy movie, Cameron made the tea and brought it over to the coffee table in the living room, where she sat nearby on the couch. "Why does Jace hate Danica?"

Harriet sighed and faced him. "What do you know about your family?"

He frowned at her. "The same as everybody else. My parents were born in California, ended up in Maine for a bunch of years, and then resettled here on the Oregon coast, where my father was a doctor in this town for decades, working at the same hospital where I now serve," he recited. "Why? What's that got to do with anything?"

"Did they ever have kids?"

"Obviously, yes, me and my brother," he pointed out, staring at her. "What are you talking about?"

Harriet nodded. "What if Jace isn't your brother?"

"What do you—what? What?" he asked, staring at her, feeling like the bad movie had just taken an even uglier turn. "What are you getting at?"

"Your brother's adopted. You know that, right?"

"No, I don't know that," he declared, shaking his head. "I'm pretty sure he's my father's son. They're the spitting image of each other."

"Oh, that could be genetically possible," she confirmed, with a nod. "He's also my grandson."

CHAPTER 19

DANICA HAD BEEN allowed into the main house, via the back door into the kitchen, her instincts driving her forward. She didn't know exactly what was wrong, but definitely something was off. As she walked into the living room, she saw both her grandmother and Cameron sitting on the couch, talking.

When the subject turned to Cameron's brother, Jace, Danica winced. No way her grandmother would keep quiet on this one. Danica reached the living room just in time to hear her grandmother drop the bomb on him.

Cameron stared at her grandmother in shock, then bounced to his feet, exclaiming, "Like hell."

She nodded sadly. "You need to hear me out," she urged.

He started pacing. "Why the hell should I hear you out?" he muttered. "Absolutely no way that's for real."

She stared at him and waited until he stopped pacing. Then she caught sight of Danica in the kitchen doorway. Nana's frown became more pronounced. "You should *not* be out of bed," she snapped.

Danica moved slowly, accepting Cameron's help, as she crossed over to the big easy chair. "Hopefully enough tea is in there for three," she muttered.

Cameron snorted. "I don't want any," he declared bitterly. "And, if you don't tell me that your grandmother is full of shit with what she just said, I'm out of here."

Danica eyed him steadily. "I didn't find out until after that whole mess with my mother."

He stared at her, then shook his head. "No, no, no, no."

Danica nodded and continued. "I think that's why Jace is so mad at me. We were making out in the back seat, when he got repeated phone calls and finally took it. Immediately he was pretty grossed out, pretty upset, moving away from me, not wanting to touch me. He was yelling at me to get out of his car and to get out of town even. I didn't even understand what he was so angry about, but he broke up with me in the harshest way possible, and I had no clue why. Then I was attacked by my own mother and left for dead. Literally," she pointed out somewhat cheerfully, finding the humor in the situation. "Ever since then, your brother can't look me in the eye. Apparently he somehow found out that I was his half-sister, even before I knew about it."

Cameron sagged down into a chair in front of her and stared.

"I'm sorry. Apparently you didn't know."

"Know? How could I know?" he asked, looking at the two of them. "How could anyone know this?"

Danica hesitated, then looked over at her grandmother. "I didn't know, and I'd gone to school with Jace, began dating him. He's, what, a year older than I am?" she asked, looking at Cameron.

"I don't know." He waved his hands. "Maybe he's a year older than you," he replied, a bit confused. "How old are you?"

"I'm twenty-nine," she replied. "Jace is thirty-two. He'll be thirty-three soon. So can you think back to your family and what it was like back when Jace was born or soon thereafter?"

He stared at her, shook his head, and said, "No, I really can't. I was a toddler."

"Is your mother even *your* mother?" Nana asked Cameron.

He looked at her in confusion, then nodded. "Yes, yes, of—"

"It may not have mattered to you, but it mattered to other people," Nana explained, "and one to whom it mattered a lot was your younger brother, once he found out."

"Good God," Cameron muttered, staring at the older woman. "I can't believe it."

"You shouldn't necessarily believe it, but there will be records that confirm it."

"Yeah, but not those kinds of records. Not adoptions. They could be sealed. They could be private adoptions." Cameron frowned and turned to Danica. "I couldn't find your hospital records from ten years ago, by the way."

"Of course not." Danica snorted. "What they don't understand, they want to destroy."

Nana continued. "I guess my question is whether your parents were married at the time."

"Yes, they were married at the time," he declared. "I was there." Yet he frowned and looked off into the distance.

"Are you sure you're not adopted too?" Nana pressed.

"Yes. No. Hell, I'm not sure of anything now," he snapped. Then he pivoted and looked at the old woman. "Unless you are saying that I am your grandson too."

She shook her head. "No, you are not."

"Thank God for that," he murmured, scrubbing his face.

Harriet's lips twitched, as she shared a knowing glance with Danica. Meanwhile Cameron glared at the old woman. "I'm glad this is all so funny to you," he snapped again, "but you're busy tearing down lives."

"No," Nana argued. "I'm not tearing down any lives. As a matter of fact, I've done my best to keep lives whole and contained by withholding this data. You're the one who's suddenly not too interested in this detail. You wanted to know everything, remember?"

He winced because, of course, he probably had told her that.

Danica motioned to the tea beside him and asked, "Could you pour it, please?"

He groaned, got up, poured tea, and served the ladies, as if that would solve all the problems in the world. As he handed her a cup, he asked Danica, "So you knew Jace was your half-brother?"

"I only found out when I came home after being killed," she shared.

"Damn," he muttered. "Do you have to put it that way?"

She shrugged. "I'm the one who survived my mother attacking me with a knife."

He stopped and frowned. "I never heard all the details of that."

"It's probably just as well," Danica murmured. "For those of us who lived through these things, it's not as if we're trying to hide them or to minimize them. However, those events definitely aren't easy things to remember."

"No. I'm sorry. That was very callous of me."

She waved it off, smiled, then pointed to the chair beside hers. "Come sit."

He sat down in a daze. "It doesn't change anything

though, does it?"

"I don't know," she admitted, with a shrug.

"Does Jace really know?" Cameron asked the old woman.

"He knows," Nana replied, much too quickly this time.

"How did he find out?" Cameron asked.

"I don't know. Probably my daughter told him," she shared in a heavy tone. "Jace did come talk to me back then. He was so angry. He wanted me to tell him that it was all lies and that he wasn't the evil spawn of the crazy lady. He had a few other choice words at the time," she added. "I had to tell him that, as far as I knew, it was true, but he didn't take it well at all."

Danica watched Cameron's face and interjected, "It does, in a way, explain why he hates me so much."

"It doesn't explain it at all." He looked at her in shock. "How the hell does learning that you were adopted also mean that you must hate your sister?" he asked, and he genuinely appeared completely dumbfounded.

She reached out and gently stroked his hand, trying to offer comfort if she could. He clasped her hand tightly, staring down at it. "I couldn't figure out why there was so much hate for you. I didn't see it before I was gone, but it does explain some of it now."

"Yes, it does, but the reality that Jace carries around such hate for me doesn't make anything easier for anyone," Danica murmured. "It would be nice if I could at least be civil with him."

"I don't know that being civil is part of his nature right now," Cameron admitted.

"No, probably not. … I suspect that he's the one who shot me."

At that, Cameron jerked upright and stared at her in shock. "Please don't say that."

She shrugged. "I don't know that for certain, but he's the only one I know of who hates me that much," she murmured. "So, I don't know what to say. Other people hate the idea of me or are frightened of me, but Jace is the only one I can think of who actively goes around hating me, spouting off his superstitions like conspiracy theories."

"It's got to be somebody else." Cameron groaned, looking back over at Danica's grandmother. "So, do you believe Jace is your grandson?"

She nodded. "Are there any other potential siblings?"

Danica jolted at that question.

Cameron frowned at Danica, as she stared at her grandmother.

"You don't know, do you?" Nana asked of Danica.

"I never thought to ask," Danica muttered. "It was always bad enough that Jace was there, hating on me nonstop. So much that it never occurred to me that there could be any more of them." She stared at her grandmother. "Did Daisy have other children out of wedlock?" Just then Danica's heart sank, as she saw the look on her grandmother's face. "Good God," she mumbled, closing her eyes. "Who? Who the hell else did Daisy give birth to, and why didn't you tell me?"

"For one, you left. For two, no good could come of it. I wasn't about to tell the townsfolk about it. Your mother wouldn't have anything to do with either child, and that was probably a good thing for both of them. I'd already lost that part of my family, and I didn't want to lose anybody else, so what was I supposed to do? You talk as if I enjoyed keeping things from you, but the contrary is true. How many secrets could I possibly keep? Particularly when they weren't mine to keep or to tell."

Danica stared at her. "I don't even know what to say," she whispered. "So, all that time when I thought I had no siblings, and then I found out that I have the one," she began, shaking her head, "but he hates me. Now I find out there's another one who I never knew about. Who is it?"

"I don't know," Nana replied, barely above a whisper.

"How can you not know?" Danica asked. "How can you know another sibling exists and not know who it is?"

"That's the truth, child. Daisy told me that she was pregnant. Next thing I knew, she was gone, and God help me," Nana added, "a part of me said, *Good riddance*. She had caused such havoc and such pain when she was here, but then she was back some six months later, and she wasn't pregnant anymore."

"So—" Danica began.

"Yes, I asked her, and, no, she wouldn't tell me. She just continued to become more and more unstable."

"Of course she did," Danica murmured, "and then had me. The last one."

"Yes, you were the last of Daisy's children." Her grandmother nodded. "After that, when she was in the hospital, she *got herself fixed*, as she put it, saying she wasn't having any more brats."

"That explains why she was never the least bit maternal to me. It seemed she never cared because she didn't," Danica shared, trying to hide the hurt in her tone.

"Apparently she wasn't maternal for any of her kids," Cameron stated, turning to look back at Danica's grandmother. "You didn't take them all in?"

"I couldn't," Nana murmured. "It was all I could do to

keep us together. Cameron, your father accepted responsibility for his transgression at the very least, and I know it was always a bit of an issue between him and his wife, but she accepted the child with good graces. Part of the reason for that, I believe, is that he never told her who Jace's mother was."

"Of course," Danica snorted. "If you were raising the crazy lady's bastard son, it's not exactly something you would want the genteel townsfolk to know about."

"Exactly," Nana murmured.

"Jeez," Danica said, looking at her grandmother. Silence fell over the room, as they all thought about the implications.

"I don't know if that explains why Jace hates you so much," Cameron interjected, "but maybe it explains why he got so weird. Back then he was hanging around your mother a lot, and I was afraid it was for the wrong reason."

She looked over at him and winced. "Yeah, I did too. Until I found out."

"Good God," Cameron added. "What if all he was doing was getting to know his real mother? … You know, after the shock of it all had calmed down a bit?"

Danica snorted. "Has he ever calmed down since high school? I would say definitely not. So I don't think he wanted to know the crazy lady who birthed him. What I would believe was that he was trying to get his birth mother off his back because, at that point, I think she realized that her three kids could all make money for her, and money was something that Daisy needed and would always need."

When Cameron stared at her in horror, she nodded. "In high school, I had a part-time job, and every time I got paid, Daisy was right there, looking for her *percentage*, as she called it."

Nana stared at her, obviously shocked to hear about this.

Danica nodded. "It was the only way I could get her off my back," she admitted, with a humorous laugh. "So I paid her from every paycheck. It was like she got her tithe."

"I am so sorry to hear that," Nana muttered, frowning at Danica. "I didn't know she was doing that."

"That's because I didn't tell you. You were struggling to put food on the table as it was."

"Yet you paid every month out of your paycheck for that too, as well."

"Sure, I was living here too," Danica noted. "Believe me that I was trying to get out of here and as far away as I could, but I also refused to be my mother," she declared, giving Nana a sad look. "That was a never-ending cycle of crises."

"Okay, so we've got a few things locked down," Cameron noted, as he now sipped the hot tea in his hand. "I can't believe that Jace had anything to do with your shooting, but obviously somebody has got that hate for you."

"Not just somebody," Danica said pointedly, "but somebody very specific."

He winced. "Fine, Jace is a possible suspect. Yet a lot of other people here hate you and what you're doing too."

"Absolutely. But most of what I do, people don't know about."

Her grandmother eyed Danica with interest.

Danica shrugged. "Some things we just can't *not* do."

Her grandmother studied her for a long moment, and then Nana brightened. "Are you healing?" she cried out in delight.

Danica shook her head and sighed. "I work with a hospital, and I work with certain patients," she shared. "I still have a lot to learn, but I'm getting there. It happened by accident, and—sometimes—sometimes it works, and I feel good when I help somebody. So, I do it," she muttered. She waved her hand at her grandmother. "Don't get too excited." Yet her grandmother laughed and laughed, way more than Danica thought she should have.

Nana smiled, ear to ear. "Oh, my dear, you don't understand. That is brilliant news."

"No, I don't understand. What's so brilliant about it?" Danica asked.

"I needed you to open up those energy pathways," Harriet exclaimed. "I *really* needed you to, and I didn't know how to make it happen. Yet you've gone and done it all on your own."

"That doesn't make me feel any better," Danica muttered, frowning at her grandmother. "What are you talking about?"

Nana hesitated and then smiled. "You'll understand when I'm gone."

"Maybe not," Danica snapped. "Enough with the secrets already." Her grandmother looked over at Cameron, but Danica shook her head. "No, enough secrets, Nana. Let's just get this all out in the open, so we can figure out what we're supposed to do from here on out."

Her grandmother groaned. "You'll be sorry."

"I've been sorry a lot in my life, but Cameron has helped me almost at every step since I came back home," she admitted, then glanced at him. "I haven't been very fair with him either."

"No, you sure haven't," Cameron agreed. "If you already work with a hospital, why the hell won't you work with this one?" Then he held up a hand. "Never mind. I get it. You don't need to answer. Nobody here would appreciate it."

"They might if their loved one was dying and if I was the last possible solution left to them. However, if I saved them or not, they would only continue to hate me—and likely you afterward."

Silence fell over the room, and then somebody pounded on the front door. Danica looked over at her grandmother, one eyebrow raised, and her grandmother shook her head.

"I'm not expecting anybody," she murmured.

The pounding happened again and then again. At that, Cameron hopped up and muttered, "Somebody's interested in talking to you, but they're certainly not being very nice about it."

"Welcome to our world," Nana said, with a shrug. "Lots of people come here banging and crying and screaming at us, sometimes for help, even if the rest of their family doesn't know. Sometimes because they want us to be gone."

Cameron looked to Danica for confirmation, and she nodded. "Ever since I was born, it's been that way,"

"Christ," he muttered, as he strode toward the front door. "No wonder you left."

She smiled at that. "Yes. No wonder."

Nana looked over at her and whispered, "Thank you for coming home."

"It's not an issue," Danica murmured. "It's a sadness that this is the way our world is now."

Nana clarified, "It's not even a case of *now.* It's always been this way and became much worse since your grandfather passed away."

Danica stared at Nana, wondering about that. "I haven't heard very much about him at all."

The old woman sighed. "Not a whole lot to tell. My father lived, he worked, he loved, and he was gone."

Such was the summation of somebody's life, someone who obviously had been well-loved, and yet, retold in such cold terms, it had a clinical sound to it and was not at all pleasant to hear. Danica wanted to say something about it, try to get more information, because she knew that, when her grandmother was gone, all this information would be gone as well. She wanted to know more about her family.

When the doctor returned, the deputy was with him. He looked at the two women and glared.

"What do you want now?" Nana sighed and muttered, "Why can't you leave an old lady in peace?"

"I would like to leave an old lady in peace," he snapped, glaring at her, "but apparently she's up to no good."

Cameron asked, "What are you talking about? What has Harriet supposedly done?"

Danica watched the deputy try to control himself, but it was obvious he had a completely different attitude toward Nana than Danica had expected. "I don't understand what the problem is, Deputy," Danica stated, "but, if you could clarify it, then both my grandmother and I could get back to resting."

His gaze pivoted to her, intensified, and then returned to her grandmother. Danica had no clue what was going on, but it was obvious something was. "The town says you did something," the deputy finally said.

Nana stared at him, a hint of a smile playing at the corners of her mouth. "Something?" she repeated. "Would you care to explain?"

"No, I don't care to explain, but they're on a tirade, and I'm having a hard time holding them back from coming here and burning your house to the ground. You should stop inciting riots."

"Whoa, whoa, whoa." Cameron stepped up, confused and dismayed. "One, you shouldn't be talking to her like that. She's still recovering from a blow to her head. And, two, what the hell are you talking about?"

Benson shrugged. "Something happened today, apparently to set somebody off. I don't know what it was, but it involves Harriet. Any damn time, anytime trouble happens around here, it involves *her*."

Cameron added, "I asked you earlier if you knew Harriet, and you said *barely*, as I recall."

"I barely do know her," he confirmed, "but she and her kind have been around, tormenting this poor town for a long time."

"Harriet and her kind?" Cameron asked. "Are you serious?"

"Of course I'm serious," Benson snapped, "and you'd best stay out of it."

"Stay out of what?" Cameron cried out. "I haven't a clue what you're even talking about."

"Good. Keep it that way." Benson turned to look at Danica. "Now what the hell are you doing?" he asked, facing her, furious. "Shooting yourself just to get attention? Are you after the good doctor here?"

She stared at him, nonplussed. "You seriously think I shot myself?"

"Yeah." He nodded. "No bullet was found on your grandmother's front porch."

"Maybe because I was shot on the front lawn. Maybe because, after I was taken to the hospital," she suggested, "the shooter came and collected it, so that there wouldn't be a bullet for you to find."

He glared at her. "Or maybe nobody else was here in the

first place."

"So, what did I do with the gun that I supposedly shot myself with?" Danica asked.

"That would be nice to know too," he declared, turning back to Nana. "Where's your old gun?"

"Where it always was," she stated calmly. "What is it you're trying to do? Arrest us? Would that make you happy? You want to take me to jail?" Nana asked, an odd note in her tone. "I wonder if I would even last the night. I certainly wouldn't if you put me in with other people, as you well know."

"I don't have accommodations for every nutjob around this place to have their own facilities," the deputy replied in a harsh tone.

Danica had never seen anybody quite so riled, but no way in hell she was letting her grandmother put up with this. As she opened her mouth to stop Benson's insane tirade, Cameron stepped in first.

"Deputy Benson," he snapped, a warning in his tone, "I'm not sure what you're playing at here, but I don't like the tone of your voice or the way you have barged into this place without warning or clarifying what you're even doing here. This is not what I would have expected from you or any local authority," Cameron explained, anger in his tone.

Cameron's disapproval was so clear, and, for many, it would have been an obvious slight, but, for the deputy, he didn't appear to even give a crap. "For all I know, you're a part of this too," the deputy shared, turning to Cameron.

"Part of what?" Cameron asked, raising both hands. "This is unbelievable."

"No, it's not unbelievable," Deputy Benson snapped. "What these weirdos here do, that's unbelievable."

"That's enough," Cameron bellowed, raising his voice. "You came barging in here, screaming all kinds of nonsense. You don't have any proof. You have absolutely nothing but accusations, yet haven't even been clear on those. Is this the way you treat the citizens of this town? I'm absolutely dumbfounded," Cameron continued.

"I don't give a crap if you're dumbfounded or not," the deputy replied, looking at him. "She's obviously got you wrapped around her heart, just like her mother had everybody else in this town bamboozled."

At that, Nana groaned. "Of course he's bringing my daughter back up again, isn't he?" she muttered. "She really made a name for herself."

"Aye, she did at that," the deputy snapped, "and a lot of people have some very long memories."

"Like you?" Danica asked.

"I wasn't here back then." Benson shrugged.

"Are you sure?" she asked, staring at him. "Because you have an awful lot of anger and hate in your tone for Daisy, someone you never had anything to do with."

"I don't need firsthand knowledge to know what's wrong," he snapped, glaring at her, "and you stick to yourself. You stop coming to that damn hospital and don't you dare go and shoot yourself anymore. I'm talking to the judge when he comes through about what we can charge you with," he openly threatened. "Until then, you stay put." He turned his gaze to Danica's grandmother and then raised a finger, the same as he did for Danica. "And you, old woman, you just need to fucking die."

And, with that, he stormed out, slamming the door, leaving the rest of them to stare at each other in silence.

CAMERON WAS STILL dumbstruck and in a fury, like he'd never known before surged through his blood. He hopped up and raced out behind the deputy. Even as he got to the front door, all he could see was the gravel fly, as the deputy pulled out and took off. Cameron slowly returned to the two women, still sitting calmly in the living room. He stared at them suspiciously. "Are you serious right now?"

They looked over at him, as if nothing had happened. Danica smiled. "Welcome to our world," she stated calmly. "You sure you want to be here?"

He sat down in a chair, more confounded at what had just happened than they appeared to be. Was it really possible that this is the behavior these two women had experienced from the locals? "He's a deputy. He's supposed to help you."

"No help for people like us, in case you hadn't gotten the message," Danica explained, staring at him. "When I tell you that we are treated horribly here, you should believe me. That's exactly what I meant."

"Which makes your wanting to buy land here even more confusing to me." He stared at her. "I can't imagine you would do anything but run for the hills when this is over."

"I probably will," Danica admitted, with a nod toward her grandmother. "Nana knows perfectly well that she's dying. She might even know exactly what day."

Her grandmother gave a cackle. "Just think how this used to be such a nice place to live."

"When?" Cameron asked, turning to look at the old woman. "I had no idea. I only came back a year ago and have never seen this side of the townsfolk."

"No, you haven't. And maybe you never will again," Harriet added, with a smile. "If you stay clear of us, you certainly would do better. However, if you insist on sniffing around my granddaughter," she noted indelicately, "then you'll definitely get the same treatment. So, you might want to consider that your job is on the line. Your career, in fact, is likely to be on the line."

He stared at her in shock, as Danica chided her grandmother. "He's not *sniffing around me*, thank you very much. He's been very good to me and to you."

"Sure," she conceded, "but you and I both know where that goes."

Danica let out a sigh. "Nana, that's not necessary."

"Maybe not," she muttered, fatigue in her voice. "I just saw so much of that with your mother."

"May I remind you, once again, that I am not, nor ever will be, my mother," Danica declared, her tone firm, but a wealth of patience was evident, as if she had said it to her grandmother time and time again.

"How can you be so calm?" he asked in wonder.

"Because we know we have no way to change it," Danica acknowledged, looking at him. "I'm not kidding. This is the behavior I've encountered ever since I woke up at the morgue. I had hoped that people would forget, but they haven't. So be it."

He stared at her and repeated, "When you woke up in that morgue—"

She looked over at him. "Yeah, what about it?"

"It's because you could heal yourself, isn't it?"

She winced and then nodded. "I guess, though it took me a long time to figure that out. I don't know the full extent of my injuries when I went in there, but I was pronounced dead and was put away in the cold room storage," she replied, with a shudder. "Somehow my body started to heal, and I'm not dead anymore," she muttered. "So, you can see how the simple folk here took that the wrong way."

"Oh, I can see. I can definitely see it," he confirmed, not fully recovered from what he had witnessed so far. "I saw your leg heal today, and I still couldn't believe it."

"Of course not, and that's another reason I question why you're still sitting here," Danica shared, with half a smile. "You're one of very few people who even know much about us and our healing energies."

"Yet I feel like there's so much more I could know," he admitted.

Danica nodded. "Probably. So much more I could know too, and my grandmother's been doing it for years. However, you can bet that nobody in town wants us to know any more *witchcraft* or whatever they call it."

"Christ," Cameron grumbled, "this is such a mess."

"No, it's not," Nana declared, looking over at him. "In your case, it's quite simple. You have a decision to make. Your life will continue as it is, if you maintain a neutral attitude toward us. However, if you stay friendly with my granddaughter or with me," Nana pointed out, "you can expect this to continue."

He shook his head. "It's wrong," he declared stoutly. "It's wrong today, and it was wrong yesterday."

Danica murmured, "It didn't stop anybody, and it definitely didn't stop your brother. He's one of the worst offenders when it comes to how he's treated us. Now that I know why and how, yes, it would be all about fear. Fear that he is like us, *gifted*. Fear that he might end up like us. The other consideration is that my mother was obviously unstable, so maybe Jace fears he has a good chance of heading down that same pathway as well."

Cameron slumped in his chair and nodded. "That's already becoming evident. I keep hoping that I can get him in for some rehab or some professional help, but, so far, he keeps refusing to even talk to me about it."

"Refusing to talk to you about it is fairly normal, given that you didn't know what he's trying to keep you from finding out."

"Of course," Cameron agreed, groaning, "and, as long as he's trying to do that, he won't open up and be honest."

"Of course not. How can he be?" Nana asked, with a gentle smile. "Yet he's still your brother. You were raised together, and, regardless of who your mothers were, Jace is still an important part of your life."

Cameron nodded at that. "Only the two of us are left. Almost a year ago my father was the doctor on shift to work the hospital on Halloween. He died of a heart attack the next day, and my mother followed soon afterward."

Danica shared a glance with her grandmother and just nodded. "I'm so sorry. That must have been tough."

"It was very tough. Jace and I were pretty shaken up by it, losing both parents in such a short amount of time," Cameron muttered, "Plus Jace was going through a divorce at the time and found out his son isn't his genetically. All of which added to his depression."

"That makes sense." Danica looked over at her grandmother. "Will you be okay if I walk Cameron out?"

"Absolutely," Nana replied, with a sigh. "Talk some sense into him. He shouldn't ruin his life right now. He has a good life. He has a chance at something other than this. You know best, but ensure he doesn't ruin his world too."

CHAPTER 20

THE NEXT DAY Cameron was shocked at how busy the ER was when he arrived at work. Everything from small things to big things. By the time he was done with his shift the next morning, and things had calmed down enough for him to hand it off, he looked around and asked, "What the hell was that?"

"Tomorrow's Halloween, so that was everybody coming in *before*," said Jenny, the nurse with the most tenure here.

"Meaning?" Cameron asked.

"It means nobody'll come in during Halloween."

Cameron sighed. "It would be nice if we had a calm evening for once, but are people really that superstitious around here?"

"They are definitely that superstitious," she confirmed. "And I wouldn't laugh if I were you because people take it seriously."

"Oh, trust me. I've gotten that impression already," he murmured. "I'm not exactly sure what to do with that level of hysteria though."

"You just accept it and carry on, realizing that these people have a reason, and they're not to be mocked for it."

He slowly turned, frowning at her, and asked, "Have I mocked anyone?"

"No, but I'm not sure you have as much understanding

as there could be."

He studied her and asked, "You've been here a long time, haven't you?"

"I have been here for a very long time," she claimed. "I'm the oldest nurse on staff and am also the backup administrator for the hospital. So, if the hospital shuts down permanently, I'm retiring because I have been here every day of my working life," she murmured, then shook her head. "The shit I have seen here has just been unbelievable. No one would believe it."

"So, you'll be here tomorrow night?"

"I should be," she said grimly. "Generally nobody else shows up for work on Halloween. So, if anybody is hurt and doesn't know about the Halloween nightmares and comes here anyway, then they still need to be treated," she explained, looking over at him. "So, I sure as hell hope you show up."

"I have every intention of showing up," he declared. "I don't have opinions or experiences with these types of esoteric events."

"You might change your mind after tomorrow night," Jenny suggested, staring at him intently. "It depends on whether you've got the guts to continue through the night or you'll be scared away."

"I don't scare that easily," Cameron stated, raising one eyebrow.

"Yeah, and maybe you've got more guts than brains, if you're going out with that crazy chick." He stiffened again, and she nodded. "I was afraid that would be your reaction."

"Why does everybody insult Danica?" he asked. "The shit she's gone through from people here? I just don't get it."

"Maybe not, but you've also got to wonder why she's

back again, if the treatment was that bad."

"She's back again because of her grandmother. It's only the two of them." He almost bit his lip on that one, stumbling over the realization how that was no longer true.

"Most people in this town will do everything they can to ensure Danica doesn't stay."

"Why is that anyway?"

"Because of her waking up dead," she snapped. "Something about finding out you have a witch in your midst, when she should have been a ghost and six feet under, makes you not want to have anything to do with her. Add to that her crazy-ass mother who was sleeping with *married* men all over town and who then supposedly tried to kill Danica, … or she killed her mother. Nobody's ever really been sure. So that just adds to the evil element as to why Danica shouldn't be around. If she tried or maybe did kill her mother, then she's a murderer who got away scot-free. If she didn't try to kill her mother, she's still somebody who escaped permanent purgatory, and nobody's happy about that either."

"Sounds like people around here just aren't happy."

"That house, that whole family," Jenny said, with a hard laugh, shaking her head, "they're just different, … so weird. And right now it seems to be getting worse. I can't come in here without listening to people going off about how Danica shouldn't be here and how she shouldn't be allowed to stay."

"I've been hearing a lot of the same thing," Cameron confirmed. "I just hadn't expected to hear it from you."

"Eventually," she replied, twisting in her chair at the front counter to look at him, "you should go with the tide instead of always fighting it. You know that old saying, *Where there's smoke, there's fire*? Something happened, and people here just don't like anything about it."

"What about Harriet?" Cameron asked.

"I think she's to blame too, but there have been just enough times that she's been helpful to the townsfolk that people hate to blame her without justification. But I think they're sorely losing on that point now too. She brought Danica back, and that's something they won't accept easily."

"Jeez," Cameron muttered, his hands on his hips, "and what if Danica didn't do anything but endure the terrible experience of waking up in the morgue, after her own mother tried to murder her?"

"That's the sad part of it," Jenny replied, "because, if Danica didn't do anything, this town hasn't treated her well at all. However, none of that will change the viewpoint of the townsfolk. They've made a stance, and that's all there is to it."

"So, whether they're right or wrong doesn't really matter?" Cameron asked.

"It absolutely does not matter, not here," Jenny declared, with a nod, "and you better get that in your head. If you decide to continue a relationship with Danica, you'll find out that everybody here will turn against you."

He stared at her for a long moment. "I see. So you're prepared to get another doctor in here then, if that's the case?"

She turned and stared at him, her gaze hooded. "I'm hoping I can talk you out of it. You really don't need that in your life."

"I don't *need* that in my life, and Danica and Harriet don't *need* it in theirs either," he stated. "This town doesn't *need* to hang on to something that fills them with so much hate that they can't see that Danica had nothing to do with any of this nonsense."

"Maybe, … but, even if they *did* see it, I don't think anybody here would treat Danica any differently. It would be hard for them to back up and to let go of all those old rumors and innuendos. So, even if Danica is innocent, I don't think they can see their way to letting her be."

Cameron sighed, as he looked around to see a couple other people staring at him. Several looked away, ashamed. Others just glared at him. "Interesting," he murmured. "Up until I met her, I had no idea that this was the level of animosity in town or right here in this hospital. And now it is directed at me." He stared down at the tablet in his hands, wondering about his decision to be here.

"As you well know, you have several more months in your contract," Jenny reminded him.

He nodded. "I do, but that doesn't mean I should stay beyond that." With that, he turned and walked back to his office, feeling a sadness deep inside. He'd come home to help out the town he had been raised in, but, at this point, he wasn't even sure that he would stay to the end of his contract. He'd had a house built, although only partially to date, and had been prepared to settle down and to make it his home, but his heart wasn't in it anymore.

He finished his shift, blocking out everything but what he needed to do. By the time he headed home, it was five in the morning. Instead of going straight to bed, he walked outside, wandering around in the fresh morning air.

Deciding he needed the exercise and a chance to destress, he put on his running shoes and headed out for an early morning jog. By the time he got back, it was definitely time for a shower, and then he crashed.

Waking up a few hours later, he had an odd sense of not being alone.

He bolted out of bed and stepped into his living room, wearing just his pajama pants, to find his brother sitting there. Jace looked disheveled, as if he'd lost his entire world.

He looked up when Cameron walked in but didn't say anything, choosing to just glare at him instead.

Not sure what to say, Cameron walked to the kitchen, put on coffee, then turned to his brother and asked, "What's the matter, Jace?"

"Everything," he muttered. "Absolutely everything."

"I gather you're having some trouble right now."

"Ya think?" he muttered.

"Please don't blame Danica anymore," Cameron said, his fatigue evident in his expression, as he prepared to listen to his brother run off at the mouth again.

"It wouldn't matter if I did or not," he snapped, "because you won't listen anyway, will you?"

"Why does everybody think I'm getting into a relationship with her?"

"Because you are. You just haven't allowed yourself to admit it."

He stared at him and shrugged. "Even if I did, what difference does it make to you? I like her."

"Yeah, well, you're nuts." Jace stared off in the distance. "She's freaky."

"Really? Is she? Or is it just you saying that?"

"It doesn't matter because the minute you're off on your own, doing whatever you're doing, everybody will just judge you anyway."

"Is that what happened to you?"

"I don't know what happened to me," Jace admitted. "I really don't. It just feels like everything is wrong these days."

"I'm sorry to hear that."

When the coffee was done, he poured two cups. He also pressed the Record button on his phone and pocketed his cell. Then he called out to Jace, "Come out onto the deck." The two of them walked outside and sat down. He looked over at his brother and asked, "What the hell's going on now? You're not here working, and you're not doing anything else, as far as I can tell."

"Don't lecture me," Jace replied irritably.

"I'm not trying to, but I really don't know what I'm supposed to do with you either."

"It doesn't matter what you do," he muttered, glaring around. "Everything's just fucked up."

"I get that. I just don't know why or how."

"I shot her."

Cameron stared at his brother, his heart sinking. "You what?"

"I shot her."

No point in even trying to pretend it wasn't true. "Why?" he asked, staring at his brother in shock. "Why would you do that?"

"I had to," he said in a miserable tone.

"You had to, but why?"

He shrugged. "I'm broke."

It took Cameron a minute to sort out just what the implication of that statement was. "When you say you're broke and that you had to, are you telling me that you shot Danica for somebody else to give you money?"

Jace nodded. "Yeah, but now I think they're after me, to ensure I don't say anything."

Cameron swallowed hard, as he stared at the brother he didn't recognize right now. "My God," he whispered. He pinched the bridge of his nose, not even sure what to say.

"You don't have to say anything," Jace noted bitterly. "I know I'm fucked."

"Ya think?" Cameron asked. "You just admitted to trying to kill somebody and that you did it for money. That makes you a paid assassin or a hitman or some godforsaken thing," Cameron yelled, staring at him. "And then there's the fact that she didn't do anything to you, which adds another completely bizarre element. Why would you would sign up for this?"

"I needed the money."

"But did you?"

"Yes, I did. My ex is trying to get my truck, so I won't even have wheels," he spat, raging on. "That stupid bitch is taking my disability money as child support even though he's not mine. I love him though. I thought he was mine and inside he is, regardless of any DNA testing. All this talk and rumors though … both poisonous."

Just too much was going on for Cameron to unpack so quickly. "So, hang on a minute. You accepted a contract to shoot Danica for money, so you could pay the money to your ex-wife, so you could keep your truck?"

He looked at him and nodded. "Yeah, that's exactly it."

"Okay, and now you think that the guy who hired you is trying to what? Get rid of you so you can't tell?"

Jace shrugged. "That makes the most sense, yes."

"Has somebody tried to go after you?"

"Not yet, but obviously they will, if that's what they want to do."

Cameron frowned. "So, you don't know for sure that somebody is after you?"

"No, I don't know for sure that somebody is after me," he repeated, with patent slowness in his tone. "But I've been followed these last few days, and I don't know who else would do that or why."

"Okay, so you've been followed, and you think it's this guy?"

"Yes."

"Did you meet him?"

"He came into my house one time, when I was not in very good shape," he acknowledged, with a snort. "When I say, *not in very good shape*, I mean piss-tank drunk."

"So, you decided, based on what this stranger told you, that you would do this?"

"Yes, and he didn't pay me either."

Cameron let out his breath. "Maybe that's a good thing because, if you weren't paid, maybe it wasn't a hired hit."

"But it *was* a hired hit. Except that I haven't seen him since. I've been trying to contact him so I could get my money."

Cameron didn't even know what to say. This was just so far beyond anything he would have expected as a conversation with his brother that it was just shocking. "I see," he murmured.

"I don't think you do see though," Jace countered. "If he is after me, then I'm screwed."

"Yes, I imagine that's possible. Did he give a reason why?"

"I don't know. I was so drunk I'm not even really sure."

Cameron hesitated, then asked, "Is there any chance that …" He paused, searching around for the right word that would answer the question but not set off his brother. "Could you have maybe imagined him?"

His brother glanced him, and Jace's gaze dropped to the patio table.

Cameron swore, as he realized his brother had already considered that option. "Have you been taking your medication? Have you been hallucinating at all?" he asked, speaking softly, trying to keep the conversation productive and under control.

"I don't have money for the medication," Jace muttered. "So, I haven't been taking them for a while."

"Damn it, Jace." Cameron stared at his brother in shock. "You know you could have come to me for that."

"Yeah, but I didn't want to," he retorted. "I'm better off without them anyway."

That was all so patently wrong, particularly about shooting an innocent woman for promised money from some guy whom Jace didn't know.

"That guy showed up out of the blue, asking me to do it."

"Christ," he muttered. "You need to tell the deputy."

"Hell no." Jace shook his head. "I ain't telling that guy nothing. Besides, he's already got a hate on for Danica, and he thinks she shot herself." He laughed. "So, it's all good. As long as Benson thinks she did it to herself, then I'm in the clear."

"You'll just let him think that?" Cameron asked.

"Sure, why not?" Jace asked. "It's better than having me going to jail for it."

"I don't know about that," Cameron murmured, staring at his brother. "It's just not right."

"Yeah, you're the one who was always held by that sense of right or wrong," Jace noted, shaking his head and sneering. "I never was."

Unfortunately that was quite true. If one of them never worried about the law, it was his brother. "You can't let the deputy think Danica did this to herself. He's looking to get her charged."

"That's her problem," Jace muttered. "It sure as hell isn't mine."

Cameron shook his head. "How is it you can just say it's not your problem when you know full well what you did?"

"Sure, but what I did has nothing to do with it. And, if *you* tell Benson, I'll just call you a liar, and he'll believe me because he wants to."

The logic in his words was a little too real. It was also sadly true because Deputy Benson did appear to have a problem with Danica, to the point that it would quite likely stop him from ever seeing her as innocent. Cameron still wanted to believe in the law and in justice, but right now? Everything seemed to be completely screwed. "I get that you'll say I'm just lying, but I do have a stellar reputation."

"Yeah, well, your *stellar reputation* is getting smeared right now," Jace said, with a laugh. "It's one of the reasons why I didn't have a problem telling you what I did because everybody's starting to think of you in a different way."

That was also true, and Cameron had seen the evidence of it already. He could only just stare at his brother in surprise. Then it hit him. "Hang on. Have you been actively spreading lies and damaging my reputation, and Danica's?" he asked in shock.

"No, why the hell should I be bothered with that?" he muttered, looking over at him. "You're doing a good enough job of that yourself. Besides, if you weren't seeing that bitch, it wouldn't have happened, but you are. So now it's your world that can spin off into a nightmare spiral, … just like mine did."

Honestly Cameron didn't have a clue what to say. He

stared at his brother and shook his head. "Has the whole fucking world gone mad?"

His brother looked at him in surprise, then shrugged. "No, I think you're just starting to see the real world that you live in."

"No, it's not. It wasn't this way before," Cameron argued. "I get that it can take time when you resettle into a place to really figure out who and what's changed, but"—he took a moment to collect his thoughts—"I never *ever* would have thought that something like this was happening here."

"That's because you were living in your happy little world," Jace pointed out. "As long as you're in your happy little world, everything is just fine and dandy, but somebody, namely *her*, pulled you out of that happy little world."

"What is it that she supposedly did?" he asked his brother curiously. "You went through all the trouble to get a gun?"

"No," Jace held up a hand. "I've always had the gun. Haven't had too many reasons to use it, so I was not all that upset about getting a chance to do something with it."

His brother sounded so completely calm. How could that be when the words coming out of his mouth were absolutely insane and made no sense to Cameron? He knew his brother was on medication—or should be. Cameron had deliberately removed himself from Jace's psychological treatments, knowing it was easier to keep his distance and to be neutral and supportive, especially if he stayed out of the details and wasn't his doctor. However, *this*—whatever this was—wasn't normal at all. "I wonder if the whole place goes mad at Halloween."

His brother laughed. "You heard all those Halloween rumors, did you?"

"Or is that something you've created too?" Cameron

asked, looking at him.

"No, but I certainly added fuel to the fire. After all, that crazy bitch Daisy died that night."

"Yes, she did. And I'm still trying to figure out how and why."

"You and the rest of the world," Jace noted, with a laugh. "It's not as though anybody really cares. She was one hell of a whore, and the best thing to happen to her was to get herself knocked off. I should be thanking Danica for that."

"Danica didn't kill her mother," Cameron stated, looking at his brother with new insights.

His brother laughed. "See? I knew you were so far gone that you would listen to all the shit she spouted."

"And what if it isn't shit that she's spouting?" he asked, staring at his brother.

He snorted. "Everybody here is pretty superstitious. I mean, Daisy was crazy, like good old-fashioned crazy. You know that, right? All the guys would talk about her constantly."

"Did that make her crazy or just sad, as in pitiful?"

"Oh, she was that too," Jace added, his tone hard.

"I know that you know," Cameron declared.

His brother looked at him in surprise and asked, "Know what?"

"I know." He didn't add anything else.

His brother looked at him, then suddenly yelled, "Those stupid fucking bitches."

Cameron's eyebrows raised. "Now who are we talking about?"

"You know exactly who I'm talking about. Are they spreading that bullshit again?"

"And what bullshit is that?" he asked, still staring at his brother.

"The bullshit that the old lady witch is my grandmother too? You know that's complete BS."

"I don't know anything at this point," Cameron replied, staring at him. "Honest to God, Jace. I don't know or understand what the hell's going on here."

"That's just because you're so fucking gullible," Jace declared, with a mock smile. "Never really thought that you would be quite that gullible though."

"Meaning?" This whole conversation was breaking Cameron's heart. To see Jace like this? … Yet Cameron had to continue this crazy conversation, as it was the only way to get answers.

Jace chuckled. "Don't tell me that you can't figure that out either. You should know that I'm your brother, and, if you can't figure that out, then, God, I can't imagine what the hell you've been doing with your life all these years. No one who knows you would be listening to you spout all this off now."

"I'm not spouting it off to anybody," Cameron stated. "I'm just trying to figure out what the hell is going on and why you would shoot Danica and then expect me to keep quiet about it."

"Even if you don't keep quiet, Deputy Benson won't listen to you anyway. Besides, what do you care? She's crazy."

"*She's* crazy?" he asked, frowning at his brother.

"Or do you think I am?" he asked, his tone turning ugly.

"I don't know what the hell I believe right now, Jace," he murmured, shaking his head.

At that, he laughed and laughed. "See? That's the thing. You should figure it out, but, because you haven't, that just makes it all the more amusing for me." Jace stood up. "Don't even begin to believe that shit they're spouting. I am not related to them." He looked over at Cameron bitterly. "The fact that you would even doubt something like that? God, Mom and Dad must be rolling in their graves." Then he laughed. "And, if they aren't, they should be."

Something in his tone just didn't make any sense. Cameron eyed his brother and whispered, "Did you have anything to do with that?"

His brother stared at him in surprise and then snorted. "You mean, because I shot Danica, now I'm supposed to be some crazed killer?" he asked, chuckling. "My God, you've really got it bad, don't you?"

"I don't have anything at the moment," Cameron admitted, "and I certainly don't have a grasp on the truth. If somebody would enlighten me on that part, I could get somewhere."

"Yeah, you might. On the other hand, you don't appear to have a very good grasp on anything, so you should probably just toddle along and let the rest of us big boys do our thing."

"Just what is your thing?" he asked, wondering at the twisted bitterness on Jace's face, even as Cameron looked for a resemblance to Danica. "Because none of this makes a damn bit of sense."

"Oh, it makes perfect sense, but you just don't see it." And, with that, he laughed again. "Don't mind me. I'll head out for a while."

"Where to?"

Jace faced him, a mocking expression on his face. "What? Now you'll start checking up on me?"

"I never thought to before, but now, all of a sudden,

you're shooting innocent people? What the hell am I supposed to do with that?"

Jace walked to the door and turned to look back at his brother. "Don't you believe in any of that shit they told you about Mom and Dad."

"They didn't say anything about Mom and Dad," Cameron clarified, eyeing his brother as if he'd never seen him before—and honest to God, he wasn't sure he ever had. "I'm still struggling with a lot of stuff they did say."

Jace nodded. "I struggled with some of it too for a long time, and then I ditched it as just weird, jealous, godforsaken rumors they decided would be fun to spread. Nobody's spreading that shit about me," he muttered. "No way in hell that anybody in this town would let any relative of theirs live peaceably who did that," he snapped. "And believe me that I won't be part of that shit." And, with that, he strode out the front door.

Cameron stared in his wake, wondering what the hell had just happened to his world. He grabbed his phone and saved the recording. As soon as his brother was gone, he called Danica.

She answered but seemed distracted. "Hey, can I call you back in a bit?"

"I don't know," he replied, trying to understand the urgency he felt. "My brother was just here. He's the one who shot you."

She gasped. "Why does he hate me so much?" she cried out.

"I don't know, but I suspect it has to do with the news that you might be family."

"So he decided to shoot me over that *now*?"

"He doesn't seem to think that *anybody would be allowed*

to live here peaceably if they were related to you," he shared. "All I can tell you is that he's gone and that I'm not comfortable with you guys being alone over there."

She gave a broken laugh. "I mean, what else can go wrong?" she muttered. "This is just one horror after another. I'm just waiting for my grandmother to wake up again. I thought we were getting somewhere with this big family secret, and then she basically fell asleep while she was talking."

"So, you still don't know what's happening?"

"No, and I keep trying to sort it out," she muttered, "but I'm not getting very far."

"Do you want me to come over?"

"No," she stated forcefully. "You have to work tonight, don't you?"

"Yeah," he replied. "I slept earlier, wanting to ensure I got at least some sleep. Apparently the hospital will be short-staffed tonight because it's Halloween."

She shivered. "I get that you don't understand the huge impact all this has had on us," she noted, "but Halloween at the hospital would definitely not be a place I wanted to be."

"No, not when you've already spent so much spooky time there," he murmured. "However, if you need me, you call me."

"I know you won't call in sick, not with your sense of duty and all," she shared, "yet, if anybody looking like my mother comes in, please don't let her grab your lab coat."

"You really think it would kill me?"

"I don't know if it would or not, but considering what happened to your father, let's not take a chance," she whispered.

"What do you mean? My father died of a heart attack."

"Yeah, after my mother left a bloody handprint on his lab coat."

"Oh no. Don't you go believing the superstitions too." Cameron moaned.

Danica sighed. "I don't want anything to happen to you. I just know that those people encountered by Daisy on Halloween don't die instantly but usually within a few months," she shared. "Believe me that everybody looked at me over that too. Some probably still do. So don't add to the body count please."

"They blamed you for it?"

"Yeah. Apparently, when you walk out of a morgue after being pronounced DOA, they seem to think that you're in the business of taking souls with you," she muttered.

"Wow, I'm really rethinking my future here."

"I'm not at all surprised," she replied, with a chuckle. "It's pretty scary to think about all that is wrong here. I'm not sure I even know the bare minimum of it."

"Meaning?"

"I think my grandmother is still hiding some pretty dark secrets, and I don't know that I'm up for seeing just how dark they may be."

"You think it's really bad?"

"Yeah, I think it's *really* bad. She's keeping secrets from me. So, hell, yes, it's bad. I just don't know how bad. She's having such a hard time telling me that I'm pretty worried she won't get it out before she goes," Danica revealed, sadness in her tone. "I suspect she'll pass on tonight, but I can't be sure."

"Tonight?"

"*Halloween* night," she noted, "and that's quite possible."

"I get it," Cameron said, hearing hesitation in her tone. "I understand, but I'm also worried about you."

She nodded and then smiled, unbeknownst to him of course. "I appreciate that. I really do."

He muttered, "Yeah, you appreciate it, yet why do I expect to hear a *but* coming?"

She chuckled. "Not so much a *but*, as much as a warning. An awful lot is going on, much of it that I still don't understand, and until I do—"

"Oh, I know," he interrupted. "I get that, and I won't push anything, but you obviously know that I like you and that I want you to stay safe. You've been hurt pretty badly already. I can't believe my brother shot you, and that already makes me feel guilty as hell," he shared, taking a moment to wrap his head around it. "I still can't believe Jace even did that."

"I'm not sure I do either."

"He did admit to it so …"

"What?"

Cameron hesitated.

"What did he say?" she asked curiously.

"He did say that somebody hired him to do it."

"What?"

"The thing is, I honestly don't really know if I can believe him or not. He explained how someone offered to pay him to take you out." He heard her cry out into the phone, and he whispered, "I'm sorry, but … no easy way to tell you that. However, when pushed, he also admitted that he didn't know if he made him up in his mind, as he was drunk at the time and hasn't seen him again."

With tears in her throat, she whispered, "God, I hate this place."

"I'm starting to be right there with you," he muttered.

He heard her softly crying, and he felt like a heel. "I don't know. I don't even know what to do. Jace seemed to think that the deputy wouldn't believe me if I told him that Jace had shot you because Benson would rather think that you did it to yourself."

She gave a choked laugh and then said, "He's correct on that because the deputy does want me to have done it, and he won't look for anybody else."

"But that's just wrong, damn it."

"There is wrong all over this world, and there's wrong all over this nightmare," she murmured. "And I'm not sure anybody gives a crap."

"I sure do," he snapped.

She whispered, "I am very grateful for that, and I don't think you even realize how much. Over the last decade I've been used to not having anyone in my corner, and you've been a light in this nightmare."

"But don't you dare put that in past tense," he warned. "I don't know what the hell's going on, but I am not giving up. We will get to the bottom of it."

She gave a broken laugh. "You say that, but so many other people say other things, and sometimes—"

"We'll figure this out. You're *not* crazy."

"Are you sure?" she whispered. "Because my mother was legitimately nuts, and it sounds to me that your brother may be as well. What if it's genetic? What if it is all just a matter of who's crazier than the other one?"

"Don't even think like that," he murmured. "We will get to the bottom of this, and it's not your fault. Whatever it is that you're thinking might be your fault, it's not. You stay safe tonight. I do have to go to work because there isn't another doctor on shift, and I don't quite know what I'm supposed to do about that. But maybe, when this is over, and when your grandmother has passed on, maybe instead of buying this other piece of property," he offered, hinting at his wishes, "maybe we can move somewhere else."

When Danica didn't respond, Cameron whispered, "I know I'm moving very quickly by even saying that, and I'm really sorry to spring this on you. Damn it," he muttered. "I'm usually—I can be a whole lot smoother than this."

"I don't know whether it's *smooth* or not," she replied, chuckling. "I couldn't tell you because I haven't had a whole lot of experience. Men tend to see me and run."

"I'm not the running kind, in case you hadn't noticed. Now I've got to get organized and get to work. That's pissing me off too because I don't want to leave you alone. But you look after yourself and your grandmother, you hear me?"

"I will. I told you how I feel as if she's almost gone, right?" she whispered.

"I know what you're saying, and that could very well be true. I'm sorry I can't be there, if that's the case," he told her. "She's had a very long inning. She's had a good inning."

"Yes," she whispered, "she has. I know. I know. I just—"

"I need to know that you'll be okay."

"I'll be fine," she whispered. "I just need her to tell me what the hell's going on."

"Good," he said, assured that she was listening to him. "I'll be at the hospital if anything crazy goes on here tonight."

She snapped back sharply, "If anything crazy goes on, you be careful. Promise me."

"I will," he murmured. "I promise I'll be careful."

She shook her head. "It doesn't sound to me like you'll

be careful enough," she countered.

He laughed. "I'm not sure how much more careful I can be. It will be over soon. Halloween is tonight, so whatever the crazy cosmos has got planned, we'll deal with it. And your grandmother, as you said, is on her last leg. So, when she's gone, everything in your world may shift as well."

"I hope so," Danica conceded. "Nana did say something about a bloody legacy though, and that's got me worried."

"Legacy? What kind of a legacy?" Then he groaned. "I would love to stay and talk. I would love to just come over and talk," he added, taking a moment, "but that's not something I can do right now."

"I understand," she whispered. "Go—just go to work. You deal with that chaos, and I will attempt to deal with my chaos. Then maybe, if we catch a break later tonight, you can give me a shout, and we'll catch up on how things are going."

"Done," he said. "And, if your grandmother has anything to say that disturbs you, where you need to talk, you call me."

"Will do," she murmured.

And, with a whispered, "Good night," he ended the call and packed up, ready to go to work.

Definitely something was going on. He felt it. A tension coiled inside him, but he didn't know why. If he was lucky, the night would be relatively harmless. Maybe the people—staff and patients alike—would be decent to deal with, and, if they weren't, he would get through it somehow.

IT'S TIME, CAME the insistent voice in the darkness of her mind.

Harriet groaned, rolled over on her bed, and whispered, "I don't think I can do it."

You have to, the voice stated forcefully. *You know that you must. There is no choice.*

"I know. I do know." Feebly she made her way to her feet, swearing that she hadn't told her granddaughter already.

We told you to, came the same insistent voice.

Interrupting that voice was another male, one that she barely recognized.

Are you all right? Stefan asked sharply.

She gave a broken laugh. "I may never be all right," she whispered, "but it is my time to go."

A softening to his tone came, when he whispered, *That isn't necessarily a bad thing.*

"No, it absolutely isn't a bad thing," she agreed, tears in her eyes. "But there are things that I was supposed to tell my granddaughter, and it's very important, but I'm getting so weak."

Stefan, his thoughts almost as clear in his head as in hers, whispered, *I might be able to help for a little bit, but I can't stave off the … inevitable.*

"I understand," she whispered. "I know. I just need a little bit of time, that's all."

Are we talking an hour or are we talking a day? he asked doubtfully. *Because I can see from the energy that you're close.*

"Exactly." She called out weakly, "Are you there? Danica, are you there?"

The bedroom door opened, and Danica walked in. "I'm here, Nana. I'm here."

"Good," she whispered. "Stefan, please just give me an hour or two."

I can try, but I can't promise anything.

Harriet whispered to Stefan, "Nobody can promise anything anymore."

Motioning Danica closer, Harriet murmured, "Come, child."

Danica sat down beside her and picked up her hand. "Nana, are you all right?"

"No," she whispered, "but the tale I should tell you, well—" Her voice faded away again.

Stefan urged Harriet, *You don't have time. I can't keep this up for long.*

"What time is it?" Nana whispered to Danica.

"It's a little late," she replied. "I wanted you to sleep and rest. Yet I didn't want you to sleep too long."

"How late is it?" Nana asked, her tone sharp.

"It's eleven p.m."

"Almost the witching hour," she whispered.

"Maybe, depending on what we're *witching* for," Danica replied, full of worry. "Nana, you're scaring me."

"I have not done you any favors by keeping this from you. I thought maybe there would be a better time to tell you, a better time to explain, but it wasn't to be, and now Benjamin is getting insistent."

"Benjamin?" she asked, not recognizing the name. "I don't think I've ever heard you mention that name before."

"My father and his father before him," she whispered. "And his father before him and further back."

"Yet you call him Benjamin," Danica noted.

"Well …" She gave a broken laugh. "All the sons down the line have been Benjamins, except for my dearly departed husband." Outside, the wind picked up, and Nana shivered. "It's coming time now. Stefan, if you can, you need to look out for Danica."

I don't even know what I'm supposed to look out for regarding her, replied the voice in her head.

"You will," she whispered. "You will. I'm sorry for not cluing you in on this too."

What have you done? Stefan asked in a sharp tone.

"It's not what I've done. It's what everybody through the ages has done," she whispered to him. "Danica, come closer. You need to know before midnight."

"What does it matter that it's midnight?" she asked.

"It's the witching hour."

"Nana," Danica said, her tone sharpening, "that doesn't mean anything to me."

"No, I understand it doesn't, but it means a lot to those people who are part of this."

"Part of what?"

"Transitioning," she whispered.

"You mean," Danica hesitated and then asked, "are you talking about death?"

"Yes, death, but not death. It's literally a transition in our family."

"Transition of what?"

"It's transition to life forever spent as part of the entity that has housed all of us for so many decades. Even centuries ago, since this house was founded."

"What are you talking about?" Danica cried out. "What has it got to do with this house?"

"Everything," Nana whispered. "Absolutely everything."

CHAPTER 21

DANICA STARED AT Nana. Danica opened her mouth several times to urge her grandmother to speak, but Nana would only hold up her hand.

Nana whispered, "I'm getting there. It's hard for me."

"I know that, but time is running out." Danica couldn't help herself from glancing at the clock.

"Oh, I'm so out of time," Nana mumbled, her voice so weak. "That's okay. Any other time I would be all right with this," she whispered. "But, Danica, you must understand that you should *not* make the same commitment that I had to."

"Commitment to what?"

"To the family community, to the family legacy," she whispered. "They'll get angry at me for saying that because, as I pass on, you are supposed to pick up the mantle and carry on, as the next bearer of this burden."

"I don't understand. … You're scaring me."

"I know. I know," Nana muttered, "and shame on me for having left it so long."

Stefan, his voice resounding around the room now, declared, "I don't even understand, and I deal in this, Harriet. You should make us understand."

Danica looked around the room and cried out, "Stefan, is that you?"

"Yes, I'm helping your grandmother stay on for just a few more minutes, so she can make peace with whatever it is she needs to make peace with, but it's an energy drain on me. I cannot keep up, and she needs to hurry."

Immediately Danica turned to her grandmother. "Please, please tell me what's going on."

"Listen, and I will explain."

And the tale that unfolded was something straight out of an Alfred Hitchcock movie.

"Many years ago," Nana whispered, "and I don't even know how many, anymore. Somebody came over from Europe. His name was Benjamin, and he loved life, and he loved the idea of living forever and more than anything, he loved his wife, and he didn't want to lose any of this when his time came. He dealt in the dark arts for a long time, trying to find a way to live forever. He definitely had psychic abilities, and his wife had psychic abilities as well. Just when he was searching for a way to live forever, he realized that they needed an anchor, a ground in a way. So, he built this house as a home for them all, for when it came time to leave, so that everybody would have a place to go to, a family to welcome them. A place of honor and a place to rest and to be together again what they could be."

"Good God," Danica said in shock. "You're talking about a haunting."

"To a certain extent, yes—but not quite. More of a possessing. I know that makes no sense to you."

"No, it really doesn't. There is no living forever."

"No, there isn't. And yet—in the same way—there is," Nana whispered. "These entities, these souls of our forebearers, they control this house, the house that you have always loved and hated, and these entities have controlled it all of your life. It is them, the collective of them, who control this house," Nana explained, looking around the room. "They call themselves *Benjamin*, as was my father's name, as was my grandfather's name. My grandfather went to join the collective—with joy in his heart, knowing he would live forever as part of it. Then my father joined the collective, knowing forever that he had garnered that promise for me to continue the line. But, as promises go, that was a hard one for me to continue."

"How are you supposed to continue that line?" Danica asked.

"How do you think?"

"You only had my mother, no son. Surely that was enough."

"It was. It was, indeed. But it gets worse. With every new transition, there must be a sacrifice. There has to be somebody, something that they use for energy, for transition energy, they would say, to make the journey. It's not an easy journey, and it requires a lot of power, and, from their perspective, it always required a sacrifice."

"What sacrifice?" Danica asked, her tone turning hard. "Is that what happened to my mother?"

"No, not really, but yes—she was supposed to be part of this. She *was* part of this. She was strong energetically, so very strong, but she was also sick. She couldn't handle the energy, and she was desperate for something other than what would be her life here, so she *wanted* to transition. She wanted to be part of this forever family and lifetime. Yet she couldn't seem to make her way to do so. And we tried." Then Nana's voice broke. "When she tried to take you, it was her attempt to cross over and to make you her sacrifice."

"Oh, my God," Danica cried out in shock. "I was supposed to be Daisy's sacrifice so Daisy could live forever as part of this house?"

"Yes, something like that. The way you've put it is far too simplistic, but the meaning is partially there."

"No meaning is here"—Danica reared back—"only insanity."

"And I get that. But you should understand that dozens of our family members are here. That's why the house protects me. That's why it looks after me. That's why it looks after you."

"You're kidding, right? It doesn't look after me. It barely even lets me in."

"Until it becomes your time, until it becomes bonded to you, then it will look after you," Nana whispered. "That's what it's waiting for. It's waiting for you to be the next in line."

Danica didn't even have a clue what to say. "My God, this is unbelievable."

"I know. I know it is. I know that, for you, it's probably too unbelievable to even begin to understand it. I should have started your training a long time ago, but you left, and you didn't want to come back. I thought that maybe we could find another way for me to become part of the house, as I was always meant to be, without it requiring you."

"What do you mean, *requiring me*?" Danica asked incredulously. "Isn't it bad enough that my mother already tried to use me as a sacrifice?"

"Instead, she became the sacrifice herself."

"What are you talking about?"

"You don't remember? What she tried didn't work for her because she wasn't already bonded to the house, which is a process to get that next soul to be *the one*," she whispered.

"She wasn't chosen to be *that one* because it was still me. Because she tried to jump ahead of time and tried to use you as a sacrifice, when you shouldn't have been used, Daisy ended up caught in-between worlds."

"Oh my God. The hauntings at the hospitals."

"Yes," Nana whispered, "she's the one haunting the two hospitals, and, God help me, it's been impossible for me to figure out how to stop her. I was hoping tonight, as I transition, that maybe I could free her and could bring her with me."

"To be your sacrifice?" Danica asked, her tone hardening.

"She's already dead," Nana whispered. "All I want is for her to find peace."

"Is that even possible now?" Danica asked, her voice breaking.

Nana sobbed slightly. "I know you don't understand, and I don't blame you. I should have told you all of this so long ago, but, once you left, I didn't know how to bring you back and not have you run away again."

"My God," Danica muttered, staring out the window into the wilderness around her.

"This house is centuries old, older than any people who settled here. The house blended in and had the ability with each new generation to recreate itself in conformity to the history of those homes around it, so that the memories blurred, and nobody understood just how long ours had been standing."

Nana sighed, then whispered, "It is a bloody legacy that I leave you. More than that, it's a soul legacy, and you are the next soul. With my transitioning, taking Daisy with me, then this house will now bond to you, and you will become the next owner and the next generation of energy. And, for that, you will carry the spirits of all the generations gone before."

"What if I don't want to?" Danica cried out.

Her grandmother opened her eyes, and there was power in them as she roared, "It is not a choice. It is ordained."

Danica stared at her, as if seeing her beloved Nana now possessed by generations of Benjamins. "So, I am to be a prisoner of this house? I can't ever leave it because all the souls of my ancestors are here?"

"Yes," Nana replied, "that's it exactly. And with those souls of your ancestors is my soul as well," she whispered. "If you do not do this, then we all perish."

In the background, she heard Stefan muttering something, but Danica was too stunned to even understand. "I don't get this. What happened to my mother?"

"I already told you. She tried to make the transition before the preparation, without being ready, and it didn't work, which left her caught in limbo. If and when I transition tonight, I'm hoping that she will make an appearance and that somehow I can free her of her frozen purgatory and take her with me back into this familial soul legacy."

"Why did you want me to get the property from Cameron?"

"Because they're all buried there," she whispered. "I had it wrong when I sold it to him. I thought incorrectly that I knew where the boundary was, but I didn't know, and I was wrong. So, Cameron has the property with the graves. I need that property back. I need our legacy whole," she wailed, tears running down her face. "You don't understand. That's very important," she said urgently, reaching out and grabbing Danica's hand.

Danica stared down at the hand of the woman she had been so close to for so much of her life. Nana had been the voice of sanity in a world gone mad, when so much had been wrong. "Did they have anything to do with me dying?"

Her grandmother hesitated. "Your mother almost succeeded in her wish to join the collective soul," Nana explained, then stopped. "She almost succeeded when she tried to make you the sacrifice."

Danica burst out into bitter laughter. "That's all I was to Daisy. Is a sacrifice always required?"

"Yes, a sacrifice is always required."

"Is that why she's haunting the hospital and taking lives there?"

Nana hesitated. "In a way, yes. She keeps trying to get the *right* sacrifice and to rejoin all of us. She is us. That's what you should understand, and, being caught in-between the process like that, she is still there. Yet she is still one of us."

"I don't know that I can accept her as one of us," Danica whispered. "I don't know what I believe anymore."

"I know that, and I'm so sorry," Nana whispered.

"Who was the sacrifice for your father? For your husband?" she asked Nana suddenly. "You said a sacrifice is required every time."

"Yes," she whispered, "and the sacrifice should be somebody who loves you."

"Oh, my God, no," she whispered. "Please tell me that you didn't sacrifice your husband."

"I did, indeed, but it wasn't my choice. It was his. He wanted to join the family. He wanted to be a part of it."

"And did he join them?"

"Yes, he did," she whispered. "That was a successful

turnover. He's waiting, and I want to go to him. … I've been waiting for this moment for a very long time. It's my turn, and I desperately want to join them," she whispered.

"That's fine and all, but I don't know what you want from me. You've been trying to tell me all this, and you could have told me a long time ago, but you didn't, which means you still have something yet to say."

She groaned. "Yes, I have something yet to say."

"What is that?"

"We need your commitment."

"My commitment? What kind of a commitment? Why would I commit to this house that doesn't even like me, this house that has shunned me most of my life?"

"But now it will be yours," Nana muttered, "and it will include me, and I will always be here for you. It's not like we will turn our backs on you. We will be here now for you forever, and that is important."

Danica just stared.

CAMERON WALKED THE halls of the hospital, looking back at Jenny. "You meant it when you mentioned how it would be dead around here."

"Yep, everybody knows to stay away," she murmured. "Doesn't mean the old witch will show up, but just the chance of it keeps most people away. One year we had a news crew in here because they'd heard the rumors about our resident witch," Jenny shared, shaking her head. "Daisy didn't show up, but the other happenings that night freaked them pretty good anyway."

"How?" he asked in confusion.

"Because just enough weird stuff was going on, amid

retelling the tales of past Halloweens, that it completely spooked the news crew," she shared, with a smirk. "Good riddance, as far as I was concerned."

He nodded. "I can see how you might feel like that."

She glanced over at him. "You just wait. It's almost time." She glanced at the clock behind him.

"What happens normally?"

"I wasn't even going to tell you that. It's pretty much the same every year. There's a slight bit of difference but not a whole lot," she replied, with a shrug.

Just then, the police scanners went off about a car accident and a woman coming in.

Immediately Jenny's expression darkened. "Here we go," she muttered.

Two nurses raced to meet the ambulance, as it screamed into the parking lot, and a young woman was unloaded from the back on a gurney.

Cameron, completely forgetting about everything Jenny and Danica had warned him about, raced out to deal with the new patient. "What happened?" he cried out.

"Car accident. She hit a telephone pole, from the looks of it," the first responder cried out. "She's stable, but she's completely covered in blood, and we're still struggling to find the source of the bleeding."

"I got it," Cameron replied, as they quickly swung her into the cubicle he'd pointed out, and he went to work, checking for vitals, and yet, the more he worked, the more puzzled he got.

Finally he became aware of the silence around him and the fact that only he was working on the patient. He looked back at the others, glaring at them. "What the hell? Since when do you stop giving aid? We have a patient."

Jenny looked over at him and nodded. "Yeah, we know. Some of us might have seen her before."

At that, he turned back to the patient, who was even now twisting in agony, and he shook his head. "No way," he muttered, going back to helping her. However, he needed to find out more. Cameron turned to two orderlies and snapped, "Get her up to X-ray right away. We need to know what the hell's going on. I don't see any visible injuries, but she's obviously in great pain."

The two orderlies, both young men, grabbed the gurney and headed out.

As the gurney went past Cameron, his patient grabbed Cameron's lab coat and called out, "Help me, please help me."

He frowned, as she let go and was wheeled away. When the earlier warnings came back to him, he stared at his lab coat, as the bloodstains slowly disappeared. He turned to face Jenny.

She nodded. "Yeah, that's why nobody's helping you."

He looked back at the other nurses, who were swallowing hard, both of them staring at each other and then at Jenny. "What about the orderlies?" Cameron asked.

Just then came a shriek, and both men came running back.

"She disappeared from the bed. She took off."

"One minute she was there, and then she was gone."

Both orderlies spoke on top of each other, as one of them just went nuts. "Call security."

Cameron stared at them, as Jenny responded first. "It's fine, guys. It's fine."

They frowned and asked, "What do you mean, *fine*?"

Jenny explained, "We won't need to call security." As

they stared at her in shock, she added, "You've just met our Halloween ghost."

In the meantime, Cameron still studied his lab coat, staring at where the blood had been but was no longer there. "Good God," he whispered.

"Yep, that's about how we all feel about the ghost of Daisy. She's here, and then she's gone. Now you," Jenny stated, pointing at him, "need to be careful."

"Why is that?"

"Because a lot of the time—and I won't say every time—but, when Daisy grabs somebody, she ends up killing them."

He shook his head. "She asked for help."

"I know, but I'm not exactly sure what it is that she expects us to help her with."

He grimaced and then told Jenny, "But I might." And, with that, he took off for his office, reaching for his cell phone, even as he slammed the door behind him, shutting out the outside world. He called Danica. "You won't believe it," he began.

"Yeah," she responded, exhausted. "I probably would. You just met the ghost of Daisy, didn't you?"

He stopped in shock and said, "Yeah, I did. How did you know?"

"Because I finally got the story out of my grandmother, and you won't believe it." She hesitated, then whispered, "Did Daisy grab you?"

"Yes, she did, and apparently that means I could soon be dead. She asked me to help her," Cameron added in frustration, "How the hell can I help her? I don't even know what happened to her."

"What happened to her is that—wait, are you sitting down?"

He walked over to a bench and sat down hard. Then she gave him a brief outline of what Nana had finally shared. "No way," he muttered.

"Yet I've been listening to my grandmother, who is, even as we speak, dying, telling me all this and expecting me to become the next part of this house."

"Don't," he replied urgently.

"The worst part of it is, apparently every time someone passes, or *transitions* as Nana puts it, there must also be a sacrifice. When it was Nana's father's turn, Nana sacrificed her own husband. Apparently he was a willing sacrifice, but what do I know?" Danica cried out in pain. "None of this makes any sense."

"So, your mother—"

"Yeah, my mother tried to kill me, making me *her* sacrifice," Danica shared bitterly, "Only it wasn't her time, it wasn't her turn, and, as such, she wasn't properly *prepared* or some such thing, so it didn't work. Then, in the end, I survived, and she's been caught in limbo."

"That's what Daisy meant by asking for help."

"Yes, but I suspect what she really meant was to let her take your soul as her sacrifice, so that she could join the rest of my family. Is she gone now?"

"I don't know," he replied in exasperation. "The orderlies were instructed to take her up to X-ray, and they came running back, saying they'd lost her."

"Right. According to my grandmother, the ghost of Daisy could still be there, as she wanders the halls for a few hours, looking for a way to make this *transition* happen, before it can't happen again."

"Why Halloween?"

"Because that's when she tried to make me *her* sacrifice,"

Danica whispered. “You need to get out of there.”

“Me? You need to get out of wherever the hell you are.”

“I know. I know,” she whispered, “but you have no idea how hard it’ll be for me to leave Nana.”

“Absolutely nothing is happening here, so I’ll come to you.”

“I don’t think … No. … That’s not a good idea,” she snapped all too fast. “That’s probably what they want. We would all be in the same house, all to be used for their sacrifices.”

Cameron declared, “They can damn well do without you. Hasn’t that family taken enough from you?”

And, with that, he ended the call.

CHAPTER 22

DANICA TURNED TO face her grandmother. "Cameron's coming here."

Her grandmother sighed. "I gather my daughter showed up."

"She did." Danica shook her head. "Freaked everybody out—but him? Not so much. He's mostly angry that I'm being asked to sacrifice my life for this house."

"Not for the house," Nana corrected. "For the souls, for the people of our family. All of them are here, all of them in need, all of them connected."

"Sure," Danica whispered under her breath, "but at what price?"

Stefan, his tone soft and gentle, whispered in her mind, *Stay strong.*

"How can I?" she asked in an outburst. "Do you hear this?"

I have a friend trying to help right now, looking for energy, looking to see what she can find.

"Somebody who sees *energy*?" Danica muttered in a dour tone, not believing that or much of anything else tonight.

She sees energy. She sees people's auras, and she heals people. And, in this case, we're looking to see if there's a way to help.

"*Good*," she whispered out of desperation. "I truly hope so. I don't know what the hell I'm supposed to do otherwise."

Don't let anything crazy go on, Stefan suggested.

Danica snorted. "It's a little late for that. You mean *crazier*, right?"

He snorted. *Your grandmother has controlled a lot of your life, whether you know it or not. Sometimes for your betterment and sometimes maybe not.*

"I'm starting to think more along the line of *maybe not.*" She repeated the conversation to Nana.

"That's not true," Nana called out. "I loved you."

Danica winced, as she noted the usage of the past tense in Nana's statement. "And my mother?" Danica asked.

"Yes, I loved her too," she whispered, "but she just wouldn't commit. She wouldn't listen. She was so out of control. She just wouldn't listen."

"And what was it she was supposed to listen to?"

"She wanted to be part of this," her grandmother began. "It's important that everybody be a part of this. We're all family."

"We're all family," Danica repeated. "But not all family members are given the same choices. You've made choices that you expect me to follow through on, choices that I may not want."

"It doesn't matter, child. You have been promised since birth. There are no choices anymore."

She gasped at that. "Seriously? You will give up your last-born grandchild to this?"

"Yes," she whispered. "That's it exactly. As it has always been done before."

"What if I don't want to, Nana?" Danica stared at the old woman, who was suddenly somebody she didn't even want to know or to be like.

"I still need a sacrifice."

Danica froze. "*You* need a sacrifice?" she cried out in horror, jumping to her feet. "Is that what this is all about? I'm to be your sacrifice?"

Dead silence came, when suddenly the front door burst open, and Cameron raced through the house. "Are you okay?" he asked, as he hugged Danica. He turned to face her grandmother. "How the hell is this even happening?"

She groaned in obvious pain. "It has to happen," she whispered. "It's been happening for decades, for centuries. It should already have happened, but I haven't done my part. I am failing my family. It's important that you follow through."

"What if I don't want to?" Danica looked over at Cameron. "Apparently I'm supposed to dedicate my life to this house, and, in return, this house will become my guardian, my protector, as it always has been for my grandmother. But now she just needs a sacrifice."

"This house?" Cameron stared at Harriet in shock.

Just then every window and every door in the house opened and slammed shut, open and slammed shut, until Nana screamed, "Stop. Stop it. He understands."

"Like hell I do," Cameron argued, staring at Harriet. "How is—" And then he stopped, shook his head, and gave an order to Harriet. "You release Danica. You let her have her own life. She's been in your shadow, in the shadow of your daughter all her life. Danica's never been free. You let her go."

Harriet groaned again, mustering great effort. Her body shook, as she fought the tide.

Stefan, his voice rippling through the room, cried out, "I can't hold this much longer."

"Nobody can," Nana added in a shriek. "Generations and generations of us are here, and it's my turn to join the rest."

"It might be your turn," Stefan noted, "but that doesn't make it right to force Danica to go too."

"She has to. She has to be the one. She has to be part of this," Harriet cried out.

Outside, the wind howled, and a storm picked up at a level that appeared to terrify Cameron. He stared around at them, at the room, and muttered, "This is just too crazy."

"I know," Danica whispered. "Believe me that I know. You would be better off without me."

"No," he declared, turning to face Danica. "That makes no sense. But what also makes no sense is that Harriet would expect you to be a willing sacrifice for her. That's not how the generations should be. She should be sacrificing for you, not the other way around. Yet nothing else she's said tonight makes any sense anyway."

"I don't think anybody cares about how the generations should be," Danica whispered. "I think they're only concerned with how their own lives should continue ad nauseam." Danica stared at her grandmother, with tears in her eyes. "I don't think it mattered one bit to her what my life has been like."

Just as she went to speak again, another loud *bang* happened, and something cold and brittle raced into the room. A spirit raced to Nana's side.

Her grandmother cried out, "Finally, Daisy, there you are."

"Daisy?" Danica asked, turning to look around in horror. "Is that really you, Mom?"

Cameron pulled Danica closer. She gripped him tightly

and whispered, "Was this who you helped at the hospital tonight?"

He nodded. "She grabbed my lab coat."

She gasped at him in horror, then back at her grandmother, and wailed, "No, no, no. Please, no."

Her grandmother looked at her with tired faded eyes. "I wish there could be another way," she whispered, "but it isn't to be. A sacrifice is required."

"But you also said that it should be of the bloodline."

"It's best if it's of blood," she replied, barely above a whisper. "We were never big on having children. It was hard for us to procreate. So sometimes the sacrifice had to be within."

"*Within*," Danica whispered. "My God." She shook her head. "Are you saying you had children just to create sacrifices?"

"No," Nana countered. "Sometimes we couldn't even create children. I only had the one."

"So, this is what you get up to in your spare time?"

Instantly more silence filled the room, right before someone else crashed inside.

Slowly Danica turned to face Jace, her half brother, who stared at her with such a ferocious hatred overtaking his facial expression. She didn't understand why he was here. She told him, "You need to leave."

He laughed. "Why the hell should I leave?" he asked hysterically. "This is perfect. This is awesome."

"What do you mean?"

He smiled. "You have no idea the power that's here. You have no idea how much power could be here."

"No," she cried out, "*you* don't understand. This is *unstable* power."

"It's still power," he cried out. "*You're* the one who doesn't understand. You won't let yourself understand," he said, looking around the room, an oddly intense look on his face. "This is special."

"No, no, no, no—" Danica whispered. "It's *not* special."

He turned to look at their grandmother and cried out, "Take me."

Her grandmother twisted, fighting against something, fighting against some power that appeared to be stronger than her.

"You can't," Danica yelled.

Her grandmother shook her head. "It's time. I have no choice."

The ghost of Daisy ripped forward and declared, "He is my sacrifice."

"No," her grandmother muttered, "there are enough sacrifices already."

"No," Daisy argued, "there isn't. He's mine," and she raced toward Jace.

Cameron held on to Daisy with a tight grip, as he yelled, "Jace, don't you understand what's happening here?"

"Oh, I do, and I'm loving every minute of it. Do you know how much power I'll wield as part of this?" Jace asked, looking from him to Harriet. "I know exactly what's going on, and I welcome it." He turned to the ghost of his mother and said, "Yes. Finally, yes. Do it."

She gave a hoarse laugh and raced toward him, even as Harriet shouted, "Stop. Daisy, stop."

Daisy cried out, "He's mine. You have your own." And, with that, she dove headfirst into Jace's body.

Jace lifted up with a cry of pain and agony, before he was tossed brutally to the ground, unconscious.

Cameron released his hold on Danica, as he checked on his brother. Even as he turned, he heard the screams, and he knew he'd made a mistake. He jumped back out of the way, as Harriet screamed at him, "You only have this moment," she cried out. "You should do something."

"Do what?" he asked, staring at this frail old lady, who even now seemed to be fighting some internal storm, her hair lifting on its ends, even as the ghostly spirit of Daisy was now gone. "I think your daughter is at peace now," he whispered.

"Aye, she is, and that is a good thing," the old woman whispered, "but I have no idea how I'm supposed to deal with this now." She groaned, clearly in pain, amid her death throes.

Just then, the front door burst open and two men, Deputy Aaron and Deputy Benson raced in.

"Stop what you're doing," Benson cried out.

Harriet looked over at him and whispered, "My other grandson. *Perfect.*"

Just as the deputy went to raise his gun, Harriet convulsed several times, then her body went stiff, and she fell back. As she did, Deputy Benson's body jolted forward and upward, as he cried out.

Cameron watched in horror and shock, as something appeared to slam through the deputy, dragging his body to the wall behind him, where he cried out once and then slowly collapsed.

Aaron, as if controlled by some invisible force around them, was also slammed to the wall, and then he too collapsed. Cameron turned to stare at the vestiges left here, then at Danica, who stood in the middle, her hand to her mouth as she stared at him.

"I think," she whispered, "I think they're all dead."

CAMERON SHOOK HIS head, as he raced to Aaron's side. "This one's not," he declared, urgency in his tone. "Hurry, Danica. Let's get him out of the house."

"Why out of the house?"

He stopped and frowned, but Stefan now yelled into the house, "Hurry and get out of the house."

She instinctively obeyed, not sure what the hell was going on. Then she smelled it. Smoke came from somewhere.

"It's on fire," Cameron urged her. "Let's go. Let's go."

She helped to drag Aaron's limp body outside, even as she turned to get her grandmother's body.

Cameron stopped her and said, "No."

She frowned at him, but Stefan's voice, gentle in her head, added, *Leave her. It's best to cremate them all together.*

Danica didn't know what to say to that. Her grandmother was obviously dead and wouldn't care and maybe would even prefer this. Danica was still stunned and unsure just what she was supposed to think of it all. Nevertheless she raced out of the house, Benji at her heels. He'd been hiding somewhere, but he was here with her now. She grabbed him, even as Cameron told her, "Get your RV out of here. Move. Move it now."

She hopped inside with Benji, while Cameron carried the deputy inside, before she backed up her RV and turned it around, watching the flames engulf the big old house from deep inside. As she raced down the driveway, she cried out, "You know the fire department won't come."

Cameron nodded, a strange expression in his gaze. "Maybe that's a good thing," he muttered. "Maybe the memories and the superstitions and the rumors and the gossip will be burned up too."

She felt tears clogging her throat, and she nodded. "Maybe it is for the best." She looked over at Aaron, one of the few who'd treated her well. "How is he?"

"Take us to the hospital," Cameron declared, his tone hard. "He's got a concussion, but I don't know whether it's more than that."

"Blood is coming out of his nose," she noted, "but I suspect it's more from the energy bursts all around him."

"The energy that somehow didn't affect us?" Cameron asked grimly, as he looked over at her. "Was that you?"

She whispered, "Maybe."

"I thank you for that." He studied her, as she pulled off to the side of the road for a moment, then looked back at the house, now a towering wall of flames. He watched it burn too, with a mixture of emotions. "I don't—I don't even know what to say," he murmured.

Danica sighed. "I'll try to explain it, but not right now." She called out, "Stefan, are you here?"

"I'm here," he murmured to all inside the RV. "Did you hear what Harriet said at the end?"

Danica groaned. "*Grandson*, … yes. Deputy Benson was my half-brother, … and so was Jace. I just lost four family members in that house tonight." And yet she couldn't help but wonder. "This really is for the best, isn't it?"

"It really is," Stefan replied in a soothing tone. "Only so much can pass from generation to generation, and they succeeded in something I had no idea was even possible," he murmured, "but honestly, I'm glad that it's over with."

"I had no idea what Nana was up to. She was looking for a sacrifice who wasn't me," Danica shared. "At least I'm hoping I interpreted that correctly."

"You did," Stefan agreed. "She was looking for anybody who could do the job. When the deputy burst inside, Harriet obviously had a very strong negative relationship with him. She also must have sensed the blood tie between them. So, when she felt the hate within Benson, she had no trouble going after him."

"He's the deputy who made my life so miserable," she whispered. "As in very miserable. So, when Nana saw him, even when I saw him, I felt the same kind of hate."

"No, not hate," Stefan whispered. "Not from you. You felt the same kind of pain. Harriet felt that pain, and she chose him. I think she recognized him on a soul level as blood and went after him, instead of you. So that you could live."

Danica muttered, "I don't want to think that I'm to blame for that."

"You aren't. Not at all. At the same time, I am not sure that this town will be big enough for all of you."

"That's just fine," Cameron agreed. "I have several more months here on my contract, and I had thought to stay. I built a house and everything, but I can't stay here, not now."

"I think you'll find your house will go up in flames next," Stefan said. Sure enough, the entire property was burning, the fire had raced off to the side, heading straight for Cameron's home.

"But why?" Danica asked in shock. "Why his house too?"

"You know why," Stefan countered.

"Because of the graves, right?" she whispered.

"Because of the graves?" Cameron looked over at her. "What are you talking about?"

"That's why Nana wanted the property back," Danica began. "Everybody, all the bodies, generations of graves are all there. I didn't even get a chance to ask her if that's where my mother was. After all these years, I don't think I ever asked her where my mother was buried. She told me that Daisy had been cremated."

Stefan added, "You need to spend some time working on a lot of healing. Yet you're strong, you're healthy, and you can do this."

"Are you sure?" she whispered. "I'm not so certain."

"I am," Stefan declared, "and you also have an awful lot of work you need to do."

"Yeah? What kind of work?" she asked, with a broken laugh. "I'm feeling very overworked and unloved."

"I'm pretty sure the solution to that is right beside you," Stefan replied, with a smile. "I've also spoken to the hospital, where you worked."

"You mean, *that* kind of work?"

"Yes, *that* kind of work. You're a healer, and the more that you turn against that energy within you, the more problems and pain and dissatisfaction you'll have out of life. But the more you go toward that healing energy, using your gifts in a positive way," Stefan explained, "the more you will flourish, and that is what Harriet wanted for you."

"You talked to her for years. Did you not have any idea what was going on?"

"No," he admitted regretfully. "I didn't see that coming at all. It didn't even occur to me that she was harboring that secret for so long. And that is something I regret not having spoken to her about—the block she had erected in her mind. I should have insisted she be honest with me long ago. She crashed into my world, shared what she wanted and no more," he noted, with a touch of humor.

"She was a force to be reckoned with."

"She was," Stefan agreed.

Danica asked him, "Do you think the family members are all angry?"

"No. I suspect that, in a way, they're all at peace," Stefan stated. "The house in itself had become bigger than all of them. It had become their own prison. What might be a nice spot to retire for someone isn't exactly the same for everyone," he murmured.

Danica asked Cameron, "Are you okay?"

Cameron nodded. "Yes, but it would be a hell of a lot less disruptive if this Stefan person would use a phone." At that, his cell rang. He frowned down at his Caller ID and answered it cautiously. "Hello?"

"Is this easier for you?" Stefan asked.

"Yes, damn it." He put it on Speaker and shook his head. "Will this stuff happen all the time with her?"

"Yep, and with you too. You have no idea, but you've been touched by all this, and you do not escape unscathed."

"What does that mean?" he asked in horror. "Personally, I'm okay to be unscathed."

"There's healing with this, as a lot of healing energy has been released, a lot of love. You'll be a better doctor for it now."

"Oh, I'm not against that." He chuckled. "It is what I do."

"I hear rumblings of some ethics violations coming for the hospital and for the local sheriff's office. So, I think you might want to change locations for doing what you do."

"I got that impression already," he noted, looking over at Danica. "As long as Danica goes with me, I'm totally okay with a move."

She smiled at him and nodded.

Just then, the deputy lying on the floor before them groaned.

She turned on the RV engine and said, "I hear you. Let's get him to the hospital." And, with that, she drove directly there. The orderlies got him unloaded and carried inside, where Cameron could work on him.

When Cameron returned over an hour later, he found the RV still sitting there in the hospital parking lot, and Danica and Benji sat on the lawn, the one green space under the early morning light. "Are you okay?" he asked, as he sat down beside her.

She nodded. "Is Aaron okay?"

"Yes," he replied, reaching out to pet Benji. "The deputy's awake, but he has no clue what happened."

She murmured, "I wonder what we'll tell him."

"We'll tell Aaron how there was an explosion at Harriet's house, right after her passing, where Deputy Benson and Jace were killed inside. The only thing we could do was run, and we grabbed Aaron as we left the house," he explained. "That's what I came up with."

She looked over in admiration and smiled. "That's not half bad. I know it'll take you a whole lot longer to come to terms with all that happened."

"Yeah, I'm not sure there's any coming to terms with all that," he murmured. "I mean, out of all your family, including your two half-brothers, the only sane person was Harriet, and I would have sworn to that. Come to find out, I can be so wrong."

"At least Nana redeemed herself somewhat by refusing to use me as her sacrifice. I still can't believe she killed her husband. How could Nana have done that, claiming he was the love of her life and how she had him for too few years?"

Cameron shook his head. "We may both need therapy, yet we can't tell anyone what really happened. It's one of those things that'll stay in our memories. We may need to be our own therapists."

She smiled at that. "I'm game."

Cameron asked her, "Do you have a dream location where you want to live?"

She looked at him and laughed. "I certainly don't have any place to live outside of my trusty wheels," she replied, motioning to her RV. "You pick a city. I'm happy to go, but I really don't want to stay here."

"That's okay. I'm pretty sure the hospital doesn't want me to stay either."

"Yet, if nothing else, I think that solved the problem of their annual Halloween hauntings."

"Agreed. So maybe they will remember me kindly after all."

"What about your brother? I'm so sorry."

"Yeah, me too, but it's another reason to go away and to start fresh somewhere else," he whispered. He reached out a hand and asked, "Coming?"

"Absolutely," she murmured, as she hopped up. She looked back over at the hospital. "Don't you need to go back inside again?"

"Not right now," he replied, with the wave of his hand. "I will finish my contract, but only if they insist. If they can find another doctor, I'm out early."

"Regardless of how the patients feel?"

He nodded. "I think it's time I did something for me and you and Benji, not just for everybody else."

"I like the sound of that," she whispered.

He grinned. "I'm hoping that you'll stick around and see what else we can sort out in our lives."

"Absolutely," she murmured. She reached up and kissed him gently on the cheek. "I'm really grateful that you came into my life."

"Ditto," he murmured, as he wrapped an arm around her and pulled her close. "It could get a little ugly over the next few weeks," he warned, looking at her intently. "There'll be inquiries and all kinds of shit. Because of that they might even let me out of my contract early."

"I wouldn't be against that either," she shared, with a smile. "As soon as you're ready to leave is good for me. You've got your house issues to deal with too, though."

"Yeah, and it was insured, but I've also got to deal with my brother's remains."

"Oh, right. I'm sorry. I forgot."

"Your brothers' too," he added, with a nudge. "How do you want to deal with that?"

"I don't even know what to do about them," she murmured. "We can't bury them, and the house cremated them. Maybe just add a stone in remembrance to the property, with all the other family members buried there? Once we figure out where that is … But what about Jace? What would you want for him?"

"He's gone, and, despite whatever was happening to him at the end there, I would like to think that he's finally at peace."

"Had he been troubled for a while?"

"Yes," he whispered. "I can look back and see it even in his early years. He was very troubled and getting worse. So, I'm good to have a memorial plaque on your family's land. If that's okay with you, it's fitting for him, as your half-brother. Plus, it's an ending. Not the ending I would have wished for him, but it's over."

She nodded. "Sometimes that's all we can ask for."

He smiled, held her close, and whispered, "Personally I'm all about beginnings."

"I'm all about beginnings if there is one in my future," she said, with sorrow in her tone. "It's been a long haul."

"But that is all over," he stated firmly. "From now on, it's you and me against the world."

She grinned. "I don't think I've ever heard that before, at least not in relation to me."

"You have now," he declared, smiling at her. "So, let's just hold on tight and get through these next few weeks. Then we'll find a place where we can start again."

CHAPTER 23

Weeks Later …

DANICA AND CAMERON shared the same chaise longue, snuggled under a huge sun umbrella, on the soft sandy private beach. She stared out across the ocean. "I know we aren't staying here permanently, poor Benji is likely hating his pet hotel," she noted, "but I must admit that I never thought Hawaii could be so beautiful."

"It is beautiful, isn't it?" he agreed, with a smile. "I hadn't been here before either. It's one of the places that I always planned to come for a holiday."

"And a honeymoon counts, doesn't it?"

He chuckled. "It absolutely does. I'm so happy to share this experience and this lifetime with you, Mrs. Danica Wingford." He gave her a kiss that warmed places deep within her. "How are you doing?"

"I'm doing pretty well," she replied with a genuine smile, knowing exactly what he referred to. "Time has helped."

He nodded in understanding. "It absolutely does help," he whispered. He kissed her on the temple.

Danica sighed and shared, "A lot of things happened that I still need to process. Maybe I'll never really get all the answers I want, but the answers that I do have don't make a whole lot of sense anyway, so I'm not sure what the point would be of looking for more."

"I totally agree. I'm still dealing with it all too."

She chuckled. "Now you know what it means to live in my world."

"What's this about Stefan reaching out to you?" Cameron asked her.

"Yeah, and he had Dr. Maddy contact me."

"Right. So, was she the one who was going through Harriet's house, looking for energy?" Cameron asked.

"Yes, and, while I doubt that anyone will admit it, I suspect she's also the one who set the house on fire. Stefan said that she's incredibly talented and that she's a magical energy worker. Anyway, he's put us in contact and suggested that I work with her. She is a healer of global renown apparently, and, according to her, I have a lot of talent."

Cameron stared at her in surprise. "Wow, okay, so I guess the woo-woo stuff will be part and parcel of our future."

She smiled. "I don't know about how much *woo-woo* there is, but healing could be," she acknowledged, "and that's what you do anyway."

He nodded. "It sure is."

"I do feel—I don't want to say stronger, more powerful, more intuitive—yet all of the above. It's as if I can almost instinctively know what's going on with somebody right now. And that's a good thing, right?"

"Definitely, yes. And, speaking of good things, I got a notice from the hospital that I am officially let out of my contract, so we never have to go back there again."

She laughed. "All in all, I've got to say that life is looking pretty damn good."

He wrapped an arm around her and tilted her chin up,

so he could look into her eyes. "Honestly, our future is looking damn wonderful, if you ask me."

And, with that, he lowered his head and kissed her.

This concluses Book 25 of Psychic Visions: Soul Legacy.

Read a sneak peek Coveted: Psychic Visions, Book 26

Coveted: Psychic Visions (Book #26)

So, what happens when one desperately wants something but can't have it? And what happens if that person puts plans into motion to get all that is coveted? And… what happens to the innocent victims along the way?

Kylie Oakwood is a new police sketch artist with an amazing talent but also a very secretive past. She's desperate to make a good life for herself and to forget all about the tragedy in her life. Not that it's easy being in the one field she should most likely avoid.

Detective Porter Hanson takes note of the nightmares in the back of this young woman's eyes, but it's so easy to forget when he sees her artwork and how well she handles the witnesses. She's a unique personality, and that rubs others in the department the wrong way. But, for him, something about her brings out his protective instincts.

The trouble is, he cannot figure out why he is supposed

to be protecting her—or maybe that should be more about *who,* or better yet, *what?* Especially when weird things start happening around her …

"HEY, KYLIE. ARE you ready for this?"

Kylie Okovi turned to look at Detective Hanson. Kind, compassionate eyes searched hers, and she realized that he must have noted her clenched fist and her white-knuckled grip on her sketch pad. She took a deep breath and said, "I will be, but I don't think any of us will walk away from this unscathed."

"We're not supposed to," he said gently, "from any crime scene."

"But this one"—she motioned at the evidence of the mass shooting all around her—"this, … this," and she stopped, the words dying in her throat.

He nodded gently. "I understand," he said. "Nobody should ever have to go through something like this, and certainly never twice."

"And this is your second, isn't it?" she asked, turning to face him.

He winced and nodded. "We're not counting or anything because I don't want to keep track of it in that way."

"No, I'm sorry," she whispered.

"I wasn't expecting to come to work today and to deal with twenty-two deaths." He hesitated, then added, "Twenty-three now. The latest victim … died in the hospital."

Kylie took a deep breath and slowly nodded. "And the killer?"

"We have no idea at the moment. They're running through videotapes, looking for him. There were eyewitnesses, but they're all fairly contradictory."

"How is that possible?" she asked, staring at him. "I know I'm fairly new to the detective side of this, just being a sketch artist, but … is that normal?"

He smiled, nodded. "Particularly under stress, people think what they see is what they're actually seeing, but often it isn't. Their minds try to make logical sense of the jumble of events in their memories, when really it doesn't work because this can never make sense. It's not intended to make sense. It's supposed to be horrific. The people doing this want it to be horrific. They're after a big show, some final ending to whatever it is that they have planned."

"How could anybody have planned this?" she whispered, her gaze going to the chaos of the masses in the casino all around her. "It's just too unbelievable."

"That's why we're here, to make sense of the chaos," he said. "If it's too much for you …"

She held up a hand immediately and said, "Don't."

"I'm just letting you know this will affect all of us."

"And I'll turn your words back on you and say it's supposed to," she replied ever-so-simply.

He patted her gently on the back and suggested, "If you need some downtime, let us know. In the meantime, I don't even know if you can do anything here."

"I was called in," she stated, turning to look around. "I'm not sure why. I think they just want sketches of the scene and more photographs."

He waved a hand at that. "You and I both know how the boss feels about that."

"I do. I'm here to put some personality into it," she confirmed. "That also makes it something we can use on the stand."

"But it's never been about the trial with you, has it?"

She winced and then shook her head. "No, I'm not so much about making them pay as making sure that they're caught," she whispered.

"So you do you, whatever that means in this instance, and I'll check in with you in a little bit." And, with that, Detective Hanson disappeared.

Kylie adjusted the cap on her head—to keep her hair from contaminating the crime scene—took a deep breath, and slowly walked forward. It was all about impressions, all about sights and sounds and scenes. Yet everything was running through her brain at top speed, and something inside her screamed that this crime wasn't something anybody could make sense of.

Kylie stood inside one of the largest casinos in Vegas. Somebody had decided to walk through with heavy artillery and had gunned down their victims in what appeared to be random shootings. Twenty-three at last count. Yet in the chaos, random people, EMTs, rescue workers, volunteers had moved the dead, had picked up the wounded, had quickly raced away with survivors and everyone else who was looking for medical assistance. Some were families and friends, who had grabbed their loved ones, some dead, some alive, and had moved them.

Yet Kylie also knew instinctively that, once the shooting began, people scattered, as the need for self-preservation kicked in. Yet, had she been here during this mass shooting, she's not sure how she would have handled it.

To even think about leaving a loved one behind, for more bullets to be riddled into their prone body, seemed so completely wrong, and yet most people would instinctively run. In this case, at least three families had grabbed their loved ones, trying to save them, and had booked it to the other side, where they had all been attacked instead of saved. Several were still alive and now in the hospital, and several others hadn't made it that far.

Kylie was here with her sketchbook to try and sort out some of this evil, at least as much of it as she could.

It was an odd case for her, and she was here more at the request of the detective than anything else. She still didn't quite understand why. She was a police sketch artist, but occasionally she had also worked crime scenes. This kind of crime scene was one she never *ever* wanted to get called in on again.

With a deep breath, she pulled out her sketch pencil, walked to one corner, figuring that that might be the easiest place to start, and turned to a clean page on her sketchbook and started drawing.

Find Book 26 here!

To find out more visit Dale Mayer's website.

https://geni.us/DMSCoveted

Simon Says...: Kate Morgan (Book #1)

Welcome to a new thriller series from *USA Today* Best-Selling Author Dale Mayer. Set in Vancouver, BC, the team of Detective Kate Morgan and Simon St. Laurant, an unwilling psychic, marries all the elements of Dale's work that you've come to love, plus so much more.

Detective Kate Morgan, newly promoted to the Vancouver PD Homicide Department, stands for the victims in her world. She was once a victim herself, just as her mother had been a victim, and then her brother—an unsolved missing child's case—was yet another victim. She can't stand those who take advantage of others, and the worst ones are those who prey on the hopes of desperate people to line their own pockets.

So, when she finds a connection between more than a half-dozen cold cases to a current case, where a child's life hangs in the balance, Kate would make a deal with the devil himself to find the culprit and to save the child.

Simon St. Laurant's grandmother had the Sight and had warned him that, once he used it, he could never walk away. Until now, her caution had made it easy to avoid that first step. But, when nightmares of his own past are triggered, Simon can't stand back and watch child after child be abused. Not without offering his help to those chasing the monsters.

Even if it means dealing with the cranky and critical Detective Kate Morgan …

Find Simon Says… Hide here!

To find out more visit Dale Mayer's website.

https://geni.us/DMSSHideUniversal

Author's Note

Thank you for reading Soul Legacy: Psychic Visions, Book 25! If you enjoyed the book, please take a moment and leave a short review.

Dear reader,

I love to hear from readers, and you can contact me at my website: www.dalemayer.com or at my Facebook author page. To be informed of new releases and special offers, sign up for my newsletter or follow me on BookBub. And if you are interested in joining Dale Mayer's Reader Group, here is the Facebook sign up page.
http://geni.us/DaleMayerFBGroup

Cheers,
Dale Mayer

About the Author

Dale Mayer is a *USA Today* best-selling author, best known for her SEALs military romances, her Psychic Visions series, and her Lovely Lethal Garden cozy series. Her contemporary romances are raw and full of passion and emotion (Broken But … Mending, Hathaway House series). Her thrillers will keep you guessing (Kate Morgan, By Death series), and her romantic comedies will keep you giggling (*It's a Dog's Life*, a stand-alone novella; and the Broken Protocols series, starring Charming Marvin, the cat).

Dale honors the stories that come to her—and some of them are crazy, break all the rules and cross multiple genres!

To go with her fiction, she also writes nonfiction in many different fields, with books available on résumé writing, companion gardening, and the US mortgage system. All her books are available in print and ebook format.

Connect with Dale Mayer Online

Dale's Website – www.dalemayer.com

Twitter – @DaleMayer

Facebook Page – geni.us/DaleMayerFBFanPage

Facebook Group – geni.us/DaleMayerFBGroup

BookBub – geni.us/DaleMayerBookbub

Instagram – geni.us/DaleMayerInstagram

Goodreads – geni.us/DaleMayerGoodreads

Newsletter – geni.us/DaleNews

Milton Keynes UK
Ingram Content Group UK Ltd.
UKHW050718010724
444982UK00014B/952

9 781778 863547